# PRISM

## MICHAEL MANOSCA

EDITED BY
**REGENA SLATER**

*For those who navigate the world with a different rhythm—*

*Who need quiet spaces to recharge, who love deeply but struggle with the unspoken rules, who feel everything intensely in a society that asks you to dim your light, your way of being.*

*You are not a flaw to be fixed, but a gift to be celebrated.*

# PREFACE

This story came about from a simple scribble of a note I made to myself while walking one day: "Character is reflecting on his end of life (he's 55) but remembering everything from his past. He actually died 30 years prior but didn't know." I promptly forgot about it.

Months later, I was rummaging through old files in search of what seemed important at the time and ran across "Idea for a book." Apparently, my important task wasn't so important after all, because this simple note to myself sparked something that poured out.

There's a lot of feeling in this story, and that's intentional—especially for those of us who have always felt like we didn't quite fit in. Not quite a nerd or geek, not carrying the "hidden shame" of being gay or the worry of growing up ostracized for some other societally perceived deficiency. No, this story attempts to share the life that grows for those of us for whom simply being part of society is often a challenge—a chore to masquerade through. Those unable to contain the strain of modern life with its bells, whistles, constant noise, and electronic clutter we fill ourselves with. And the constant need to feel connected, to understand how just being social "works."

The premise of life and death doesn't really matter for this story. What does matter is the idea that the most trivial moments of life often result in the most fundamental and phenomenal changes that bring us joy—and allow us, especially those of us for whom trying to describe our realities is often so very difficult, to find that these simple life glimpses can become elements of love, strength, support... the very definition of family.

# CHAPTER 1
# SUMMER HOME

"So what's the plan, Josh?" Rebecca asked, stirring her coffee as she watched her twenty-one-year-old son methodically arrange his breakfast. Two pieces of wheat toast, cut diagonally. Orange juice in the blue glass, never the red one. Butter spread to exactly the edges, no further. Some things never changed.

Joshua shrugged, not looking up from his precise butter distribution. "I don't know. Maybe catch up on some reading. Work on that coding project I started last semester."

"That's it? That's your entire summer vacation plan?" Rebecca leaned back in her kitchen chair, studying her son's face. "Jesus, Josh, you're twenty-one. Shouldn't you be planning some epic road trip with your buddies? Backpacking through Europe? Getting arrested in Tijuana?"

"Language, Mom." Joshua's mouth quirked slightly—the same almost-smile that always reminded Rebecca so sharply of someone else. "And no, I'm not really the 'epic road trip' type. You know that."

"I know, but..." Rebecca waved her hand vaguely. "What about your friends from school? Surely someone's doing something interesting this summer."

Joshua finally looked up, those serious eyes that were so familiar it sometimes stopped Rebecca's breath. "They all talk about these amazing plans—Jake's supposedly doing some internship in London, Marcus is 'traveling Europe'—but I think half of it's bullshit. They just don't want to admit they're going home to work at their dad's law firm or whatever."

"And you're okay with that? Just... staying here?"

"I like it here." Joshua took a precise bite of toast, chewed thoughtfully. "Besides, I've got projects I want to work on. That 3D printer's been sitting idle since Christmas, and I had some ideas for new miniatures."

Rebecca felt that familiar pang. The 3D printer had been Joshua's obsession senior year of high school—he'd begged them to go halfsies on it for Christmas, used it constantly for months, creating elaborate miniatures for his Dungeons & Dragons campaigns. Then he'd gone to college, and like everything else Joshua threw himself into completely, it had been abandoned the moment something new caught his interest.

The pattern was so painfully familiar. Piano at fourteen—from zero to near-virtuoso in less than a year, then sudden, complete disinterest. The 3D printing obsession. Before that, it had been astronomy, with star charts covering his bedroom walls until he'd mastered the constellations and moved on. And before that, origami, which had progressed from simple cranes to impossibly complex dragons in a matter of weeks.

"You know," Rebecca said carefully, "your Uncle Prism used to do that same thing. Pick up hobbies, master them completely, then just... move on to something else."

Joshua's hand stilled halfway to his mouth. "Really?"

"Really. Drove your Uncle Ken absolutely nuts. One month Prism would be building these incredible birdhouses—like, architectural marvels that belonged in a magazine. The next month, he'd be teaching himself watercolor painting and the garage would be full of half-finished canvases."

"What happened to all his stuff?"

Rebecca felt her chest tighten. "I... well, you know how it is. When people move around a lot for work, they can't keep everything."

It was a weak answer, and she could see Joshua filing it away with all the other weak answers she'd given over the years about his uncles. The truth was, she had boxes of Tyler's things in the attic—the birdhouses he'd made, sketchbooks full of those precise architectural drawings, even some of his diving medals. Things she couldn't bear to get rid of but couldn't bear to look at either.

"Maybe I should call him," Joshua said suddenly. "It's been forever since I talked to Uncle Prism. I keep meaning to, but college is so crazy, and then I feel bad that I haven't called..."

Rebecca's coffee cup rattled slightly as she set it down. "He's... they're both really busy with work right now. You know how it is."

"But I could just send a quick text. Or an email." Joshua was getting that stubborn look she recognized. "I feel like they think I don't care anymore, like I just forgot about them when I went to college."

"They don't think that, honey." Rebecca's voice came out strained. "They know you care about them."

"Then why don't they ever call me? It used to be Uncle Prism would call every few weeks, just to check in. Now it's like..." Joshua trailed off, that hurt look crossing his face that broke Rebecca's heart every time. "It's like I don't exist to them anymore."

Rebecca wanted to crawl under the table. The birthday cards she and David had been sending, signed with Tyler and Ken's names. The five-dollar bills for good grades, carefully forged notes about being proud of Joshua's accomplishments. All of it a fiction they'd built to avoid telling their son that the two people he'd adored most in the world were gone.

"People get busy," she said weakly. "Adult life is complicated."

Joshua stood abruptly, his breakfast half-finished. "I'm going to go work on my coding project."

Rebecca watched him go, noting the familiar signs of overwhelm—the way his shoulders tensed, the careful controlled movements that meant he was holding himself together through sheer force of will. In another few minutes, he'd be in his room with the door closed, noise-canceling headphones on, losing himself in the precise logic of code.

Just like Tyler used to do with his spreadsheets when the world became too much.

"Josh," she called after him.

He turned in the doorway, and for a moment Rebecca almost told him everything. Almost ripped off the bandage and let twelve years of grief and lies spill out across the kitchen floor.

"Your Uncle Prism and Ken..." she started, her heart hammering.

Joshua turned fully around, something shifting in his expression. "What about them?"

"Well..." Rebecca felt the words stick in her throat. She could see something in Joshua's eyes—a careful wariness, like he was preparing himself for disappointment. Like he'd been expecting this conversation for years.

She hated herself. It had been too long. Way too fucking long. She was actually surprised Joshua still bought all their bullshit. He wasn't stupid. It was like he was playing along, the way kids pretend Santa Claus is real because they don't want to disappoint their parents. But why? Why was he protecting her feelings when she'd been lying to him for over a decade?

"I uh... I may need your help," she said quickly, chickening out completely.

"With what?" Joshua's voice was careful, neutral.

Think, Rebecca, she told herself frantically. "I uh... I need to clean out the attic, and since you're home..."

"Ugh, really?" Joshua's shoulders slumped.

Rebecca almost said forget about it, but then it dawned on her. Maybe it might actually be good for Josh to help. At least he'd see all of Prism and Ken's old stuff up there. All the things she'd been hiding. Maybe... hell, she didn't know... maybe he'd finally understand what had happened without her having to find the words.

Rebecca felt like a chickenshit, but she nodded anyway. "Yeah. Maybe tomorrow."

After Joshua disappeared upstairs, Rebecca sat alone in the kitchen, staring at his abandoned breakfast. The toast cut in perfect diagonal halves, the orange juice glass placed exactly parallel to his plate. Even his napkin was folded and placed just so.

Every mannerism, every careful habit, every need for things to be just right—it was like watching Tyler grow up all over again. But Tyler had been thirty-three when he died, and Joshua was only twenty-one. How much more of Tyler would she see emerging in her son? How much longer could she keep up this elaborate fiction?

And what would happen to Joshua when he finally learned the truth?

⊏⊐

That night, Rebecca lay in bed next to David, both of them staring at the ceiling while the television murmured unwatched in the background. They'd had this conversation a dozen times over the years, but it never got easier.

"We have to tell him," David said quietly. "He's twenty-one, Becca. He's not a little boy anymore."

"I know." Rebecca's voice was barely a whisper.

"It's been twelve years. Twelve fucking years of lying to our son about why his uncles never visit, never call, never show up for anything important in his life."

Rebecca flinched. "They do show up. The cards, the money for good grades—"

"Rebecca." David's voice was gentle but firm. "You know that's not the same thing. And Josh is starting to notice the gaps. Today he wanted to call Tyler. What happens when he tries to look them up online? For all I know, he already has. What happens when he graduates and wants them at his graduation?"

Rebecca was quiet for a long moment, tears sliding silently down her cheeks. "I couldn't do it, David. When he was nine and asking why Uncle Prism didn't come to his birthday party, I just... I couldn't be the one to tell him they were never coming back."

"I know why you started this, Becca. But it's been twelve years."

"I panicked again today," Rebecca whispered. "He was asking

about them, and I almost told him. I got as far as 'Your Uncle Prism and Ken...' and then I just froze."

David reached over and took her hand. "What did you tell him?"

"That I needed help cleaning out the attic." Rebecca's voice was small, ashamed. "I made it up on the spot. Completely chickened out."

David was quiet for a moment. "Do you think that'll work? Maybe seeing their things will help ease into it?"

"I don't know. Maybe. Or maybe it'll just make everything worse." Rebecca turned to face him in the dark. "David, he's so much like Tyler. You see it too, right? The way he gets overwhelmed, his need for everything to be just so."

David nodded. "He's exactly like Tyler at that age."

"What if I panic him? What if telling him about the accident, about all the lying, what if I hurt him when I didn't mean to? I can't..." Rebecca's voice broke. "I can't be responsible for breaking him the way I broke myself when they died."

"Tyler would have understood him," David said softly. "They would have connected in ways we can't. And you've robbed them both of that relationship."

"Tyler's dead, David. You can't have a relationship with someone who's dead."

"No, but Josh could have had the memory of loving him. He could have had stories about his uncle who understood what it was like to be different. Instead, he has abandonment and confusion."

Rebecca was crying harder now, years of grief and guilt finally breaking through. "I just missed them so much. I couldn't accept that they were really gone. And Josh was so little, and he loved them so much..."

"I know, baby. I know." David pulled her close, letting her cry against his chest. "But you have to fix this. Somehow, you have to find a way to tell him the truth."

"What if he never forgives me?"

"Then we'll deal with that when it happens. But you can't keep lying to him. It's not fair to Josh, and it's not fair to Tyler and Ken's memory."

Rebecca nodded against David's chest, knowing he was right but terrified of what came next. How do you tell your adult son that two of the most important people in his childhood have been dead for over a decade? How do you explain twelve years of elaborate deception, no matter how well-intentioned?

And how do you prepare yourself for the possibility that your son might never trust you again?

Outside their bedroom window, the Seattle night was quiet and peaceful, full of the kind of calm that made difficult truths seem possible to bear. But inside, Rebecca lay awake long after David's breathing had evened out into sleep, wondering how to unravel a lie that had become the foundation of her son's understanding of love and family.

Tomorrow, she decided. Tomorrow she would start figuring out how to tell Joshua the truth.

But even as she made the promise to herself, Rebecca knew she'd made the same promise dozens of times before. And every morning, facing her son's trusting face across the breakfast table, she'd found another reason to wait just one more day.

# CHAPTER 2
# THE CONVERSATION

Joshua's bedroom looked like it could belong to a sixteen-year-old, despite its occupant being twenty-one. He'd always looked young for his age—could easily pass for a high schooler if he tried—and his room reflected the same careful simplicity that defined everything about him.

The clothes he'd brought home from his dorm were already put away with methodical precision. Four pairs of Diesel jeans, tapered, hung in the closet alongside his single hoodie. He'd been wearing that same style of jeans since he was thirteen and saw no reason to change now just because some fashion magazine declared them passé. In his dresser, everything had its place: a dozen white Gap t-shirts in one drawer, six navy ones in another. Twenty-four pairs of white ankle socks, because anything that went higher than his ankles gave him the jitters. A dozen pairs of gray Calvin Klein briefs, because boxers bunched and twisted in ways that made him want to crawl out of his skin, and he didn't care what other guys thought about his underwear choices—they weren't the ones who had to wear them.

His two pairs of white Reeboks with blue stripes sat perfectly aligned by his bedroom door, freshly hand-washed from his weekend routine. Everything was exactly where it should be, exactly how he'd left it at spring break. The familiar order of it all was like slipping into a warm bath after a long day.

"She's worried about you."

Joshua turned toward his uncle Tyler, seeing those two brilliant, differently colored eyes that had given rise to his nickname "Prism."

"Mom?"

"Of course. It's been years and she still doesn't know how to tell you."

Joshua looked down. Prism was the only person he could make eye contact with and feel okay doing so, but even now it felt awkward. His uncle understood that feeling, though.

"You know, I used to think I would just come out and tell her I already know."

"What stopped you?"

"I'm chicken, I guess. I mean, I knew she was signing your name and stuff on cards, and I don't know... I just... it seemed like if I did, it'd hurt her more. Like make her even sadder. That's probably not making any sense."

Prism crossed the room and rested his hands on his nephew's shoulders, giving him an encouraging squeeze. Joshua felt the weight and warmth of them, solid and real. "It does. I feel you."

"But..."

"You don't know how to keep pretending?"

"Yeah."

"Then don't."

"Easy for you to say."

"Yes, it is easy. But, Joshua..."

"Yeah?"

"You know I'm always here for you, right? I'm not going anywhere."

"Aren't you?"

That took Tyler aback.

"Uncle Tyler, no offense, but I'm old enough to know that either I've been hallucinating you, or I'm crazy, or you're a ghost, or something."

Prism stood there, listening.

"And I don't care if you are a figment of my imagination or not, but Uncle Ken is gone. One day you'll be gone too, right?"

Joshua didn't come across as angry or sad or anything really— just honest, like Tyler himself would be.

Tyler considered this before responding by sitting down on Joshua's bed, causing it to sag slightly under his weight. Something Joshua noted.

"Josh, come sit next to me." He patted the twin bed.

Joshua settled beside his uncle, the familiar comfort of having someone who understood washing over him.

"I honestly don't know exactly why your Uncle Ken moved on and I'm still here. And I'll be honest, it used to scare me a bit."

"Do you miss him?" Josh asked innocently.

"More than I can ever express." Tyler looked like a truck had rolled over him for a moment before recovering. "But I took it that I was here for a reason, and perhaps it was because I was here for you."

"Me?"

"Yeah. You were little when..."

"It happened?"

"Yeah."

"Do you remember it?"

"Not really. I remember Ken being gone and I woke up walking along the road. I couldn't find him and no one would stop to help me."

"I didn't even know it happened."

"I think that was because your mom and dad were trying to protect you, Joshua. But that's all in the past."

"I guess."

Josh jumped up and changed the subject. "Oh, did I tell you? Mom got all weird earlier and said she wants to clean out the attic tomorrow or something. Isn't that where all your old stuff is?"

"How did you know about that?"

"I used to go up there looking for where they'd hide my

Christmas presents when I was like twelve and figured out Santa was a thing."

Tyler laughed. "You're too much like me!"

Joshua grinned. He liked this banter with his Uncle Prism.

"I think I'm gonna tell her I already know."

"Do it gently, Joshua. She was really devastated when it happened."

"I know, but that was like a billion years ago."

"Seems like just the other day."

"You know what I mean."

"Yes, I do."

"I wonder if there's anything cool in your old boxes?"

"Probably. Some of my best stuff was packed away. I didn't stick around to watch them do it. Too..."

"Painful to watch?"

"Yeah." Joshua and Prism were on the same wavelength in many ways.

"Any porn in there you think?"

"Joshua!"

He laughed. "Just asking! You never know—vintage porn might sell for a lot these days!"

"Vintage?! I'm not that old!"

"You're not old at all, Uncle Tyler. You're dead!"

Prism laughed alongside his nephew. "Don't let your mom hear you talking like that. She'd box your ears."

"I know, I know. But we've got to quit playing this fake game around each other."

"Just be gentle with her, Joshua."

"I will."

# CHAPTER 3
# DISCOVERY

Joshua stood at the foot of the pull-down ladder in the second-floor hallway, looking up into the yawning darkness of the century-old attic alongside his mother. Their Victorian home was one of those old beauties that Rebecca and David had purchased in a part of town that had seen better days, but had caught the attention of up-and-coming hipsters and was becoming gentrified faster than Starbucks could build coffee shops on every goddamn corner. Consequently, a home equity loan against the newfound value of the old house had allowed them to add a few modern touches—new bathrooms that actually had decent water pressure, central air conditioning that didn't sound like a dying rhinoceros, and a kitchen that wouldn't have looked out of place in a magazine. Nothing fancy, but functional. It had also allowed them to take advantage of the sprawling attic space, framing it out properly so it had actual floors instead of just joists and insulation, and cedar-lined sloping ceilings in some areas to store old winter clothes and the accumulated detritus of domestic life.

Rebecca wondered when the hell she and David had become so ridiculously domestic, and recalled that day she'd sat with Tyler crying just before her wedding, worrying about becoming exactly this: a suburban mom who was genuinely proud of her cedar-lined wardrobe storage and organized holiday decoration system. How fucking bourgeois! Tyler would have laughed his ass off at the irony.

Climbing the ladder and throwing the light switch, Josh made a good show of being amazed at all the carefully organized chaos—boxes labeled in Rebecca's meticulous handwriting, clothes hanging in garment bags, old toys of his from various childhood phases, furniture draped in sheets like ghosts, rolled-up Persian rugs that had cost more than his first car, decorations sorted by holiday and color scheme. There was even that ridiculous light-up jack-o'-lantern that David had found at a flea market and insisted they buy despite the fact that it barely fit in their car and took three people to wrestle up the ladder into the attic.

Josh didn't want his mom to know his secret—he'd been up here countless times before. When he was younger, conducting covert Christmas present reconnaissance missions with the dedication of a CIA operative. Then, when he was fifteen, needing privacy for the kind of activities that fifteen-year-old boys require privacy for, and his bedroom walls were unfortunately thin. And sometimes, when life got particularly overwhelming, when he felt the world closing in too fast and too loud, he'd escape up here, unroll one of the expensive rugs and drag over his old bean bag chair and lose himself in a book, surrounded by the quiet ghosts of family history.

"I've been meaning to clean this place out for years," Rebecca began, her voice carrying that particular tone of maternal determination that Joshua recognized meant she was about to assign him manual labor.

Josh just nodded, not saying much. It was funny, really, how they were both dancing around wanting to admit the same things to each other, circling the truth like wary cats.

Rebecca gestured toward the far corner where two tall windows flanked the old turret, casting diamond-patterned shadows across the worn floorboards. "Why don't you start going through those old boxes piled up over there, Josh? I honestly forget half of what's stuffed up here anymore. Go through everything and make an inventory." She handed him a clipboard—because of course she had a clipboard ready—along with a Sharpie marker. "Label each box clearly so we actually know what the hell is in them. Put the obvious junk over by the wall for the donation pile, but anything we're keeping goes over by the windows where we can see it properly."

Josh grumbled a little, but nothing more dramatic than any typical college kid being "voluntold" to do household chores, and began making his way across the creaking floorboards. Rebecca busied herself pulling aside old holiday decorations, tossing faded wrapping paper remnants toward the discard pile alongside a canvas bag full of David's old clothes from his more experimental fashion phases.

"Any interest in Dad's vintage hippie collection?" she asked, holding up a tie-dyed shirt that looked like it had survived Woodstock.

"God, no," was all Josh responded, which was exactly what she'd expected. He might be David's biological son, but David was all flowing scarves and vintage band t-shirts while Josh had never met a basic white Gap t-shirt he didn't love. If Rebecca wasn't absolutely certain Joshua had David's DNA, she would have sworn somehow Tyler's genes had magically transferred themselves to her son through sheer force of personality.

"I'm going to head downstairs and throw together some lunch," Rebecca announced, her voice carefully casual as she pointed toward what was obviously Tyler and Ken's carefully preserved corner. "Why don't you tackle those boxes over there while I'm gone?"

This was it, she knew. She was completely chickening out, but she couldn't physically be present for whatever was about to happen. Lunch was as plausible an excuse as any, and besides, this conversation—whatever form it took—had been twelve years overdue. Time to let the chips fall where they fucking would.

Josh just shrugged with practiced twenty-one-year-old indifference and ambled over toward the designated corner, kneeling down beside a box whose cardboard flaps had been carefully tucked under themselves to keep the contents secure.

Rebecca had just stepped off the ladder back into the relative safety of the hallway when she heard her son's voice drifting down: "Mom? What... is this stuff?"

Her heart clenched. "What stuff, honey?" She knew exactly what he was looking at but played innocent anyway, because apparently that's who she was now—a woman who'd built an entire relationship with her son on elaborate pretense.

"It's like a bunch of binders and papers and..." she could hear him shifting things around, the whisper of pages turning, "there's like, I don't know, keepsake things or something. Personal stuff. Are these yours and Dad's?"

"Oh, those must be your Uncle Prism's old writing project from years ago," she said, her throat tight as she realized which particular box he'd stumbled upon first. Of course it would be that one.

"Writing project?"

Rebecca managed a laugh that sounded almost natural. "Well, I used to tell your Uncle Prism all the time that he should write a book because he knew so many interesting people and had all these incredible stories from his travels. Must be his old research materials."

Meanwhile, up in the attic, Joshua had carefully lifted out a thick three-ring binder that bore all the hallmarks of Tyler's meticulous organizational style—neatly labeled, if a bit dusty and carrying that particular smell of aged paper and memories. Inside, clipped to the first page, was a small note written in Tyler's precise, architectural handwriting: "Needs Preface."

"Jesus, Uncle Prism," Josh murmured to himself. "You really went all out on this thing."

The box was heavier than he'd expected, and when he dragged it across the floor toward the windows, it made that distinctive scraping sound of old cardboard against worn wood—a sound that carried clearly through the floorboards to where Rebecca stood frozen in the hallway below. She knew that sound meant he was settling in to really examine what he'd found, and this was the moment that would change everything, ready or not. She nearly broke down right there, but forced herself to get moving toward the kitchen before her resolve completely crumbled.

Joshua hauled his old bean bag chair over to the windows and positioned himself with his back to the natural light, the way he'd done countless times before when this attic had served as his secret reading sanctuary. The binder felt substantial in his hands, heavy with the weight of whatever Tyler had been trying to capture. As he began flipping through the carefully organized pages, a picture started to emerge—this wasn't just random notes or travel journals. This looked like Tyler had been conducting actual interviews, recording conversations with people who mattered to him.

His heart nearly stopped when he came across a section labeled "Rebecca Brennan" in Tyler's unmistakable handwriting.

"Holy shit," he whispered. "He interviewed Mom?"

Turning more pages, his excitement building like Christmas morning, he found another section: "Ken Takeshi." Uncle Ken! Josh's chest tightened with a mixture of joy and old grief. He remembered Uncle Ken, but it had been so long, and he'd been just a kid when... well, when whatever had happened, happened. He missed Uncle Ken terribly, and whenever he got to spend time with Uncle Prism, he tried not to mention Ken too much. He didn't want to make his uncle sad by bringing up painful memories.

But here was Uncle Ken's voice, preserved in Tyler's careful documentation. Josh felt like he'd discovered buried treasure.

He kept reading, finding more familiar names and completely new ones. Mom and Dad's wedding—he'd heard stories about that legendary disaster with the storm. But who was this Kit Lee guy from Hong Kong? And Miss Evangeline from New Orleans? What the hell was all this about voodoo and tarot cards? His Uncle Tyler was apparently way more fascinating than anyone had ever let on.

But something was nagging at him, some detail that felt off, though he couldn't quite put his finger on what.

"You found it."

Joshua looked up to see Tyler standing there, watching him with those distinctive mismatched eyes, a soft smile playing at the corners of his mouth as he took in the sight of his nephew surrounded by the carefully preserved pieces of his life.

"What?" Josh asked, though something in his uncle's expression told him this moment was more significant than it appeared.

"My life," Tyler said simply, gesturing toward the binder in Josh's hands. "All of it. The important parts, anyway."

Josh felt a strange sensation wash over him—not quite understanding, but the beginning of understanding. He was holding more than just interviews and stories. This was Tyler's attempt to capture something essential, something that mattered deeply enough to document with his characteristic thoroughness.

"I feel like I'm snooping," Josh said, suddenly self-conscious. "Like I'm going through your private stuff without permission."

Tyler's smile widened, taking on that mischievous quality that Josh remembered from childhood. "Don't be sorry. I'm pretty sure I wrote it for you, actually, though I didn't realize it at the time."

"Really?"

"Really. It's been sitting up here waiting for the right moment, the right person to find it." Tyler moved closer, settling onto the floor across from Josh with that easy grace that had always made everything seem manageable. "There are more binders, you know. I was... thorough."

Just then, Rebecca's voice echoed up from the hallway: "Honey, who are you talking to up there?"

Tyler's grin turned positively devilish, the expression of someone who knew exactly how much the world was about to change. "Busted," he whispered conspiratorially.

"Uh... nothing, Mom!" Josh called back, thinking quickly. "Just... did you say something about lunch?"

"Yeah, whenever you're ready, sweetie!"

Joshua looked back at his uncle, lowering his voice to barely above a whisper. "Would you mind if I...?"

"Read it?" Tyler finished. "Be my guest. It's yours anyway. Has been all along, really."

"Mine?" Josh felt that strange sensation again, stronger this time

—like puzzle pieces clicking into place, though he couldn't see the full picture yet.

"Yes, Joshua. Like I said, I think I wrote it for you. It's been a while since I looked at it myself, but there are several more binders in those boxes. I was, as you well know..."

"Incredibly thorough. Yeah, I figured that out about you when I was like ten," Josh finished with a grin.

"Are you absolutely certain you're not mine?" Tyler laughed, the sound carrying more warmth than Josh had heard from him in years.

"Uncle Prism!" Josh giggled, quickly shushing his uncle. "You're going to get us both in trouble!"

But he was smiling as he said it, that particular smile reserved for the people who truly understood him. Tyler had always been that person—the one who got his need for order, his social awkwardness, his way of seeing the world slightly differently than everyone else.

"Keep exploring, kiddo," Tyler said, nodding toward the remaining boxes stacked in the corner. "There's a lot more where that came from. Lots of memories, lots of stories. Lots of truth."

The last word carried extra weight, and Josh felt his pulse quicken. "You're sure it's okay for me to read all this?"

"More than okay," Tyler said, his voice carrying a certainty that made Josh feel like they were standing at the edge of something important. "I have a feeling this is exactly what you need right now. And Joshua?"

"Yeah?"

Tyler's expression grew serious, but not scary-serious. More like the kind of serious that came before good news, before explanations that made everything make sense. "Whatever you discover in those pages, whatever questions come up, whatever doesn't quite add up the way you expected... just remember that the important stuff, the stuff that really matters, that's all true. The love, the friendship, the family we built together—all of that is completely real."

Josh felt a shiver run down his spine, not unpleasant but significant, like his body was preparing for something his mind hadn't caught up to yet. "Uncle Tyler, what are you trying to tell me?"

Tyler stood up, brushing imaginary dust off his jeans. "I'm telling you to read the story, Josh. Read it all. And when you're ready, when you've processed everything and you have questions —and trust me, you will have questions—we'll talk. Really talk. About everything."

"Everything?"

"Everything," Tyler confirmed. "But for now, just read. Let the story unfold the way it wants to. Don't try to solve all the puzzles at once. Just... experience it. Get to know the people who loved you before you were even born, who helped shape the world you grew up in."

Tyler started to fade slightly around the edges, the way he sometimes did when their conversations were ending, and Josh felt a familiar pang of abandonment.

"You're not leaving, are you?"

"I'm never really gone, kiddo. You know that by now. I'll be around when you need me." Tyler's smile was infinitely gentle. "But this part, this discovery, this is something you need to do on your own. For now."

And with that, Tyler was gone, leaving Josh alone in the attic with his bean bag chair, the diamond-patterned window light, and a box full of stories that were apparently written just for him.

Josh looked down at the binder in his hands, then at the boxes that held the rest of Tyler's carefully documented life. Whatever secrets they contained, whatever truths were waiting to be uncovered, he was ready.

Or at least, he was ready to try to be ready.

He opened the binder to the first page and began to read.

# CHAPTER 4
# KEN TAKESHI

**Ken:** *[Flopping dramatically into chair]* Okay, okay, I'm sitting! You happy now?

**Tyler:** Thank you. Now, can you please just—

**Ken:** *[Interrupting]* Wait, is this thing recording? Do I need to do my good side? Should I have worn something nicer? This is going in your fancy book, right?

**Tyler:** *[Sighing]* Ken...

**Ken:** What? I'm just saying, if I'm gonna be immortalized in the Tyler Anderson memoir, I want to look good doing it.

**Tyler:** It's not a memoir, and you know it. Rebecca just thinks I should write down some of our stories, starting with how we met. So if you could please just—

**Ken:** *[Grinning]* Oh, you want me to tell you the story of how we met? Babe, you were there. You literally lived through this with me. Did you hit your head or something?

**Tyler:** *[Slight smile]* I know I was there. But Rebecca's been nagging me for years that I should write down all my travel stories and experiences, and she thinks our story would make a good opening chapter. So humor me.

**Ken:** *[Leaning back]* Ah, so this is for the Tyler Anderson memoir project, huh? Rebecca finally wore you down with all that "Prism, you should really put those stories together" stuff?

**Tyler:** Something like that. She said, and I quote, "They'd make a wonderful book, Prism!"

**Ken:** *[Laughs]* That's our Rebecca. Okay, fine, I'll play along with your little interview here. But you owe me dinner for making me relive my awkward nineteen-year-old self.

**Tyler:** Deal. So... the diving meet?

**Ken:** *[Bursts out laughing]* Oh man, you really want me to spill the tea on our meet-cute, babe? This is gonna be good. Okay, okay, buckle up buttercup, because your boy Ken has THOUGHTS about that day.

**Tyler:** *[Smiling]* I'm ready.

**Ken:** So there I am, January '99, first day back from break, and Rebecca – oh my GOD, Rebecca back then was like a force of nature, right? – she literally DRAGS me to this diving meet. And I mean drags. I'm talking full-on arm yanking because she wants to "scope out the merchandise."

*[Does exaggerated Rebecca voice]* "Ken! There's going to be college boys! In teeny tiny Speedos! This is better than Christmas!"

**Tyler:** She did not say that.

**Ken:** Babe, she absolutely said that. Word for word. I have witnesses! Well, I HAD witnesses, but they've all probably blocked out the trauma of early Rebecca by now.

*[Grins widely]*

So there we are, and Rebecca's got her little notepad – yes, she brought a NOTEPAD – and she's literally scoring these guys like Olympic judges. "Ooh, nice form! Seven point five! Wait, is that a tattoo? Minus half a point!"

**Tyler:** A notepad? Really?

**Ken:** I swear on my mother's miso soup recipe. Anyway, I'm sitting there being the good wing-woman – because at this point I'm still pretending I'm straight as a board, right? – when suddenly this tiny little dude appears on the high dive and I'm like... *[trails off]*

**Tyler:** What?

**Ken:** *[More quietly]* I just... stopped talking. Which, for me, you know that's like a medical emergency waiting to happen.

**Tyler:** What made you stop?

**Ken:** *[Leaning forward, getting more serious]* You did, babe. You were up there and it was like... okay, you know how everyone else was goofing around? Splashing, doing belly flops, being idiots? But you... you had this whole ritual. Like you were preparing for something sacred.

The goggles had to be exactly right. The shoulder thing you do. That little bounce. It wasn't showing off – it was like watching someone pray, you know?

**Tyler:** I never thought of it that way.

**Ken:** *[Voice softening]* When you dove, Rebecca literally grabbed my arm and goes "Holy shit, did you SEE that?" But I wasn't watching the dive anymore. I was watching your face when you came up. Those crazy beautiful eyes of yours, and for just a second you looked up and I thought... I thought you were seeing something the rest of us were missing.

**Tyler:** And then what happened?

**Ken:** *[Grins again, but softer]* I turned to Rebecca and said, "I need to meet him." And she went FULL Rebecca mode – bouncing, clapping, probably planning our wedding in her head. "YES! Operation Get Ken Laid is a GO!"

**Tyler:** She did not say that either.

**Ken:** *[Laughing]* Okay, maybe not those exact words, but the energy was there, babe. Trust me.

But then... *[gets serious again]* then I actually had to walk down there. And I've never been nervous about talking to anyone in my life, you know? I'm the guy who makes friends in bathroom lines. But you were sitting there, alone, looking like the noise was about to make your head explode, and I realized all my usual Ken tricks weren't gonna work.

**Tyler:** What do you mean?

**Ken:** *[Quietly]* I mean you looked real, babe. Like, actually real. And I was so tired of being the performance version of myself all the time. Japanese Ken at home, American Ken at school, fun Ken for parties... I looked at you and thought, "This guy might actually want to meet the real one."

**Tyler:** Did that scare you?

**Ken:** *[Long pause, then soft smile]*

Terrified me. Best kind of scared I ever felt.

**Tyler:** So what did you actually say to me?

**Ken:** *[Laughs and covers face with hands]* Oh God, this is embarrassing. I walked over there with like seventeen different opening lines in my head, right? I was gonna be smooth, charming, all that Ken magic...

**Tyler:** And?

**Ken:** And I got there, you looked up with those eyes, and my brain just went *BZZT* - total system failure. I think what came out was something super profound like, "That was... um... really good."

*[Throws hands up]*

REALLY GOOD! Like I was commenting on a sandwich or something! Mr. Smooth over here, ladies and gentlemen!

**Tyler:** *[Quietly]* I remember you said it was beautiful.

**Ken:** *[Stops mid-gesture, expression softening]*

Oh. Yeah. Yeah, I did say that, didn't I?

*[More seriously]*

Because it was, babe. It really was beautiful. Not just technically perfect – though holy crap, that entry was clean – but like... you made it look like art, you know? Like the dive was just this extension of who you are.

**Tyler:** Most people just said "nice dive" or asked about my score.

**Ken:** *[Shaking his head]* Most people are idiots. They see the surface stuff but miss the... the essence, I guess? You weren't just diving, you were being Tyler. And I'd never seen anyone be so completely themselves in front of a crowd before.

**Tyler:** Is that when you knew you wanted to get to know me better?

**Ken:** *[Grins]* Babe, I knew I was in trouble the second you said "Tyler. Prism" in that quiet voice of yours. No BS explanation, no trying to downplay the eye thing – just matter-of-fact honesty. Like, "Yeah, I'm different, deal with it."

*[Leans back]*

Meanwhile I'm standing there thinking, "Holy shit, when's the last time I introduced myself without putting on some kind of show?" You know what I mean?

**Tyler:** Actually, no. What kind of show?

**Ken:** *[Pauses, thinking]*

Like... okay, you know how I am with new people, right? Big smile, lots of energy, make everyone laugh? That's not fake, exactly, but it's... performed. Safe. People like fun Ken, so that's who I give them.

But you just stood there, dripping wet in your little Speedo, and said your name like it was the most natural thing in the world. No armor, no performance. Just... you.

**Tyler:** I was terrified.

**Ken:** *[Laughs]* You were terrified? Babe, you had the most serene expression! I thought you were this zen master of confidence!

**Tyler:** I was overwhelmed by the noise and the crowd, and then this gorgeous guy walks up to me...

**Ken:** *[Preening]* Gorgeous, huh? I mean, I knew I was bringing the heat that day, but it's nice to get confirmation...

**Tyler:** *[Soft laugh]* Ken.

**Ken:** *[Grinning but getting serious again]*

Sorry, sorry. But for real though, you seemed so... centered, I guess? Like all the chaos around you couldn't touch you. I wanted to know how you did that.

**Tyler:** What happened next?

**Ken:** Rebecca happened next, that's what. She comes bouncing down like a golden retriever who spotted a tennis ball, practically vibrating with excitement. "Hi! I'm Rebecca! Ken's best friend! Are you single? Are you gay? Do you want to get coffee?"

*[Does Rebecca voice again]*

Poor girl had no filter back then. Still doesn't, really, but now we love her for it.

**Tyler:** I remember being overwhelmed.

**Ken:** *[More gently]*

Yeah, I could see that. You got that look you get when there's too much input coming at you. So I told Rebecca to dial it back a notch – which, for Rebecca, meant she only asked three more personal questions instead of twelve.

But you were sweet about it. Answered her honestly, even though I could tell you wanted to disappear into the pool tiles.

**Tyler:** And that's when you asked if I wanted to get dinner sometime?

**Ken:** *[Shakes head]*

Nope! I chickened out completely. We talked for maybe ten more minutes, Rebecca grilled you about your major and your diving coach and probably your childhood pets, and then your teammates started leaving and you had to go.

I just... watched you walk away. Like an idiot.

**Tyler:** So how did we end up going out?

**Ken:** *[Grinning sheepishly]*

Rebecca. Obviously. She got your number while I was standing there with my mouth hanging open, and then she spent the next three days texting me things like "ASK HIM OUT YOU COWARD" and "I'M GOING TO DIE OF SECONDHAND EMBAR-RASSMENT."

**Tyler:** She gave me your number too.

**Ken:** *[Sits up straighter]*

Wait, she did? I never knew that! That sneaky...

*[Pause]*

Did you think about calling me?

**Tyler:** Every day for a week.

**Ken:** *[Softly]*

Really?

**Tyler:** Really. But I kept talking myself out of it.

**Ken:** *[Leaning forward]*

What changed your mind?

**Tyler:** You did. You called me first.

**Ken:** *[Laughs]* Oh right! God, I was such a mess that night. I must have picked up the phone like fifteen times before I actually dialed.

**Tyler:** What finally made you do it?

**Ken:** *[Grinning]* Rebecca threatened to call you herself and ask you out on my behalf. And knowing Rebecca...

**Tyler:** She absolutely would have done that.

**Ken:** *[Nodding emphatically]* One hundred percent! She probably would have shown up at your dorm with a PowerPoint presentation about why you should date me. "Exhibit A: He's cute. Exhibit B: He's funny. Exhibit C: He makes really good ramen."

*[Gets more serious]*

But honestly? I called because I couldn't stop thinking about that moment when you looked up at me after your dive. Like, for three seconds, we just... saw each other. Really saw each other. And I thought maybe, if I was really lucky, you might want to see me again.

**Tyler:** I did. Want to see you again, I mean.

**Ken:** *[Softly]* I was hoping you'd say that.

**Tyler:** So what did you say when you called?

**Ken:** *[Covers face again]* Oh God, more embarrassment. I had this whole script planned out, right? Casual, confident, asking if you wanted to grab coffee or something low-key...

**Tyler:** And?

**Ken:** And you answered the phone with "Hello?" in that quiet voice of yours, and I immediately blurted out, "Hi, it's Ken from the pool, do you want to go to dinner with me Friday night?"

*[Peaks through fingers]*

No build-up, no small talk, just straight to asking you out like some kind of caveman. "Ken want dinner. You come?"

**Tyler:** *[Laughing]* I remember thinking it was sweet. Direct.

**Ken:** *[Looking up]* Sweet? I was mortified! I was supposed to be smooth! Charming! Instead I sounded like I'd never talked to another human being before.

**Tyler:** I liked that you were nervous. It made me feel less nervous.

**Ken:** *[Pausing]* Really?

**Tyler:** Really. Most people who approached me were either overly confident or they were making fun of me. You were just...

real. Like you actually wanted to get to know me, not just hook up or whatever.

**Ken:** *[More seriously]*

I did want to get to know you. Everything about you. The way you moved, the way you thought, what made you laugh, what made you feel safe...

*[Trails off]*

Man, I had it bad for you right from the start, didn't I?

**Tyler:** We both did.

**Ken:** *[Grinning]* True. So what did you say when I asked you out?

**Tyler:** I said yes, but then I panicked and asked if Rebecca could come too.

**Ken:** *[Bursts out laughing]* YES! Oh my God, you were so scared it was going to be a real date! And I was like, "Sure, of course Rebecca can come," while inside I'm thinking, "Nooo, I want you all to myself!"

**Tyler:** You were very gracious about it.

**Ken:** *[Shrugs]* I figured if that's what it took to spend time with you, I'd take it. Plus, let's be honest, Rebecca was going to insert herself into our relationship whether we invited her or not.

**Tyler:** She did seem pretty invested in us getting together.

**Ken:** *[Laughing]* Invested? Babe, she appointed herself our personal matchmaker. I think she had our whole relationship time-line mapped out before we even went to dinner.

**Tyler:** And Friday night?

**Ken:** *[Settling back with a fond expression]*

Friday night was... perfect. Even with Rebecca there asking you about your life story and trying to play footsie with me under the table to get me to ask you more personal questions.

**Tyler:** I remember you telling her to stop kicking you.

**Ken:** *[Grinning]* She had zero subtlety! But you... you started to relax as the night went on. Started talking more, making little jokes. And when you laughed – really laughed, not just being polite – I thought, "Okay, I'm definitely falling for this guy."

*[Waves hand]*

And you know the rest of that night, babe. We walked you back to your dorm, I was too chicken to kiss you goodnight, Rebecca spent the whole way back to my place planning our second date...

**Tyler:** Yes, but they don't know the rest. So why don't you tell them anyway?

**Ken:** *[Laughs]* Right, right. The mysterious "they" who are going to read about our epic love story. Okay, for the sake of your future readers...

**Tyler:** When did you know for sure? That you were falling for me?

**Ken:** *[Long pause, expression growing tender]*

You really want to know?

**Tyler:** Yeah.

**Ken:** *[Softly]*

It was about two weeks later. We'd been hanging out pretty regularly – always with Rebecca as our unofficial chaperone – and you invited me to study with you at the library. You had this big accounting exam coming up.

**Tyler:** I remember that.

**Ken:** *[Leaning forward]*

You had all your notes laid out in this perfect system, color-coded and organized, and you were so focused. But about an hour in, the library got really crowded and noisy, and I could see you starting to get overwhelmed.

You kept trying to push through it, but your hands were getting shaky and you couldn't concentrate. So I suggested we go back to your dorm room to study instead.

**Tyler:** You noticed I was struggling.

**Ken:** *[Nodding]*

And when we got to your room, you just... collapsed on your bed and said, "Thank you. I couldn't think in there anymore." No shame, no apology for being different. Just honest gratitude.

*[Voice getting quieter]*

That's when I knew, babe. You trusted me enough to let me see you when you were struggling, and you didn't try to hide who you were or pretend to be someone else. You were just... Tyler. Beautiful, honest Tyler.

*[Pause]*

And I realized I was completely, utterly gone for you.

**Tyler:** That's sweet. But wait, I just realized something. How did you and Rebecca even become friends in the first place? You never told me that story.

**Ken:** *[Groans]* Oh God, you want that story too? Babe, this is supposed to be about us meeting, not the Ken and Rebecca origin story!

**Tyler:** Well, she's part of our story. She's the one who dragged you to the diving meet, right? The readers should probably know how you two became friends.

**Ken:** *[Sighs dramatically]* Fine, but I'm warning you, this story makes me look even more ridiculous than the diving meet one. And that's saying something.

**Tyler:** Now I'm really curious.

**Ken:** *[Covering face with hands]* You're going to laugh at me. Actually, you know what? You've probably already laughed at me about this. Multiple times.

**Tyler:** Just tell the story, Ken.

**Ken:** *[Peeking through fingers]*

Okay, so picture this: freshman year, first week of classes. I'm trying to be Cool College Ken, right? New school, fresh start, nobody knows I'm the kid who skipped two grades and still lives with his parents because Oregon State is like twenty minutes from home.

**Tyler:** Mm-hmm.

**Ken:** So I'm in this psych class, and there's this girl sitting next to me. Tall, pretty, light brown hair, wearing this cute sweater - you know how Rebecca always wears sweaters.

**Tyler:** I know exactly the type.

**Ken:** And I'm thinking, "Okay Ken, this is your moment! Time to be Mr. Super Fabulous!" You know, all with-it and charming, like everyone wants a piece of me, ya know?

*[Dramatic pause]*

So I'm sitting there, being my usual charming self, cracking jokes, making her laugh...

**Tyler:** *[Starting to smile]* Oh no.

**Ken:** *[Nodding emphatically]* Oh yes. Class ends, and she turns to me with this big smile and goes, "Hey, I'm Rebecca. You want to grab coffee sometime? Like... a date?"

And I look at her - because she's cute and sweet and everything - and I just say, "Oh honey, I'm totally gay. But we can absolutely be best friends!"

**Tyler:** *[Laughing]* Just like that?

**Ken:** *[Throwing hands up]* Just like that! No beating around the bush, no awkward buildup. Just boom - "I'm gay, wanna be besties?"

**Tyler:** What did she say?

**Ken:** *[Grinning widely]* Without missing a single beat, she goes, "Oh my god, even better! We can be best friends and you can help me find hot guys AND we can check out guys together!"

*[Mimicking Rebecca's excited voice]*

Like, her whole face just lit up. Zero disappointment, zero weird pause. Just instant pivot from "I want to date you" to "We're gonna be BFFs and talk about boys!"

**Tyler:** *[Cracking up]* That's so Rebecca.

**Ken:** *[Nodding enthusiastically]*

Right? And then - I swear this happened in the same conversation - she starts asking me about what kind of guys I like, if I've dated anyone, whether I think the TA is cute...

We went from her hitting on me to full-blown best friend girl talk in like thirty seconds flat.

**Tyler:** And you two have been inseparable ever since.

**Ken:** *[More seriously]*

Pretty much. She just... accepted me completely, you know? No judgment, no weirdness. Just pure Rebecca enthusiasm redirected from "potential boyfriend" to "gay best friend who's gonna help me navigate college boys."

*[Pause]*

You know, I don't think we would have made it without

Rebecca. Especially in those early years when being gay was still... complicated for other people, even if it wasn't for us.

**Tyler:** She really was our protector.

**Ken:** *[Suddenly sitting up straighter, grinning mischievously]*

Okay, hold up. Time out. I've been doing all the talking here, spilling my guts for your little book project. Don't you think it's my turn to ask some questions?

**Tyler:** Ken, that's not how this works—

**Ken:** *[Waving hands dramatically]* Nope! I'm grabbing the microphone now, babe. My interview, my rules.

*[Leans forward with that troublemaker grin]*

So, Mr. Future Author, let me ask you something. What was it really like for you when Rebecca met David? Because I remember you being all weird about it.

**Tyler:** I wasn't weird about it.

**Ken:** *[Snorting]* Oh please! You totally were! The first time she brought him around, you barely said two words all night. And then afterwards you kept asking me if I thought he was "good enough for her."

**Tyler:** I was being protective.

**Ken:** *[Teasing]* You were being jealous! Admit it! You thought some random guy was gonna steal your sister away from us.

**Tyler:** *[Quiet for a moment]* Maybe a little.

**Ken:** *[Triumphantly]* I KNEW IT! And then what happened when she told us she was pregnant with Joshua?

**Tyler:** *[Smiling despite himself]* You know what happened.

**Ken:** *[To the imaginary readers]* Oh no, babe, they don't know! You literally cried. Happy tears, but still. Big old Tyler tears right there in Rebecca's living room.

**Tyler:** I was emotional.

**Ken:** *[Softly, but still playful]* You were perfect. You immediately started planning how to be the best uncle in the world. Remember? You spent like three hours that night talking about college funds and teaching him to swim and whether we should move closer to them.

**Tyler:** We did move closer.

**Ken:** *[Nodding]* Two months later. Because God forbid little Joshua grow up without his Uncle Prism nearby.

*[Pause, getting more serious]*

You know what I loved most about that time, babe?

**Tyler:** What?

**Ken:** Watching you with David. Once you decided he was worthy of Rebecca, you just... adopted him. Like, full Tyler protection mode. He became part of our family because you said so.

**Tyler:** He was good to her. And he accepted us without question.

**Ken:** *[Grinning again]* Remember his bachelor party?

**Tyler:** *[Groaning]* Oh no, we're not telling that story.

**Ken:** *[Laughing]* Why not? It's a good story! You got so drunk you started giving everyone relationship advice!

**Tyler:** Ken...

**Ken:** *[To the readers]* He stood up on a chair in some dive bar and started lecturing a room full of straight guys about the importance of emotional communication in marriage!

**Tyler:** I was trying to help.

**Ken:** *[Wiping away tears from laughing]* You were amazing! David's friends thought you were the wisest person they'd ever met. Half of them asked for your number!

**Tyler:** They did not.

**Ken:** *[Still giggling]* They absolutely did! And I had to keep telling them, "Sorry boys, he's taken!"

*[Settling back, expression becoming fond]*

Those were good years, weren't they babe? The four of us, then the five of us when Joshua came along.

**Tyler:** They really were.

**Ken:** *[Not ready to give up the microphone yet, eyes sparkling with mischief]*

Okay, one more question before you wrestle this thing away from me. What was the exact moment you knew you wanted to move in with me?

**Tyler:** Ken...

**Ken:** *[Holding up a finger]* Ah ah ah! I'm still conducting this interview, Mr. Anderson. And I have a theory about this, but I want to hear your version first.

**Tyler:** [*Sighing but smiling*] Fine. It was... it was when you made me soup.

**Ken:** [*Practically bouncing*] YES! The Great Flu Incident of 2001! Tell them about it!

**Tyler:** I had the flu, and I was miserable in my tiny apartment. You showed up with homemade miso soup and...

**Ken:** [*Interrupting*] And camping gear! Don't forget the camping gear!

**Tyler:** [*Laughing*] And camping gear. Because you said my couch was "an insult to furniture everywhere" and you weren't leaving until I was better.

**Ken:** [*Proudly*] I set up a tent in your living room and nursed you back to health like some kind of gay Florence Nightingale.

**Tyler:** You stayed for four days.

**Ken:** [*More softly*] Best four days ever. Just us, terrible daytime TV, and me force-feeding you soup every two hours.

**Tyler:** When I woke up on day three and saw you sleeping in that ridiculous tent, still wearing the same clothes because you refused to leave...

**Ken:** [*Grinning*] You knew you were stuck with me.

**Tyler:** I knew I never wanted to be sick without you again. Or healthy without you, for that matter.

**Ken:** [*Dramatically wiping fake tears*] And that, ladies and gentlemen, is how Tyler Anderson asked me to move in with him. Through the power of influenza and camping equipment.

**Tyler:** I didn't ask you that day.

**Ken:** [*Waving hand dismissively*] Details! You asked me two weeks later, but we both knew. The tent sealed the deal.

[*Pause, getting more serious*]

You know what I really loved about living together, babe?

**Tyler:** What?

**Ken:** [*Thoughtfully*] How we figured out our rhythms. Like, I learned that you needed forty-five minutes of quiet time when you got home from work, and you learned that I needed to talk through my entire day or I'd explode.

**Tyler:** You would literally follow me around the apartment narrating your day.

**Ken:** *[Laughing]* I was processing! And you'd just nod and make little "mm-hmm" sounds until you were ready to actually engage. It was perfect.

**Tyler:** It was perfect.

**Ken:** *[Mischievous grin returning]* Even when I rearranged all your books by color instead of subject that one time?

**Tyler:** *[Groaning]* You nearly gave me a panic attack.

**Ken:** *[Giggling]* But you looked so cute frantically reorganizing them! And I learned never to touch your organizational systems again.

**Tyler:** Good lesson.

**Ken:** *[Settling back with a satisfied expression]*

Okay, I think I'm done being the interviewer. You can have your microphone back, babe. But only because I've thoroughly embarrassed you enough for one chapter.

**Tyler:** Thank you for your restraint.

**Ken:** *[Winking]* Don't mention it. So what else do you want to know for your fancy book?

**Tyler:** *[Quietly, after a pause]* Actually... there's something I've always wondered about, but it's not really for the book. It's more personal.

**Ken:** *[Leaning forward, curious]* Oh? Now you've got my attention, babe. What's up?

**Tyler:** Do you remember that day at the hospital when Rebecca was in labor with Joshua? We were sitting in the cafeteria, just... waiting.

**Ken:** *[Smiling fondly]* Of course I remember. We were there for like eight hours, talking about everything and nothing. You kept checking your watch every five minutes like that would somehow speed things up.

**Tyler:** We were talking about your family, your heritage... and you told me your Japanese name. Kenshin.

**Ken:** *[Nodding]* "Wise heart." My grandmother chose it. She said I had an old soul even as a baby.

**Tyler:** And then you said I should have a Japanese name too. You spent all that time going through options until you settled on Akira.

**Ken:** *[Voice softening]* "Bright" and "clear." It was perfect for you, babe. Those eyes of yours, the way you see things... it just fit.

**Tyler:** *[Quietly]* I asked you to teach me how to write it.

**Ken:** *[Long pause, expression growing tender]*

You did. I was... I was actually surprised when you asked that. I mean, you'd just learned this name that I'd given you, and immediately you wanted to know how to make it yours. Really yours.

**Tyler:** I remember you going to find paper and a pen.

**Ken:** *[Chuckling softly]* I had to ask three different nurses before someone finally gave me a napkin and a ballpoint pen. Not exactly traditional calligraphy materials, but...

**Tyler:** You sat there for over an hour, teaching me stroke by stroke.

**Ken:** *[More seriously]*

You were so methodical about it, babe. Like you approached everything - careful, precise, wanting to get it exactly right. I'd show you the character, break it down piece by piece, and you'd practice it over and over until your hand knew the movement.

**Tyler:** When you went to get coffee, I kept practicing.

**Ken:** *[Soft smile, eyes distant]*

I know. I saw you when I was walking back. You were sitting there at that little table under those awful fluorescent lights, tongue sticking out just slightly the way it always did when you were concentrating really hard. You had that napkin covered in attempts, just... writing your name. Your Japanese name.

*[Pause]*

I stood there for maybe five minutes just watching you, and I felt this wave of... God, Tyler, I felt so much love in that moment I thought my chest might explode.

**Tyler:** *[Softly]* Really?

**Ken:** *[Nodding]*

You were so focused, so passionate about learning this completely foreign thing just because... because I'd given it to you. Because it connected you to my culture, to my family, to me. And watching you practice writing "Akira" with such care and determination...

*[Voice getting quieter]*

It was like watching you choose to become part of my world in the most beautiful way possible.

**Tyler:** Why did you really choose that name for me? Not just what it meant, but... why that one?

**Ken:** *[Long pause, thinking]*

You want the real reason?

**Tyler:** Yeah.

**Ken:** *[Leaning back, looking at Tyler intently]*

Because you'd always been bright to me, babe. From that very first day at the pool. But not just smart-bright, you know? You were... illuminating. You made everything clearer just by being yourself. The way you saw people, the way you understood things that the rest of us missed...

*[Pause]*

And "clear" because you never hid who you were. Even when it was hard, even when it made you uncomfortable, you were always just... Tyler. No pretense, no performance. Just clear, honest truth.

**Tyler:** *[Quietly]* And how did you feel about being Japanese? I mean, really feel about it?

**Ken:** *[Surprised by the question, then smiling]*

You know, no one ever asked me that before. Not directly.

**Tyler:** I'm asking now.

**Ken:** *[Thoughtfully]*

I was proud, but it was complicated pride, you know? At home, I was proud to speak Japanese with my parents, to understand the culture, to carry on traditions. But at school, sometimes I felt like I had to downplay it to fit in.

*[Pause]*

But that day in the hospital, watching you want to learn my language, want to write your name in characters that meant something to my family... I felt purely proud for the first time. Like all the parts of me could finally exist in the same space.

**Tyler:** It bonded us together.

**Ken:** [*Softly*]

It did, babe. In a way I didn't even fully understand at the time. You didn't just accept who I was - you wanted to become part of it. And I wanted to share it with you.

[*Grinning*]

Plus, you looked ridiculously cute concentrating on those brush strokes. Even with a crappy ballpoint pen.

**Tyler:** [*Laughing*] Okay, I think we've gotten way too sentimental here. This is supposed to be a fun interview, remember?

**Ken:** [*Perking up immediately*] Oh, you want fun? I've got fun stories, babe! Like, do you want to hear about the time you tried to cook me dinner for our six-month anniversary?

**Tyler:** [*Groaning*] Oh no. Please don't tell them about the pasta incident.

**Ken:** [*Bouncing in his chair*] THE PASTA INCIDENT! Oh, this is perfect! So picture this - Tyler decides he's going to make me this fancy Italian dinner, right? He's been planning it for weeks, researching recipes, buying special ingredients...

**Tyler:** I wanted it to be special.

**Ken:** [*Grinning widely*] And it was special, babe. Just not in the way you intended. So he's making this elaborate seafood pasta, and everything's going fine until he gets to the part about cooking the lobster.

**Tyler:** I'd never cooked lobster before.

**Ken:** [*Dramatically*] He calls me at work - I'm in the middle of a study group - and he's in full panic mode. "Ken, the lobster is still moving! I put it in the pot but it's trying to climb out! What do I do?"

**Tyler:** It was traumatic!

**Ken:** [*Doing Tyler's panicked voice*] "I can't kill it, Ken! It looked at me! I swear it looked right at me with its little lobster eyes!"

**Tyler:** [*Defensive*] It did look at me!

**Ken:** [*Laughing*] So I have to abandon my study group and rush home to find Tyler sitting on the kitchen floor, having a full crisis of conscience about this lobster. Meanwhile, the pasta is burning, the sauce is boiling over, and there's seafood smell everywhere.

**Tyler:** You saved dinner.

**Ken:** [Proudly] I did! We ended up ordering pizza and keeping the lobster as a pet for three days.

**Tyler:** [Smiling] We named him Giuseppe.

**Ken:** [Grinning] Giuseppe the Lobster! We put him in the bathtub and Tyler insisted on talking to him every morning before class.

**Tyler:** I felt guilty!

**Ken:** [Affectionately] You gave him little pep talks. "Good morning, Giuseppe! I hope you have a lovely day in the tub!"

**Tyler:** [Laughing despite himself] Rebecca thought we'd lost our minds.

**Ken:** [Nodding enthusiastically] Oh, she did! She came over to borrow a textbook and found us having a serious conversation with a lobster about whether he preferred jazz or classical music.

**Tyler:** We eventually took him to the coast and released him.

**Ken:** [Softly] Two-hour drive each way, but you insisted. You said Giuseppe deserved to see his family again.

**Tyler:** It was the right thing to do.

**Ken:** [Looking at Tyler fondly] That's my boyfriend. Can't hurt a lobster, but will absolutely destroy someone in a business negotiation.

**Tyler:** Those are completely different situations!

**Ken:** [Laughing] I know, babe. That's what made you perfect. You had this huge heart for everything, but you could be ruthless when you needed to be.

**Tyler:** Speaking of ruthless, what about you and Rebecca ganging up on me about my wardrobe?

**Ken:** [Eyes lighting up] Oh! The Great Makeover Intervention of 2000!

**Tyler:** They ambushed me.

**Ken:** [Grinning mischievously] We did not ambush you. We

staged a loving intervention because your idea of "dressy" was a clean polo shirt.

**Tyler:** My clothes were perfectly functional.

**Ken:** *[To the imaginary readers]* He had three pairs of khakis. Three! In the exact same shade of beige! And like twelve identical polo shirts in different colors!

**Tyler:** Organization is efficient.

**Ken:** *[Laughing]* Rebecca took one look in your closet and declared it "a crime against fashion and humanity." She literally called it a "beige emergency."

**Tyler:** She dragged us to the mall for six hours.

**Ken:** *[Nodding]* Six glorious hours of Rebecca playing dress-up with her favorite gay boys. She was in heaven, you were in hell, and I was just enjoying the show.

**Tyler:** You were supposed to be on my side!

**Ken:** *[Grinning]* Babe, I was on the side of seeing you in clothes that actually fit! Do you remember the first time you wore that dark blue button-down she picked out?

**Tyler:** *[Quietly]* You said I looked handsome.

**Ken:** *[Softly]* You looked incredible. Like, I literally forgot how to form words for a minute.

**Tyler:** Rebecca was very proud of herself.

**Ken:** *[Laughing]* She took credit for our entire relationship after that. "If I hadn't fixed Tyler's fashion sense, you two never would have made it!"

**Tyler:** She wasn't entirely wrong.

**Ken:** *[Mock gasping]* Tyler Anderson! Are you saying you only stayed with me because I helped you buy better shirts?

**Tyler:** *[Smiling]* I'm saying Rebecca has good taste in makeovers. And boyfriends.

**Ken:** *[Preening]* Well, she did pick the best one for you, didn't she?

**Tyler:** *[Laughing]* You're impossible.

**Ken:** *[Eyes absolutely lighting up]* OH! And what about the rainbow briefs! How could I forget the rainbow briefs?

**Tyler:** *[Covering face]* I can't believe you're going to tell this story.

**Ken:** *[Grinning wickedly]* Oh, I am absolutely telling this story. So there we are at the mall, right? Rebecca's gathered like a dozen outfits, I'm holding this mountain of clothes that's taller than Tyler, and Rebecca's got both arms full of hangers with different pants.

**Tyler:** They had me completely surrounded.

**Ken:** *[Continuing]* So we all pile into this dressing room - which, by the way, was way too small for three people - and we're standing there looking at Tyler, and he's looking at us, and nobody's moving.

**Tyler:** It was the world's most awkward staring contest.

**Ken:** *[Doing Rebecca's voice]* Finally Rebecca goes, "Get undressed and try these on!" because her arms are clearly dying from holding all those hangers.

And I'm shuffling under this pile of clothes going, "What's wrong, babe? Why aren't you moving?"

**Tyler:** I was mortified.

**Ken:** *[Continuing]* But Tyler just stands there, shuffling his feet, looking everywhere except at us. So we start asking questions, right? "Are you okay?" "Do you feel sick?" "Is something wrong with the clothes?"

**Tyler:** You two were like detectives trying to solve a case.

**Ken:** *[Laughing]* We kept guessing! "Is it the lighting?" "Are you claustrophobic?" "Do you not like the shirts Rebecca picked?"

Poor Rebecca's practically groaning under the weight of all these pants, and I'm about to drop everything, and Tyler finally just... drops his shorts.

**Tyler:** *[Groaning]* And there they were.

**Ken:** *[Practically shouting with joy]* RAINBOW BRIEFS! The brightest, most beautiful rainbow underwear I'd ever seen in my life!

**Tyler:** *[Mumbling]* If I'd known I was going to be changing clothes today, I might have worn something different.

**Ken:** *[Still grinning]* I nearly dropped every single piece of clothing trying to applaud! I was like, "Babe! You're representing! You're showing your pride!"

**Tyler:** You were so loud the people in the next dressing room could hear you.

**Ken:** *[Nodding proudly]* Because I was proud! My boyfriend was wearing rainbow underwear! Do you know how amazing that was?

**Tyler:** Rebecca was mortified for me.

**Ken:** *[Chuckling]* Poor Rebecca cleared her throat and tried to be diplomatic. She goes, "Well... they look good on you, Tyler. Now let's try on these pants."

**Tyler:** She was trying so hard to be supportive.

**Ken:** *[Fondly]* But years later, over wine at dinner, she admitted how cute you looked in those super bright rainbow undies. Said she hadn't expected it at all, but it was absolutely perfect for you.

**Tyler:** And then you made it a tradition.

**Ken:** *[Grinning widely]* Every birthday! Rainbow underwear became your signature gift from me. I'd find the most outrageous, colorful pairs I could.

**Tyler:** Whether I wanted it or not, the rainbow became my symbol.

**Ken:** *[Softly]* You embraced it though. You said it complemented your nickname - Prism. Light breaking into all those beautiful colors.

**Tyler:** And Joshua picked up on it when he was little.

**Ken:** *[Nodding]* Oh, he loved it! Every birthday, every holiday, little Joshua would give you rainbow stickers, rainbow cards, rainbow everything. He thought it was just Uncle Prism's favorite thing.

**Tyler:** *[Smiling]* He never knew the real origin story.

**Ken:** *[Laughing]* Until now! When he reads this, he's going to die laughing, making all those connections. All those years of rainbow gifts, and it started because you were embarrassed about your underwear in a mall dressing room.

**Tyler:** *[Shaking head but smiling]* I can't believe that's going to be in print forever.

**Ken:** *[Teasingly]* Hey, you're the one who wanted to write down our stories, babe. You said I should tell them everything!

**Tyler:** I may have to edit that part out.

**Ken:** *[Mock gasping]* You wouldn't dare! That's the best story! Besides, it shows how you went from being embarrassed about something to making it part of who you are. That's character growth, baby!

**Tyler:** *[Laughing despite himself]* You're impossible.

**Ken:** *[Winking]* Impossibly charming. There's a difference.

**Tyler:** *[Smiling, but checking his notes]* I think we've probably covered enough embarrassing stories for one chapter.

**Ken:** *[Mock disappointment]* Aw, but I haven't even gotten to the time you tried to surprise me with karaoke night and ended up singing the same song seventeen times because you couldn't figure out how to change it!

**Tyler:** *[Firmly]* We are NOT telling that story.

**Ken:** *[Grinning]* Fine, fine. Save something for the sequel, right?

**Tyler:** *[Laughing]* There's not going to be a sequel, Ken.

**Ken:** *[More seriously, but still smiling]* You know what, babe? This was actually really nice. Talking about all this stuff, remembering... I don't think we ever really sat down and went through our whole story like this before.

**Tyler:** *[Softly]* Me neither. I'm glad we did it.

**Ken:** *[Leaning back in his chair]* Alright, alright, I think I've given you enough material to make me look absolutely irresistible in your little memoir. Did you get what you needed from the fabulous Ken Takeshi show?

**Tyler:** *[Smiling]* I think I got more than I expected.

**Ken:** *[Bouncing up from his chair]* Of course you did! I'm a treasure trove of amazing stories and devastatingly good looks. Joshua's gonna read this and think, "Damn, Uncle Prism really scored with that Ken guy!"

**Tyler:** *[Laughing]* You're ridiculous.

**Ken:** *[Grinning widely]* Ridiculously awesome, you mean. Anyway, I've got places to be, people to dazzle, you know how it is.

*[Suddenly gets that mischievous look]*

But first...

*[Before Tyler can react, Ken swoops in and plants a big, dramatic kiss on him - the kind that would make Tyler squirm if anyone else tried it]*

**Tyler:** *[Flustered but laughing]* Ken!

**Ken:** *[Pulling back with a huge grin]* What? I always kiss you goodbye, babe. It's tradition! Plus, now your readers know exactly how lucky you were to have me.

*[Winks and heads for the door]*

Have fun writing about how amazing I am!

*[The sound of Ken's laughter fades as he leaves, leaving Tyler shaking his head but smiling.]*

# CHAPTER 5
# AKIRA

Joshua looks up from the binder he just finished reading and mouths out the word "Akira," staring off across the attic, but his mind is tracing back to the night in the hospital cafeteria... the night he had been born. He had no idea that was the name Uncle Ken gave Uncle Tyler... he always thought Tyler's nickname, Prism, was a cool name... I mean, what with the two colored eyes... but... Akira... something just sang with it... and he said it again, this time a little louder.

"Akira."

The name felt different on his tongue now that he understood its meaning. Bright. Clear. Like the way Uncle Tyler saw everything, understood people in ways that cut straight through the bullshit to what really mattered. Joshua could almost feel the weight of that hospital night, Tyler and Ken sharing something sacred while waiting for him to be born, Tyler learning to write his name in careful Japanese characters...

"Honey..." he heard from the bottom of the ladder... It was Rebecca... she had been reluctant to interrupt him... knowing full well what he was doing. It had gotten quiet since he slid the box over on the floor and she made lunch... but... well, she couldn't stand the wait so she made another excuse. "Your lunch is getting cold..."

Of course it was getting cold, stupid, she thought. It was a fucking tuna sandwich. It was supposed to be cold. God, she hated this whole excuse trap she'd built for herself. It all started with good intentions—protecting a nine-year-old boy from unbearable grief—and then morphed into this elaborate house of cards that got more impossible to maintain every goddamn day. Why the fuck couldn't she have just told him years ago? Back when the wound was fresh but the lie was small? She would've been herself then... instead of whatever the fuck this was that she'd let herself turn into. This woman who lied to her own son about the most important people in their lives, who signed dead men's names to birthday cards like some kind of deranged secretary to ghosts.

"Coming, Mom..."

Joshua climbed down the ladder and looked at her slightly, in his typical non-locking eye cast and moved around her on the way down to the kitchen... no expression... no "guess what I found?"... no excited babbling about Uncle Tyler's incredible documentation project... nothing. Just that careful, controlled politeness that meant he was processing something too big to discuss yet.

She followed him downstairs, her heart hammering with dread and anticipation. Sitting at the table, she popped open a can of Coke Zero for him and added exactly 3 ice cubes—she'd learned that he preferred that specific ratio, but wouldn't say anything if you deviated... he'd just quietly endure whatever you gave him rather than make a fuss. But she knew. Just like she knew he'd want the grilled cheese cut diagonally, not straight across, and that he'd eat the crust first to get it out of the way. All those little Tyler-isms that had been showing up in Joshua since he was tiny.

She sat down to her own pathetic lunch—a bowl of canned tomato soup and a handful of Doritos because apparently she'd given up on being an actual adult who prepared real food. Healthy as fuck, Rebecca, she thought bitterly.

"So... how's the... uh... cleaning up there?" she asked, trying to sound casual while her stomach churned with anxiety.

"Mmmm," Joshua said, pulling his phone out and scrolling through it with the kind of focused attention that meant he was actively avoiding conversation. He normally didn't even bring his phone to meals—wasn't part of the social media generation, usually just reading his nerd sites about coding and occasionally playing some puzzle game that required actual thinking. But right now he clearly needed something to do with his hands, some excuse to not make eye contact while his brain processed whatever the hell he'd discovered in those boxes.

He was too focused on everything he'd just learned. Akira... Uncle Tyler... the way Ken had given him that name with such love, such careful thought. The way Tyler had practiced writing it over and over on hospital napkins until he got it perfect.

"I was thinking..." Rebecca started, but Joshua paid no attention... typical for him when he was overwhelmed, but it still stung...

"Maybe later when your dad gets back, we could go out for dinner. Would you like that?"

The words were out of her mouth before she remembered, and she wanted to kick herself. She knew Josh was just like Tyler when it came to restaurants—the noise, the unpredictability, the sensory overload of trying to eat while strangers moved around you and servers interrupted every five minutes. Goddammit. Here it was again, her brain making the same fucking mistakes Tyler would have hated.

"What about grilling out?" he countered without looking up from his phone. Joshua always liked to grill... even more than David, actually. There was something about the precise control, the predictable timing, the way you could manage all the variables that appealed to his need for order.

"Oh... uh... sure... I'll call your dad and ask him to pick up some burgers on the way home..."

"American cheese," Joshua said automatically, still scrolling.

"Right... American cheese..."

Just like fucking Tyler. If he were standing here right now, he'd be loving this, wouldn't he, that little shit? The way Joshua instinctively knew exactly what he wanted, the way he avoided restaurants without making a big deal about it, the way he could make simple requests without explaining or justifying or apologizing for his preferences. Tyler had taken years to get comfortable doing that, but Joshua had somehow been born with that particular brand of quiet confidence.

Tyler indeed was loving it. And he was also breaking apart watching Rebecca struggle with her own guilt and grief, seeing how the years of lying had twisted her into knots. He whispered encouragement to Joshua, reminding him to be gentle with her... she was trying, even if she was fucking it up spectacularly... Joshua only kept his eyes on his phone to give himself an excuse to look distracted... otherwise, his mom would think he was completely nuts, making eye contact with empty air and having conversations with his dead uncle who was sitting right there across from him... laughing at their exchange while simultaneously wanting to reach across the table and comfort Rebecca in ways he couldn't.

"Josh, go on... give her a bone..." Tyler murmured, his voice thick with empathy for both of them.

"Fine!" Joshua said, forgetting for a moment that he was supposed to be responding to Tyler silently.

"What, honey?" Rebecca looked up, confused.

Josh felt heat creep up his neck as he recovered. "I mean, grilling is great. Hey, Mom... I found Uncle Tyler's notebook of... writing stuff you said... and... well..."

"Oh you did?" Rebecca's voice went up half an octave, that fake-casual tone she used when she was trying to seem surprised by something she already knew was coming.

She knew he had found Tyler's papers, obviously, but she was still playing this ridiculous game of pretending she didn't know exactly what was happening upstairs. God... why did she keep drawing this out? Why couldn't she just rip off the fucking bandage and tell him the truth?

"Yeah... and... well, do you mind if I finish cleaning everything up later? I'd like to read more of it. Please?"

And there were those eyes. They weren't chromatic like Tyler's incredible mismatched gaze, but goddamn if they didn't make her heart melt every single time. Joshua rarely made direct eye contact

—it was clearly difficult for him, just like it had been for Tyler—but when he did, when he deliberately chose to look at her straight-on like this, it was like being hit by a truck of pure affection. He rarely showed that vulnerability, preferring to keep his emotions carefully controlled, but when he did... Rebecca nearly melted, her life flashing back to her youth and feeling the exact same way when Tyler would occasionally grace her with one of his rare, unguarded moments of connection.

But Joshua was his own person... his own man... and she was no longer "mommy" who could fix everything with hugs and ice cream. He was twenty-one fucking years old, and she'd been lying to him about fundamental aspects of his family history for more than half his life.

"Of course... you're an adult... you don't need my permission, honey. Besides... I'm kinda happy you..."

"What?" Josh interrupted, a little too eager, leaning forward in his chair like he was waiting for her to finally, finally tell him what he desperately wanted to hear. He hoped that perhaps she was finally going to tell him what he already knew... or at least suspected... the truth about Tyler and Ken and why they'd really disappeared from his life.

"Uh... I'm happy... you... uh... are enjoying reading it. I haven't even read it myself," she said, the words falling flat and evasive even to her own ears.

"Really? Why not?" Joshua seemed genuinely surprised, and there was something in his tone that suggested this wasn't just casual curiosity.

"Well... Tyler was still working on it when..."

Here it comes, Josh thought, his heart racing as he leaned forward expectantly. Finally, maybe, she'd tell him the truth.

Rebecca felt suddenly trapped, her heart jumping into her throat like she was about to confess to murder. The words were right there—Tyler was still working on it when he died, when they both died, when I lost the two most important people in my life and couldn't figure out how to explain that to a nine-year-old who loved them more than anyone else in the world. Even Tyler leaned forward from his invisible position at the table, his expression full of desperate empathy for his best friend's obvious pain, though Rebecca couldn't see him. Joshua kept flicking quick glances toward Tyler, but Rebecca was too caught up in her own panic to notice her son's divided attention.

"Uh... well, when... we... uh... had to move to Seattle and then everything was so crazy with work and relocating and trying to get you settled in a new school and well..." she diverted, clearly coming unraveled, her voice getting higher and more strained with each word. The lie was so thin it was practically transparent, and they both knew it. Moving to Seattle didn't explain twelve years of not reading Tyler's writing. Being busy with work didn't explain why she couldn't bear to look at his careful documentation of their friendship.

Joshua hated seeing her this way—watching his strong, fierce mother reduced to stumbling through obvious lies because the truth was too painful to speak out loud. And for the first time, sitting this close and really watching her face, he realized that her lies had morphed from trying to protect him into really protecting herself. She hadn't read Uncle Tyler's papers because she couldn't bring herself to. Because reading Tyler's words would make his absence real in ways that signing his name to birthday cards didn't.

He looked over at Tyler, who had leaned back in his chair with his eyes downcast, his entire posture radiating grief and helplessness. Tyler was watching his best friend fall apart and couldn't do a damn thing about it—couldn't reach across the table and take her hand, couldn't tell her "it's okay, Rebecca, I'm here, I'm still here, you don't have to carry this alone anymore." Instead, Tyler just had to sit there and watch her suffer, feeling so fucking lost at his inability to comfort the person who'd been his chosen sister for over two decades.

The pain on Tyler's face was almost unbearable to witness, and it hurt Joshua deeply—he was the only person in the room who could see Tyler's anguish, who understood that Tyler would give anything to be able to tell Rebecca that things would be okay. Yet

Joshua was still learning the rules of whatever this was, still trying to understand how any of it worked.

Tyler suddenly disappeared completely, like he couldn't stand to watch Rebecca's pain anymore, making Joshua flinch slightly at the abrupt absence.

"Honey, are you okay?" Rebecca asked, grateful for any distraction that moved the spotlight off her obvious emotional breakdown. She thanked whatever gods might be listening for small mercies.

"Yeah... just... I'm finished with lunch... gonna go back up..." Joshua said, addressing both his visible mother and his invisible uncle, wherever Tyler had gone.

Rebecca wanted to say more—wanted to grab Joshua's hand and spill everything, wanted to tell him about the accident and the grief and the twelve years of missing Tyler and Ken so desperately that she'd rather lie than admit they were really gone. But she had no words that felt adequate to the magnitude of what she'd done. What could she say? How could she possibly explain that she'd been so fucking selfish in her grief that she'd denied her son the chance to properly mourn the two people who'd loved him most?

It was still in progress, this slow-motion disaster she'd created, and she knew she needed to let it continue unfolding. Joshua was still reading, still discovering, still putting together the pieces of a puzzle she should have helped him solve years ago.

# CHAPTER 6
# REBECCA BRENNAN

**Tyler:** Okay, Rebecca, you're the one who insisted I write all this down, so you don't get to be camera shy now.

**Rebecca:** [*Settling into her chair with a cup of tea*] Camera shy? Are you fucking kidding me, Prism? I've been nagging your ass about this for months. I'm not backing down now.

**Tyler:** [*Slight smile*] Language, Rebecca.

**Rebecca:** [*Grinning wickedly*] Oh, shut up. You love it when I talk dirty. Remember when I taught you to swear properly?

**Tyler:** [*Blushing slightly*] We are not telling that story.

**Rebecca:** [*Laughing*] Why not? It's adorable! You were twenty years old and had never said "fuck" out loud. Not once!

**Tyler:** I had a sheltered upbringing.

**Rebecca:** [*Snorting*] Sheltered my ass. You were just too polite for your own good. Still are, actually.

**Tyler:** So you decided to corrupt me?

**Rebecca:** [*Proudly*] Damn right I did! Someone had to teach you that it's okay to have edges, to get a little rough around the corners. Life's too fucking short to be polite all the time.

**Tyler:** You literally said, and I quote, "Prism, you really should put those stories together. They'd make a wonderful book!"

**Rebecca:** [*Waving her hand*] Yeah, yeah, I said that. Multiple times. At dinner, over the phone, in texts... I may have been a relentless pain in the ass about it.

**Tyler:** A little persistent? You've been campaigning for this project like your life depended on it.

**Rebecca:** *[Leaning forward, more serious but still with attitude]* Because it fucking matters, Prism! You have all these incredible experiences, these connections with people all over the world, and you just... carry them around like they're nothing special.

**Tyler:** They're just stories, Rebecca.

**Rebecca:** *[Getting fired up]* Bullshit! They're not just stories. They're your life, and your life is pretty goddamn remarkable. The way you see people, the way you connect with them despite all the social bullshit that makes you want to crawl under a rock...

**Tyler:** *[Quietly]* You think people would actually want to read about that?

**Rebecca:** *[Firmly]* Hell yes, they would. People need to read about someone who's different but doesn't apologize for it. Someone who figured out how to build real relationships despite having a brain that works like a beautiful, complicated machine.

**Tyler:** *[After a moment]* Okay. So where do you want to start?

**Rebecca:** *[Settling back with a smirk]* How about you start by asking me something? This is your interview, remember? Don't go all shy on me now.

**Tyler:** Right. Okay... How did we really become friends? I mean, I know you dragged Ken to that diving meet, but what made you decide I was worth keeping around?

**Rebecca:** *[Bursting out laughing]* Oh, that's fucking easy. You were standing there dripping wet in your tiny little Speedo, and I practically interrogated you poolside like you were applying for the CIA.

**Tyler:** You did not interrogate me poolside.

**Rebecca:** *[Raising an eyebrow]* Prism, I dragged Ken to that meet to look at hot boys, saw you nail that dive, and marched my ass right down to the pool deck to get the full story on Tyler "Prism" Anderson.

**Tyler:** You were... very direct.

**Rebecca:** *[Grinning]* I was relentless! Poor Ken was trying to be all smooth and charming, and there I was asking you about your major, your family, your diving coach, and probably your fucking zodiac sign while you're standing there in practically nothing trying to towel off.

**Tyler:** You did ask a lot of very personal questions.

**Rebecca:** *[Nodding proudly]* Damn right I did! Ken was clearly smitten - I could see it written all over his face when you surfaced from that dive. So I needed to make sure you weren't some closet case who was going to break his heart or some prissy little perfectionist who thought he was too good for us.

**Tyler:** And what was your conclusion?

**Rebecca:** *[More seriously]* You answered every single one of my ridiculous, invasive questions honestly. Even when I asked about your family and you had to tell me about your grandparents dying, about being essentially alone... you didn't get defensive or tell me to mind my own fucking business. And you're standing there half-naked and still dripping chlorine water, being more polite than most people are fully clothed.

**Tyler:** I wanted you both to know me.

**Rebecca:** *[Softly]* Yeah, you did. Right there at the pool, you just told us the truth about everything. That's when I knew you were good people. Most guys would have either gotten pissed off at my interrogation or tried to charm their way through it.

**Tyler:** What made you decide I could stay in your lives?

**Rebecca:** *[Chuckling]* When Ken asked if you wanted to get dinner and you immediately asked if I could come too.

**Tyler:** I was nervous about a real date.

**Rebecca:** *[Laughing]* You were fucking terrified! But instead of making some excuse or trying to get rid of me, you actually wanted me there. Like you understood that Ken and I were a package deal, and you were okay with that.

**Tyler:** I wanted to be part of whatever you two had.

**Rebecca:** *[Grinning]* And then I got to be your chaperone for like the first month of your relationship! Remember that? Ken was trying to be all romantic, and there I was third-wheeling every single date.

**Tyler:** You were very thorough in your... supervision.

**Rebecca:** *[Laughing]* I was making sure Ken didn't rush you into anything you weren't ready for! You were so sweet and nervous, and Ken was so obviously head-over-heels...

**Tyler:** Ken eventually told you to back off a little.

**Rebecca:** *[Grinning]* He told me to "dial down the interrogation because Tyler's going to think we're both crazy." But by then I already knew you were perfect for him.

**Tyler:** When did you really decide you wanted me as a friend, not just Ken's boyfriend?

**Rebecca:** *[Thinking]* Remember the first time you came to my dorm room? This was like a week after we met, and Ken wanted to study together for that psych exam.

**Tyler:** Your room was... chaotic.

**Rebecca:** *[Laughing]* My room was a fucking disaster zone! Books everywhere, clothes on every surface, papers scattered like confetti. And you walked in and got this expression like you were in physical pain.

**Tyler:** It was a lot to process visually.

**Rebecca:** *[Grinning]* But instead of just ignoring it or making some smartass comment about my messiness, you very politely asked if you could organize my bookshelf while Ken and I studied.

**Tyler:** It seemed presumptuous to just start rearranging your things.

**Rebecca:** *[Nodding]* See? That's what I mean! You saw a problem, you wanted to fix it, but you asked permission first. You respected that it was my space.

**Tyler:** And you said yes.

**Rebecca:** Hell yes, I said yes! And then I got to watch you work for two hours. Ken was supposed to be helping me study, but we both just sat there watching you create this beautiful, logical system out of my book explosion.

**Tyler:** That wasn't weird for you?

**Rebecca:** *[Shaking her head]* Weird? Prism, it was fucking mesmerizing. You had this whole process, this rhythm. Like watching an artist work. And when you were done, you looked so goddamn satisfied.

**Tyler:** Your books finally made sense.

**Rebecca:** *[Softly]* That's what made me want to be your friend. You cared about making things better, even my stupid little problems. You made my chaos into something beautiful.

**Tyler:** When did you realize I was... different? That I processed things differently than other people?

**Rebecca:** *[Long pause, thinking]* You know what? I never really thought of you as "different." I just thought of you as Prism. But if I had to pick a moment...

**Tyler:** What moment?

**Rebecca:** *[Settling back]* Remember that party at David's frat? This was way before David and I were together - just some random college party Ken dragged us to.

**Tyler:** I remember leaving early.

**Rebecca:** *[Nodding]* But I watched you that night, really watched you. You were doing fine at first - talking to people, even laughing at someone's dumb joke. But then the place got packed, music got louder, and I could see you starting to... shut down.

**Tyler:** It got overwhelming.

**Rebecca:** *[More gently]* You found Ken and me and said, "I think I need to head home now," in this very careful voice. No bullshit explanation about how the party sucked, no drama. Just honest communication about what you needed.

**Tyler:** I didn't want to ruin your night.

**Rebecca:** *[Leaning forward]* And that's exactly what I mean! You knew your limits, you told us clearly, and you took care of yourself without making it anyone else's problem. Most people either suffer through shit they hate or make a big scene about leaving.

**Tyler:** It took me years to see that as a good thing.

**Rebecca:** *[Firmly]* Well, Ken and I saw it right away. We knew your brain worked differently, but we didn't give a shit because different doesn't mean broken.

**Tyler:** When did you learn about the autism spectrum stuff?

**Rebecca:** *[Smiling]* When you called me at eleven fucking PM all excited because you'd finally found the words for what you'd always known about yourself.

**Tyler:** I was really excited.

**Rebecca:** *[Laughing]* Excited? Babe, you were bouncing off the walls! You'd been reading about it, and suddenly everything clicked. I just sat there thinking, "Well, duh. This explains everything, but it doesn't change jack shit about who you are."

**Tyler:** Did it worry you? Having a friend who was... neurologically different?

**Rebecca:** *[Looking genuinely puzzled]* Why the fuck would that worry me? Prism, you were already my friend. You were already the guy who remembered exactly how I like my coffee, who helped me study without making me feel stupid, who listened to me bitch about boys without ever once telling me I was being ridiculous.

*[Pause]*

Learning you were on the spectrum didn't change you. It just gave us better language for understanding how to be good friends to you.

**Tyler:** Like what?

**Rebecca:** *[Counting on her fingers]* Like knowing you needed a heads-up before we dragged you to parties. Like understanding that when you went quiet during dinner, you weren't pissed off - you were just processing all the input. Like realizing that your crazy attention to detail wasn't you being obsessive, it was just how your beautiful brain works.

**Tyler:** You and Ken got really good at... accommodating me.

**Rebecca:** *[Shaking her head firmly]* We got good at being your real friends. The kind who understand that friendship means working with each other's needs, not forcing everyone into the same fucking mold.

**Tyler:** You were always very... supportive when it came to encouraging me to try new experiences.

**Rebecca:** *[Snorting]* Oh, for fuck's sake, Prism. Just say it - I pushed you to do shit you were scared of. You don't have to be all diplomatic about it.

**Tyler:** Like when you... encouraged me to try drinking.

**Rebecca:** *[Laughing]* "Encouraged you to try drinking"? Jesus Christ, Prism, just say I got you drunk! You sound like a fucking health pamphlet.

**Tyler:** I didn't see the point.

**Rebecca:** *[Snorting]* The point was learning to let go of that iron control you keep on yourself. You needed to see that it was okay to be a little messy sometimes.

**Tyler:** You made me do shots.

**Rebecca:** *[Proudly]* I made you do ONE shot. And then I spent the rest of the night making sure you didn't die while you experienced your first hangover.

**Tyler:** Ken was horrified.

**Rebecca:** *[Grinning]* Ken was a fucking mother hen! "Rebecca, what if he gets sick? Rebecca, what if he doesn't like it? Rebecca, what if he never forgives us?"

**Tyler:** You told him to calm his tits.

**Rebecca:** *[Bursting out laughing]* I did! I told him to calm his goddamn tits and trust me. And what happened?

**Tyler:** I had fun.

**Rebecca:** *[Triumphantly]* You had a blast! You got giggly and started telling us all these stories about your diving competitions, and you laughed so hard you snorted, and it was fucking adorable.

**Tyler:** And then I threw up in your bathroom.

**Rebecca:** *[Waving her hand]* Details! The important thing is you learned that letting go a little bit wouldn't kill you.

**Tyler:** You did that a lot, didn't you? Found ways to... well, you knew when I needed a push.

**Rebecca:** *[More seriously]* Because I could see when you were holding yourself back out of fear instead of just not wanting to do something. I wasn't going to let you miss out on life because you were scared, but I also wasn't going to push you into shit that would actually hurt you.

**Tyler:** Like what?

**Rebecca:** *[Thinking]* Like that time in senior year when you didn't want to go to the career fair because there would be too many people and too much noise.

**Tyler:** It was going to be overwhelming.

**Rebecca:** *[Nodding]* Yeah, it was going to be a nightmare. So Ken and I put our heads together and figured out how to make it work for you.

**Tyler:** Wait, you two planned that whole thing?

**Rebecca:** *[Grinning]* Of course we did! We had signals for when you needed to step outside, we researched which companies would actually be worth your time, we even mapped out the quietest route through the building.

**Tyler:** I... I had no idea you did all that.

**Rebecca:** *[Laughing]* You think it was just a coincidence that we kept "randomly" suggesting coffee breaks right when you were starting to look overwhelmed?

**Tyler:** I thought you were just being... social.

**Rebecca:** *[Snorting]* Social, my ass. We were running interference so you could actually focus on the companies that mattered instead of burning out on small talk with every random booth.

**Tyler:** And I got three interviews out of it.

**Rebecca:** *[Proudly]* Including KPMG! You almost bailed on the whole fucking thing because you thought it would be too overwhelming.

**Tyler:** I didn't realize you two were... managing all of that for me.

**Rebecca:** *[Softly]* That's what friends do, Prism. We figure out how to make things work so you don't miss out on good shit just because your brain processes differently than ours.

**Tyler:** *[Quietly, after a long pause]* Rebecca... I had no idea. All these years, I thought I just... got lucky that day. That somehow I managed to handle it better than I expected.

**Rebecca:** *[Gently]* You did handle it, babe. We just made sure the conditions were right for you to succeed.

**Tyler:** That job fair... that interview... it literally changed my entire career path. My whole life. And you and Ken orchestrated all of that without me even knowing.

**Rebecca:** [*Shrugging*] We saw an opportunity that could be good for you, and we figured out how to make it happen. No big deal.

**Tyler:** [*Voice getting emotional*] It is a big deal, Rebecca. It's a huge deal. Thank you. I don't think I ever properly thanked you for... for seeing what I needed before I even knew I needed it.

**Rebecca:** [*Softly*] You don't need to thank me, Prism. But you're welcome.

**Tyler:** [*Taking a breath, composing himself*] Okay, let me ask you about something lighter before I start crying. Tell me about when David came into the picture.

**Rebecca:** [*Face lighting up with mischief*] Oh, you want to hear about Operation David?

**Tyler:** Operation David?

**Rebecca:** [*Grinning*] That's what Ken called it when I started obsessing over this guy in my literature class. I may have been slightly... intense about it.

**Tyler:** What do you mean by "intense"?

**Rebecca:** [*Laughing*] I had fucking spreadsheets! Color-coded analysis of compatibility factors, shared interests, potential red flags...

**Tyler:** [*Surprised*] You made spreadsheets about dating David?

**Rebecca:** [*Proudly*] I approached that man like a military campaign. And it worked, didn't it? But I was terrified about introducing him to you and Ken.

**Tyler:** Wait, why were you scared? I thought you liked him.

**Rebecca:** [*More seriously*] I did like him. That's exactly why I was scared shitless. You two were my family. If David couldn't handle that, couldn't accept you as part of the package, then he could fuck right off.

**Tyler:** What were you worried would happen?

**Rebecca:** [*Sighing*] Honestly? I was worried he'd be weird about you two being gay. This was 2001, remember? Not everyone was cool with it, even if they pretended to be.

**Tyler:** And we weren't exactly subtle about being together.

**Rebecca:** *[Smiling fondly]* You were fucking adorable together. Always sitting close, Ken making you laugh until you got that soft expression... anyone with eyes could see you were crazy about each other.

**Tyler:** So what happened when you brought David around?

**Rebecca:** *[Face glowing]* Magic happened. You remember that dinner at your place? You cooked something amazing - thankfully not lobster this time - and Ken was being his usual charming self, and David just... fit.

**Tyler:** He asked good questions about my work.

**Rebecca:** *[Nodding]* Real questions! Not just polite small talk. And when you started explaining some complex accounting thing, he actually listened and asked follow-up questions.

**Tyler:** He seemed genuinely interested.

**Rebecca:** *[Warmly]* And then Ken started telling that embarrassing story about your first apartment with the broken heater, and David laughed at all the right parts and looked at you two like he thought you were the cutest fucking couple ever.

**Tyler:** That's when you knew he was a keeper.

**Rebecca:** *[Softly]* That's when I knew he got it. That loving me meant loving my chosen family. That you and Ken weren't just my friends - you were my brothers.

**Tyler:** We got pretty protective during the engagement.

**Rebecca:** *[Bursting out laughing]* Protective? You two interviewed him like he was applying to join the fucking FBI!

**Tyler:** We wanted to make sure his intentions were serious.

**Rebecca:** *[Grinning]* You made him explain his five-year plan, his thoughts on joint finances, and his position on hypothetical future children. Ken asked him about his family's medical history!

**Tyler:** Ken did not ask about medical history.

**Rebecca:** *[Laughing]* Okay, maybe not medical history. But you two definitely put him through the wringer. Poor bastard was sweating by the end of it.

**Tyler:** And he passed with flying colors.

**Rebecca:** *[Softly]* You know what he said to me after that dinner?

**Tyler:** What?

**Rebecca:** *[Voice getting tender]* He said, "I can see why they're so protective of you. You're lucky as hell to have people who love you that much. I hope someday they'll consider me family too."

**Tyler:** *[Quietly]* Really?

**Rebecca:** *[Nodding]* Word for fucking word. And that's when I knew I was going to marry his ass.

**Tyler:** Because he wanted to join our family.

**Rebecca:** Because he understood that marrying me meant joining something bigger than just the two of us. He got that you and Ken weren't just my past - you were my present and my future too.

**Tyler:** Tell me about the wedding planning.

**Rebecca:** *[Groaning dramatically]* Oh, sweet Jesus, the wedding planning! You turned into this incredibly efficient wedding coordinator, and Ken became my personal therapist.

**Tyler:** Your planning was complete chaos.

**Rebecca:** *[Laughing]* I had notebooks everywhere with ideas scattered like confetti! You took one look at my "system" and had a small nervous breakdown.

**Tyler:** It wasn't a nervous breakdown. It was organizational horror.

**Rebecca:** *[Grinning]* You created these beautiful, detailed spreadsheets with timelines and vendor contacts and backup plans for the backup plans for the backup plans.

**Tyler:** Weddings are complex logistical operations.

**Rebecca:** *[Fondly]* You treated my wedding like you were planning the fucking D-Day invasion. Everything color-coded, cross-referenced, with contingency protocols.

**Tyler:** And it worked perfectly.

**Rebecca:** *[Warmly]* It did work perfectly. Everything went off without a hitch because you had thought of every possible detail. You even had backup shoes in my size in case my heels broke.

**Tyler:** Ken's idea.

**Rebecca:** [Softly] You two were the perfect team. You handled all the logistics, Ken handled all my emotional meltdowns when I started freaking out about whether the flowers would match the tablecloths.

**Tyler:** You would have figured it out without us.

**Rebecca:** [Shaking her head firmly] Bullshit, Prism. I would have had a nervous breakdown and eloped to Vegas. You gave me the gift of a perfect wedding day because you cared enough to make sure every single detail was exactly right.

**Tyler:** What was your favorite part of the wedding?

**Rebecca:** [Without hesitation] Your speech.

**Tyler:** My speech was terrible. I was shaking like a leaf.

**Rebecca:** [Firmly] Your speech was fucking perfect. You stood up there, in front of all those people, and you talked about chosen family and unconditional love and how David was gaining a sister but also gaining two brothers who would always have his back.

**Tyler:** My hands were shaking so badly I could barely hold the paper.

**Rebecca:** [Softly] I remember you being nervous, but I also remember crying happy tears because you put into words something I hadn't even been able to articulate - that our little family was growing, not changing.

**Tyler:** And then Ken made everyone laugh with that story about you trying to teach him to waltz.

**Rebecca:** [Laughing] Poor Ken! I was so fucking determined that he needed to know how to dance for the wedding. We spent hours in my living room with me counting steps and him stepping on my toes.

**Tyler:** You were very patient with him.

**Rebecca:** [Grinning] Patient, my ass! I was determined! I wanted my boys to be able to dance with me, and Ken has two left feet and the rhythm of a broken washing machine.

**Tyler:** He tried very hard.

**Rebecca:** [Fondly] He did try. Because it mattered to me. Just like you learned to make small talk with my relatives even though it made you want to hide under a table.

**Tyler:** Your Aunt Margaret cornered me for twenty minutes.

**Rebecca:** *[Sympathetically]* She did! And you were so gracious about it, even though I could see you getting that glazed look you get when you're hitting your social interaction limit.

**Tyler:** Worth it to see you happy on your wedding day.

**Rebecca:** *[Voice getting emotional]* That's what I fucking love about you, Prism. You pushed yourself way outside your comfort zone because you wanted my day to be perfect.

**Tyler:** Let's talk about something happier. Tell me about finding out you were pregnant.

**Rebecca:** *[Face absolutely glowing]* Oh shit! The pregnancy! You want to hear about your complete emotional breakdown when I told you?

**Tyler:** I did not have an emotional breakdown.

**Rebecca:** *[Grinning widely]* Prism, you cried for ten minutes straight and then immediately started planning the baby's college fund before I was even done talking!

**Tyler:** Those were happy tears. And it's never too early to start saving for education.

**Rebecca:** *[Laughing]* You had fucking spreadsheets again! Before I was even showing, you had full financial projections for eighteen years of expenses!

**Tyler:** Children are expensive. You needed to be prepared.

**Rebecca:** *[Fondly]* David and I were still wrapping our heads around the idea of becoming parents, and you were already researching pediatricians and preschools.

**Tyler:** I wanted to help.

**Rebecca:** *[Softly]* You did help. More than you know. Having you and Ken so excited and supportive made everything feel... safe. Like this baby was going to be born into this huge network of people who already loved him.

**Tyler:** Our first baby. The first baby in our chosen family.

**Rebecca:** *[Nodding]* And you immediately started talking about being uncles. Not "Rebecca's friends who would help out some-times" - uncles. Real family.

**Tyler:** That's what we were going to be.

**Rebecca:** [*Voice getting tender*] Do you remember what you said when I asked if you wanted to be in the delivery room?

**Tyler:** I said I wanted to be wherever you needed me to be.

**Rebecca:** [*Softly*] You said, "This is our baby too. Our family's baby. Of course I want to be there."

**Tyler:** Ken said he'd handle the emotional support while I handled the logistics.

**Rebecca:** [*Laughing through tears*] You brought an actual labor bag checklist! You had backup phone chargers and snacks and magazines and probably a fucking first aid kit.

**Tyler:** Hospital food is terrible, and David was too nervous to remember basic human needs.

**Rebecca:** [*Warmly*] You took care of everyone. Even the nurses loved you because you had everything organized and you stayed calm when the rest of us were losing our shit.

**Tyler:** Someone had to stay calm.

**Rebecca:** [*Softly*] And when Joshua finally arrived...

**Tyler:** [*Quietly*] You let me hold him first. After David, you let me hold him first.

**Rebecca:** [*Voice full of love*] Because you were his Uncle Prism. Because this was your nephew, and you had been waiting for him just as much as we had.

**Tyler:** He was so tiny and perfect.

**Rebecca:** [*Smiling*] And you held him like he was made of spun glass, talking to him in that gentle voice you use when something is really precious to you.

**Tyler:** What did I say to him?

**Rebecca:** [*Softly*] You said, "Hello, Joshua. I'm your Uncle Prism, and I've been waiting my whole life to meet you."

**Tyler:** [*Quietly*] I meant every word.

**Rebecca:** [*Through tears*] I know you did. And that's when I knew that little boy was going to grow up with the most incredible uncle in the fucking world.

**Tyler:** Tell me about Joshua as a little kid. What was he like?

**Rebecca:** [*Wiping her eyes, then grinning*] Oh, he was something else, Prism. Curious about everything, fearless as hell, always asking questions that made you think...

**Tyler:** He definitely got that from you.

**Rebecca:** *[Laughing]* The curiosity and the smart mouth, maybe. But that fearless thing? That was all his own. Remember when he was three and decided he was going to "help" you rebuild the deck?

**Tyler:** He wanted to use the power tools.

**Rebecca:** *[Nodding]* And instead of just telling him no and sticking him in front of cartoons, you got him his own little plastic tool set and spent two hours teaching him about construction safety.

**Tyler:** He was genuinely interested. It would have been disrespectful to dismiss that.

**Rebecca:** *[Fondly]* That's what made you such an incredible uncle. You always took him seriously. You treated his questions and interests like they actually mattered, not like cute kid stuff to humor.

**Tyler:** They did matter.

**Rebecca:** *[Softly]* And he knew that. Even as a tiny kid, he knew Uncle Prism would never brush him off or talk down to him like he was stupid.

**Tyler:** What was his favorite thing to do when he was little?

**Rebecca:** *[Without hesitation]* Build shit with you. Legos, blocks, blanket forts... anything that involved creating something together.

**Tyler:** He had excellent spatial reasoning skills for his age.

**Rebecca:** *[Laughing]* He had excellent Uncle Prism training! You taught him to think through problems step by step, to plan before building, to be patient when something didn't work the first time.

**Tyler:** Important life skills.

**Rebecca:** *[Warmly]* They are. And watching you two work together was... fuck, it was beautiful, Prism. You were so patient with him, so encouraging. You made him feel capable and smart and important.

**Tyler:** He was all of those things.

**Rebecca:** *[Softly]* But not every adult would have seen that in a four-year-old who wanted to build a blanket fort "as tall as the ceiling and strong enough for elephants."

**Tyler:** We figured out the engineering.

**Rebecca:** [*Grinning*] You engineered a blanket fort with actual structural supports and proper ventilation. Most uncles would have thrown a sheet over two chairs and called it good enough.

**Tyler:** Joshua deserved better than a basic fort.

**Rebecca:** [*Fondly*] He got the goddamn Fort of Dreams because his Uncle Prism doesn't do anything halfway.

**Tyler:** He deserved something special. Most kids don't get to build something that elaborate.

**Rebecca:** [*Grinning*] You know what your nephew asked me for last week? A calendar. Not just any calendar - one of those big wall ones so he can mark off the days until his thirteenth birthday when you take him to Disneyland like you promised.

**Tyler:** [*Surprised*] Really? He's that excited about it?

**Rebecca:** [*Laughing*] Excited? Prism, that kid has been planning that trip for years! Ever since you told him thirteen would be the perfect age to really appreciate it.

**Tyler:** He's been very patient about it.

**Rebecca:** [*Grinning*] Patient? You should see his room - he's got that calendar marked up with red X's for every day that passes. And he keeps adding little notes about things he wants to remember to ask you about the trip.

**Tyler:** Really?

**Rebecca:** [*Nodding*] He's been researching everything - which rides he wants to go on first, what snacks he wants to try, even the optimal walking routes through the park. Wonder where he gets that organizational obsession from?

**Tyler:** I may have mentioned the importance of proper planning.

**Rebecca:** [*Grinning*] You've created a monster! He's got lists, Prism. Multiple lists. And he keeps asking me questions about what you were like when you were his age so he can "prepare for the trip properly."

**Tyler:** What kind of questions?

**Rebecca:** *[Fondly]* Like whether you preferred roller coasters or dark rides, what your favorite Disney movie was, whether you get motion sick... He wants this trip to be perfect because it's with his Uncle Prism.

**Tyler:** It's going to be amazing. I've been planning it too.

**Rebecca:** *[Softly]* I know you have. And watching him get so excited about something that's still two years away... it's beautiful, Prism. You've given him this incredible thing to look forward to.

**Tyler:** He deserves something magical.

**Rebecca:** *[Voice getting emotional]* He's going to remember that trip for the rest of his life. Just like he remembers every birthday gift you've carefully picked out, the way you teach him things without making him feel stupid, how you never rush him when he's trying to explain something complicated to you.

**Tyler:** He's easy to love.

**Rebecca:** *[Softly]* So are you, Prism. So are you.

**Tyler:** *[After a moment]* Can I ask you something that might be difficult?

**Rebecca:** *[Straightening up]* Shoot.

**Tyler:** How do you want people to remember our friendship? When you think about everything we've shared, what matters most to you?

**Rebecca:** *[Long pause, thinking carefully]*

You know what I want people to understand about our friendship?

**Tyler:** What?

**Rebecca:** *[Leaning forward intensely]* That chosen family isn't some consolation prize. It's not what you settle for when you don't have "real" family. It's what you create when you're brave enough to build something based on actual love and understanding instead of just biology and obligation.

**Tyler:** We built something pretty incredible, didn't we?

**Rebecca:** *[Firmly]* We built everything, Prism. We built a family that survived college, career changes, my marriage, Joshua's birth, distance, time... We built something that could adapt and grow and weather any fucking storm.

**Tyler:** What made it work?

**Rebecca:** *[Thoughtfully]* Absolute honesty. Complete, sometimes uncomfortable honesty. You never pretended to be someone you weren't, and you never let Ken or me get away with pretending either.

**Tyler:** I'm not good at pretending.

**Rebecca:** *[Smiling]* Exactly! And that taught the rest of us to be real too. No performance, no trying to be the "perfect" friend. Just... authentic love and support, even when it was messy.

**Tyler:** Especially when it was messy.

**Rebecca:** *[Nodding]* Like when I was stressed about wedding planning and took it out on you. Or when Ken got that job offer in Seattle and we all had to figure out how to stay close across distance.

**Tyler:** We always figured it out.

**Rebecca:** *[Warmly]* We always figured it out. Because that's what real family does - they work through the hard shit instead of bailing when things get complicated.

**Tyler:** What do you want Joshua to know about all this? About our family, our friendship?

**Rebecca:** *[Voice getting tender]* I want him to know that love comes in all different forms. That the people who choose to be in your life, who show up consistently and give a damn about your happiness... those people are just as much family as anyone you're related to by blood. Sometimes more.

**Tyler:** He's always seemed to understand that instinctively.

**Rebecca:** *[Softly]* Because he grew up seeing it. He grew up watching his Uncle Prism and Uncle Ken love him and me and David without question, without obligation. Just because we mattered to each other.

**Tyler:** And he matters to us. So much.

**Rebecca:** *[Through tears]* He does. And I want him to carry that forward - the understanding that family is something you create and maintain and choose every single day.

**Tyler:** *[Quietly]* Rebecca?

**Rebecca:** Yeah, babe?

**Tyler:** Thank you. For everything. For accepting me from day one, for protecting our little family, for pushing me when I needed it, for letting me be Joshua's uncle...

**Rebecca:** *[Firmly]* Prism, stop right fucking there. You don't thank family for being family.

**Tyler:** I don't?

**Rebecca:** *[Shaking her head]* You don't thank people for loving you when that love is genuine and freely given. Family doesn't keep score.

*[Pause]*

If anything, I should be thanking you.

**Tyler:** For what?

**Rebecca:** *[Softly]* For showing me what unconditional love looks like. For being the most consistent, caring, generous person I've ever known. For making my son feel like the most important kid in the world every time he's with you.

*[Voice breaking slightly]*

For being exactly who you are, without apology, and teaching the rest of us that it's safe to be ourselves too.

**Tyler:** *[After a long moment]* I love you, Rebecca.

**Rebecca:** *[Through tears]* I love you too, Prism. Always and forever, no matter what. You're stuck with me, you beautiful bastard.

**Tyler:** *[Softly, with a small smile]* Always and forever.

**Rebecca:** *[Wiping her eyes and suddenly laughing]* Okay, enough of that shit! Jesus Christ, I can't believe I actually talked you into doing all this interviewing and writing crap. What the fuck was I thinking? Now I'm sitting here crying like some kind of sentimental asshole.

**Tyler:** *[Laughing]* You said my stories would make a wonderful book.

**Rebecca:** *[Grinning]* Yeah, well, I didn't know you were going to make me get all emotional and weepy in the process. This is your fault for being such a good interviewer, you bastard.

# CHAPTER 7
# THE POLAROIDS

Joshua let the heavy binder rest in his lap and stared out the window, watching the late afternoon light stretch across the neighborhood. Everything felt weird and suspended, like he was caught between then and now, holding pieces of a puzzle that was way bigger than he'd realized.

God, there was so much he didn't know about Uncle Tyler and Ken. All these years, he'd just figured Tyler was his mom's brother —I mean, it made sense, right? Ken was clearly Japanese, so unless someone had been adopted somewhere along the line, he wouldn't be Mom's biological brother. That left Uncle Tyler. And when you're a kid, you don't really question that stuff. Family is family, blood or not.

But now, reading these interviews, learning about how they'd all actually met in college... Joshua could feel his brain scrambling to catch up, like puzzle pieces were rearranging themselves into a completely different picture than he'd been carrying around his whole life.

The sun had shifted just enough to catch something shiny in the box next to him. Joshua reached down and pulled out this colorful binder clip holding a stack of what looked like old flyers. The papers were yellowed and beat up, with permanent dents where the clip had been squeezing them for years.

"Oregon State Swim Invitational, Saturday, January 23, 1999." Just a basic photocopied program—nothing fancy, but it had all the events listed out in neat little columns.

Joshua flipped through more of them, not bothering to take off the clip. More swim meet programs from different dates, different colored papers, some so faded you could barely read them. And then he saw it buried in the event listings:

"Tyler Anderson - 1m Springboard, 3m Springboard, Platform."

Wait, what? Uncle Tyler was on the diving team? That had never come up in any of their conversations. Joshua felt this weird hollowness in his chest—how much of Tyler's life had he just... never thought to ask about?

Digging deeper, he found a stack of old Polaroids held together with a rubber band. Classic faded Polaroid look—that slightly blurry, dreamlike quality they all had. Most were just typical team photos: guys hanging around with their coach before a meet, celebration shots after what was probably a win, the whole team lined up for some official picture.

But there were four at the bottom that made Joshua's breath catch. These weren't group shots.

The first one was Tyler getting ready to dive, caught right at that moment of total focus before he launched. The next couple showed him just after getting out of the pool—all lean muscle and dripping water, looking like some kind of athlete from a magazine. And the last one... Tyler with his arm around Uncle Ken, both of them grinning like idiots, probably after Tyler had just nailed his dives.

Holy shit. Uncle Tyler looked absolutely ripped. Was it weird that Joshua thought he looked good? Like, really good? He felt awkward even thinking it, but come on—they weren't actually related, and Tyler had clearly been in incredible shape.

Joshua looked back at the binder in his lap, his mind racing. Everything he'd been reading—Ken's story, his mom's interview—it was all starting to click. They weren't related by blood. Tyler had met Ken and Mom in college. They'd basically created their own family from scratch.

And then it hit him like a freight train.

He stared back at the Polaroid of Tyler on the diving platform, water still beading on his skin, that look of total concentration that Joshua recognized from watching Tyler approach literally everything in his life.

Tyler had met them at the pool. At a diving meet. Joshua could practically see it—his mom and Ken going to check out college guys in Speedos (which was hilarious and totally something his mom would do), and there was Tyler, up on that platform, making something incredibly difficult look like pure art.

This was it. This was the beginning of everything.

The whole thing gave Joshua chills. If Tyler hadn't been on that diving team, if Ken and Rebecca hadn't decided to go to that specific meet, if Tyler hadn't caught their attention with whatever magic he was doing up there... would any of this have happened? Would Joshua even exist?

It was like holding the DNA of his own life in his hands.

He set the photos down carefully and flipped back to the beginning of Tyler's binder, suddenly desperate to find the full story of that first meeting. There had to be more details about how three random college students had looked at each other and somehow known they were going to build something lasting.

And that's when it really hit him—this wasn't just Uncle Tyler documenting his friendships. This was like a love letter to the whole concept of chosen family. A carefully preserved record of how love could create bonds that were stronger than biology, more real than anything genetics could offer.

Joshua found himself thinking about his mom's words from the interview: "I want him to know that love comes in all different forms. That the people who choose to be in your life, who show up consistently and give a damn about your happiness... those people are just as much family as anyone you're related to by blood. Sometimes more."

She'd been talking directly to him across time. Tyler had somehow known Joshua would be sitting here one day, reading this, needing to hear exactly those words. It was like Tyler had given his mom a microphone to the future.

And there was something else that made Joshua's throat tight: "He grew up watching his Uncle Prism and Uncle Ken love him and me and David without question, without obligation. Just because we mattered to each other."

That hit different than just learning embarrassing stories about his parents' college days. This wasn't ancient history. This was the explanation for why Uncle Tyler and Uncle Ken had always felt more like family than most of his actual relatives, why their love had felt so solid and unconditional.

They had chosen him before he was even born. When he was just a possibility in his mom and dad's future, Tyler and Ken had already decided to be his uncles, his people, his backup. Not because they had to, but because Joshua would matter to the people they loved, which automatically meant he'd matter to them.

Sitting there in the dusty attic with afternoon shadows getting longer, surrounded by all these preserved pieces of a love story that had basically created his entire world, Joshua finally got what Uncle Tyler had been trying to tell him about family being something you build instead of something you're stuck with.

He picked up that Polaroid again—Tyler and Ken with their arms around each other, both looking so young and happy and completely clueless that they were about to become the foundation of something incredible. They were just kids, really. College students figuring out love and friendship and what it meant to choose your people.

Joshua grabbed the binder again, suddenly dying to find the full story of that first meeting, that moment when three strangers became the beginning of everything that mattered in his life.

But first, he looked back at his mom's words one more time: "What do you want Joshua to know about all of this?"

Everything, he thought, his heart racing with anticipation. I want to know absolutely everything.

# CHAPTER 8
# DIVING

Rebecca Brennan had been planning this mission for three days.

"Ken!" she called, bursting into his dorm room without knocking, her light brown sweater practically vibrating with excitement. "Get your sexy ass up. We're going to the natatorium."

Ken looked up from his psychology textbook, already grinning. "The what now?"

"The diving meet! Oregon State versus University of Washington! College boys! In tiny little Speedos!" She was already pulling his jacket off the back of his chair. "This is better than fucking Christmas, Ken. Better than Christmas."

"Rebecca, I have studying to—"

"Bullshit!" She thrust his jacket at him. "You've been moping around here for weeks bitching about how you never meet anyone interesting. Well, today's your lucky day because I am personally delivering you to a building full of athletic, practically naked college boys."

Ken's face lit up as he tossed his textbook aside. "Well, when you put it like that... Why didn't you lead with the practically naked part?"

"Because I knew once I mentioned Speedos, you'd be putty in my hands!" Rebecca beamed. "I'll do all the terrifying social interaction stuff. You just have to show up and look devastatingly handsome. Which, let's be honest, is not exactly a hardship for you."

Twenty minutes later, they were settling into the bleachers overlooking the pool deck, their laughter echoing off the high ceiling. The natatorium was packed—more crowded than Rebecca had expected, but that just meant more options. She pulled out a small notepad and pen.

"Oh my God," Ken said, delighted as he watched her flip to a fresh page. "Please tell me you actually brought a fucking scorecard."

"Scientific scoring system!" she announced proudly. "Technical merit, artistic impression, and general fuckability. Very thorough."

"Rebecca Brennan, you magnificent bitch." Ken was practically bouncing in his seat. "This is why we're friends."

"This is research!" Rebecca was already scanning the pool deck through the warm-up activities. "Ooh, look at number seven! Nice shoulders. And that one by the starting blocks has an ass you could bounce a quarter off of."

Ken followed her gaze appreciatively. "Mmm, very nice. But what about the one stretching by lane four? Hello, gorgeous."

The pool deck was delicious chaos—swimmers doing warm-up laps, divers practicing on the lower boards, coaches shouting instructions over the echoing din of voices and splashing water. The air was thick with chlorine and humidity, testosterone and possibility.

"I love college athletics," Ken sighed happily. "It's like a buffet for the eyes."

"Speaking of buffets," Rebecca grinned wickedly, "diving's starting. Time for the main course."

The first few divers were competent but unremarkable. Rebecca dutifully made notes—"Good entry, seven point five," "Nice height, but too much splash, six point eight"—while Ken provided color commentary.

"Ooh, that one's trying too hard," Ken critiqued as a diver over-rotated. "Honey, less is more."

"Points off for desperation," Rebecca agreed, scribbling. "Never attractive."

They were having a blast, being just loud enough to earn some disapproving looks from more serious spectators, when a small figure climbed the ladder to the high platform.

Ken's commentary died mid-sentence.

The diver was tiny—probably no more than five-foot-four—but moved with an economy of motion that made everyone else look clumsy by comparison. While the other divers had been loose and casual in their preparation, this one had a ritual.

Goggles adjusted to exactly the right position. A slow roll of both shoulders. Three small bounces on the balls of his feet. Then complete stillness, staring down at the water with an intensity that seemed to quiet the entire natatorium.

"Holy fucking shit," Rebecca whispered, her pen frozen above her notepad.

Ken couldn't speak at all.

When the diver launched, it wasn't just a dive—it was sculpture in motion. The pike was impossibly tight, the rotation controlled and precise, and the entry... Ken had never seen anything like it. The water barely rippled.

The entire crowd erupted in cheers, but Ken was watching the diver's face as he surfaced. For just a moment—maybe three seconds—those mismatched eyes looked up toward the bleachers, and Ken felt something shift fundamentally in his chest.

"Did you see that?" Rebecca was practically bouncing. "Did you fucking see that? That was... that was art!"

Ken was still staring at the pool. The diver had swum to the edge and was pulling himself out, water streaming from his compact frame. Even from this distance, Ken could see the careful way he moved, the slight pause as he oriented himself away from the noise of the crowd.

"I need to meet him," Ken heard himself say, his usual performative confidence completely stripped away.

Rebecca's head whipped around, recognizing something different in his tone. "What?"

"That guy. The diver. I need to meet him." Ken's voice was quieter now, almost reverent.

A slow, knowing grin spread across Rebecca's face. This wasn't Ken's usual "ooh, cute boy" reaction. This was something else entirely.

"Well, shit," she said softly. "Operation Get Ken Laid just became something way more fucking interesting."

"Rebecca!"

But she was already standing, gathering her things with military efficiency. "Come on, lover boy. We're going to the pool deck."

"We can't just—"

"We absolutely fucking can. That's what these things are for!" She was already pushing past people in their row. "Social interaction! Meeting people! Besides, I want to tell him that dive just made me believe in God again."

Ken followed her down to the pool deck, his heart doing something completely unfamiliar in his chest. Usually he was the one leading these social expeditions, but something about this felt different—more important, more fragile. The noise level down here was overwhelming—coaches shouting, swimmers splashing, the echo of voices bouncing off the high ceiling. He could see the diver sitting alone on a bench near the diving well, toweling off with the same careful precision he'd shown on the platform.

"There!" Rebecca pointed. "He's alone. Perfect fucking opportunity."

"Becca, maybe we should—"

But Rebecca was already marching across the deck with the determination of a woman on a mission. Ken had no choice but to follow, acutely aware that his usual social superpowers had completely abandoned him.

The diver looked up as they approached, and Ken got his first good look at those eyes—one blue, one green, startling in their intensity. There was something almost vulnerable about his expression, like the noise and chaos of the pool deck was too much input to process comfortably.

"Hi!" Rebecca said brightly. "That dive was absolutely fucking incredible! I'm Rebecca, and this is my friend Ken."

The diver's gaze flicked between them, settling somewhere around Ken's left shoulder. "Thank you. Tyler. Prism."

His voice was quiet, almost lost in the ambient noise, but there was something in the careful way he spoke that made Ken want to lean closer.

"Prism?" Rebecca asked, her curiosity immediately piqued. "That's your name?"

"Nickname." Tyler gestured vaguely toward his eyes. "The... color thing."

Ken found his voice, though it came out softer than usual. "That was... really beautiful. The dive."

Tyler's gaze moved to Ken's face for just a moment—direct eye contact that lasted maybe two seconds—and Ken felt that same fundamental shift in his chest.

"Thank you," Tyler said again, then seemed to struggle for what to say next.

Rebecca, bless her perceptive soul, jumped into the silence. "Are you a student here? What's your major? Do you always dive like that, or was that just showing off for all us horny college kids in the stands?"

Ken watched Tyler's face as Rebecca launched into her friendly interrogation. There was something about the way he processed each question—a slight pause, like he was translating from one language to another—that was oddly endearing.

"Business administration," Tyler answered. "Oregon State. And... I wasn't showing off. That's just how I dive."

"Just how you dive?" Rebecca laughed. "Like that's fucking normal? That was poetry in motion, sweetie!"

A tiny smile flickered across Tyler's face. "Language, Rebecca."

"Oh, please. Like you've never heard the word 'fuck' before."

"I've heard it." The smile got a little wider. "I just don't use it much."

Ken realized he was staring and tried to think of something intelligent to contribute. "How long have you been diving?"

"Since I was eight." Tyler's posture relaxed slightly, like this was safer conversational territory. "My high school coach said I had good spatial awareness."

"Good spatial awareness?" Rebecca snorted. "That's like saying Michelangelo had decent hand-eye coordination."

Tyler actually laughed—a quiet sound, but genuine. "That's... that's a really nice compliment. Thank you."

Ken was completely gone. The laugh, the slight blush, the way Tyler held himself like he was ready to bolt at any moment but was choosing to stay—it was all impossibly attractive.

"So," Rebecca continued, settling onto the bench next to Tyler like they were old friends, "what do you do when you're not making us question our life choices with your diving skills? Hobbies? Interests? Secret fucking talents?"

"Rebecca," Ken said quietly, recognizing the signs of Tyler getting overwhelmed again. The pool deck was getting more crowded as events finished, and Tyler kept glancing toward the exits.

"What? I'm just being friendly!"

"I should probably go," Tyler said, confirming Ken's instinct. "It's getting loud, and I have studying to do."

"Wait!" Ken said, then immediately felt like an idiot for how eager he sounded. "I mean... would you maybe want to get coffee sometime? Or dinner?"

Tyler looked directly at him again—another one of those brief, intense moments of eye contact. "I... yes. I'd like that. But could Rebecca come too?"

Rebecca's eyebrows shot up. "Me?"

"If that's okay," Tyler said quickly. "I'm not... I don't really do well with... I mean, I'd feel more comfortable if..."

"Of course I can come!" Rebecca beamed. "The more the merrier! Right, Ken?"

Ken felt a flicker of disappointment—he'd been hoping for something more like a date—but one look at Tyler's relieved expression told him this was the right answer. "Absolutely. The three of us."

Tyler's smile was radiant. "Thank you. That's... thank you."

They exchanged numbers—Rebecca taking charge of the logistics with her usual efficiency—and made plans for Friday night. As they were saying goodbye, Tyler looked at Ken one more time.

"I'm glad you came to the meet," he said quietly.

Ken felt his heart do that irregular thing again. "Me too."

As they walked back toward the parking lot, Rebecca was practically vibrating with excitement. "Holy fucking shit, Ken! He's perfect! Did you see how sweet he was? And those eyes! And the way he dove! You're going to fall so goddamn hard for this guy it's not even funny."

Ken realized he already had.

"Yeah," he said, watching Tyler disappear into the crowd of departing spectators. "I think I am."

Rebecca looped her arm through his. "Operation Get Ken Laid just became Operation Get Ken the Love of His Fucking Life. This is going to be so much better."

Ken laughed despite himself. "Don't get ahead of yourself, Becca."

"Too late!" she grinned wickedly. "I can already see it. You two are going to be disgustingly perfect together. I'm going to be the best goddamn wingwoman in the history of wingwomen."

As they walked to Rebecca's car, Ken found himself replaying those moments of eye contact, the careful way Tyler spoke, the vulnerable smile. But something was nagging at him.

"Becca," he said quietly, his usual confidence wavering. "Do you think... I mean, when he asked if you could come to dinner too... do you think maybe I read this all wrong? Maybe he's straight?"

Rebecca stopped walking and turned to stare at him. "Are you fucking kidding me right now?"

"I'm serious! Maybe I just—"

"Ken." Rebecca grabbed his shoulders. "Honey, whoever gave that boy his nickname was spot fucking on, because those prism eyes of his were all over you. He may have had a hard time looking at you directly, but trust me, he was checking you out."

Ken felt a flicker of hope. "Really?"

"Really. That wasn't straight boy politeness, that was 'holy shit this gorgeous guy is talking to me and I don't know what to do with myself' behavior." Rebecca started walking again, pulling Ken along. "I don't think he's straight. I think he's just... different. Like, socially different. He doesn't know how to date, or maybe just how to be social in general."

"What do you mean?"

"I mean he probably asked me to come because he sensed I take charge of social situations, and that feels safer to him." Rebecca's voice got gentler. "Some people need training wheels for this shit, Ken. Doesn't mean he's not interested."

Ken was quiet for a moment, processing. "I really like him, Becca. Like, really fucking like him. And I don't... I'm never at a loss for words, you know? But with him..."

"You were absolutely tongue-tied," Rebecca grinned. "It was adorable and completely unlike you."

"What if I fuck this up?"

Rebecca stopped at her car and looked at Ken seriously. "You won't. Because for the first time since I've known you, you're not performing. You're just being real. And that's exactly what he needs."

Ken felt something settle in his chest. Rebecca was right. This felt different because it was different.

"Friday can't come fast enough," he said.

"It's going to be perfect," Rebecca promised. "Trust me on this one."

# CHAPTER 9
# THE FIRST DINNER

Ken had changed his shirt three times.

"It's just dinner," he muttered to himself, checking his reflection in the mirror for the fifth time in ten minutes. "With Rebecca there. Not even a real date."

But his hands were shaking slightly as he adjusted his collar, and his stomach felt like it was hosting some kind of gymnastic competition. He'd been on plenty of dates before—hell, he was usually the confident one, the one who made other people nervous. This was completely backwards.

The phone rang, making him jump.

"You ready, lover boy?" Rebecca's voice crackled through the receiver. "I'm picking you up in fifteen minutes, and I swear to God, if you're having some kind of fashion crisis, I'm dragging you out in whatever you're wearing."

"I'm ready," Ken lied, taking one more look in the mirror. "Just... be cool tonight, okay? Don't embarrass me."

Rebecca's laugh was loud enough to hurt his ear. "Me? Embarrass you? Ken, honey, I'm going to be the picture of fucking discretion. You won't even know I'm there."

"That's what I'm afraid of."

Fifteen minutes later, Rebecca was honking her horn outside his dorm, and Ken was walking across campus with sweaty palms and a nervous energy he didn't recognize. They'd chosen a small Italian restaurant off-campus—somewhere quiet, Rebecca had suggested, not too overwhelming. Ken was grateful for her thoughtfulness, even if he was too nervous to say so.

Tyler was already waiting when they arrived, sitting alone at a corner table, looking small and slightly out of place in his carefully pressed khakis and blue button-down. He'd clearly put effort into his appearance, and something about that made Ken's chest tight.

"There's our diving superstar," Rebecca said warmly as they approached the table. "You clean up nice, Prism."

Tyler stood up quickly, almost knocking over his water glass. "Hi. You both look... nice too."

Ken slid into the seat across from Tyler, hyperaware of every movement. "Thanks for meeting us. I mean, for agreeing to dinner. With us."

"Thank you for asking," Tyler replied, his voice quiet but steady. "I don't... I don't really go out to restaurants very often."

"Why not?" Rebecca asked, settling into her chair and immediately commandeering the menu. "Food's one of life's great fucking pleasures."

Tyler's mouth quirked slightly. "Language, Rebecca."

"Sorry, sorry. Food's one of life's great pleasures," she corrected with exaggerated primness. "Better?"

"Much."

Ken watched this exchange with fascination. There was something about the way Tyler interacted with Rebecca—gentle correction without judgment, genuine amusement at her dramatics. It was... sweet. Really sweet.

"So," Ken said, trying to contribute something meaningful to the conversation, "what kind of food do you usually eat? When you're not at restaurants, I mean."

Tyler considered this with the same careful attention he'd given everything at the pool. "Simple things, mostly. I'm not really... I don't cook much. Pasta, sandwiches, things that don't require a lot of..." He gestured vaguely.

"Skill?" Rebecca suggested.

"Complexity," Tyler corrected. "I like things to be straight-forward."

The waitress appeared—a cheerful college-aged girl with too much energy for the quiet atmosphere Tyler seemed to prefer. "Hi there! Welcome to Romano's! Can I start you folks off with some drinks? Maybe an appetizer? Our calamari is absolutely amazing tonight, and we've got this fantastic wine special—"

Ken watched Tyler's face as the waitress launched into her enthusiastic spiel. He could see the exact moment when it became too much—the slight tension around Tyler's eyes, the way he gripped his menu just a little tighter.

"Water's fine for me," Ken interjected gently. "Tyler? Rebecca?"

"Water sounds perfect," Tyler said, shooting Ken a grateful look.

Rebecca, bless her perceptive soul, seemed to pick up on the dynamic immediately. "Three waters, please. And maybe just a few more minutes with the menu?"

"Of course! Take your time!" The waitress bounced away, leaving blessed quiet in her wake.

Tyler's shoulders relaxed visibly. "Thank you."

"For what?" Ken asked.

"The waitress was..." Tyler paused, seeming to search for the right words. "A lot. Very energetic."

"Some people are," Rebecca said matter-of-factly. "Nothing wrong with needing a breather from that."

Ken felt something warm settle in his chest. This was why Tyler had wanted Rebecca here—she understood things without needing explanations, made space for his needs without making a big deal about it.

They ordered simply—pasta for Tyler, chicken for Rebecca, something with too much garlic for Ken because he was too nervous to really process the menu. But as the evening progressed, something magical happened: Tyler began to relax.

It started small—a genuine laugh at one of Rebecca's stories about her psychology professor, a question about Ken's major that showed he'd been paying attention. By the time their entrees arrived, Tyler was leaning forward slightly, more engaged, making eye contact that lasted longer than those quick flickers from the pool.

"So you grew up in Oregon too?" Tyler asked Ken as they shared the bread basket.

"Born and raised. My parents moved here from Japan before I was born, so I'm like... culturally confused. Very Japanese at home, very American everywhere else."

"That sounds complicated."

Ken was surprised by Tyler's directness. Most people either changed the subject or made some awkward comment about his heritage. "It can be. But mostly it's just... part of who I am, you know?"

Tyler nodded thoughtfully. "I understand feeling like you don't quite fit the expected mold."

Something in his tone made Ken lean forward. "Yeah?"

"The eyes," Tyler said simply, gesturing toward his mismatched gaze. "People notice. They have... reactions."

"Good reactions or bad reactions?" Rebecca asked.

Tyler considered this. "Curious reactions, mostly. Like I'm some kind of interesting puzzle to figure out."

Ken felt a surge of protectiveness. "That must get old."

"Sometimes." Tyler's smile was soft. "But sometimes people see something they like. Something worth getting to know."

The eye contact that followed lasted maybe five seconds, but Ken felt it everywhere. There was something in Tyler's expression —vulnerability, hope, maybe a question he wasn't quite ready to ask yet.

"Okay," Rebecca announced, breaking the moment with characteristic timing, "I need to know more about this diving thing. How the hell did you get so good at it?"

Tyler turned to her, grateful for the safer topic. "Practice, mostly. My coach says I have good spatial awareness, but I think it's really about patterns. Understanding the physics of rotation, entry angle, the way your body moves through space..."

As Tyler talked, his whole demeanor changed. The careful,

hesitant quality disappeared, replaced by genuine enthusiasm. His hands moved as he explained the mechanics of a reverse somersault, his eyes lit up when he described the feeling of a perfect entry.

Ken was completely captivated. This was Tyler without his guard up—passionate, articulate, beautiful in his intensity.

"...and when you get it exactly right," Tyler was saying, "when the entry is clean and the water barely moves, it's like... like everything makes sense for just that moment."

"That's fucking beautiful," Rebecca said softly.

Tyler blushed. "Language."

"Sorry. That's beautiful. No fucking."

Ken laughed—actually laughed, the nervous energy finally breaking. "She's hopeless, Tyler. You're never going to cure her."

"I don't want to cure her," Tyler said, smiling at Rebecca with genuine fondness. "I like her exactly the way she is."

Rebecca looked like she might cry. "Okay, that's it. I'm adopting you. You're officially part of the family now."

"Is that how adoption works?" Tyler asked, deadpan.

"It is in Rebecca's world," Ken grinned. "Fair warning—she's very territorial about her people."

"Good," Tyler said simply. "I'd like to be one of her people."

The rest of dinner passed in a warm haze of easy conversation. Tyler asked thoughtful questions about Ken's psychology studies, listened with genuine interest to Rebecca's complaints about her statistics class, and slowly, gradually, began to seem more like himself—whatever that was.

When the check came, Ken reached for it immediately, but Tyler's hand shot out to stop him.

"I can pay for myself," Tyler said quietly.

"I know you can," Ken replied. "But I asked you out. I pay."

Tyler's fingers were still touching Ken's hand on the check. "Is this a date?"

The question hung in the air between them. Ken could feel Rebecca holding her breath.

"Do you want it to be?" Ken asked softly.

Tyler's mismatched eyes searched Ken's face. "I think so. But I don't really know how dating works."

Ken's heart did something complicated in his chest. "We can figure it out together."

Tyler's smile was radiant. "I'd like that."

The walk back to Tyler's dorm was slower than necessary, all three of them reluctant to end the evening. Rebecca chattered about weekend plans and upcoming exams, but Ken was acutely aware of Tyler walking beside him, the way their hands occasionally brushed, the way Tyler seemed more comfortable with each step.

"This is me," Tyler said when they reached his building. He turned to face them both, looking suddenly uncertain again. "Thank you. For dinner. For... this."

"Thank you for saying yes," Ken replied.

They stood there for a moment, the weight of potential heavy in the air. Ken wanted to kiss him—had been wanting to kiss him all evening—but something held him back. This felt too important to rush, too fragile to risk with too much too soon.

"I'll call you," Ken said instead.

Tyler's smile was soft and hopeful. "I'd like that."

Rebecca linked her arms through both of theirs as they watched Tyler disappear into his dorm. "Well, fuck me sideways," she said quietly. "That was the most adorable thing I've ever witnessed."

Ken was still staring at the door Tyler had disappeared through. "I'm in trouble, aren't I?"

"Oh honey," Rebecca laughed, squeezing his arm. "You're in so much fucking trouble. And it's going to be beautiful."

As they walked back to Rebecca's car, Ken felt like the world had shifted slightly on its axis. Everything looked the same, but something fundamental had changed. He was falling for Tyler Prism Anderson, and for the first time in his life, that felt like the most natural thing in the world.

"Rebecca," he said quietly.

"Yeah?"

"Thank you. For coming tonight. For... understanding what he needed."

Rebecca stopped walking and turned to look at him seriously. "Ken, that boy is special. Like, really fucking special. And if you hurt him, I will personally kick your ass from here to next Tuesday."

Ken smiled. "I'm not going to hurt him."

"Good. Because I think he might be exactly what you've been looking for."

Ken thought about Tyler's careful honesty, his gentle humor, the way he'd looked when talking about diving—like everything made sense for just that moment.

"Yeah," he said softly. "I think he might be."

# CHAPTER 10
## FINDING EACH OTHER

Joshua looked up from the binder where he'd just finished reading about that first dinner at the Italian restaurant—his mom, Uncle Ken, and Uncle Tyler navigating the careful dance of new friendship and budding romance. It was fascinating to see them all at his age, just college kids figuring out life and love and how to be around each other. He could picture them so clearly: his mom with her boundless energy and zero filter, Ken with his easy charm and secret nervousness, and Uncle Tyler trying to process it all without melting down from social overload.

The three of them had been his age back then—twenty, twenty-one, just kids really. And reading about them felt like discovering that the foundations of his entire world had been built by people who could have walked up to him on campus and asked him to join them for pizza. It felt... good. Like family wasn't this ancient, untouchable thing, but something young people created when they were brave enough to choose each other.

"What are you smiling at?"

Josh startled, looking across the room to see Tyler digging through one of the boxes, searching for something.

"Could you at least give me notice before you scare the shit outta me like that?"

Tyler grinned, adopting an exaggerated Elizabethan accent: "Sir

Joshua of Seattle, the right honorable Tyler of Portland is awaiting your keep..."

Joshua looked around for something to throw at his uncle while his smile betrayed him. Only Uncle Tyler could get away with this kind of ridiculous banter with him. Most people's humor felt forced or awkward, but Tyler's teasing always hit exactly the right note.

"Why did you ask Mom to come with you and Ken on your first date?"

Tyler paused for a moment, that familiar processing look crossing his face as he rearranged his thoughts to sync with the change in conversation. Joshua appreciated it—he was the same way, needing time to shift mental gears before responding. Most people got impatient with the pause, but Tyler never rushed him, and Joshua returned the courtesy.

Tyler put down whatever he'd been searching for and came over to sit cross-legged on the floor in front of Joshua's bean bag chair, looking up at him like a kindergartner settling in for story time. The light had faded, and Tyler's face was cast in the orange glow of the streetlamp outside the window.

"I was scared," Tyler said. "Your mom... she could just talk to people when I had no clue what to say."

Josh considered this, struggling to sit up in the bean bag chair while weighed down by the heavy binder. He carefully folded it and placed it on the floor next to Tyler's crossed feet, then scooted down to sit on the floor so they could be eye-to-eye, his back resting against the bean bag chair.

"Did you love Ken at first sight?"

The back-and-forth between them always included these built-in periods of patience where each had time to process and respond. Most people would have been prodding for a quick answer, but they felt comfortable in this cadence. It was the right pace.

"I don't know if it was love at first sight," Tyler said. "I was too focused on my diving. But he... you ever see something that just makes you feel really good? Like you want to know everything about it? Like you're gonna burst from happiness just being around it? But you don't know what to say or do... you just know you wanna be there?"

"Umm... yeah, I suppose... I guess..."

"It was like that."

Joshua considered this before Tyler interrupted him: "Josh, have you ever been in love?"

The question took Josh by surprise. He'd grown up—really grown up—after Uncle Ken and Tyler had "gone away," and he only saw Uncle Tyler occasionally now. They hadn't had much opportunity to really talk about his relationships, or if he even had any, or romance, or likes, or anything. Hell, Josh hadn't even told him if he was interested in boys or girls. So this was new territory. He wasn't really embarrassed, per se, but it was something... well, it was the first time.

"I don't think so."

"Mmm..."

"I'm pretty far behind, aren't I?" Josh said, looking down slightly ashamed. He was twenty-one now. Shouldn't he already be a pro at this stuff? Multiple relationships? Countless experiences? He was debating whether to volunteer that he remained a virgin before his uncle continued.

"Joshua, one day someone's gonna find you... just like Ken found me... and it might be scary and exciting and amazing... but yeah, scary."

"Find me? You mean, one day I'll find someone, right?"

"No, I mean they'll find you. When you're out there looking, you usually miss the people who were there all along. The ones that really connect... they just show up in your life when you're not even expecting it. Just like Ken did that day. I'd spent weeks stressing about that meet, and even when I was diving, I wasn't paying attention to him or your mom up in the bleachers. I was too worried about my routine, my dive... too focused to notice or care. But when your mom came up and started firing all those questions at me..."

"Sounds like she was really a nosy bitch," Josh laughed.

"Well... she is your mother... but yeah," Tyler laughed too.

"Seriously, when she came up and hit me with all her questions, I started to panic a little, like I do... like I think you do sometimes too, right?"

Josh just looked at his uncle. He knew Tyler was right, and he knew that only his uncle understood.

Tyler continued, "So there I was, kinda shutting down—wet, just finished my meet, and your mom's creating all this chaos around me with people starting to crowd the platform—and there's Ken, standing quietly behind her. And I did something that's usually really hard for me..."

"What?"

"I allowed him to catch my eye."

Josh smiled. He knew exactly what his uncle meant. "So that's... love?"

"I didn't know it then, but... yeah."

"But... what about Mom?"

"What about her?"

"Why did you ask her to come on your first date again?"

"Oh," Tyler laughed, "because I figured I wouldn't know what to say or how to act... I was scared, you know? I liked Ken, but I didn't really know him. He didn't know me. And I was worried he'd think I was some kind of..."

Tyler got quiet and looked down. Even though it had been years and he'd since found words to describe himself and his brain's way of working, it was still difficult at times to admit the pain people had caused through their misunderstanding at best, or downright cruelty at worst, simply because of his autism—though he didn't know what it was back then.

"Uncle Tyler... are you okay?" Josh began to reach over to touch his uncle's hand instinctively, but paused just shy of contact, the hairs on his arm standing up as they drew near, as if there were a magnetic energy surrounding Tyler that he couldn't see.

"Sorry... I was just so worried Ken would think I was a freak or something..." Tyler looked tense when he said "freak," and Josh caught it. He felt the pain too.

"But he didn't... and he became your biggest cheerleader, right?" Josh added, trying to cheer him up.

"Yes, yes he did," Tyler said, lifting his head and smiling as if remembering Ken in that very moment.

"But your mother helped too. That first date and the first few weeks, she helped keep the conversation going... and without knowing it, helped me get to know Ken by simply watching and listening... and having time to understand him."

"Really?"

"Yeah. Your mom's got this thing where she can make social stuff just... work. She could ask Ken questions I was too nervous to ask, and I'd listen to his answers and learn about him without feeling pressured to respond right away. And when Ken asked me stuff, your mom would jump in if she saw I was struggling, give me time to think."

Josh nodded slowly. "Like a translator."

"Exactly like a translator. Someone who speaks both languages fluently." Tyler's expression grew fond. "She did that for years, actually. Not just with Ken, but in lots of situations. She'd run interference when things got too overwhelming, or create space for me to process when I needed it."

"That's why you three became so close."

"One of the reasons, yeah. We weren't just friends—we became a team. Each of us had something the others needed. Your mom had the social confidence I lacked, I had the organizational skills she... well, let's say she appreciated, and Ken had this way of making everything feel possible, even when it seemed scary."

Joshua shifted against the bean bag chair, processing this. "So when you met Dad..."

"David just fit right in because he got that loving your mom meant loving the whole package. He didn't try to break up our friendship or make her choose between us. He just... joined the family." Tyler smiled. "Plus, Ken and I put him through the full interrogation to make sure he was good enough for our Rebecca."

"You interrogated Dad?"

"Oh, thoroughly. Asked him about his five-year plan, his

thoughts on joint finances, his intentions toward your mother..."
Tyler's grin turned mischievous. "Ken asked about his family's
medical history."

"No way."

"Your mother was not amused, but David passed with flying
colors. Said he could see why we were so protective of her, and
that he hoped someday we'd consider him family too."

Josh felt something warm settle in his chest. "And you did."

"Of course we did. Anyone who loved your mom automatically
became our family too. That's how chosen family works—it keeps
growing when the right people come along."

They sat in comfortable silence for a moment, the streetlight
casting shifting shadows as the evening deepened. Josh could hear
his parents moving around downstairs, the familiar sounds of
dinner preparation and domestic life.

"Uncle Tyler?"

"Yeah?"

"When I do meet someone... when someone finds me, like you
said... will I know? Like you did with Ken?"

Tyler's expression grew gentle. "You'll know, kiddo. Might not
click right away, but you'll feel it. That sense of everything being
right, of possibility. Of wanting to be better because someone sees
something in you that's worth loving."

"Even if I'm... you know... awkward about it? Like you were?"

"Especially then. The right person won't be put off by your
need to process things, or your careful way of approaching new
situations. They'll appreciate that you take relationships seriously,
that you don't just jump into things without thinking them
through."

Josh nodded, filing this away with all the other wisdom Uncle
Tyler had shared over the years. "Can I ask you something else?"

"Always."

"Do you think I'm like you? I mean, really like you?"

Tyler studied Josh's face in the streetlight glow. "What do you
mean?"

"The way my brain works. How I need things to be... organized. The way crowds make me feel like crap. How most people totally exhaust me but some people, like you, don't." Josh's voice got quieter. "Am I autistic too?"

Tyler was quiet for a long moment, and Josh could see him choosing his words carefully.

"I think," Tyler said finally, "that your brain works perfectly, exactly the way it's supposed to. Whether there's some clinical name for it doesn't change the fact that you see things clearly, you care about stuff deeply, and you think everything through with real integrity."

"But that's not really an answer."

Tyler smiled. "No, it's not. Because that's something you'll have to figure out for yourself, when you're ready. Just like I did. But Josh?"

"Yeah?"

"Whatever you figure out about yourself, whatever words you find or don't find to describe how your mind works... you're already perfect exactly as you are. Any future someone who finds you is gonna be incredibly lucky."

Josh felt tears threaten, the same overwhelming gratitude he always felt when Uncle Tyler saw him so clearly, so completely.

"Now," Tyler said, his tone shifting back to playful, "what do you say we find out what other embarrassing stories I documented about your mother? I'm pretty sure there are some good ones in the wedding planning section."

Josh grinned, reaching for another binder from the box. "Only if you promise to tell me the parts you didn't write down."

"Deal. But fair warning—some of these stories might change how you see your dignified suburban mother forever."

"I'm counting on it," Josh said, settling in for another evening of discovering the beautiful, chaotic, imperfect love that had created his family.

Outside, the Seattle night grew darker, but in the attic, surrounded by preserved memories and the gentle presence of his uncle, Joshua had never felt more connected to the story of where he came from—and more excited about where he was going.

# CHAPTER 11
# WEDDING PLANNING

"So we're thinking something really chill," Rebecca said, giggling as she nearly knocked over her beer reaching for the nachos. "Like maybe Silver Falls State Park? Just our buddies, something outdoors and super simple."

David grinned, already a little loose from their third round. "Yeah, just Becca and me gettin' hitched in the woods! Ceremony by the waterfall, then we party in the pavilion with some decent beer and maybe find a band that doesn't completely suck."

Tyler chuckled, watching his friends with fond amusement. "That sounds perfect for you guys."

Ken, who had been suspiciously quiet while demolishing his burger, suddenly froze mid-chew. He swallowed slowly, set down his food, and stared at Rebecca like she'd just announced she was joining a cult.

"I'm sorry, what now?" Ken said carefully.

Rebecca blinked at him, still smiling. "What what?"

"Did you just say..." Ken paused dramatically, "...*low-key*?"

"Uh, yeah?"

Ken clutched his chest like he'd been shot. "Rebecca Marie Brennan. You get ONE wedding in your entire fucking life. ONE! And you want to have it in a goddamn *park*?"

"Hey, it's a really nice park!" David protested, laughing.

"Oh, sweet baby Jesus, no." Ken swiveled in his seat, eyes lighting up with pure theatrical joy. "Do you have ANY idea what kind of fairy tale extravaganza you could have instead? Picture this, darling—and I mean REALLY picture this..."

Ken gestured grandly, nearly knocking over Tyler's water glass. "A cathedral! With actual stained glass windows throwing rainbows all over the place! You floating down the aisle in layers and layers of ivory chiffon that cost more than Tyler's car—"

"Ken—" Rebecca started, but she was grinning.

"—with like fourteen bridesmaids in perfectly coordinated gowns that I personally select! And David standing there in a tux so gorgeous it should be illegal! Then afterward—oh honey, AFTERWARD—we rent some ridiculous ballroom with crystal chandeliers and gold fucking everything, and we have a sit-down dinner with more courses than a French restaurant, champagne fountains, and a wedding cake so tall it needs its own zip code!"

"Language," Tyler said, but he was trying not to laugh.

"And THEN," Ken continued, getting more animated, "we get you a horse-drawn carriage for photos because you only live once and you deserve to feel like Cinderella having the most fabulous day of your entire goddamn life!"

Rebecca and David were doubled over laughing as Ken painted his vision of wedding extravaganza, complete with increasingly wild hand gestures and descriptions of floral arrangements that sounded like they belonged at Versailles.

"And the flowers!" Ken continued, on a complete roll now. "We're talking arrangements so massive they need their own structural engineering! Roses, peonies, orchids flown in from fucking Hawaii—"

"Okay, okay!" Rebecca gasped, wiping tears from her eyes. "Ken, you magnificent lunatic, that sounds absolutely insane and wonderful, but it's really not... us."

Ken pouted dramatically. "But it could be! Just for one day! You could be the most ridiculously fabulous bride in the history of brides!"

David was still chuckling. "I gotta admit, Ken's got a point about the whole 'you only do this once' thing. Maybe we could bump it up a notch? Like, still chill but not completely bare-bones?"

Tyler watched this whole exchange with growing amusement, these three slightly drunk people he loved most in the world debating wedding logistics like it was a matter of national security.

"Alright, what do you think, Tyler?" Rebecca asked, gesturing with her beer bottle. "You're the voice of reason here. Talk some sense into somebody."

Tyler held up both hands, laughing. "Oh hell no. I'm not touching this one with a ten-foot pole. This is Rebecca and David's party, not mine."

"But surely you think—" Ken started, looking hopeful.

"I think," Tyler said, grinning at all of them, "that when this whole circus is over, what's gonna matter isn't whether the cake has seven tiers or the flowers cost more than my monthly rent. What's gonna matter is the people who showed up to celebrate with you guys."

Ken paused, his beer halfway to his mouth. "Okay, that's... actually really fucking sweet."

"Exactly," Tyler continued. "So whatever makes you two happy is the right call. Fairy tale wedding, backyard barbecue, Vegas drive-through chapel—doesn't matter to me."

Rebecca beamed at him. "See? This is why we keep you around." She turned to David. "What if we split the difference? Still do the outdoor thing at Silver Falls, but invite more people and get actual catering? Fancy enough to make Ken happy, relaxed enough to keep us sane?"

David brightened. "I like it! Best of both worlds."

Ken perked up immediately, and Tyler could practically see the wheels turning. "Ooh! Can I coordinate the catering? And decorations? I promise I won't go completely batshit crazy!"

Rebecca laughed. "Sure, Kenny. Just remember—elegant, not extravagant. We want people to remember the wedding, not require therapy afterward."

Ken raised his beer solemnly. "I can do elegant. Elegant with just a tiny touch of completely fabulous."

What followed were two months of the most entertaining wedding planning Tyler had ever witnessed. Ken threw himself into the coordination role with the enthusiasm of a Broadway director, complete with color-coded binders and vendor meetings that resembled auditions.

"The catering manager is absolutely gorgeous," Ken announced after one particularly successful meeting. "Seriously, this man has an ass you could bounce quarters off of. And his suggestions for the appetizer selection? *Chef's kiss*"

Tyler raised an eyebrow. "Should I be concerned about how much attention you're paying to the catering manager's... assets?"

Ken immediately swooped in to plant a dramatic, sloppy kiss on Tyler's cheek. "Jealous, babe? Don't be. You know you're the only one for me. I'm just appreciating the aesthetics of fine catering management."

Tyler wiped his cheek, blushing furiously while Rebecca howled with laughter. "You're impossible."

"Impossibly devoted to you," Ken grinned, then turned back to his wedding planning with renewed energy.

But as the wedding date approached, Tyler began to notice changes in Rebecca. The confident, take-charge woman who usually had opinions about everything had become oddly quiet during planning meetings. She'd defer to Ken's suggestions, seem distracted during vendor appointments, and had a distant quality that wasn't like her at all.

Tyler found her one evening sitting alone in the pavilion at Silver Falls, three weeks before the wedding. They'd come to do a final walkthrough with the caterers, but Rebecca had wandered off during the meeting.

"Hey," Tyler said softly, settling beside her on the picnic bench. "Everything okay?"

Rebecca was quiet for a long moment, staring out at the waterfall. "Tyler, can I ask you something? And will you give me a really honest answer?"

"Always."

"Do you think I'm making a mistake?"

Tyler blinked, surprised. "What kind of mistake?"

Rebecca turned to look at him, and Tyler could see she'd been crying. "This whole thing. Getting married. Growing up. I love David, I really do, but... God, Tyler, what if this is it? What if this is the moment my real life starts and everything else was just... practice?"

Tyler waited, recognizing that Rebecca needed to get this out.

"I keep thinking about what comes next," she continued. "After the wedding, we'll buy a house. Then probably kids. Then we'll be those people who talk about mortgage rates and school districts and... and I'll turn into my mother, won't I? Worried about lawn care and retirement planning and whether the kids are eating enough vegetables."

Tyler smiled softly. "Would that be so terrible?"

"I don't know!" Rebecca threw her hands up. "I thought I'd have more time to be young and carefree and... I don't know what I thought, but it feels like all these adult responsibilities are just slamming down on me at once. Marriage, house, kids, getting old, dying..." She laughed shakily. "Jesus, listen to me. I'm having a full existential crisis over wedding planning."

Tyler was quiet for a moment, processing. This wasn't like Rebecca—she was usually so certain about everything. But Tyler understood something about fear, about the weight of big decisions.

"Rebecca," he said gently, "can I tell you what I see when I look at you and David?"

She nodded.

"I see two people who make each other laugh every day. I see David bringing you coffee exactly the way you like it without being asked, and you defending him from Ken's fashion critiques with absolute ferocity. I see you two planning this wedding and compromising and supporting each other through every decision."

Rebecca wiped her eyes. "But what if—"

"What if you're exactly the same person after you get married as you are right now?" Tyler interrupted. "What if having a house just means you get to paint the walls whatever color you want? What if kids just means more people to protect and love the way you've protected and loved Ken and me?"

Rebecca looked at him with surprise. "You think I've protected you?"

"Rebecca, you've been taking care of everyone around you since the day we met. You pushed Ken and me together because you saw something we were too scared to see ourselves. You've been our fierce defender, our voice of reason, our family." Tyler smiled. "Those aren't skills you lose when you get married. If anything, you'll probably get better at them."

"Really?"

"Really. And honestly? I can't wait to see what kind of mother you'll be. Those kids are going to be the luckiest, most fiercely loved children in the world."

Rebecca started crying again, but these were different tears. "God, Tyler, what would I do without you?"

"You'll never have to find out," Tyler said simply. "That's what family means."

The day of the wedding dawned gray and humid, with threatening clouds that Ken kept eyeing nervously as he directed the setup crew.

"It's going to be fine," Tyler assured him as they supervised the placement of tables under the pavilion. "We have the backup plan, remember?"

"But the photos," Ken moaned. "Rebecca's going to look gorgeous, and if it's all gray and gloomy—"

At 11:47 AM, thirteen minutes before the ceremony was scheduled to begin, the sky opened up.

Not a gentle Pacific Northwest drizzle. Not a brief summer shower. A full-on downpour that sent guests scrambling for cover and turned the carefully arranged ceremony space into a muddy disaster.

Tyler's crisis management instincts kicked in immediately.

"Ken! Help me get the catering tables moved under the pavilion! We need to create a ceremony space in here!"

"But the decorations—"

"Forget the decorations! We need dry space for sixty people!"

What followed was twenty minutes of controlled chaos as Tyler and Ken worked with the catering staff to completely reconfigure the pavilion. Tables were moved, chairs were wiped down, the flower arrangements were rescued from the downpour, and somehow they managed to create a makeshift chapel under the roof of the pavilion.

The band set up in the corner, worried about their equipment getting wet. The catering staff bumped into each other as they tried to rearrange their service station. The wedding cake had water spots on the frosting. Rebecca's dress had muddy hem from running through puddles.

Tyler looked around at the chaos—the cramped space, the dripping decorations, the guests crowding together on folding chairs—and prepared to deliver the bad news to Rebecca.

Instead, he found her standing in the doorway of the pavilion, looking out at the disaster, and laughing.

Not crying. Not panicking. Laughing so hard she could barely stand up.

"Rebecca?" David appeared beside her, his tuxedo soaked and his hair plastered to his head. "Are you okay?"

"This is perfect," Rebecca gasped between laughs. "This is absolutely fucking perfect."

"Perfect?" Ken stared at her for about two seconds, then threw his head back and cackled. "Oh my God, you're right! This is HILARIOUS!"

And then Ken did the most Ken thing possible—he ran straight out into the downpour, arms spread wide, spinning around in his perfectly coordinated wedding outfit while getting completely drenched.

"If we're doing disaster wedding, we're doing it RIGHT!" Ken shouted over the rain, doing a little dance move that sent water flying everywhere.

Tyler watched Ken's theatrical rain dance and something inside him just... broke. In the best possible way. He started laughing—really laughing, the kind that starts in your chest and takes over your whole body until you can barely stand up.

The laughter was infectious. David started cracking up at the sight of Ken performing what looked like a Broadway number in a thunderstorm. The catering staff, who had been frantically trying to save the food, stopped what they were doing and started laughing too. Pretty soon the entire pavilion was filled with people doubled over with laughter at the beautiful absurdity of it all.

"You know what?" Rebecca yelled over the noise, grinning so wide her face hurt. "Forget saving the wedding! This IS the wedding now!"

She gestured around the chaos—guests dripping wet but chatting and laughing, Ken still dancing in the rain like Gene Kelly, Tyler wiping tears of laughter from his eyes, the band gamely trying to tune their instruments while chuckling at the whole situation.

"Welcome to the fucking family, everyone!" Rebecca hollered, raising her water-spotted bouquet in the air. "Where everything goes sideways and we party anyway!"

The cheer that went up from the crowd was probably audible three counties over.

The ceremony itself was unlike anything any of them had ever experienced. Crammed into the pavilion with rain drumming on the roof like nature's own percussion section, there was an intimacy and joy that no fancy church could have matched. When the minister—who was also soaking wet and loving every minute of it —asked if anyone objected to the marriage, someone in the back called out, "Only the weather!" and everyone dissolved into laughter again.

Rebecca and David exchanged vows while standing in a puddle, their voices barely audible over the storm, but their faces absolutely radiant. When they kissed, the entire pavilion erupted in cheers and applause that somehow managed to be louder than the thunder.

Ken, who had finally come in from his rain dance but was still dripping everywhere, shouted "THAT'S MY GIRL!" so loudly that it startled the minister into laughing.

The reception was equally chaotic and wonderful. The catering staff threw the formal service plan out the window and just started passing around food family-style. Guests shared tables with complete strangers and became instant friends. The band played acoustic sets because their full electric setup wouldn't fit in the cramped space, which turned out to be perfect for sing-alongs.

Tyler found himself standing beside a thoroughly soaked but absolutely glowing Ken, watching Rebecca and David dance on the tiny makeshift dance floor, both of them muddy and wet and completely radiant.

"Well," Ken said, wringing water out of his shirt, "this definitely wasn't in my wedding coordinator binder."

"It's better than anything in your binder," Tyler replied, still grinning.

Ken looked at him with mock offense. "Excuse me? My binder was a work of art."

"Your binder didn't account for Rebecca being completely perfect in a crisis," Tyler said, watching their friend spin around in her muddy wedding dress like she was wearing a ballgown at the Met Gala.

Tyler watched Rebecca throw her head back and laugh at something David whispered in her ear, saw the way everyone in that crowded pavilion had rallied around them to turn disaster into magic.

"You know what?" Ken said, following Tyler's gaze. "You're absolutely right. This is going to be the most amazing wedding story ever."

"The only wedding story worth telling," Tyler agreed.

Later, as they helped clean up the soggy decorations and stack the borrowed chairs, Rebecca found Tyler trying to save the water-damaged programs.

"Tyler," she said softly.

He looked up. "Yeah?"

"Thank you. For everything. For letting me have my existential crisis, for helping me realize that this—" she gestured around at the beautiful aftermath of their chaotic day "—this is exactly what I needed. Even when I didn't know it."

Tyler smiled. "That's what family does."

"Yeah," Rebecca said, pulling him into a fierce, slightly damp hug. "It fucking is."

And standing there in the muddy pavilion, surrounded by the beautiful disaster of Rebecca's perfect wedding day, Tyler understood something fundamental about love and life and the importance of being flexible when storms hit your best-laid plans. The best memories don't have a script.

# CHAPTER 12
# NIGHT THOUGHTS

Joshua lay in bed thinking about everything that had happened that day. The bullshit excuse to get him up in the attic to find Uncle Tyler and Ken's boxes. The tension between him and his mom at lunch, her almost telling him the truth before chickening out. The way Uncle Tyler had looked so helpless when he couldn't comfort her. The way Josh felt knowing he couldn't either.

But reading about how Uncle Tyler and Ken met... and to think it was all because of his mom and her sassy mouth, dragging Uncle Ken to that swim meet to gawk at guys in Speedos. He smiled to himself, propping his head up with his hands behind his head, staring at the ceiling of his darkened room. Shadows from the streetlight outside crept through his curtains, creating familiar patterns on the walls. He did this often—lay here unable to get his brain to slow down enough for sleep, not until he'd worked through everything from the day.

And then there'd been Uncle Tyler himself showing up while he was reading...

It wouldn't be surprising to see him, especially when Josh was going through all his old stuff. Hell, he'd probably come back from the dead too if someone was messing through his shit. Josh giggled slightly, thinking about himself as a ghost. Would he look like

Casper the friendly ghost or just some bullshit floating white sheet?

God, could his brain just shut the fuck up long enough for him to go to sleep?

But something kept gnawing at him. When he'd asked Prism if he might be... well... like him too...

Goddammit, Josh, he mumbled to himself. Why can't you just say the word? What are you afraid of?

"Special?" "Different?" "Unique?" He hated all those euphemisms, but he used them himself. Chickenshit, just like his mom's inability to tell him the truth about Uncle Tyler and Ken. Hell, he couldn't even tell himself the truth about... well...

Autistic. There. He thought it.

He felt—no, knew—he was like Uncle Tyler. It just fit. But when he'd asked earlier, Uncle Tyler had been careful, said Josh had to figure it out for himself. Made sense. It's like someone telling you "You're gay"—you've got to know yourself.

How the hell did he even start thinking about all this? God, he was tired and just wanted to sleep.

He shifted onto his side, staring at where he knew his desk was in the darkness. The digital clock read 12:47. Fuck. He'd been lying here over an hour already.

This was so typical. Brain going a million miles an hour when all he wanted was to just... stop. Think about nothing. Dream about something normal, like flying or being naked in class or whatever normal people dreamed about.

Instead, his mind kept circling back to that wedding story and how his mom had been such a mess. That was weird. His mom was always the one with her shit together. She could talk her way out of speeding tickets, make friends with random people at the grocery store, handle any social situation like she'd been born for it.

But Uncle Tyler's story about her freaking out before the wedding, sitting alone at that park, crying about growing up... it seemed so vulnerable. Human.

Like she really did need Uncle Tyler just as much as he needed her.

Those sentences kept replaying in his head:

"God, Tyler, what would I do without you?"

"You'll never have to find out. That's what family means."

Except she did have to find out, didn't she? When Uncle Tyler and Ken went away. Whatever the hell that meant.

Maybe that's why she couldn't tell him the truth. Maybe without Uncle Tyler there to help her process the hard stuff, she'd been just as lost as Josh got in crowds. Just making it up as she went along, hoping the lies would somehow get easier to maintain.

The clock now read 1:15.

Come on, brain. Please. Just shut up for a few hours.

But his mind wouldn't let it go. All those little details from the interviews, the photos, the careful way Uncle Tyler had documented everything—it was like putting together a puzzle where half the pieces had been missing his whole life.

His mom hadn't been lying to hurt him. She'd been lying because she was drowning and didn't know how else to swim.

Josh rolled onto his back again, hands behind his head, staring up at the ceiling. The house was quiet except for the usual settling sounds—pipes creaking, furnace humming, probably the neighbor's cat knocking over trash cans outside.

He wondered if Uncle Tyler slept. Did ghosts need rest? Did they dream?

"You're thinking pretty loud over there."

Josh turned his head, unsurprised to see Tyler sitting in the desk chair. In the dim streetlight, he looked younger. Less like the put-together adult from the photos and more like someone Josh's age.

"Can't turn it off," Josh whispered.

Tyler nodded. "I know that feeling."

"Does it ever get easier? The whole brain-won't-shut-up thing?"

"Sometimes. When you learn to work with it instead of fighting it." Tyler leaned back in the chair. "Ken used to say I had two bedtimes—when my body got tired and when my brain finally agreed to cooperate."

"What did you do when it wouldn't cooperate?"

"Usually? Exactly what you're doing. Lie there and let it run through everything until it was done." Tyler smiled. "Sometimes I'd get up and write stuff down. Make lists. Organize my thoughts on paper so they'd stop bouncing around in my head."

Josh considered this. "Is that why you wrote all those interviews? To organize your thoughts?"

"Partly. Writing helped me understand what I was feeling, what things meant." Tyler paused. "Your mom always said I should write a book. Guess I finally did, sort of."

They sat in comfortable quiet for a moment. Josh could feel his eyelids getting heavier, but his brain was still churning.

"Uncle Tyler?"

"Mm?"

"I think I get it now. Why Mom couldn't tell me about you guys."

Tyler waited.

"She was used to having you help her figure out the hard stuff. When you weren't there anymore, she probably had no idea how to handle something that big. So she just kept putting it off, hoping it would get easier."

"Probably."

"But it didn't get easier. It got more complicated. Harder to explain."

Tyler's voice was soft. "Yeah."

Josh yawned, finally feeling his body start to relax. "I'm not mad at her. I mean, I wish she'd told me, but I get why she didn't."

"You're pretty wise for twenty-one."

"I learned from someone pretty wise." Josh pulled his pillow more comfortably under his head. "I think I need to tell her I know. Not to be mean about it, just to let her know it's okay."

"That sounds right."

Josh's breathing was starting to even out, his thoughts finally beginning to blur at the edges. "Will you help me figure out what to say?"

"You already know what to say, kiddo. You've got a good heart."

As sleep finally started to take hold, Josh felt something he hadn't experienced in a long time. Not just tiredness, but actual peace. Like he was starting to understand his place in all of this. Who he was, where he came from, why certain things made sense.

"Love you, Uncle Tyler," he mumbled into his pillow.

"Love you too, Josh."

The last thing Josh was aware of was Tyler still sitting there, keeping watch in the darkness. Tomorrow would bring more discoveries, more difficult conversations, more pieces of the puzzle.

But tonight, for the first time in a long time, his brain finally agreed to let him rest.

# CHAPTER 13
## A STUDY SESSION

It had been two weeks since their first dinner, and Ken was starting to understand Tyler's rhythms.

They'd fallen into a pattern of studying together—sometimes with Rebecca, sometimes just the two of them—and Ken had become fascinated by the way Tyler's mind worked. Methodical, precise, beautiful in its organization. Tyler approached his accounting coursework the same way he approached diving: with ritual, focus, and an attention to detail that bordered on art.

"Want to hit the library tonight?" Ken asked after catching up with Tyler outside the business building. "I've got a psychology exam coming up, and you mentioned having that big accounting assignment due."

Tyler paused, considering. Ken had learned to recognize this—Tyler always took a moment to process social invitations, weighing variables that Ken was only beginning to understand.

"The library gets pretty crowded on Wednesday nights," Tyler said finally. "But... yes. I could use the study time." He hesitated, then added, "I need to go back to my room first to get my accounting books and change. Would you... want to come with me? We could figure out dinner plans on the way."

Ken's heart did a little skip. This was the first time Tyler had invited him to his dorm room. "Yeah, that sounds great."

The walk to Tyler's building was filled with easy conversation about their respective assignments, but Ken could sense Tyler working up to something. There was a careful quality to his voice, like he was rehearsing words in his head.

"So," Tyler said as they climbed the stairs to his floor, "I was thinking... after we study... maybe we could get dinner? Just the two of us this time?"

Ken grinned, recognizing Tyler's attempt at asking him on a proper date. "Are you asking me out, Tyler Prism Anderson?"

Tyler's cheeks flushed pink. "I'm trying to. I'm not very good at this."

"You're doing fine," Ken said gently, then couldn't resist adding, "Though I have to say, your technique could use some work. Maybe start with 'Ken, you devastatingly handsome man—'"

Tyler looked genuinely panicked for a moment, and Ken immediately realized his humor had missed the mark.

"Sorry, sorry," Ken said quickly. "I was joking. You don't need to change anything about how you ask. I'd love to have dinner with you. Just us."

Tyler's relief was visible. "Good. That's... good."

Tyler's room was exactly what Ken had expected—meticulously organized, everything in its proper place. Textbooks arranged by subject, pens lined up with military precision, diving medals hung in perfect alignment on the wall. It was so fundamentally Tyler that Ken felt a wave of affection just looking at it.

"Make yourself comfortable," Tyler said, gesturing toward the desk chair. "I just need to change and grab my books."

Ken settled into the chair, trying not to seem too interested as Tyler pulled a clean shirt from his dresser. "So, how's that cost accounting class going? I know you mentioned Professor Williams can be pretty... uh..."

Tyler began changing, pulling off his day shirt to reveal the lean muscle definition Ken had only glimpsed at the pool. Ken forced himself to keep talking. "Pretty demanding with the... the assignments and..."

Then Tyler started unbuttoning his khakis.

"...and the, um, the workload seems really..." Ken's voice faltered as Tyler stepped out of his pants, standing there in just his underwear and an undershirt. Ken tried to look anywhere else, but Tyler's wall mirror betrayed him, offering a perfect view of Tyler's compact, athletic frame as he carefully folded his khakis with the same precision he brought to everything else.

Ken cleared his throat and attempted to continue. "Really intensive this semester, from what I've... what I've heard..."

Tyler hung the pants on a wooden hanger, adjusting them until they hung perfectly straight, then placed them in his meticulously organized wardrobe. The whole process took maybe thirty seconds, but to Ken it felt like an eternity of trying not to stare at Tyler's legs, at the way his muscles moved as he reached for a pair of navy shorts from his dresser drawer.

"Professor Williams is tough," Tyler agreed, completely oblivious to Ken's struggle as he pulled on the shorts, "but fair. I like that he's straightforward about expectations."

Ken blinked, realizing he'd completely lost the thread of conversation. "Right. Straightforward. That's... that's good."

"So where were you thinking for dinner?" Ken asked, forcing himself to focus on the conversation rather than Tyler's physique.

Tyler paused, his hands stilling on his textbooks. "I... honestly, I'm not sure. I don't really know many restaurants around here."

"Oh! Well, there's this great pizza place downtown—Mario's. You literally shout your order to the guys behind the counter, and they yell back at you, and there's this whole interactive thing with loud music and—" Ken stopped mid-sentence as he watched Tyler's face go slightly pale. "Or... maybe not that one."

Tyler looked apologetic. "It sounds fun, it's just..."

"No, no, you're totally right," Ken said quickly, mentally kicking himself. "That place is insane. Like, genuinely chaotic." He thought for a moment. "There's this little diner I've heard about—Mabel's, I think? Never been there myself, but people say it's good. Supposed to be really low-key, like home cooking. More... conversational."

Tyler's relief was visible. "That sounds perfect."

Ken felt a surge of protectiveness mixed with uncertainty. He wanted Tyler to be comfortable, but he also didn't want Tyler to think he was being... managed. Or that Ken saw him as fragile. "I mean, it'll give us a better chance to actually talk and get to know each other better than shouting over pizza ovens," he added, trying to make it sound like a natural preference rather than an accommodation.

Tyler's smile was warm and grateful. "I'd like that. Getting to know each other better, I mean."

Tyler gathered his accounting textbooks with the same methodical care he applied to everything, and Ken found himself charmed by the ritual of it. Even packing a backpack was precise and purposeful for Tyler.

"Ready?" Tyler asked, shouldering his bag.

"Ready," Ken replied, though he was starting to realize he'd never be fully ready for the effect Tyler had on him.

The library was indeed crowded when they arrived. The main study area buzzed with the low hum of conversation, the rustle of pages, the scrape of chairs against linoleum. Students claimed tables with territorial efficiency, spreading textbooks and notebooks like they were marking their domain.

Ken watched Tyler's face as they stood in the entrance, looking for available seats. He was starting to recognize the signs—the slight tension around Tyler's eyes, the way his shoulders went rigid, the careful scan of the room like he was calculating variables in some complex equation.

"There," Tyler said quietly, pointing to a table near the back corner. "That one's free."

They made their way through the maze of occupied tables, Ken following Tyler's precise navigation toward the quieter section. Tyler had all his materials perfectly organized—color-coded notebooks, pens arranged by type, textbooks stacked in order of use. Ken found it oddly soothing to watch him set up his workspace.

For the first hour, everything went smoothly. Tyler was in his element, working through accounting problems with the same focused intensity Ken had seen at the pool. His handwriting was precise, his calculations methodical, and he had this habit of tapping his pen in a gentle rhythm when he was thinking through complex problems.

Ken tried to focus on his psychology reading, but he kept getting distracted by Tyler. The way Tyler's brow furrowed when he encountered a difficult accounting concept. The tiny smile that appeared when he solved something particularly challenging. The unconscious way Tyler organized his workspace throughout the evening, keeping everything in perfect alignment.

But as the evening wore on, the library filled up. What had been a manageable buzz of activity became a cacophony of competing sounds. Students talking in increasingly loud whispers. The scrape and slam of chairs. The percussion of textbooks being dropped onto tables. Someone's music bleeding through head-phones. A study group near the periodicals having an animated discussion about European history.

Ken noticed Tyler's change before Tyler seemed to realize it himself. The pen tapping became more frequent, more urgent. Tyler started glancing up from his work, scanning the room with growing agitation. His handwriting, normally so precise, began to look strained.

"Tyler?" Ken said quietly. "You okay?"

Tyler looked up, and Ken could see the overwhelm in his mismatched eyes. "It's getting... there's a lot of..." Tyler gestured vaguely at the room around them.

Ken understood immediately. The noise, the crowded space, the unpredictable sounds—it was too much input for Tyler to process while trying to concentrate on complex material.

"Want to get out of here?" Ken asked gently.

Tyler's relief was visible. "Could we? I know we just got settled, but—"

"Of course." Ken was already gathering his things. "You know what? Let's just go to that diner now. We can eat and then find somewhere quieter to study after."

"Are you sure? I don't want to impose—"

"Tyler." Ken looked at him seriously. "You're not imposing. I want you to be comfortable."

The walk to Mabel's Diner was quiet, Tyler visibly decompressing as they moved away from the library's overwhelming environment. Ken found himself stealing glances at Tyler's profile, noting how his shoulders gradually relaxed, how his breathing became less careful.

"Thank you," Tyler said as they approached the small, warmly lit building. "I couldn't think in there anymore."

"I could tell," Ken replied. "It was pretty overwhelming, even for me."

Tyler shot him a look of gratitude that made Ken's chest tight. This was new territory for both of them—Tyler trusting Ken enough to admit when he was struggling, Ken learning to read the subtle signs of Tyler's discomfort and respond without making it a big deal.

Mabel's was exactly what Ken had hoped—small, cozy, with mismatched chairs and the comfortable hum of quiet conversation. The lighting was warm rather than harsh, and the smell of home cooking filled the air. Only about half the tables were occupied, mostly by locals who seemed to know each other.

"This is nice," Tyler said, settling into a corner booth. "Peaceful."

"Thanks. I hoped it would be." Ken slid into the seat across from him. "More comfortable?"

Tyler nodded, already looking more like himself. "Much. I can actually think here."

They ordered simply—Tyler got the meatloaf special, Ken chose a burger—and spread their books on the table between them. The change in environment had shifted something between them. In the library, they'd been just study partners maintaining careful distance. Here, in this cozy booth with the warm lighting and quiet atmosphere, it felt more like a date.

Ken found himself watching Tyler work with new fascination. Without the stress of the overwhelming library environment, Tyler moved with natural grace. He had a way of organizing his materials in precise arrangements, creating order from textbooks and notebooks. His concentration was beautiful to watch—complete focus that seemed to quiet everything else in the world.

"Ken?" Tyler's voice broke through his reverie.

"Yeah?"

Tyler hesitated for a moment, glancing up from his textbook. "I know you're not an accounting major, but... could you read this paragraph and tell me what you think it means? I've read it about five times now, and my brain keeps interpreting it three different ways."

Ken blinked, a little surprised by the request, but pleased Tyler was asking for his input. "Sure, I can try."

What Ken didn't know was that Tyler had been stealing glances at him for the past ten minutes, trying to figure out some socially acceptable way to interact. Tyler knew it was probably lame to use homework as an excuse, but his logical brain couldn't come up with any other plausible reason to get Ken's attention. Social skills had never been his strong suit.

Ken moved around to Tyler's side of the booth, close enough to see the accounting textbook but careful not to crowd him. Any excuse to be close to Tyler was fine with him. Tyler smelled like that clean scent Ken was beginning to associate with him—soap and something indefinably Tyler.

"Which part?" Ken asked, trying to focus on the accounting text rather than Tyler's proximity.

Tyler pointed to a passage about cost allocation methods, and even though Ken wasn't an accounting major, he could see where the textbook's explanation was confusing. "I think they're trying to say..." Ken began, working through the logic step by step.

But as Ken talked through the accounting concept, he became aware of Tyler's attention—not just on the material, but on Ken himself. Tyler was listening with the same focused intensity he brought to everything, but there was something else in his expression. Something that made Ken's pulse quicken.

"That makes sense," Tyler said softly when Ken finished explaining. "You're good at breaking things down, even when it's not your subject."

"Thanks. You're a good student."

They were sitting close enough in the booth that Ken could see the flecks of gold in Tyler's blue eye, the subtle differences in color that made his gaze so striking. Close enough that when Tyler smiled—one of his rare, unguarded smiles—Ken felt it like a physical sensation.

The waitress came by to refill their coffee, and they reluctantly moved apart, but something had shifted permanently between them. The careful distance they'd been maintaining had closed by degrees, and Ken found himself thinking less about his psychology studying and more about the boy sitting across from him, carefully working through accounting problems with the same precise attention he brought to everything else.

When they finally left the diner, close to nine o'clock, they walked slowly back toward campus, neither wanting the evening to end.

"This was nice," Tyler said as they reached the quad. "Different from what I expected when we planned to study."

"Good different?" Ken asked hopefully.

Tyler's smile was soft and wondering. "Very good different."

Ken's heart did that irregular thing it had been doing around Tyler. "Maybe we could do it again sometime? The studying together part, I mean. Though maybe not at the library."

"I'd like that," Tyler said. "Maybe somewhere quiet again?"

"Definitely somewhere quiet."

They stood there for a moment outside Tyler's dorm, the weight of potential heavy in the air. Ken wanted to kiss him—had been wanting to kiss him all evening—but something held him back. This felt too important to rush, too fragile to risk with too much too soon.

"I'll call you tomorrow?" Ken said instead.

Tyler's smile was radiant. "I'd like that."

# CHAPTER 14
## QUESTIONS

"Why didn't you kiss Uncle Ken?"

Josh was back in his bean bag chair, looking up at Uncle Tyler, who'd been pacing back and forth in front of the boxes like he was waiting for a book review or something.

"Excuse me?"

"Kiss! Kiss!" Josh puckered up and made exaggerated kissing sounds, which made Prism turn about three shades of red and Josh crack up laughing. "When Ken walked you back from your first date—you know, without Mom chaperoning—why didn't you kiss him? I mean, come on. I totally would've."

"You would've kissed your Uncle Ken?"

"Oh my god, you know what I mean!" Josh threw his hands up, but he was grinning. This was the kind of back-and-forth they both loved.

"I... I dunno. I was probably just... innocent? Naive?"

"Wait." Josh sat up like someone had just turned on a light bulb over his head. "You'd never been kissed before."

It wasn't really a question, and Tyler still got embarrassed talking about this stuff, even all these years later. But this was Josh, and... he took a deep breath. "No. I was still a virgin."

"Even kissing?"

"Even kissing."

"So when did you finally—"

"When did I what?"

"Kiss Ken!"

"Well..." Tyler started rocking back and forth on his heels without realizing it. "Actually, Ken kissed me first."

"Ooh, details!"

"What, you want the play-by-play?" Tyler laughed nervously. "This is like having the sex talk with you."

"We never had that talk," Josh pointed out.

"We didn't?"

"Nope! Wanna have it now?" Josh knew exactly which buttons he was pushing and had zero intention of stopping.

"Uh... well... you're twenty-one, so I figured you'd already..."

"Nope! Virgin. Guilty as charged. Never even kissed anyone."

Tyler stopped pacing and stared at his nephew, trying to figure out if he was being played. "Seriously?"

"Scout's honor," Josh said, making an exaggerated cross over his heart and flashing the most innocent smile in his arsenal.

"Well... um... are you sure you want to—"

Josh started giggling, totally blowing his cover.

"You little shit!" Tyler grinned, starting toward him like he was gonna give him a noogie before stopping just short. "You had me going there."

"Okay, okay, but seriously though... I do have something I've been wondering about."

"Sure."

"It's kinda personal."

"Josh, you can ask me anything. You know that."

"Even about SEX?" He said it extra loud just to watch Tyler squirm.

To his credit, Tyler pulled it together and plopped down on the floor so they were eye-to-eye. "Yeah. I'll do my best. I'm no expert, but I picked up a few things along the way."

"You sure?"

"Positive." Tyler got that focused look he got when he was really listening. "What's up?"

Josh started to ask, then got nervous. Some of his fidgeting started, and Tyler noticed.

"Hey, take your time. And remember—there's literally nothing you could ask that would be shameful or wrong."

Josh thought about that, then just blurted it out before he could chicken out. "How did you know you liked boys?"

Tyler looked right at him—really looked at him, which he almost never did with anyone. "I was probably... ten? Eleven maybe?"

"What happened?" Josh leaned forward, totally hooked.

Tyler had never told this story to anyone. Not even Ken, really. "So I was at swim practice one afternoon. I'd been moved up to train with the junior high kids, and I was always watching them, trying to figure out how they got so fast."

"Uh-huh."

"Well..." Tyler's face went bright red and he started smiling despite himself, which made Josh grin even wider.

"What? Come on!"

"I finished practice and was walking into the changing room behind all the older kids. And there was this boy—Billy Straughton—taking off his swim trunks right in front of me."

"And?"

Tyler was practically glowing red now. "Do I really have to—"

"YES!"

"You're exactly like your mother, you know that?"

"Best compliment ever. Keep going!"

"Fine! So Billy turned around and... well... there was his..." Tyler gestured vaguely.

"Dick?"

"Yeah."

Josh was dying laughing.

"And I got my first..." Tyler covered his face with his hands. "Oh god, I can't believe I'm telling you this."

"Uncle Prism! You promised!"

"Fine! I got my first boner, okay? There. Happy?"

"You got a hard-on from Billy what's-his-name and that made you gay?" Josh was practically falling out of his chair.

"It didn't make me gay," Tyler said, laughing too now. "I was always gay. I just finally had a word for what I was feeling."

Josh sat back, looking at his uncle like he was seeing him completely differently. "Huh."

Tyler decided to turn the tables. "What about you? Ever think about what you might be? And it's totally okay whatever the answer is. Or if you don't want to answer."

Josh opened his mouth, then closed it. He bit his lip and looked away, making Tyler worry he'd pushed too hard.

"Sorry, I didn't mean to—"

"No, it's fine. I just... honestly? I don't know. That's kinda why I asked. I wanted to know how you figured it out."

Tyler nodded. "There's no formula, trust me. I wish there had been. But I think deep down I just knew I was attracted to boys. The hard part was finding the words for it, then getting over being scared and ashamed about it."

"Yeah, that makes sense."

"Can I ask you something now?"

"Shoot."

Josh turned bright red. "Those pictures in the box..."

"Oh, those old Polaroids? Your mom took those. She and Ken used to collect pictures of guys they thought were cute and put them up on her dorm wall."

"Wait, what? That's hilarious, but hang on." Josh was getting redder by the second. "I saw some of you in your... Speedos... and you were kinda... hot."

Now Tyler was blushing too. "Oh."

"I don't mean it weird or anything!" Josh waved his hands around. "I just... you looked really good."

"Well... thanks, I guess? Your mom used to tease me about that stuff all the time. Don't even get me started on the rainbow underwear incident."

"Rainbow underwear? What the hell?"

"Long story. But Josh? Whatever you feel toward anyone—

random people, classmates, guys, girls, divers in tiny bathing suits —it's all normal. Nothing to be ashamed of."

"I know that up here," Josh tapped his head.

"But you need to know it in here too," Tyler pointed to his heart. "And that takes time."

"Uncle Tyler?"

"Yeah?"

"Did people ever give you shit for being gay?"

Tyler's whole body language changed. Josh could see the answer before he said anything.

"Your mom handled most of that for me."

"Mom? Really?"

"Yep. I learned real quick—you never mess with Rebecca."

Josh giggled. "Were you about to say 'fuck'? Like, never fuck with Mom?"

Tyler couldn't deny it. "She... taught me how to swear, actually."

"WHAT? Mom taught you to say fuck?"

Tyler nodded.

"Oh my god, that's the best thing I've ever heard! Mom corrupted innocent little Uncle Tyler!"

"It was actually pretty liberating."

"Fuck yeah it is!" Josh yelled.

"Fuck yeah," Tyler agreed, though way more quietly.

They both started cracking up, and Josh felt something he'd never experienced before—like he could ask anything, say anything, be anything, and his uncle would just love him exactly as he was. It was the best feeling in the world.

# CHAPTER 15
# THE PROTECTIVE SISTER

"I know this is totally lame," Rebecca said, sliding into the booth across from Ken and Tyler with her beer, "but I promise this isn't your real housewarming gift. I just haven't had time to find you something proper for the apartment yet."

Ken grinned, raising his wine glass. "Are you kidding? Free pizza and drinks? This is perfect."

Tyler nodded, sipping his diet soda. "Really, Rebecca. You didn't need to get us anything at all."

"Bullshit," Rebecca said cheerfully. "You two finally living together in sin is definitely worth celebrating. Even if it's just with Mario's pizza and cheap beer."

They'd been at Mario's for about an hour, catching up on classes and apartment life, when the table of frat boys next to them started getting louder. What had begun as typical college guy banter was slowly escalating into something more obnoxious as their pitcher emptied.

"Don't drop your fork, Todd," one of them said with exaggerated concern, "or you might feel something poke you in the ass!"

The whole table erupted in juvenile laughter, and Tyler could feel his cheeks burning. Ken rolled his eyes and took another sip of wine, clearly trying to ignore them.

"Classy," Rebecca muttered, but she kept her voice low. They'd all been through this before—drunk college guys making stupid jokes. Best to just ignore it and wait for them to move on to something else.

But they didn't move on.

"Hey, maybe we should sit somewhere else," one of the frat boys said loudly, clearly intending to be overheard. "I don't want to catch anything from the couple of fags in the next booth."

Rebecca's entire demeanor changed in an instant. One moment she was relaxed, laughing, taking a casual sip of her beer. The next, she looked like she'd grown six inches and gained fifty pounds of pure fury. Her eyes went cold, her jaw set, and Tyler watched her transform into someone he'd never seen before.

Before Ken or Tyler could even register what was happening, Rebecca was on her feet and moving toward the frat boys' table.

"Rebecca—" Ken started, but she was already there.

Tyler couldn't see much from his position in the corner of the booth, but he could hear everything.

"Excuse me," Rebecca said, her voice carrying a pleasant tone that somehow managed to sound absolutely terrifying. "Did I just hear you correctly?"

"What's it to you?" one of them replied, clearly emboldened by alcohol and his friends' presence.

"Well, those are my friends you're talking about," Rebecca said, still in that eerily calm voice. "And I don't appreciate the language you're using."

"What are you gonna do about it?" Tyler heard another voice sneer. "What are you, their fag hag?"

That's when Ken jumped up, clearly worried things were about to get violent. But by the time he could see around the booth wall, the situation had already shifted dramatically.

Rebecca was leaning down close to the largest guy at the table —obviously their ringleader—and whatever she was doing, he looked like he was in serious pain. His face was red, sweat beading on his forehead, and his eyes were wide with shock and something that looked like terror.

The other guys at the table sat frozen, staring at their friend being taken down by this girl they'd clearly underestimated. They looked like they had no idea what to say or do.

"Do we have an understanding?" Rebecca asked in the most authoritative voice Ken had ever heard from her. Her arm was doing something Ken couldn't see, but whatever it was made the guy wince and grunt.

"Do we?" she asked again, her voice rising slightly as she apparently increased whatever pressure she was applying.

"Yes," the guy gasped out, his voice strained.

"Good. And if ANY of you sick fucks ever cross me or my friends again..." Rebecca didn't finish the sentence, but the threat hung in the air like a storm cloud. She looked like she could have sprouted horns and Ken wouldn't have been surprised.

Then, as quickly as it had started, it was over. Rebecca straightened up, her face returning to its normal pleasant expression, and gestured for Ken to come back to their booth.

The transformation was so complete and so sudden that Ken wondered if he'd imagined the whole thing. Rebecca slid back into her seat and picked up her beer like nothing had happened. The pizza place returned to its normal sounds—conversations, music, clinking glasses. No more loud laughter or crude comments from the neighboring table.

Tyler looked between Ken and Rebecca, completely bewildered. "What happened?"

Rebecca was mid-sip, so Tyler looked to Ken for answers.

"I have no idea," Ken said honestly, still processing what he'd witnessed.

After some cajoling from both of them, Rebecca finally shrugged and explained matter-of-factly, "I told him that if he or any of his friends ever used the word 'fag' or 'gay' or any other derogatory term, or made any insults about you two in any way, I'd personally tear off his dick and shove it up his ass so he could literally go fuck himself."

Ken and Tyler both burst into laughter. "No!" Ken insisted. "You didn't actually say that!"

"Did you really?" Tyler asked, not even bothering to correct her language.

Rebecca looked at them with an expression that clearly asked whether they thought she was joking.

Ken remembered the guy's pained expression. "He looked like he was really hurting..."

"Oh, that?" Rebecca said casually, taking another sip of beer. "Well, I grabbed his balls and twisted when he didn't think I was serious. You two are not to be messed with."

Both Ken and Tyler reflexively grabbed their own crotches, wincing in sympathy.

"Prism, can you pass me another slice?" Rebecca asked cheerfully. "I'm hungry after all that."

Tyler started to mouth something, but Rebecca caught it. "What did you say?"

"Uh... well... I was just saying not to mess with you."

"You mean don't fuck with me," Rebecca corrected.

"Language, Rebecca."

Rebecca set down her beer and looked at Tyler seriously. "Tyler, honey, I appreciate when you correct my language. And more often than not, you're right. But this time, you're wrong. Those assholes were wrong to treat you both like that, and I'm not going to let them or anyone else do that to you. Ever. So yes, I am correct. They, and anyone else who ever makes fun of or treats either of you like that, is going to face the wrath of me. Don't FUCK with me. That's the right word. And you can say it."

Tyler smiled slightly, recognizing that she was right. But Rebecca wasn't done.

"It's okay, Prism. You can say it."

Tyler looked embarrassed. "Oh... I..."

"What? It's just a word. I mean, surely you've said it a thousand times. Lord knows Ken and I would get rich with your proverbial swear jar!" They laughed. "I think I practically said it coming out of the womb!"

"Yeah, I know... but..."

"But what, Tyler? Sometimes, especially when people deserve

to know you mean business, words matter. What those frat boys were doing wasn't right. And it's not only okay to say it, it's the right thing to say! Come on, say it with me!"

"I... uh... I don't..."

"Oh, don't be a pussy on me, Prism!" Rebecca said, which made Ken nearly spit out his pizza laughing.

"I can't believe you're trying to get Tyler to cuss!" Ken said.

"I already cuss!" Tyler protested indignantly.

"Oh yeah, you say 'damn' and 'hell,'" Rebecca teased in an exaggerated prissy voice. "Ohhhhh, such words for my dainty ears!"

Tyler's face turned red.

"It's okay, Tyler. Those assholes deserved it. Fuck them!"

Ken looked at Rebecca and repeated enthusiastically, "Yeah, fuck them!"

Both looked expectantly at Tyler, who stared down at his pizza before glancing back at them. "You're not letting me out of this, are you?"

"Nope!" they said in unison.

Taking a deep breath, Tyler mumbled something inaudible.

"What? I didn't catch that," Rebecca teased.

Tyler mumbled again, slightly louder but still incomprehensible.

"What?" Ken joined in the playful harassment, though he nudged his boyfriend affectionately to help him loosen up.

Realizing he was defeated, Tyler finally gave up and spoke clearly: "Fine... F... F... Fuck them!"

"What? My virgin ears!" Rebecca gasped dramatically. "Did our innocent Prism just say 'fuck'? I'm going to be forever scandalized!"

Ken played along, clutching his chest in mock horror, before they all dissolved into laughter.

"Seriously, Tyler," Rebecca said when the laughter died down, her tone becoming genuine again. "You both mean too much to me to have anyone treat you like shit. So yes, fuck them. I will hurt them if they so much as joke about hurting you."

Tyler, who had been embarrassed about saying what he'd

always thought of as the mother of all curse words, suddenly felt less embarrassed and more... safe. Knowing he had an ally like Rebecca, someone who would literally grab a guy by the balls to defend him, made something tight in his chest relax.

And honestly? It felt kind of good to properly curse. Like he'd been given permission to use a tool he'd been denied his whole life.

"You know," Tyler said thoughtfully, taking another sip of his soda, "I think I understand now why you use those words so much."

"Because they're fucking useful," Rebecca grinned.

"Because they're fucking useful," Tyler repeated, and this time he didn't blush at all.

Ken beamed at both of them. "I love my family."

"Damn right you do," Rebecca said, raising her beer. "And now anyone who messes with any of us knows exactly what they're dealing with."

As they finished their pizza, Tyler kept glancing over at the frat boys' table. They'd been completely quiet since Rebecca's intervention, speaking in hushed tones and shooting nervous glances their way. Whatever Rebecca had done, whatever she'd said, had clearly made a lasting impression.

But more importantly, Tyler felt something he'd never quite experienced before—the absolute certainty that someone had his back, no matter what. Not just Ken, who loved him, but Rebecca, who had claimed him as family and would apparently commit violence on his behalf without hesitation.

It was a good feeling. A very fucking good feeling, actually.

And when they left the pizza place that night, Tyler walked a little taller, knowing that anyone who wanted to mess with him would have to get through Rebecca first. And based on what he'd witnessed, that was not a battle anyone in their right mind would want to fight.

# CHAPTER 16
## TRUTH

Rebecca kept pacing in the kitchen like a caged tiger, alternating between topping off an already overflowing coffee cup and staring out the window at their pathetic excuse for a backyard. Neither she nor David were worth shit as gardeners—hell, they could kill a plastic plant—so there wasn't much to admire except a jungle of weeds, the sad skeleton of what used to be a flower bed from her brief "domestic goddess" phase a few years back, and Joshua's beat-up Honda parked crooked in front of the garage like he'd been texting while pulling in.

She remembered the day he got his license... Jesus Christ, what a shitshow that had been. Neither she nor David had the patience of saints required to teach a teenager to drive without losing their ever-loving minds, but she'd gritted her teeth and powered through. Good thing she didn't smoke, because goddamn if that whole experience didn't make her want to take up a pack-a-day habit. Joshua would freeze up at four-way stops like a deer in headlights, desperately waving at other drivers to go first, while they'd wave back at him in that polite "no, after you" dance that could go on for fucking ever. "Just GO already!" he'd yell at the windshield in frustration. "It's okay, honey, it's your turn," she'd say through gritted teeth, her right foot instinctively searching for a passenger-side brake pedal that didn't exist. He'll figure it out eventually, she kept telling herself like a mantra.

And he did figure it out... and somehow they all survived without anyone getting arrested or divorced. With the help of a few therapeutic beers for her and David after each white-knuckle practice session, and Joshua's signature obsessive studying—the kid probably memorized the entire DMV handbook, driver's ed videos, and every "What to Expect When Your Teen Is Driving" article on the internet. The actual test was a joke. Rebecca didn't even sweat it, knowing Josh would nail a perfect score because that's how his brain worked. But being alone in a car with some DMV stranger who was judging every turn signal and parallel parking attempt while Joshua's anxiety went through the roof? Fuck, she nearly popped one of those little pink "mommy's helpers" when he drove off with the examiner. But twenty minutes later, he came strutting back with a shit-eating grin that could've powered the neighborhood.

"Mom?"

Rebecca turned to see her son standing by the fridge, rummaging through.

"Yes, honey?"

"Do we have anything for lunch?"

Well... she got a kick out of how he still approached her like she was the magical lunch fairy who could conjure food from thin air...

Ten minutes later they were sitting down to a proper fucking feast: Campbell's potato soup, half a pastrami sandwich, and a pickle that had seen better days. Gourmet dining at its finest. Both of them ate in comfortable silence for a while—nothing earth-shattering to discuss, just the usual mother-son lunch vibe.

Except there was everything to talk about. A whole goddamn elephant tap-dancing in the middle of the kitchen that they'd been ignoring for years.

Rebecca finally caved like a house of cards...

"Did you... find anything... interesting upstairs?"

"I think it's funny as hell that you taught Uncle Tyler how to say 'fuck'," her son said cheerfully while chomping down on half a pickle, causing her to nearly choke on her sandwich and spray pastrami across the table.

After a coughing fit that would've made a tuberculosis patient proud, Rebecca gulped some water and came up for air. "What the hell?"

"One of his stories said you grabbed some frat dude's balls and told him not to fuck with you. Classic Mom move."

Holy shit. Rebecca had completely forgotten about that day... yet suddenly she was transported back like someone had grabbed her by the scruff of the neck and dropped her right into that pizza place. She could practically smell the grease, hear the chaos, feel that asshole's face going beet red when she squeezed his nuts like she was juicing a lemon. What a douche. A wicked grin spread across her face that Joshua caught immediately, and he grinned right back.

"You're a badass bitch, you know that?"

"Joshua! Don't call your mother that!" she gasped in mock horror.

"Okay... you're a badass. Better?"

"Why you little shit! I oughta..." But she was laughing, and so was he. They had that kind of relationship—the apple didn't fall far from the sarcastic tree with her son, and she wouldn't have it any other way. But her mind was already racing back to Tyler and Ken, remembering how fierce she'd felt protecting them from those homophobic assholes who threw around words like "fag" like they were confetti.

She'd do it all over again in a heartbeat.

"I would've killed to see Uncle Tyler's face when you made him say 'fuck'! I bet he turned redder than a fire engine!" Joshua was practically bouncing in his chair with glee.

The easy laughter between them felt good, natural—like old times when things were simpler and she didn't have to watch every word. For a moment, it was just mother and son sharing hilarious stories, the kind of comfortable intimacy she'd always treasured with Joshua. But then...

It had been so long since her son began cussing she hadn't even given two thoughts about it. She remembered him coming home from Kindergarten once complaining about one of the boys being mean to him, impatient because Joshua had taken too long in thinking about what side he wanted to play kickball on, and taken to yelling at him for seemingly going quiet. Rebecca had attempted to comfort her little boy, telling him that it's okay to think things through, and that some people just get excited and can't wait until it's their turn. Josh's response had been to say that the boy was "an asshole", prompting spontaneous laughter from his mother followed quickly by inquisition as to where he learned that word. Of course, Josh had heard it from her. Buckle up, she thought. Just look what other words and phrases he was going to come home with soon.

And boy did he! By 3rd grade, he'd moved well beyond H-E-Double Hockey Sticks to "Son of a Bitch". By 7th grade, his nom-de-plume was "mother fucker"... he particularly found that one funny, for no other reason, she learned, that it just seemed odd that anyone would fuck their mother. Of course, he wasn't sure what "fuck" meant really... but he thought it meant doing something mean, like hitting or spanking. Oh, this definitely was her son. They had a little talk about when he could use those words and in what company. If nothing else, so she didn't have to pay any visits to the Principal's office.

Rebecca thought of that day when she'd put the screws on those assholes to protect Tyler, only to end up making him uncomfortable by forcing him to cuss. But he needed both—the protecting and the loosening up. Sometimes, you just needed to be able to say "fuck it" in this world, didn't you? It felt good. It released something inside that only that word could touch.

"Well, it was kinda' funny. He was always so..."

"Uptight?"

"Well... sorta'..." Rebecca's voice grew softer, more careful. "Your uncle Tyler was... special... he liked things... well... ordered... in place."

"Kinda' like me?"

The question hit her like a sucker punch. Rebecca hadn't really given much thought to the comparison, but now that her son mentioned it, she could see so much of Tyler in Joshua it was almost painful. The way they both organized everything just so. The way they both got overwhelmed in crowds. The way they both needed time to process before responding.

"Yeah... I guess... you remind me a lot of him, now that you say it," she said, and tried to smile. But the smile felt wrong, forced, because suddenly she wasn't thinking about funny stories anymore. She was thinking about Tyler himself—really thinking about him—and all the grief she carried came rushing back like a tidal wave.

The laughter died in her throat. Her face changed, the warmth draining away as that familiar ache settled back into her chest like an old wound reopening. She tried to push it down, tried to get back to the safety of casual conversation, but it was too late. She was drowning again, just like always when Tyler stopped being a funny memory and became the person she'd lost.

Joshua watched his mother's face transform from joy to devastation in real time. He'd seen this look before—dozens of times over the years—whenever their conversations about Tyler or Ken went on too long, or got too real, or touched too close to whatever truth she was hiding. The way her eyes would go distant and pained, the way she'd suddenly need to find something else to do, somewhere else to be.

He looked down at his plate, his appetite completely gone now. His stomach was twisting into knots because he knew what he was about to do, and there would be no taking it back once the words were out.

The kitchen fell into a suffocating silence. Rebecca stared blindly out the window, fighting to pull herself back from the edge of the grief that always threatened to swallow her whole when she let herself remember too much. She could feel Joshua watching her, could sense his concern, but she couldn't seem to find her way back to normal.

"Mom?" Joshua's voice was different now—quieter, more careful, like he was approaching a wounded animal.

"Mmm?" She couldn't look at him. Couldn't trust herself not to fall apart completely.

The pause stretched between them, heavy with twelve years of unspoken truth.

"I know."

Two words. That's all it took.

Rebecca's world stopped. The coffee cup in her hands suddenly felt impossibly heavy. The air in the kitchen became thick, unbreathable. Everything—the humming refrigerator, the distant traffic, even her own heartbeat—went silent as those two words hung in the space between them like a guillotine blade, ready to sever everything she'd built.

"Know what, honey?" she managed, though her voice came out strangled, barely a whisper.

"About Uncle Ken and Tyler."

The fork clattered against her plate. The kitchen went completely silent except for the hum of the refrigerator and the sound of Rebecca's heart hammering against her ribs so loudly she was sure Joshua could hear it. Twelve years of carefully constructed lies, of birthday cards signed in Tyler's handwriting, of made-up excuses and deflected questions—all of it crumbling in the space between those five words.

She couldn't speak. Couldn't breathe. Couldn't do anything but stare at her son's bent head while her entire carefully constructed world collapsed around her. The walls of lies she'd built so meticulously, brick by brick, year after year, were falling down in slow motion, each piece hitting the ground with a deafening crash.

"What... what do you know?" she whispered, though every fiber of her being already knew the answer.

Joshua was still looking down at his plate, methodically arranging the remnants of his pickle with the same careful precision Tyler used to organize everything. "I know they're dead, Mom."

She felt the room spinning, her vision blurring as tears she'd been holding back for over a decade finally broke free. The careful composure she'd maintained through thousands of conversations about Uncle Tyler and Uncle Ken shattered completely, leaving her gasping and raw and utterly exposed.

"How long have you known?" she whispered.

"A while," Joshua said quietly, finally looking up at her with those gentle eyes that reminded her so much of Tyler it was like a knife in her chest. "I'm not sure exactly when I figured it out, but... the cards always came on the same day every year. Your handwriting when you were trying to be neat. They never called anymore, never visited..."

Rebecca's face crumpled completely. "Josh, I'm so sorry. I'm so fucking sorry—"

"Mom, it's okay." Joshua reached across the table and took her trembling hand. "I get why you didn't tell me. I was nine. You probably had no idea how to explain that they were never coming back."

"I couldn't," Rebecca sobbed. "I just couldn't break your heart like that. You loved them so much, and they loved you, and I thought... I thought maybe if I just... if I kept them alive for you somehow..."

He paused. "And maybe protecting yourself too. Like if you didn't say it out loud, it wouldn't be real."

Rebecca stared at her son. Jesus, when had he gotten so perceptive?

"What happened to them?" Joshua asked quietly. "I mean, what really happened?"

Rebecca's voice came out shaky. "Car accident. Black ice on I-84, coming back from some weekend trip to the coast." She wiped her nose with the back of her hand. "I got the call the next morning from the state police."

Joshua nodded slowly. "Were you there when it happened?"

"God, no. David had to drive me to the hospital to..." Her voice broke completely.

They sat there crying for a minute, neither one knowing what the hell to say. Finally, Joshua reached over and squeezed her hand.

"I'm not pissed at you, Mom."

Rebecca looked up, surprised. "You're not?"

"No. I get it. I was just a kid. You probably had no fucking clue how to tell a nine-year-old that his favorite people in the world were never coming home." He paused, his voice getting quieter. "But I'm not nine anymore. I want to know about them. Really know them. Not just my kid memories, but who they actually were. What made them tick, what they fought about, what stupid shit they did in college."

Rebecca felt something break open in her chest—not bad broken, but like finally being able to breathe after holding her breath for twelve years. "Yeah," she said, wiping her eyes with her sleeve. "Yeah, I can tell you about them. They were... fuck, Josh, they were the best people I ever knew. They would've been so damn proud of you."

What Joshua didn't say—what he figured would just freak his mom out even more—was that Uncle Tyler was standing right behind her chair. Tyler had tears streaming down his face and looked like he was dying to wrap his arms around Rebecca, but his hands just hovered there, inches from her shoulders, unable to touch her. The look on Tyler's face was pure heartbreak—for Rebecca's pain, for all the years she'd carried this alone, for everything they'd all lost.

Josh caught Tyler's eye and saw the relief there, the gratitude that finally, finally, the bullshit was over and they could just be real with each other. But that conversation would have to wait. Right now, his mom needed him to just be her son.

"So tell me," Joshua said, settling back in his chair. "Tell me everything."

And for the first time in twelve years, Rebecca did.

# CHAPTER 17
# MOVING IN TOGETHER

"It's perfect," Rebecca declared, hands on her hips as she surveyed the small two-bedroom apartment. "Close to campus, quiet neighborhood, decent kitchen... and most importantly, it's got two bedrooms so Ken's parents won't have a fucking heart attack when they visit."

Ken shot her a look. "Becca."

"What? I'm being practical!" She grinned wickedly. "Though we all know you two are going to end up sharing one bedroom anyway."

Tyler, who was methodically measuring the living room with a tape measure, looked up with pink cheeks. "Rebecca..."

"Oh please, like it's not obvious you're crazy about each other," she said, flopping dramatically onto the couch that came with the furnished apartment. "I'm just saying, having the extra bedroom gives you options. Ken's family gets their propriety, you get your privacy."

It had been Rebecca's idea to help them apartment hunt. Three weeks after Tyler's declaration of love during the flu incident, they'd been spending every night together anyway—either in Ken's dorm or Tyler's studio. The camping incident had broken down the last of their careful boundaries, and they'd both realized that separate living spaces were just a formality at this point.

"My parents are pretty traditional," Ken said quietly, testing the firmness of the mattress in what would theoretically be his bedroom. "Having separate rooms will make the whole 'roommate' thing more believable."

Tyler looked up from his measuring. "Are you... nervous about them meeting me?"

Ken's expression softened. "Not about them meeting you. You're incredible. I'm nervous about..." He gestured vaguely. "The coming out part. They've probably suspected for years, but actually introducing them to my boyfriend is different."

"We could keep it simple," Tyler offered. "Just say we're roommates. I don't mind."

"No." Ken's voice was firm. "I'm not hiding you. I'm not hiding us. I just... need to figure out the right way to tell them."

Rebecca sat up straighter. "When are they coming?"

"Next weekend. They want to see the new place, meet my 'roommate,' make sure I'm not living in squalor." Ken ran his hands through his hair. "My mom's already planning to cook for us. She's bringing enough food to feed a small army."

"That's sweet," Tyler said softly.

"It is. And she's going to love you." Ken looked at Tyler seriously. "They both will. I just need to prepare them for the fact that you're not just my roommate."

Tyler nodded, then went back to his measuring. Rebecca watched him for a moment, recognizing the focused energy Tyler put into organizing when he was processing something emotional.

"Prism," she said gently, "you okay?"

Tyler paused his measuring. "I've never... I mean, I've never met anyone's parents before. As their... boyfriend."

Ken moved to sit beside Tyler on the floor where he'd been measuring. "They're going to love you," he repeated. "My mom's been asking about who I'm dating for years. She'll probably cry happy tears when she realizes I found someone as amazing as you."

"What if I say something wrong? What if I'm too... different?"

Rebecca snorted. "Tyler, honey, you're perfect. If Ken's parents can't see that, they're blind."

Ken reached for Tyler's hand. "You're not too anything. You're exactly right."

They signed the lease that afternoon, Rebecca insisting on being their witness and unofficial decorator. She had opinions about everything—the placement of furniture, the organization of the kitchen, the absolute necessity of good curtains for privacy.

"Trust me on this one," she said, eyeing the large living room windows. "You do not want your neighbors seeing everything that goes on in here."

Moving in took two days, mostly because Tyler insisted on organizing everything systematically while Ken and Rebecca provided entertainment through increasingly ridiculous commentary on Tyler's method.

"Babe," Ken said, watching Tyler arrange books by subject, then by author, then by publication date, "it's okay if the books aren't in perfect order."

"They need to make sense," Tyler replied, not looking up from his work. "How will we find anything if there's no logical system?"

Rebecca, who was sprawling on the couch eating pizza, grinned. "Ken, you're about to learn so much about living with Prism. Everything has a place, and everything goes in its place."

"I like organization," Tyler said defensively.

"We know, sweetie. It's one of your most endearing qualities." Rebecca took another bite of pizza. "Along with your complete inability to leave dishes in the sink overnight and your habit of folding fitted sheets perfectly."

Ken looked intrigued. "You can fold fitted sheets?"

Tyler paused in his book organizing. "There's a technique. I could show you."

"Of course there is," Ken said fondly. "I love that your brain works like that."

The first week of living together was an adjustment period that felt like the most natural thing in the world. Tyler had his routines —morning coffee made exactly the same way every day, evening study time with materials arranged just so, a specific order for getting ready for bed. Ken found Tyler's precision soothing rather than restrictive. There was something comforting about the predictability, the way Tyler created order and calm in their shared space.

Ken's parents arrived Saturday morning, his mother bearing enough food to feed half the campus and his father carrying flowers "for the new apartment." Tyler had been awake since five AM, nervous energy manifesting in an apartment so clean it practically sparkled.

"They're going to think I'm weird," Tyler muttered, adjusting the coffee table arrangement for the third time.

"They're going to think you're wonderful," Ken said firmly. "Just be yourself."

When the doorbell rang, Tyler froze. Ken squeezed his hand before going to answer it.

"Kenshin!" His mother swept him into a hug, then immediately began looking around the apartment with maternal approval. "Oh, this is lovely! So much space! And so clean!"

Ken's father, more reserved but equally warm, shook Ken's hand and handed him the flowers. "The neighborhood seems nice. Safe."

"It is. And I want you both to meet Tyler." Ken gestured for Tyler to come forward. "Tyler, these are my parents, Hiroshi and Michiko Takeshi. Mom, Dad, this is Tyler Anderson."

Tyler stepped forward with that careful politeness Ken loved, bowing slightly in a gesture that made Michiko's face light up. "Mr. and Mrs. Takeshi, it's an honor to meet you. Ken speaks of you often."

"Oh!" Michiko clasped her hands together, clearly delighted by the respectful greeting. "You're so polite! And Ken has told us wonderful things about you."

Ken took a deep breath. "Actually, there's something I need to tell you both. Tyler isn't just my roommate. He's my boyfriend."

The silence that followed felt endless to Ken, but lasted maybe five seconds. Then Michiko burst into rapid Japanese, throwing her arms around a startled Tyler, while Hiroshi smiled and put a hand on Ken's shoulder.

"Finally," Hiroshi said quietly. "We wondered when you'd trust us enough to tell us."

"You... knew?" Ken asked, bewildered.

Michiko released Tyler and turned to her son. "Kenshin, we've known you were gay since you were fifteen. We just waited for you to be ready to share that part of your life with us."

Tyler looked between Ken and his parents, amazed. "You've been waiting for him to come out?"

"We want our son to be happy," Hiroshi said simply. "If Tyler makes you happy, then we're happy."

Ken felt his eyes getting watery. "I was so scared you'd be disappointed."

"Disappointed?" Michiko looked genuinely confused. "Why would we be disappointed? You found someone who clearly adores you, who keeps a beautiful home, who shows proper respect..." She beamed at Tyler. "He's perfect!"

The rest of the visit was a whirlwind of Michiko cooking in their kitchen while interrogating Tyler about his family, his studies, his intentions toward her son. Tyler answered every question with patient honesty, and Ken watched his mother fall in love with Tyler's gentle sincerity.

"He's good for you," Hiroshi told Ken quietly while Tyler was helping Michiko with dinner preparations. "Calm. Steady. You need someone who centers you."

"I love him," Ken said simply.

"We can see that. And we can see he loves you back." Hiroshi smiled. "You chose well."

That evening, after Ken's parents had left with promises to have Tyler and Ken over for dinner soon, they sat together on their couch in their apartment, still processing the day.

"That went better than I expected," Ken said, pulling Tyler closer against his side.

"Your parents are wonderful," Tyler replied. "Your mother wants to teach me Japanese."

"She likes you. I told you she would."

Tyler was quiet for a moment. "Ken?"

"Yeah?"

"I love that this is ours now. This place, this life... us."

Ken turned to look at Tyler, seeing something new in his expression—a settled contentment, but also something deeper. Something that looked like decision.

"Me too," Ken said softly. "I love coming home to you every day."

Tyler shifted to face Ken more fully. "I want to ask you something, but I'm not sure how."

Ken waited, recognizing Tyler's careful approach to difficult topics.

"I want... I want us to be together. Really together. But I don't..." Tyler struggled with the words. "I've never done this before. Any of this. And I'm worried I might not be good at it, or that my... the way my brain works might make things difficult."

Ken's heart did that familiar flutter it always did when Tyler trusted him with vulnerability. "Tyler, are you asking about sex?"

Tyler's cheeks flushed pink, but he nodded. "I know you've been with other people before. And I know I'm probably over-thinking it, but I have so many questions and worries..."

Ken shifted so he was facing Tyler completely. "What kinds of questions?"

Tyler looked down at his hands. "Like... what if I get over-whelmed by the sensory aspects? What if I freeze up and can't think clearly? What if I'm terrible at it because I don't know what I'm doing? What if you get bored with me because I'm not experienced like the people you've been with before?"

Ken reached for Tyler's hands. "Okay, first of all, you're not going to be terrible. Trust me on that one."

Tyler looked up, uncertain. "How do you know?"

"Because you're you. You pay attention to everything, you care about doing things right, and you actually give a damn about how I feel." Ken grinned. "Plus, you're gorgeous and I'm already crazy about touching you, so we're starting with major advantages here."

Tyler blushed but smiled slightly. "What about the other stuff?"

"The sensory thing? Babe, we'll figure it out as we go. If something feels like too much, you tell me and we adjust. Or stop completely. No big deal." Ken's voice got gentler. "And if you freeze up, which honestly might happen because it's a lot the first time, then we just pause until you're ready again."

"What about your... past experiences?" Tyler asked quietly.

Ken was quiet for a moment. "You really want to know about that?"

Tyler nodded.

"Okay. I've been with three guys before you. Two were just hookups - fun, but nothing serious. One was a relationship that lasted about four months." Ken looked directly at Tyler. "None of them were anything like this."

"What do you mean?"

"I mean with them, it was just physical. Good physical, but that's all." Ken squeezed Tyler's hands. "With you, I'm not just attracted to your body - though I definitely am. I'm attracted to your mind, your heart, the way you organize your books, the face you make when you're concentrating..."

Tyler was blushing harder now. "Ken..."

"What? I'm being honest. You asked if I'd get bored with you, and that's honestly ridiculous. I can't get bored with someone I'm completely in love with."

Tyler considered this. "So it really doesn't bother you that I don't know what I'm doing?"

Ken's smile was soft but mischievous. "Tyler, it means I get to be the one to show you everything. Do you have any idea how incredible that is? I get to be your first everything."

"When you put it like that..." Tyler's smile was shy but real.

"Plus," Ken added with a grin, "you're a very fast learner. I have high expectations."

Tyler laughed despite his nerves. "No pressure or anything."

"No pressure," Ken agreed, leaning forward to kiss Tyler softly. "Just us figuring it out together. And honestly? I think we're going to be really, really good at this."

Tyler considered this. "Would you... would you be patient with me? If I need to stop or ask questions or if I can't figure something out?"

"Tyler." Ken's voice was soft but firm. "I would wait forever for you to be ready. And when you are ready, we'll go as slow as you need. We'll talk through everything. There's no rush."

Something relaxed in Tyler's shoulders. "I think... I think I'd like to try. Tonight. If that's okay."

Ken's pulse quickened, but his voice stayed gentle. "Are you sure?"

Tyler nodded. "I'm sure. I trust you completely."

Ken leaned forward to kiss Tyler softly. "Then let's go to bed and see what happens. No pressure, no expectations. Just us."

In their bedroom—the one they'd been unofficially sharing since move-in day—they started slowly. But Ken noticed when Tyler tensed as they began undressing each other, saw the moment Tyler's breathing became shallow.

"Hey," Ken said softly, stopping his movements. "Talk to me. What's going on in your head right now?"

Tyler looked embarrassed. "I'm overthinking everything. Wondering if I'm doing it right, if I look okay, if I'm supposed to know what to do next..."

Ken sat back, giving Tyler space. "You know what? Let's just talk for a while. No pressure to do anything else."

"You wouldn't mind? I know this probably isn't very sexy..."

"Tyler, you being honest with me is the sexiest thing in the world," Ken said, settling beside him on the bed. "What's really worrying you?"

Tyler was quiet for a long moment. "I want this. I want you. But I don't know how to... I mean, I know I want you to..." He stopped, frustrated.

"Want me to what?" Ken asked gently.

Tyler's cheeks burned. "I want you inside me. But I feel stupid saying that."

"Why do you feel stupid?"

"Because I don't even know what that really means. Or how it works. Or if I'll be able to..." Tyler covered his face with his hands. "God, I sound like a child."

Ken gently pulled Tyler's hands away from his face. "You sound like someone who's never done this before. That's completely normal."

"But you have. Done this before."

"Yeah, I have. And honestly? I'm horny as hell right now because you're gorgeous and I love you and I want you so much it's kind of ridiculous." Ken's honesty made Tyler look up in surprise. "But I'm also not going anywhere. We have all night, all week, the rest of our lives to figure this out."

Tyler smiled slightly. "You're horny?"

"Very. Are you?"

Tyler nodded, blushing again. "Very. It's just... my brain won't shut up long enough to just feel it."

"Then let's give your brain something to do. Ask me anything you want to know."

Tyler considered this. "Does it hurt? When you... when someone..."

"When I'm inside you?" Ken finished matter-of-factly. Tyler nodded. "It can, if you're not prepared properly. But it doesn't have to hurt at all if we take our time."

"What kind of preparation?"

Ken explained, simply and honestly, about stretching and lubrication and patience. Tyler listened with the same focused attention he brought to learning anything new.

"But what if I can't relax?" Tyler asked. "What if my body just... tenses up?"

"Then we stop and figure out what you need to feel comfortable. Maybe more time, maybe a different position, maybe just more talking." Ken reached for Tyler's hand. "The goal isn't to have perfect sex tonight. The goal is to learn about each other."

Tyler was quiet for a moment. "Ken?"

"Yeah?"

"I love you. And I trust you completely. And I really, really want to try."

They started again, more slowly this time. Ken's patience was extraordinary, checking in constantly, making sure Tyler was comfortable. When they finally tried to join together, Tyler tensed immediately.

"Stop," Tyler said quickly. "It's... it's uncomfortable."

Ken stopped instantly, pulling back. "You okay?"

Tyler nodded, but looked frustrated. "I want this to work. I just... how do I relax myself so you can..."

"Enter you?" Ken finished without embarrassment.

"Yes. That." Tyler's relief at Ken's directness was visible. "I feel like I'm fighting my own body."

Ken settled beside Tyler again. "Okay, so here's the thing. Your body is trying to protect you because this is new and unfamiliar. That's totally normal."

"So how do I make it stop?"

"Well, first, we use more lubrication. Like, a lot more. And second, you need to focus on relaxing those muscles." Ken's tone was matter-of-fact, instructional. "Think of it like diving. Remember how you had to learn to control your body position in the air?"

Tyler's eyes lit up slightly. "You want me to think of this like diving?"

"Why not? It's another physical skill that requires practice and body awareness. You wouldn't expect to master a new dive the first time you tried it."

Tyler considered this. "So this is just... learning a new technique."

"Exactly. And like diving, once you understand the mechanics and get comfortable with the movements, it becomes natural. Even enjoyable."

"I want to learn," Tyler said quietly. "I want to learn because I want to make love with you. Really make love. Not just... figure out the physical parts."

Ken's expression softened. "The love part is already there, babe. That's the easy part. The physical stuff is just... logistics."

Tyler laughed despite his nerves. "Logistics?"

"Very important logistics," Ken grinned. "But still just the practical details of how two people who love each other share their bodies."

"Can we try again?" Tyler asked. "But maybe... more logistics and less pressure?"

"All the logistics you need," Ken promised. "And Tyler? There's no shame in any of this. Not in wanting it, not in asking questions, not in needing to stop and start again."

"Really?"

"Really. This is just us, learning each other. Nothing to be embarrassed about."

When they tried again, Tyler's new mindset - thinking of it as a skill to master rather than a test to pass - made all the difference. Ken's patient guidance, his willingness to explain every step, his complete lack of embarrassment about the messy, awkward, sometimes silly aspects of physical intimacy, helped Tyler relax into the experience.

And when they finally succeeded in joining together completely, both of them understood that they'd created something entirely their own - a way of being intimate that honored Tyler's need to understand and Ken's desire to care for him completely.

"As slow as you need," Ken promised.

What followed was unlike anything either of them had experienced before. For Tyler, every sensation was new and overwhelming in the best possible way. Ken's patience and tenderness, the careful way he checked in constantly, the absolute focus on Tyler's comfort and pleasure—it was more than Tyler had ever imagined possible.

For Ken, making love with Tyler was a revelation. Tyler's complete trust, his openness to new experiences, the way he approached physical intimacy with the same thoughtful attention he brought to everything else—it was profound in a way that had nothing to do with technique and everything to do with love.

When they finally came together completely, Tyler understood why people wrote poetry about this feeling. The physical sensation was incredible, but it was the emotional connection that undid him

—the feeling of being completely known and accepted and cherished.

Afterward, lying tangled together in their bed, Tyler felt fundamentally changed.

"That was..." Tyler started, then shook his head. "I don't have words for that."

Ken pulled him closer. "Good different?"

Tyler laughed softly. "Very good different. Life-changing different."

"For me too," Ken said quietly. "I've never felt anything like that before."

Tyler looked up at him. "Really?"

"Really. Being with you is nothing like being with anyone else." Ken brushed hair from Tyler's forehead. "I love you so much it still scares me sometimes."

Tyler settled against Ken's chest, listening to his heartbeat. "I love you too. And I love that this is ours now. All of it."

As they drifted off to sleep in their shared bed in their shared apartment, both of them knew they'd crossed another threshold. They weren't just boyfriends anymore, or even just partners. They were building a life together, one careful, loving step at a time.

And tomorrow, they'd wake up and do it all over again.

# CHAPTER 18
## SWEET

Joshua was propped up in his bed with one of the heavy binders, or had been. Now he was staring out the window into space as if imagining what he'd just read, a wicked little smile playing at the corners of his mouth like he'd just discovered a delicious secret.

It had been a little while before Tyler decided to clear his throat to announce his presence, not wanting to break his nephew's thoughts—which looked positively... well, let's just say there was definitely something brewing behind those eyes. Tyler even considered just disappearing—sometimes discretion was the better part of valor.

But Joshua slowly turned his head in Tyler's direction without changing that expression one bit, as if he'd known his uncle had been there all along. That same devilish grin... definitely sly now... and oh hell, this was a side of Joshua that Tyler had never seen before.

"Find anything... interesting?" Tyler didn't know what else to say. There was definitely something charged in the air—not bad, not wrong, just... electric. Like Joshua had caught him red-handed in something scandalous.

"I'm a little surprised, Uncle Prism," his nephew practically purred while looking right through him with those knowing eyes.

For a ghost, Tyler felt ridiculously exposed—and the irony was absolutely not lost on him.

Playing innocent, Tyler raised an eyebrow. "Surprised by what?"

"I had no idea you wrote such..." Joshua paused, drawing out the suspense with air quotes, "steamy material."

Tyler wasn't sure what Joshua was referring to and looked down at the heavy binder full of his old papers, meticulously ordered and color-coded with bookmark flags. But this was different. A few pages, still typed, mind you, but laying loose, having never been three-hole punched, tagged and bound—as if they were outsiders, something Tyler must have either not gotten around to filing... or...

Oh. My. God.

It suddenly came back to him. *That.*

And Joshua's eyebrows lifted with unmistakable mischief, indicating that he knew that Tyler knew that he knew exactly what he'd stumbled upon.

"I... uh..." Tyler found himself sitting on the edge of Joshua's bed without realizing it, his hand nearly brushing his nephew's feet. Joshua's eyes flicked down to where that magnetic tingle sparked between them, then back up with an amused smirk that said he'd caught that little reaction too.

"Tyler..." Joshua sat up slowly, deliberately, pushing the binder aside and laying those tellingly loose pages on top with a theatrical flourish. "Relax. I'm not scandalized."

"How did you even find..."

"I was hunting for that fort story Mom mentioned—you know, when you were sick and Uncle Ken played nursemaid?" Joshua's grin turned absolutely wicked. "But I found something much more... educational."

Tyler was mortified and didn't know where to look. Did it even matter? Joshua had obviously read every delicious detail, so the cat was thoroughly out of the bag. Still, he hadn't exactly planned on anyone discovering his private... musings.

"Uncle Tyler, breathe," Joshua said with mock seriousness. "I'm not going to blackmail you or anything."

Tyler managed to meet his nephew's eyes. "I just... I forgot those pages were mixed in with everything else. If I'd remembered..."

"You'd have hidden the good stuff?" Joshua's tone was pure mischief. "And why exactly are you so flustered? It's not like you wrote anything dirty."

"Because..." Tyler felt his non-corporeal cheeks burning. "Because it's private. Personal. And you're my nephew, for crying out loud."

"No... it's... okay. I mean, I wrote it. I guess I should've expected it to be read someday. I guess... well... I'm not very good at this, Josh."

As empathetic as he felt, his voice sounded even more so. His nephew risked it and scooted closer, feeling the energy surrounding his uncle like pulses of electricity coming from a wall outlet—not exactly terrible, but nothing he'd want to touch.

"Uncle Tyler... it's normal. Besides, it just shows how much you loved Uncle Ken, is all."

Tyler looked over at his nephew with misty, embarrassed eyes and bitten lips, holding back his shame. He only nodded his head, unable to allow himself to be "human" with "needs" and "urges." For all Tyler's qualities, he often felt most careful about his sexuality, particularly about desires. He felt awkward, like he was fourteen again.

"Tyler," Joshua dropped the "Uncle" entirely, his voice taking on that smooth, adult-to-adult tone that caught Tyler completely off guard. "I'm twenty-one, not twelve. And honestly? What I read was beautiful. Hot as hell, sure, but beautiful."

Tyler stared at his nephew, seeing him differently—not as the kid he'd been mentoring, but as a young man who was clearly more worldly than Tyler had given him credit for.

"You really think so?" Tyler asked quietly.

"Hell yes. The way you wrote about trusting Ken enough to be that vulnerable with him? The way you described wanting him that close to you?" Joshua's eyes went a little dreamy. "That's not just sex, Uncle Tyler. That's making love. There's a difference."

Tyler felt something warm bloom in his chest. "You don't think I'm... I don't know... perverted for writing it all down?"

Joshua actually snorted. "Perverted? Tyler, you wrote about love and intimacy with your boyfriend. If that's perverted, then every romance novel ever written is basically pornography." He paused, that wicked grin returning. "Which, now that I think about it, some of them totally are."

"I can't believe we're having this conversation," Tyler said, but he was smiling now.

"Why not? We're both adults. Well, you're a dead adult, but still." Joshua scooted closer, and Tyler felt that electric tingle intensify. "Besides, it's not like we can't discuss the finer points of... physical intimacy."

Tyler's eyes widened. "Joshua..."

"What? I'm just saying, reading about how you and Uncle Ken figured things out was actually pretty educational." Joshua's tone turned playfully innocent. "I mean, I am still a virgin, you know."

"Christ, Joshua, you can't just say things like that," Tyler said, but he was laughing now.

"Why not? It's true. And honestly, after reading your... memoirs... I have to say, you and Uncle Ken had something pretty incredible." Joshua's voice got softer, more serious. "The way you trusted him completely, the way he took care of you... I want that someday. Someone who'll be that patient, that loving."

Tyler looked at his nephew—really looked at him—and saw a young man who understood far more about love and intimacy than Tyler had given him credit for.

"Josh, you're going to find someone amazing. Someone who appreciates that brain of yours and that heart of yours."

"Yeah? You think so?" Joshua's confidence flickered for just a moment, showing the vulnerable young man underneath.

"I know so. And when you do find them..." Tyler paused, then grinned wickedly, "just remember what you learned from my very educational writing."

Joshua burst out laughing. "Oh my God, are you giving me sex advice based on your own erotic memoir?"

"It's not erotic! It's... romantic!"

"Uncle Tyler, sweetie, when you write about wanting someone 'inside you' and how it felt when they—"

"Okay, okay! Maybe it was a little steamy," Tyler admitted, his ghostly cheeks burning again.

"A little? I'm pretty sure I need a cold shower after reading that."

"Joshua!"

"What? I'm just saying, you two definitely knew how to... connect." Joshua's grin was absolutely sinful now. "In fact, I'm starting to think you should have written romance novels instead of whatever boring academic stuff you were planning."

After a few moments of comfortable silence, Joshua broke it with that trademark mischievous look.

"You know what you and Uncle Ken should have done?"

Tyler raised an eyebrow warily. "I'm almost afraid to ask..."

"OnlyFans!" Joshua announced with theatrical flair. "Think of the money you could have made! I mean, based on what I just read, you two were clearly very... photogenic in your activities."

"JOSHUA!"

"I'm serious! 'Hot Academic and His Athletic Boyfriend: An Intimate Documentation.' You would have made millions!"

"This conversation has officially gone off the rails," Tyler said, but he was grinning.

"Come on, admit it. You're a little flattered that your nephew thinks you and Uncle Ken were hot enough for amateur porn."

Tyler covered his face with his hands. "I cannot believe I'm dead and still having the most embarrassing conversation of my life."

"Embarrassing? Tyler, I just paid you the ultimate compliment! I basically said you two were so sexy together that people would pay money to watch!"

"That's... that's really not the compliment you think it is."

"Oh, it totally is. Trust me."

# CHAPTER 19
# THE FLU INCIDENT

Tyler's voice on the phone was barely above a whisper, hoarse and congested in a way that made Ken's chest tighten with concern.

"I'm sorry to cancel," Tyler said, pausing to cough. "I know we had plans to study tonight, but I think I'm coming down with something."

Ken was already reaching for his jacket. "How bad is it? Have you eaten anything today?"

"I'm fine, really. Just need to sleep it off. I'll call you when—" Tyler's words dissolved into another coughing fit.

"Tyler," Ken said firmly. "I'm coming over."

"You don't need to—"

"I'm coming over," Ken repeated, already halfway out the door. "I'll bring soup."

What Ken didn't mention was that he was going to make the soup himself. His grandmother's miso soup recipe, the one she'd taught him when he was twelve and homesick during his first sleepover. If Tyler was sick, he deserved better than canned Campbell's.

An hour later, Ken stood outside Tyler's apartment door with a thermos of homemade soup, a bag of groceries, and his camping gear. He'd thrown the tent and sleeping bag into his car almost as an afterthought—Tyler's apartment was tiny, barely more than a studio, and Ken had seen that pathetic excuse for a couch. If he was going to take care of Tyler properly, he needed somewhere decent to sleep.

Tyler answered the door looking absolutely miserable. His usually precise hair was disheveled, his face flushed with fever, and he was wrapped in a blanket that had seen better days. But what struck Ken most was how small Tyler looked—fragile in a way that made every protective instinct Ken possessed flare to life.

"Ken," Tyler said, his voice scratchy with surprise. "You didn't have to come. I told you I was fine."

Ken took one look at Tyler's pale face and the disaster zone of his apartment—tissues scattered everywhere, empty tea mugs on every surface, textbooks still spread across his desk like he'd been trying to study through the fever—and made a decision.

"You're not fine," Ken said gently, pushing past Tyler into the apartment. "And I'm not leaving until you are."

Tyler's protest died on his lips as Ken began unpacking groceries with military efficiency. "I brought everything you need—more tea, throat lozenges, actual tissues instead of those scratchy paper towels you've been using. And soup. Real soup, not the canned stuff."

"You made soup?" Tyler's voice was soft with something that might have been wonder.

"My grandmother's recipe. Miso base with ginger and scallions. It's good for congestion." Ken was already heating the soup on Tyler's tiny stove, moving around the cramped kitchen like he belonged there. "When's the last time you ate something?"

Tyler had to think about it. "Yesterday? Maybe?"

Ken turned to look at him seriously. "Tyler. You can't fight off illness if you don't eat."

"I know, I just... I don't really cook when I'm sick. Or ever, really." Tyler pulled his blanket tighter around himself. "Mostly I just sleep until it goes away."

Ken felt that protective surge again, stronger this time. "Well, not this time. This time you're going to eat soup and drink tea and actually take care of yourself properly."

As Ken ladled the soup into a bowl, Tyler noticed the camping gear by the door. "Ken, is that a tent?"

Ken paused, suddenly uncertain. Maybe this was too much, too presumptuous. "I thought... your couch doesn't look very comfortable, and if I'm going to stay—"

"Stay?" Tyler's eyes went wide. "You're planning to stay?"

"If that's okay," Ken said quickly. "I mean, someone should keep an eye on you. Make sure your fever doesn't spike, that you're drinking enough fluids. But if you'd rather be alone—"

"No." Tyler's response was immediate and surprisingly firm. "No, I... I'd like you to stay."

Ken's relief was visible. "Good. Then the tent stays too, because there's no way I'm spending the night on that torture device you call furniture."

Tyler actually smiled at that, the first real smile Ken had seen since arriving. "You brought a tent because my couch is uncomfortable?"

"Your couch is an insult to furniture everywhere," Ken said solemnly, handing Tyler the bowl of soup. "Now eat this before it gets cold."

The soup was perfect—warm and savory with just enough ginger to clear Tyler's sinuses without being overwhelming. Tyler found himself eating more than he had in days, partly because it tasted so good and partly because Ken was watching him with such focused attention, like Tyler's wellbeing was the most important thing in the world.

"This is really good," Tyler said between spoonfuls. "Your grandmother taught you to make this?"

Ken settled onto the floor beside Tyler's chair, close enough to monitor but not crowd. "She said good soup could cure anything except a broken heart, and even then it helped." He paused, watching Tyler carefully. "How are you feeling? Any better?"

Tyler considered this. The soup had warmed him from the inside out, and having Ken here made everything seem less overwhelming. "Better. Thank you."

"Good. When you're done eating, you're going back to bed. Doctor's orders."

"You're not a doctor," Tyler pointed out, but he was smiling again.

"I'm the closest thing you've got right now," Ken replied. "And Dr. Ken says you need rest."

What followed were four of the strangest, most wonderful days of Tyler's life. Ken transformed Tyler's tiny apartment into a recovery center, setting up his tent in the living room with the efficiency of someone who'd done this before. He made soup twice a day, kept Tyler hydrated, and somehow managed to make being sick feel less like suffering and more like being cared for.

Ken had a routine for everything. Morning temperature checks with a thermometer he'd bought at the pharmacy. Afternoon tea service with honey and lemon. Evening doses of cold medicine administered with the seriousness of a nurse. He even organized Tyler's medicine bottles and tissues with the same precision Tyler applied to his own belongings.

But it was the small things that undid Tyler completely. The way Ken would check on him every few hours, just appearing in the doorway to make sure he was breathing comfortably. How Ken insisted on doing Tyler's laundry so he'd have clean pajamas and sheets. The fact that Ken had brought his own textbooks and studied quietly in the living room so Tyler wouldn't feel abandoned but wouldn't be disturbed either.

On the third day, just when Tyler had started to feel like he was turning a corner, everything went sideways.

Ken woke to the sound of something crashing in the bedroom —a water glass hitting the floor, followed by a low, confused moan. He was out of his sleeping bag and moving before he was fully conscious, muscle memory from years of being the responsible one kicking in.

Tyler was on the floor beside his bed, disoriented and shaking, trying to crawl toward the kitchen. Sweat poured from his face and his eyes were glassy with fever delirium.

"Tyler!" Ken dropped to his knees beside him, immediately

reaching for his forehead. Tyler's skin was burning, far hotter than it had been when Ken checked on him just hours earlier.

"Water," Tyler mumbled, not seeming to recognize Ken. "Need... water..."

Ken's hands flew to Tyler's face, trying to get his attention. Normally he was so careful about touch—Tyler liked physical contact but seemed to need to initiate it, needed to be in control of when and how. They'd barely kissed beyond gentle good-night pecks, despite both of them wanting more. Ken had been willing to wait, to follow Tyler's lead in everything.

But this wasn't about boundaries or comfort zones. This was about Tyler's life.

"I've got you," Ken said firmly, pulling Tyler against his chest. Tyler was trembling violently, his body wracked with chills despite the fever radiating from his skin. "We need to get this fever down. Now."

Tyler tried to protest something, but his words were incoherent. Ken didn't need a thermometer to know this was dangerous territory—Tyler's fever had spiked to the point where he could barely think straight.

"Come on, baby," Ken murmured, half-carrying, half-dragging Tyler toward the bathroom. Tyler's legs weren't supporting him properly, and Ken found himself bearing most of his weight. "We're going to cool you down."

In the bathroom, Ken didn't hesitate. Tyler's fever-damp clothes had to come off, and Ken's own pajamas were already soaked from supporting Tyler's sweating body. He stripped them both efficiently, his mind focused entirely on the medical emergency at hand.

Tyler mumbled something that might have been embarrassment, but he was too weak to resist as Ken maneuvered them both into the bathtub and turned on the shower. Ken kept the water cool but not shocking—enough to bring Tyler's temperature down without sending his body into shock.

"I know, I know," Ken soothed as Tyler shivered against him. Ken positioned himself to take the brunt of the spray, shielding

Tyler while still allowing the cool water to do its work. He rubbed Tyler's back gently, feeling the fever-heat slowly, gradually beginning to recede.

Tyler drifted in and out of awareness, sometimes seeming to recognize Ken, other times staring at him with confused, glassy eyes. But he stayed relaxed in Ken's arms, trusting even when he wasn't fully conscious.

After what felt like hours but was probably only ten minutes, Tyler's shivering became less violent and his skin felt marginally cooler. Ken carefully helped him out of the tub, wrapping him in clean towels and drying him with the gentleness usually reserved for newborns.

"Better?" Ken asked softly as he helped Tyler into fresh pajamas. Tyler's eyes were clearer now, more focused.

"Ken?" Tyler's voice was barely a whisper, but he was actually looking at Ken now, seeing him.

"Right here," Ken confirmed, relief flooding through him. "Your fever spiked. Scared the hell out of me."

Tyler looked confused, embarrassed. "Did you... did we...?"

"I had to cool you down," Ken explained gently, helping Tyler back to his bed with fresh sheets. "You were burning up, delirious. I was worried about brain damage."

Tyler's cheeks flushed, but whether from fever or embarrassment, Ken couldn't tell. "I'm sorry you had to—"

"Stop," Ken said firmly, settling Tyler against clean pillows. "You have nothing to apologize for. Nothing."

Ken administered a careful dose of fever reducer and coaxed Tyler to drink some lukewarm tea. But when Tyler's eyes started to flutter closed again, Ken made a decision that surprised them both.

Instead of returning to his tent on the floor, Ken carefully slid into bed beside Tyler.

"Ken?" Tyler's eyes opened, uncertain.

"Is this okay?" Ken asked softly. "I want to monitor your temperature. Make sure the fever doesn't spike again."

Tyler nodded, too exhausted to overthink it. Ken settled beside him, not quite touching but close enough to feel Tyler's body heat, to know immediately if the fever returned.

Tyler fell asleep almost instantly, but it was different sleep this time—deeper, more peaceful. And sometime in the early morning hours, in his sleep, Tyler turned toward Ken, unconsciously seeking warmth and comfort.

Ken woke to find Tyler curled against his side, Tyler's head on his shoulder and one arm draped across Ken's chest. For the first time in days, Tyler's breathing was clear and even, his skin cool and dry.

This was their first real physical intimacy—not romantic, not sexual, but something deeper. The kind of raw trust and care that stripped away pretense and showed what love actually looked like when everything else fell away.

Tyler stirred as Ken shifted slightly, blinking up at him with clear, fever-free eyes.

"Hi," Tyler said softly.

"Hi yourself," Ken replied, brushing a strand of hair from Tyler's forehead. "How do you feel?"

Tyler considered this, becoming aware of their position—how naturally he'd gravitated toward Ken in sleep, how right it felt to wake up in Ken's arms. "Better. Really better." He paused. "You saved my life last night, didn't you?"

Ken's throat tightened. "You scared me. When I found you on the floor like that..."

"I'm sorry."

"Don't apologize for being sick, Tyler. Just... don't ever scare me like that again."

Tyler looked up at Ken, seeing something new in his expression —a depth of care and commitment that went beyond casual dating or even serious boyfriends. This was the look of someone who would strip them both naked and sit in a cold shower at three in the morning without a second thought. Someone who would sleep beside him just to monitor his breathing.

"Ken?"

"Yeah?"

"I love you."

The words hung in the air between them, Tyler's first time saying them, Ken's first time hearing them. Ken's smile was radiant and relieved and full of everything he'd been holding back.

"I love you too," Ken replied softly. "So much it terrifies me sometimes."

Tyler shifted closer, if that was possible, tucking his face against Ken's neck. "I never want to be sick without you again. Or healthy without you."

Ken's arms tightened around him. "You won't have to be. I promise."

And lying there in the morning light, both of them knew something fundamental had changed. They'd crossed a line the night before—not into romance or sexuality, but into something deeper. Into the kind of love that showed up in crisis, that held on through delirium and fever dreams, that would strip away dignity and comfort for the sake of keeping someone safe.

It was the most intimate either of them had ever been with another person. And it had nothing to do with sex and everything to do with love.

"You know," Tyler said as Ken delivered another perfect bowl of soup, "you didn't sign up for this when we started dating."

Ken paused in arranging Tyler's afternoon medications. "What do you mean?"

"Playing nurse to your sick boyfriend. It's not exactly romantic."

Ken looked at him seriously. "Tyler, taking care of you isn't a chore. It's..." He searched for the right words. "It's what you do when you care about someone."

Tyler felt something shift in his chest, something that had nothing to do with congestion. "Really?"

"Really." Ken sat down on the edge of Tyler's bed, close enough to brush that persistent strand of hair from Tyler's forehead. "I want to take care of you. I want to be the person you call when you're sick or scared or happy or anything else."

Tyler stared at him, processing this declaration. "Even when I'm gross and congested and my apartment smells like a pharmacy?"

Ken's smile was soft and sure. "Especially then."

Later that morning, as Ken made breakfast and Tyler sat up in bed feeling more human than he had in days, something deeper than physical recovery had taken place between them.

Tyler lay in bed for a moment, listening to Ken hum quietly as he worked, and realized something that made his heart race. He didn't want Ken to leave. Not just today, but ever. The thought of going back to his solitary routine, of being sick alone or healthy alone, felt unbearable.

"Ken?" Tyler called out.

Ken appeared in the doorway immediately, coffee mug in hand and that familiar look of concern on his face. "How are you feeling? Any lingering symptoms?"

"I'm better," Tyler said, sitting up carefully. "Thanks to you."

Ken's relief was visible. "Good. I was starting to worry about pneumonia."

Tyler gathered his courage. "Ken, I need to tell you something."

Ken set down his coffee and moved to sit on the bed, giving Tyler his full attention. "What is it?"

"I don't want you to leave," Tyler said quietly. "I mean, I know you have your own dorm room and your own life, but these past four days... I've never felt so taken care of. So..." He struggled for the word.

"Safe?" Ken suggested gently.

"Yes. Safe." Tyler looked directly at Ken, one of those moments of sustained eye contact that still made Ken's heart skip. "I've been alone for most of my life, and I thought I was okay with that. But having you here, knowing you're going to be here when I wake up... I don't want to go back to being alone."

Ken felt his chest tighten with emotion. "Tyler..."

"I know it's fast," Tyler continued, "and maybe I'm still a little fever-addled, but I want you to move in with me. Or I could move in with you. Or we could find a place together. I just... I never want to be sick without you again. Or healthy without you, for that matter."

Ken's smile was radiant. "Are you asking me to move in with you, Tyler Prism Anderson?"

Tyler's cheeks flushed pink, but his voice was steady. "I'm trying to. I'm still not very good at this."

"You're perfect at this," Ken said, leaning forward to brush his lips gently against Tyler's forehead. "And yes. Yes, I want to live with you."

Tyler's relief was overwhelming. "Really?"

"Really. Though we're definitely getting you a better couch."

Tyler laughed—the first real laugh he'd had in days. "Deal."

As Ken began breaking down his tent that afternoon, both of them planning their next steps toward a shared living space, Tyler realized that being sick had given him the greatest gift of his life: the knowledge that he never had to face anything alone again.

And Ken, folding up his sleeping bag with a permanent smile on his face, knew that camping in Tyler's living room had been the most important four days of his life. They'd moved from dating to something deeper, something real. Something that felt like forever.

# CHAPTER 20
# HONG KONG DISCOVERY

The Saturday morning sun streamed through the southwest-facing attic window, casting golden rectangles across the unfurled carpet where Rebecca and Joshua sat cross-legged, surrounded by scattered boxes and memories. Rebecca's phone lay beside her, quietly playing her "Fun Music" playlist—just loud enough to fill the comfortable silence, just soft enough not to disturb Joshua when he got into one of his focused moods.

And he was definitely in one of those moods. Rebecca loved doing projects like this with her son, felt privileged that they could finally tackle Tyler's belongings together, but once Joshua got going on a task, idle chitchat became impossible. He'd dive so deep into whatever he was examining that she might as well have been talking to herself.

Which left Rebecca with her own restless energy and nowhere to put it. She couldn't go two minutes without wanting to crack a joke or share some random thought, but Joshua would give her *the look* whenever she got too chatty. At least the music kept her humming along.

The old Florsheim shoebox at her feet had been calling to her for the past ten minutes. Carefully cutting through the aged tape with her box cutter, she lifted the lid to reveal layers of tissue paper protecting what looked like a collection of pamphlets, folded letters, and small trinkets. Her fingers found items that were clearly from Hong Kong—something with Chinese characters, a faded ticket that read "Star Ferry," and a small box about the size of a pencil case.

The pencil box contained a tourist's calligraphy set, complete with ink stone and brush. Setting it aside, she uncovered what made her breath catch: a small photo album with plastic sleeves, each Kodak picture carefully placed alongside white stickers with precise handwritten descriptions.

But this wasn't Tyler's handwriting. She knew Prism's style—meticulous, detailed, perfectly controlled. This was equally precise but different, like someone who did calligraphy had turned their attention to English characters. The letters had just enough flourish to be slightly artistic, beautiful in their own way.

Maybe fifteen photos at most. "The Giant Buddha on Lantau Island," read one caption. "The Peak at Hong Kong," said another, showing the famous skyline view. Rebecca felt a familiar pang of jealousy—Tyler's fabulous work trips to exotic places while she was stuck in suburban domesticity. But she also knew Tyler wasn't the type to party it up, so the existence of this carefully curated photo album surprised her.

When he'd returned from Hong Kong, he'd spoken fondly of the trip but hadn't gone into detail. He certainly hadn't shown pictures. This was a glimpse into his world that even she hadn't seen.

Then she found the photo that made her pause.

A young Chinese man, probably Tyler's age, smiling with what looked like embarrassment. The shot was close up, taken in front of what appeared to be a temple. He was squinting against the sun, eyes nearly closed, which gave him a stereotypical look that made Rebecca immediately chastise herself for even thinking such a thing. Ken would have made the same observation, probably with some joke about how being Japanese gave him permission to say such things, but still...

God, she missed Ken.

But looking back at the picture... damn, this guy was cute.

Actually, really cute. And there was something about that shy smile...

The handwritten caption simply read "Kit."

His name, she assumed. She didn't remember Tyler ever mentioning anyone named Kit, though he hadn't talked much about Hong Kong beyond the basic work details.

"Whatdya find?" Joshua's voice broke through her thoughts. He'd been absorbed in another interview from Tyler's binder but must have noticed her rummaging.

"Oh, just some stuff from one of Tyler's trips."

"Where?"

"Hong Kong, I think," she said, still staring at the album.

"Hong Kong? Damn! I didn't know Uncle Prism went there."

"Yeah, for work. They sent him all over the place."

"Lucky bastard!"

"Josh!" But she was grinning. "Yeah... he really was, wasn't he?"

*Was.* There it was again. Tyler had been lucky. Until he wasn't. Until the accident.

"What are you looking at?" Joshua's curiosity pulled her back from the grief.

"A photo album. But it's not Tyler's pictures."

"Whose is it?"

"Some friend of his, I guess? I honestly have no clue."

Joshua stood and crossed over to kneel beside her, leaning in to get a look.

"Who's that? Kit?"

"Your guess is as good as mine..."

Together, they flipped through the pages. Another photo showed Kit with several other young Chinese men, all appearing to be in their twenties except for one who looked closer to thirty and clearly seemed to be the leader of the group. They varied in poses and expressions—one extremely campy, another passport-photo serious, two others caught mid-laugh looking at each other as if someone had just delivered a punchline, with Kit standing in the middle grinning like he'd just told the joke.

The caption simply said "Your Dancing Queens."

Joshua snorted. "Holy shit, did Tyler have a whole gay posse in Hong Kong?"

"Language," Rebecca said automatically, but she was laughing too. "I have no fucking idea. Tyler never said a word about any of this."

The next few photos showed the same group at a restaurant, but now Tyler was in the shots, sitting between Kit and the apparent ringleader.

"Look at Uncle Prism!" Joshua pointed. "He looks so happy."

"He really does..." Rebecca said, studying Tyler's face. She'd never seen him look quite so... relaxed? Carefree? "What the hell was he up to over there?"

The last photo made them both go quiet. It was taken in the same restaurant booth, but this was just Tyler and Kit, Tyler's arm around Kit's shoulders, both of them smiling at the camera like they were sharing some private joke. The caption read "Prism and Kit" with a little heart drawn next to it.

"Wait." Joshua's voice got careful. "Were they...?"

Rebecca stared at the heart symbol, her mind racing. This was completely new territory. She'd never heard Tyler mention Kit, never knew about this friendship or... whatever the hell this was.

"I... honestly, Josh, I have no idea. This is the first I'm hearing about any of it."

"Do you think Uncle Ken knew?" Joshua sounded worried, like maybe his whole understanding of Tyler was shifting.

"I don't know." Rebecca shook her head, feeling unsettled. "But look, I know Tyler. He would never cheat on Ken. That's just not who he was."

"Wasn't," Joshua corrected quietly, and Rebecca felt the familiar stab of grief.

Joshua's eyes darted over to the bean bag chair by the window.

From that direction came Tyler's quiet voice: "Ken and Kit were great friends." He nodded toward the binder, as if to say the whole story was waiting there.

"You know what?" Joshua said, getting to his feet. "I bet they were just really good friends. Uncle Prism probably wrote all about it somewhere in here." He went back to his spot and started flipping through the binder tabs. "And knowing him, he probably called Ken every single night with a play-by-play of everything that happened."

"Oh god, you're right." Rebecca felt herself relax. "Tyler would've given Ken a full report every night at exactly the same time. Poor Ken probably knew what Kit had for breakfast."

She started laughing at the thought. Tyler's need for detailed schedules and complete information sharing. It was so him.

"What's funny?" Joshua asked, looking up from the papers.

"Just thinking about how incredibly Tyler your uncle was about everything."

"Yeah," Joshua grinned. "He really is."

"Aha! Found it!" Joshua suddenly shouted.

"What?"

"Uncle Prism's interview with Kit."

Rebecca hauled herself up and walked over to lean against Joshua's shoulder.

"Well, I'll be damned. I had no idea he'd even interviewed this guy."

# CHAPTER 21
# WAI "KIT" LEE

Tyler had been staring at the KPMG assignment letter for three days, reading and re-reading the details like they might change if he looked at them long enough.

"Hong Kong," he said for probably the fifteenth time that week, sitting at their kitchen table with his morning coffee. "Two weeks. International consultation with the Hong Kong office."

Ken looked up from his newspaper, trying to hide his smile. Tyler had been cycling through the same mixture of excitement and terror since the assignment came through. "It's a good thing, babe. A really good thing. They wouldn't send you if they didn't trust you completely."

"I know that. Logically, I know that." Tyler carefully folded the letter along its original creases. "It's just... it's so far away. And I don't speak Cantonese. And I've never been anywhere that foreign before."

"You'll figure it out," Ken said gently. "You always do."

Tyler was quiet for a moment, then: "I wish you could come with me."

Ken felt his chest tighten. He'd been thinking the same thing for days, but his work schedule made it impossible. "Me too. But this is your moment, Tyler. Your chance to show them what you can do on the international stage."

"What if I completely mess up the cultural stuff? What if I'm rude without meaning to be? What if I can't navigate the city and just get lost and overwhelmed?"

Ken reached across the table and took Tyler's hand. "Then you'll figure it out. You're the most adaptable person I know, even when you don't feel like it."

Two weeks later, Tyler was sitting in United flight 896 from San Francisco to Hong Kong, clutching his briefcase like a lifeline and trying not to think about how many time zones he was crossing. The fourteen-hour flight felt endless, filled with fitful sleep and airplane food that made his nervous stomach even more unsettled.

Hong Kong International Airport was a marvel of modern architecture—gleaming, efficient, overwhelmingly large. Tyler followed the signs to immigration, processed through customs, and emerged into the arrivals area feeling disoriented and slightly nauseous from the combination of jet lag and anxiety.

But there, exactly as KPMG had promised, was a driver in a crisp uniform holding a placard with "TYLER ANDERSON" written in clear block letters.

"Mr. Anderson?" The driver smiled professionally. "Welcome to Hong Kong. I'm David, from the car service. How was your flight?"

"Long," Tyler said gratefully, following David toward the exit. "Very long."

The humidity hit him the moment they'd stepped outside the airport—thick and enveloping, like being wrapped in a warm, damp blanket. The drive from Lantau Island began along the harbor, past mountains and gleaming skyscrapers that rose impossibly tall from the water's edge. Tyler watched in fascination as boats of all sorts came and went—ancient-looking junks with weathered sails sharing the water with sleek modern ferries and massive cargo ships, a perfect blend of old world and new.

But it was when they circled past Kowloon that Tyler got his first glimpse across Victoria Harbour at Hong Kong Island itself, lit up in all its majesty. The skyline was breathtaking—towers of light piercing the evening sky, neon signs creating rivers of color against the darkness, the whole cityscape reflected in the dark water of the harbor. It was awe-inspiring, nothing like he'd ever seen before.

"First time in Hong Kong?" David asked, navigating through traffic with practiced ease.

"First time in Asia, actually."

"You'll love it. Very exciting city. Never sleeps."

Tyler nodded politely, though at the moment the idea of a city that never slept sounded more exhausting than exciting.

The hotel KPMG had arranged was everything Tyler had hoped for—clean, modern, efficiently air-conditioned, and mercifully quiet after the sensory assault of the journey. The front desk staff were professional and spoke perfect English, making check-in painless.

In his room on the twenty-third floor, Tyler stood at the window looking out at the lights of Hong Kong spread below him like a circuit board. It was 6:47 PM local time, and his body had no idea what time it thought it was supposed to be.

He ordered room service—something simple and familiar, a club sandwich that wouldn't challenge his travel-stressed system—and calculated the time difference while he waited. Hong Kong was sixteen hours ahead of Oregon. If it was nearly 7 PM here, that made it about 3 AM back home. Ken would be asleep.

Tyler showered, letting the hot water wash away the staleness of fourteen hours in an airplane seat, then sat on his hotel bed in a bathrobe, staring at his phone. He could call Ken later, when it was morning in Oregon. But the silence of the hotel room, after two days of constant travel noise, felt almost oppressive.

He'd gotten so used to Ken's presence—not just in their bed, but as a constant in his daily life. Someone to process experiences with, to help him make sense of new situations. Being alone in a foreign country felt more isolating than he'd expected.

The room service arrived, and Tyler ate mechanically while reviewing his schedule for the next few days. KPMG had built in a free day tomorrow, which Tyler appreciated—time to adjust to the time zone before diving into work responsibilities.

At 9 PM Hong Kong time—5 AM in Oregon—Tyler finally gave

in and called Ken's cell phone, hoping Ken's alarm hadn't gone off yet.

"Tyler?" Ken's voice was sleepy but immediately alert. "Are you okay? How was the flight?"

"Long but fine. I'm at the hotel now. Just wanted to hear your voice."

"What time is it there?"

"Nine at night. You're sixteen hours behind me."

Tyler could hear Ken doing the math. "Jesus, that's quite a time difference. How are you feeling?"

"Tired but wired. Jet lag is weird." Tyler settled back against the hotel pillows, Ken's familiar voice making the foreign room feel less lonely. "The city is incredible, Ken. Like nothing I've ever seen. So many lights, so much energy..."

"Tell me about it."

Tyler described the airport, the drive through the city, the view from his hotel window. Ken listened patiently, asking questions that helped Tyler process what he was experiencing rather than just feeling overwhelmed by it.

"You're going to be amazing," Ken said when Tyler finished. "I can already hear the confidence in your voice."

"I miss you," Tyler said quietly. "Is that pathetic? I've been gone less than twenty-four hours and I already miss sleeping next to you."

"It's not pathetic. I miss you too. The bed feels too big without you."

They talked for another twenty minutes, Ken filling Tyler in on mundane details from home that somehow felt precious across the distance. When they finally hung up, Tyler felt more centered, more like himself.

He was asleep within minutes of hanging up, his body finally surrendering to exhaustion.

The phone rang at 8:15 AM, jolting Tyler from deep sleep with the violence of an alarm clock. For a moment, he had no idea where he was—the hotel room was too bright, too quiet, and Ken wasn't in bed beside him.

The absence of Ken's familiar presence hit him with unexpected force. They'd been sleeping together for over two years now, and Tyler realized he'd completely adjusted to the comfort of another person's breathing, the warmth of Ken's body next to his. Waking up alone in the unfamiliar room made him feel unmoored in a way he hadn't anticipated.

"Mr. Anderson?" The voice on the phone was crisp, professional. "This is Jennifer from KPMG Hong Kong. I wanted to check that your flight arrived safely and that everything is satisfactory with your hotel accommodations."

Tyler sat up, trying to shake off the disorientation. "Yes, everything's fine. Thank you for arranging the car service—that made arrival much easier."

"Excellent. I also wanted to remind you that a car will collect you tomorrow morning at 8:30 AM for your first day at our offices. The driver will be waiting in the hotel lobby."

"8:30, got it. Thank you."

"Enjoy your day off today, Mr. Anderson. Hong Kong has much to offer, but do be careful not to overdo it—jet lag can be more challenging than people expect."

After hanging up, Tyler lay in bed for several more minutes, processing the strangeness of being alone, being so far from everything familiar. The room service menu was filled with unfamiliar options, the sounds outside his window were completely foreign, and even the quality of light through the hotel curtains felt different.

But KPMG had given him a free day, and Tyler was determined not to waste it hiding in his hotel room.

After a breakfast of coffee and pastries from room service—the safest options he could identify—Tyler approached the concierge desk with his guidebook and hotel map.

"I have a free day to explore," Tyler told the concierge, a polished young woman who spoke impeccable English. "What would you recommend for someone who's never been to Asia before?"

"Ah, wonderful! You must see some of our cultural sites. I

recommend taking the MTR to Tsim Sha Tsui in Kowloon—it's just across the harbor. There are temples, museums, excellent shopping, and some of the best street food in Hong Kong. Very authentic Hong Kong experience."

She marked several locations on Tyler's map, explaining the MTR system and giving him detailed directions. "The subway is very efficient and clean. You'll have no trouble navigating."

Tyler thanked her and studied the map. The MTR system looked straightforward enough—color-coded lines, English signage, clearly marked stations. How hard could it be?

An hour later, Tyler emerged from the Tsim Sha Tsui MTR station into what felt like sensory chaos.

The streets of Kowloon were a maze of narrow alleys and towering buildings, but it wasn't just the architecture that overwhelmed him. The noise level was unlike anything Tyler had ever experienced—vendors calling out in Cantonese, car horns blaring constantly, construction sounds echoing off concrete, music bleeding from shop fronts, the general roar of thousands of people talking, shouting, laughing, arguing.

The smells were equally intense—unfamiliar spices from street food stalls, exhaust fumes, incense from nearby temples, something that might have been fish or might have been something else entirely. And the visual input was staggering—neon signs with characters he couldn't read, storefronts packed with merchandise, people everywhere, moving in patterns Tyler couldn't predict or understand.

Tyler tried to follow the concierge's directions, but within ten minutes he was completely turned around. The street names on his map didn't match what he was seeing—or rather, he couldn't read the Chinese characters to confirm where he was. The few English signs he spotted seemed to point in contradictory directions.

The crowds pressed around him—not threatening, just dense and purposeful and completely indifferent to the confused American clutching a tourist map. People flowed past him like water around a stone, everyone seeming to know exactly where they were going while Tyler stood frozen on a corner, trying to figure out which direction he'd come from.

His chest began to tighten. This was exactly the kind of situation that triggered his worst anxiety—too much sensory input, no clear way to process or organize the information, no familiar landmarks to orient himself. And worse, he was completely alone. No Ken to help him think through the problem, no Rebecca to take charge of the situation. Just Tyler, overwhelmed and lost, in a place where he couldn't even read the street signs.

The panic started as a flutter in his stomach and quickly escalated. His breathing became shallow, his palms started sweating despite the air conditioning from nearby shops, and he could feel that familiar sensation of his brain starting to shut down when faced with too much stimulus.

Tyler tried to retrace his steps, but every street looked the same —narrow, crowded, lined with shops whose signs meant nothing to him. He'd been walking for fifteen minutes, maybe twenty, and now he couldn't even find the MTR station he'd emerged from.

The thought of being stranded here, of having to somehow navigate back to his hotel without being able to communicate properly, made Tyler's panic spike. He could feel tears of frustration threatening, and the knowledge that he was about to have an emotional breakdown in the middle of a crowded Hong Kong street only made everything worse.

Tyler found himself gravitating toward a small noodle stand where the crowds seemed less dense, where the noise level dropped just slightly. He stood at the edge of the covered seating area, clutching his map and trying to steady his breathing, when a voice spoke up beside him.

"Eh, you okay, mate?"

Tyler looked up to see a young Chinese man about his age, sitting alone on a plastic stool with a bowl of noodles and what looked like an English-language newspaper. The guy was compact and lean, with pronounced Cantonese features, short black hair, and deep black eyes that seemed to take in everything at once. He was wearing a loose button-up shirt and brown khaki shorts, cheap rubber flip-flops, and had an easy, confident demeanor that Tyler immediately envied.

But what struck Tyler most was the guy's smile—wide and genuine, with a dead front tooth that somehow made the whole expression more charming rather than less.

"You look like someone dropped you on an alien planet," the guy said, his English accented but perfectly clear. "Very lost tourist face happening there."

Tyler felt his cheeks flush with embarrassment. "I... yes. I'm trying to find my way back to the MTR station, but I can't..." He gestured helplessly at his map. "Everything looks the same and I can't read the signs."

The young man's expression immediately shifted from amused to concerned. "Aiya, first time in Hong Kong?"

"First time in Asia," Tyler admitted, and was mortified to hear his voice crack slightly.

"Wah." The guy stood up, abandoning his noodles without hesitation. "No wonder you look ready to cry, lah. This area can be pretty intense if you're not used to it."

Tyler blinked, startled by the casual observation. Was his distress really that obvious?

"I'm Kit," the guy said, extending his hand. "Kit Lee. And you're having what we call culture shock, which is totally normal but also pretty shit to deal with alone."

"Tyler," Tyler managed, shaking Kit's hand gratefully. "Tyler Anderson."

"Right, Tyler." Kit studied Tyler's face with obvious concern. "You want to sit down for a minute? Have some tea? You look like you need to catch your breath."

Tyler nodded, not trusting his voice. Kit quickly pulled up a plastic chair next to his own spot and gestured for Tyler to sit. Within moments, Kit had signaled the noodle stand owner and was pouring Tyler a cup of hot tea from a metal pot.

"Drink," Kit instructed gently. "Deep breaths. Nobody's chasing you, yeah? We got time to figure this out."

Tyler wrapped his hands around the warm cup, using it to

anchor himself. The tea was hot and slightly bitter, nothing like what he was used to, but the ritual of drinking it gave him something to focus on besides the chaos around him.

"Better?" Kit asked after Tyler had taken several sips.

"A little. Thank you." Tyler looked at Kit with genuine gratitude. "I don't know what came over me. I'm not usually..."

"Usually what? Human?" Kit's tone was matter-of-fact, not unkind. "Mate, I've lived here my whole life and Tsim Sha Tsui still gives me headaches sometimes. Too many people, too much noise, too much everything. And you're dealing with jet lag on top of it, yeah?"

Tyler nodded, surprised by Kit's immediate understanding.

"Right, so here's what we're gonna do." Kit pulled Tyler's map over and studied it. "First, we're gonna finish your tea and let your brain calm down a bit. Then we're gonna walk somewhere quieter where you can actually think straight."

"You don't have to—" Tyler started.

"Course I do. Can't have beautiful tourists wandering around Kowloon having panic attacks on my watch." Kit's grin was teasing but warm. "Besides, helping confused foreigners is my civic duty."

Tyler felt his face heat up at the casual compliment, but Kit's easy confidence was already making him feel calmer. There was something about Kit's presence—the way he took charge without being pushy, the way he seemed to understand Tyler's distress without making a big deal about it—that made Tyler feel less alone.

"You know what?" Kit said, glancing around at the crowded street. "This place is mental busy today. You want somewhere actually civilized? We could walk over towards the harbor. There's the Peninsula Hotel—bit fancy, but they do proper afternoon tea service. Very quiet, very... what's the word... refined."

"Quiet sounds amazing," Tyler said immediately, not caring about fancy or refined.

Kit's smile became more genuine. "Thought it might. Come on

then, let's get you somewhere you can actually hear yourself think."

Kit left money on the table for both their teas—waving off Tyler's attempt to pay—and led Tyler through the maze of streets with the confidence of someone who'd grown up here. As they walked, Kit kept up a steady stream of commentary, pointing out landmarks and explaining local customs, but he seemed to instinctively understand that Tyler needed the conversation to be one-way for now.

"That's the Star Ferry pier," Kit said as they approached the harbor. "Been running since 1888, if you can believe that. And there —" he pointed to an elegant hotel building "—that's the Peninsula. Been the fancy hotel in Hong Kong since forever."

The Peninsula Hotel lobby was exactly what Tyler needed— spacious, quiet, elegantly appointed, with staff who moved efficiently but without hurry. Kit led Tyler to the afternoon tea service area, where they were seated at a small table by windows overlooking the harbor.

"Better?" Kit asked as Tyler visibly relaxed in the calm environment.

"So much better. Thank you." Tyler looked around the refined space, then back at Kit. "I can't believe how patient you're being with a complete stranger having a meltdown."

Kit shrugged. "Had a few meltdowns myself over the years. Never fun to deal with alone."

"Why were you having meltdowns?" Tyler asked, then immediately felt rude for prying. "Sorry, that's none of my business."

"Nah, it's fine." Kit signaled the waitress for tea service. "Family issues, mostly. You know how it is."

Tyler found himself leaning forward slightly. "What kind of family issues? I mean, maybe I could... I don't know, sometimes talking through problems helps figure out solutions." He paused, looking embarrassed. "Sorry, that's probably none of my business. I have this habit of trying to fix things for people, and sometimes it gets me in trouble."

Kit's smile turned distinctly cheeky. "Fix things, eh? Oh darling, that's adorable." He leaned back in his chair, studying Tyler with obvious amusement. "But what about you then, sweet boy? You always this wound up, or is Hong Kong just bringing out all your adorable neuroses?"

Tyler felt his cheeks flush. Kit was being polite about it, but he was clearly asking about Tyler's earlier meltdown. "I'm not usually... I mean, I can handle most situations fine, it's just when there's too much..." He gestured vaguely. "Too much input all at once. Crowds, noise, unfamiliar places. It's harder when I'm alone."

"Alone?" Kit picked up on that immediately, eyebrows arching dramatically. "Oh honey, you're traveling by yourself then?"

Tyler blinked at the casual endearment, suddenly noticing something different in Kit's tone—something more theatrical, more... was Kit flirting with him? The thought hadn't occurred to Tyler while he was panicking, but now, sitting in the calm environment of the Peninsula, he was starting to pick up on nuances he'd missed before.

"Yeah, but I'm not usually alone. At home, I mean. I'm used to having..." Tyler stopped, then decided to be honest. "I'm used to having someone special help me navigate social situations."

"Someone special?" Kit's tone was casual, but Tyler caught the curiosity underneath—and the slight theatrical lean forward. "Ooh, do tell. Wife?" He paused dramatically. "Girlfriend?" Another pause, his eyes twinkling with mischief. "Boyfriend?"

The last word was delivered with such theatrical emphasis that Tyler felt his face flush bright red. Kit was letting him know, without saying it explicitly, that he'd figured Tyler out.

Kit's grin widened at Tyler's obvious blush. "I thought so..." He leaned back in his chair, looking pleased with himself. "What's his name then?"

Tyler studied Kit's expression, the way he seemed so delighted by the revelation, the animated gestures. There was no doubt now —Kit was definitely gay, and that explained his immediate understanding, his quick offer of help.

Tyler hesitated for a moment, then took a breath. "Ken. His name's Ken, and we've been together for three years."

Kit's expression shifted—not surprised exactly, but pleased, like a puzzle piece had just clicked into place. "Ah. Boyfriend." He grinned, and Tyler noticed that charming broken tooth again. "Well, that explains the gaydar absolutely pinging off the charts."

Tyler blinked. "Gaydar?"

"Mine's practically legendary, darling. Though you're more subtle than most—very understated." Kit leaned back in his chair, looking more relaxed now. "So I was right about the family issues being complicated—just not yours, mine. Parents keep asking when I'm bringing home a nice girl to give them grandbabies."

"You're gay too?"

"Oh sweetie, very gay. And very single, which is why the parents keep living in hope." Kit's grin was mischievous now. "Good thing you mentioned Ken early, or I might have spent the whole afternoon trying to chat you up properly. And trust me, I can be very persuasive when I put my mind to it."

Kit's expression shifted slightly—not disappointed exactly, but something more complex. "Serious relationship?"

"Three years. We live together."

"Good for you," Kit said, and Tyler could tell he meant it. "Must be hard being so far away from him."

"Harder than I expected," Tyler admitted. "I woke up this morning and for a second I didn't understand why he wasn't in bed with me. We've been sleeping together for so long, I'd forgotten what it feels like to wake up alone."

Kit nodded understandingly. "That's love, mate. When someone becomes part of your normal, being without them feels wrong."

The tea service arrived—delicate sandwiches, small pastries, and proper English tea in bone china cups. Tyler found himself relaxing further as Kit chatted easily about Hong Kong, his work, his family, asking gentle questions about Tyler's life in Oregon.

"So what brings you to our fair city?" Kit asked, biting into a cucumber sandwich. "Business or pleasure?"

"Business. I work for KPMG—accounting firm. They sent me here for a consultation with the Hong Kong office."

"Very impressive. International businessman and everything." Kit's eyes sparkled with mischief. "I do love a man in a suit who knows his way around spreadsheets."

Tyler laughed. "I don't feel very impressive. I feel like I'm completely out of my depth."

"Oh darling, everyone feels out of their depth sometimes," Kit said with a theatrical wave of his hand. "The trick is not letting it stop you from doing fabulous things."

"Is that what you do? Fabulous things?"

Kit grinned wickedly. "I try to, sweet boy. Work in advertising, travel when I can afford it, rescue gorgeous confused tourists when they need saving..." He gave Tyler a look that was definitely flirtatious. "Meet absolutely fascinating people."

Tyler felt that familiar heat creep up his neck. Kit was attractive —very attractive—and clearly interested. Under different circumstances, Tyler might have been tempted. But the mention of Ken had clarified things for both of them, and Kit seemed to accept the boundaries without any awkwardness.

"Tell me about this Ken of yours," Kit said, settling back with his tea and giving Tyler his full attention. "What's he like, this lucky man?"

Tyler found himself talking about Ken more openly than he usually did with strangers—describing Ken's humor, his patience, the way he could navigate any social situation with ease. Kit listened with genuine interest, asking thoughtful questions that showed he was actually paying attention.

"Sounds like you really love this guy," Kit said when Tyler finished.

"I do. More than I thought I could love anyone."

Kit nodded approvingly. "Good for you, honey. Too many people settle for okay relationships. Better to have something absolutely real."

They spent the next two hours talking, the conversation flowing easily between Tyler's work, Kit's life in Hong Kong, their respective experiences with family and relationships and the complicated business of being young gay men in different parts of the world.

Kit was funny and charming, with an irreverent sense of humor that made Tyler laugh more than he had since arriving in Hong Kong. But more than that, Kit seemed to instinctively understand Tyler's temperament—when to push him to be more social, when to give him space to process, when to fill the silence and when to let Tyler think.

"You know," Kit said as they finished their tea, "you're not what I expected when I saw you looking lost this morning."

"What do you mean?"

"I thought you'd be typical uptight businessman. All work, no personality." Kit grinned. "But you're actually quite delicious. Sweet, funny when you relax... and those eyes of yours are absolutely criminal."

Tyler felt heat creep up his neck again. "Kit..."

"Relax, darling, I'm just making honest observations." Kit's expression was playful but somehow also serious. "Your Ken is one very lucky man."

"I'm the lucky one," Tyler said quietly.

Kit studied him for a moment, then nodded. "Yes, sweetie, I think you both are."

As they prepared to leave the Peninsula, Kit insisted on making sure Tyler could find his way back to his hotel safely.

"I'll walk you to the Star Ferry," Kit said. "From there, it's easy—straight shot across the harbor to Central, then five-minute walk to your hotel."

"You don't have to escort me everywhere," Tyler protested. "I should be able to navigate basic transportation."

"Of course you should, gorgeous. But you've had a rough day, and I don't mind the company." Kit's smile was warm. "Besides, I want to make sure you don't disappear into the Hong Kong chaos never to be seen again. Ken would never forgive me."

The Star Ferry ride across Victoria Harbour was exactly what Tyler needed—peaceful, scenic, with the city lights beginning to twinkle as evening approached. Kit pointed out landmarks and told stories about Hong Kong's history, but mostly they sat in comfortable quiet, watching the water and the city skyline.

"Thank you," Tyler said as they approached the Central pier. "For everything. For rescuing me, for the tea, for making Hong Kong feel less foreign."

"My absolute pleasure, darling," Kit said, and Tyler could tell he meant it. "You doing anything tomorrow evening? I could show you more of the city if you want. Somewhere divine for dinner, maybe some of the night markets."

Tyler hesitated. He'd enjoyed Kit's company more than he'd expected, but there was something about Kit's attention that made him feel off-balance in ways that had nothing to do with being in a foreign country.

"I start work tomorrow," Tyler said. "I should probably see how the first day goes before making evening plans."

Kit's smile was understanding rather than disappointed. "Of course, love. Work first, then play. Very responsible of you."

He handed Tyler a business card with his contact information. "If you change your mind, or if you get lost again, or if you just want someone to show you where the absolutely best dim sum is, give me a call."

"Thank you," Tyler said, tucking the card into his wallet. "Really. I don't know what I would have done without you today."

"You'd have figured it out, sweet boy," Kit said confidently. "You're tougher than you think."

There was a moment of awkward silence as Tyler prepared to leave, both of them aware that this felt like the end of something, though neither was quite sure what.

"Well," Tyler said finally, "goodnight. And thank you again."

"Goodnight, beautiful. Sweet dreams."

Tyler turned toward his hotel, but Kit's voice stopped him.

"Tyler?"

He turned back.

"Your Ken really is one very lucky man," Kit said quietly. "Don't forget to tell him that."

In his hotel room that night, Tyler sat on the edge of his bed with his phone, calculating time zones. It was 9 PM in Hong Kong, which made it 5 AM in Oregon. Too early to call Ken.

Instead, Tyler found himself thinking about the day—the panic in Kowloon, Kit's unexpected kindness, the way a complete stranger had seen his distress and responded with such immediate care. Kit was attractive, clearly interested, and under different circumstances...

But Tyler pushed that thought away. He loved Ken completely, was committed to their relationship absolutely. Kit had been kind, had helped him navigate a difficult day, and that was all there was to it.

Tyler typed out a quick email to Ken instead: *First day of exploring Hong Kong was overwhelming but ended well. The city is incredible but intense. Miss you. Can't wait to talk tomorrow when you're awake. Love you.*

Ken's response came within hours: *Glad you're having adventures! Can't wait to hear all about it. Love you too. Get some sleep.*

But as Tyler lay in the unfamiliar hotel bed, he found himself thinking about Kit's easy confidence, his immediate understanding of Tyler's distress, the way he'd made Hong Kong feel less foreign and overwhelming. And Tyler realized that tomorrow evening, after his first day at the KPMG office, he might very well find himself wanting company for dinner after all.

# CHAPTER 22
# KIT'S INTERVIEW

**Tyler:** Okay Kit, I need you to be serious for this interview. This is going into a real book.

**Kit:** *[Voice crackling over the international phone line, clearly grinning]* Aiya, Tyler! You sound so... how you say... businessman-like! Very sexy, this serious voice of yours.

**Tyler:** *[Laughing despite himself]* Kit, come on. I'm trying to be professional here.

**Kit:** *[Playfully]* Professional is boring, lah! You want boring book? Besides, I can hear you smiling through the phone. You like when I tease you, admit it!

**Tyler:** *[Still laughing]* I'm not admitting anything. Can we please just—

**Kit:** *[Interrupting with exaggerated sigh]* Okay, okay! Fine! I be good boy for your fancy book. But only because this international call is costing me fortune already, and my parents will kill me if phone bill is too high.

**Tyler:** *[Settling down]* Thank you. Now, when I started this whole book project, I never expected to learn so many things I didn't know about my own life.

**Kit:** *[Still with hint of mischief in his voice]* Ah, now we getting somewhere! Tyler, darling, you think you know everything that happened, but wah, you were so blur sometimes. Very sweet, but completely blur.

**Tyler:** Rebecca said the same thing. Apparently everyone was managing my life behind the scenes.

**Kit:** *[Laughing]* Not managing, lah! Just... helping things work more smooth. You were so nervous about everything back then, like scared little rabbit.

**Tyler:** This was my first big international assignment. I was terrified.

**Kit:** *[Making sympathetic sound]* Aiya, I could tell, lah! When I first saw you in Kowloon, you looked like... like someone drop you on alien planet and say "figure out the local customs by yourself!"

**Tyler:** That's exactly how I felt. Ken wanted to come with me, but there was no way he could take that much time off work.

**Kit:** *[Voice getting softer]* And you were so worry about being far from him, right?

**Tyler:** We'd never been apart for more than a few days. Two weeks felt like forever.

**Kit:** *[Understanding tone]* Wah, I remember when you first tell me about Ken... I can see how much you love him just from way you say his name. But also can see you were so kancheong - so anxious - about being away from him.

**Tyler:** Ken was worried too, though he tried to hide it with jokes and bravado.

**Kit:** *[Giggling]* Ah yes, the famous Ken humor! Wah, I got to experience that one firsthand, you know.

**Tyler:** *[Confused]* What do you mean?

**Kit:** *[Pausing, then voice getting mischievous again]* Tyler, my darling friend, this is where your story becomes very interesting. Because got things that happened that you never know about.

**Tyler:** What kind of things?

**Kit:** *[Getting excited, speaking faster]* Wah, okay lah, let's start from beginning. Tell me what you remember about those first few days we spend together.

**Tyler:** I remember you rescuing me from being completely lost, taking me to Mrs. Chen's noodle stall, showing me around the city...

**Kit:** *[Making "correct" sound]* Mm-hmm, and what you do every night?

**Tyler:** Called Ken. We had our scheduled ten-minute calls.

**Kit:** *[Voice getting playful again]* And what you tell him about me?

**Tyler:** *[Thinking]* That I'd made a friend, that you were helping me navigate Hong Kong, that you were funny and kind...

**Kit:** *[Laughing, sound crackly through phone]* Wah, and how Ken react to hearing about your new friend?

**Tyler:** *[Slowly]* He seemed... well, he asked a lot of questions. Wanted to know what you looked like, how old you were, whether you were gay...

**Kit:** *[Making knowing sound]* Ah yes, lah! Ken was very very interested in the details about me.

**Tyler:** I thought he was just being protective. Maybe a little worried.

**Kit:** *[Snorting with laughter]* Tyler! Ken was jealous like hell! Completely, totally jealous!

**Tyler:** *[Surprised]* Really? But when you talked to him on the phone that one time, everything seemed fine.

**Kit:** *[Voice getting mischievous]* Aiya, that phone call. Yes, let's talk about that phone call. And all the other phone calls that happen that you don't know about.

**Tyler:** *[Confused]* Other phone calls?

**Kit:** *[Settling in, clearly enjoying this]* Tyler ah, after you had me talk to Ken to "reassure" him, I could tell he was even more jealous than before. You were completely blur, thinking everything okay, but I could hear it in his voice, you know?

**Tyler:** I don't understand.

**Kit:** *[Making dramatic sound]* So lah, I got phone number from you - told you I need for emergency - and I call Ken directly. Without you knowing.

**Tyler:** *[Staring, though Kit can't see]* You called Ken? When?

**Kit:** *[Matter-of-factly]* Next night. Call him at home in Oregon. Wah, we had quite the conversation, I tell you.

**Tyler:** What kind of conversation?

**Kit:** *[Laughing]* Well ah, it start with him basically accusing me of trying to steal his boyfriend, and me telling him he being ridiculous...

**Tyler:** *[Shocked]* Ken accused you of trying to steal me?

**Kit:** *[Waving hand, forgetting Tyler can't see]* Not exact words lah, but yes! He was very... how you say... territorial. Very "hands off my Tyler" energy, you know?

**Tyler:** I had no idea he was that worried.

**Kit:** *[Voice getting softer]* Tyler ah, he loved you so much. The thought of you being halfway around the world with some good-looking guy who showing you around, making you laugh... wah, it was killing him inside.

**Tyler:** *[Quietly]* I never meant to make him worry like that.

**Kit:** *[Gently]* You didn't do anything wrong, darling. Ken knew that. But his heart was completely tied to yours - he cannot imagine life without you.

**Tyler:** So what happened during this phone call?

**Kit:** *[Getting excited again]* After we get past the territorial nonsense, we actually talk! Really talk. About you, about what you meant to both of us, about how I got no intention of coming between you two.

**Tyler:** And?

**Kit:** *[Warmly]* We become friends! Real friends. Ken was actually damn funny once he stop being jealous. We end up talking for like two hours, can you believe?

**Tyler:** *[Amazed]* Two hours? About what?

**Kit:** *[Laughing]* About you, mostly! He tell me stories about your relationship, about how you two meet, about your little quirks and habits. And I tell him about showing you around Hong Kong, about how sweet you were, how respectful of everything.

**Tyler:** I can't believe you two had secret a conversation.

**Kit:** *[Proudly]* Not just one conversation! We talked several more times while you were here. Ken wanted updates on how you doing, and I wanted make sure he know I taking good care of you.

**Tyler:** *[Shaking his head in disbelief]* All this time, I thought that one phone call solved everything.

**Kit:** *[Giggling]* You were so innocent! But in sweet way. You just assume everyone getting along because you wanted them to.

**Tyler:** What else did you and Ken talk about?

**Kit:** *[Mischievously]* Well, he was very interested in whether I found you attractive.

**Tyler:** *[Blushing]* Kit...

**Kit:** *[Laughing]* Oh, look at you blushing! Just like you did back then whenever I flirted with you!

**Tyler:** You were very... forward.

**Kit:** *[Proudly]* I was! And Ken wanted to know if I was hitting on you. So I was honest with him.

**Tyler:** What did you tell him?

**Kit:** *[Looking directly at Tyler]* I told him that yes, I found you very attractive. That if you weren't completely devoted to him, I would absolutely have tried to take you to bed.

**Tyler:** *[Face getting redder]* Kit!

**Kit:** *[Grinning]* But I also told him that anyone with eyes could see how much you loved him, and that I would never try to interfere with that. You were off-limits, and I respected that completely.

**Tyler:** And Ken was okay with that?

**Kit:** *[Nodding]* Once he understood that I wasn't a threat to your relationship, he actually found it funny how I could make you blush just by being a little flirtatious.

**Tyler:** He found it funny?

**Kit:** *[Laughing]* He said it was adorable how flustered you got! Like you weren't used to people being openly attracted to you.

**Tyler:** I wasn't. I'm not.

**Kit:** *[Fondly]* I know. That's part of what made you so appealing. You had no idea how cute you were.

**Tyler:** *[Quietly]* I thought you were cute too.

**Kit:** *[Delighted]* Really? You never said anything!

**Tyler:** *[Still blushing]* Of course I didn't! I had a boyfriend. I loved Ken.

**Kit:** *[Softly]* I know you did. But it's nice to know the attraction was mutual, even if nothing could come of it.

**Tyler:** It was definitely mutual.

# CHAPTER 23
# A SECRET PHONE CALL

Ken was staring at his phone, willing it to ring. It was 7:15 PM in Portland, which made it... he did the math again... 11:15 AM in Hong Kong. Tyler would be in meetings all morning, but maybe he'd have a break soon.

They'd managed four brief phone calls over the past week, snatched conversations between Tyler's work schedule and the impossible time difference. Twenty minutes here, fifteen minutes there, just enough time for Tyler to sound increasingly confident and settled while Ken felt increasingly... what? Lonely? Abandoned?

Jealous?

Ken tried to push that thought away, but it kept returning. He was jealous. Desperately, miserably jealous. Yes, he was proud of Tyler for handling such a major international assignment, and yes, he was grateful someone was being kind to his boyfriend. But he was also eaten alive by the thought of some attractive Hong Kong guy who got to spend entire afternoons with Tyler, who got to see Tyler laugh and relax and discover new things, while Ken sat in their empty apartment calculating time zones and feeling utterly replaceable.

The rational part of Ken's mind knew he was being ridiculous. Tyler loved him. They had a solid relationship. But the irrational part - the part that had been growing stronger with each enthusiastic phone call about Kit's kindness and knowledge of the city - whispered that maybe Tyler was realizing he didn't need Ken as much as he'd thought.

The phone rang, making Ken jump.

"Hello?"

"Ken? Sorry, I know I'm calling earlier than usual, but I had a break between meetings and wanted to hear your voice."

Ken felt that familiar warmth at hearing Tyler's voice, followed immediately by the now-familiar stab of loneliness. "Hey, babe. How's your day going?"

"Really well, actually. The Hong Kong team is incredible - they're so organized and efficient. And Kit's taking me to Macau this weekend, which should be amazing. He says the Portuguese influence makes it completely different from Hong Kong proper."

There it was again. Kit. Ken forced his voice to stay light. "That sounds great. You two are really hitting it off."

"He's been incredibly kind. Yesterday he took me to this dim sum place that was..." Tyler launched into an enthusiastic description of his latest adventure with Kit, and Ken found himself gripping the phone tighter with each detail.

Kit had rescued Tyler from a panic attack. Kit was showing Tyler the "real" Hong Kong. Kit knew exactly how to help Tyler navigate overwhelming situations. Kit was everything Ken wanted to be for Tyler but couldn't be from seven thousand miles away.

"Ken? You okay? You've been really quiet."

"I'm fine. Just tired, I guess. The time zone thing is harder than I expected."

There was a pause. "Ken, you sound... are you sure you're okay? You've seemed off the last few calls."

Ken forced a laugh. "I'm just missing you, that's all. It's weird being here without you."

"I miss you too. But Ken, is there something else? You can tell me."

Ken hesitated. Tyler's voice had that careful quality it got when he was reading between the lines, picking up on things Ken thought he was hiding. "No, really, I'm just tired. And I miss sleeping next to you."

Another pause. "Okay. Well, I should probably get back to my meeting. I love you."

"Love you too. Have fun in Macau."

After they hung up, Ken sat in their silent apartment, staring at the phone and hating himself. He was being ridiculous. Tyler was having an amazing professional experience, making friends, proving himself capable of handling international assignments. Ken should be nothing but supportive.

Instead, he was sitting here like a jealous boyfriend, resenting someone who was taking care of Tyler in ways Ken couldn't.

The phone rang again, startling him out of his brooding. Tyler calling back?

"Hello?"

"Is this Ken?" The voice was unfamiliar, accented, clearly long-distance.

"Yes, who is this?"

"This is Kit. Kit Lee. From Hong Kong."

Ken sat up straighter, every nerve suddenly alert. "Kit. Tyler's... friend."

"His very good friend, yes. Listen, darling, I hope you don't mind me calling, but I got your number from Tyler for our Macau trip paperwork, and I thought... wah, I thought maybe we should talk, lah."

Ken's chest tightened. "About what?"

"About the fact that you're feeling terrible and trying to hide it from Tyler, and Tyler's starting to worry that our friendship is causing problems in your relationship."

Ken's jealousy and fear exploded into anger. "Look, I don't know what your game is, but Tyler loves me. We've been together for three years, and some attractive guy showing him around Hong Kong isn't going to change that. Are you calling to tell me you're trying to steal my boyfriend?"

"Whoa, whoa," Kit interrupted gently. "Ken, I'm not trying to steal your boyfriend, lah."

"Then what are you doing? Why are you spending so much time with him? Why are you calling me?" Ken's voice was getting louder, all his careful control slipping away.

Kit's voice became even gentler, almost soothing. "Because Tyler mentioned you seemed 'off' on your calls, and I could see him getting all worried and analytical about it. Look, if I were in your position - if my boyfriend was halfway around the world spending time with some good-looking guy who clearly adores him - I'd be losing my mind too, lah."

Ken felt his defensive anger wavering slightly. "So you admit you're attracted to him."

Kit laughed, a sound that was both camp and completely genuine. "Honey, your boyfriend is absolutely stunning. Those mismatched eyes? That sweet smile when he gets embarrassed? The way he lights up when he talks about you? Any gay man with working eyeballs would find him gorgeous, lah."

Ken didn't know whether to be flattered or more worried. "So you are attracted to him."

"Of course I am. But here's the thing, love - and this is why I'm calling at eleven in the bloody morning after staying up all night to catch you at decent hour - what you two have is very special. Like, really special, lah. I've spent four days with Tyler now, and I can tell you with absolute certainty that man is completely, utterly devoted to you."

Something tight in Ken's chest began to loosen slightly. "He is?"

"Are you kidding? He talks about you constantly. 'Ken would love this restaurant.' 'Ken has the best stories about his family.' 'Ken makes me feel safe in crowds.' It's actually quite adorable, though I did threaten to charge him extra if he mentioned your name more than ten times during dim sum."

Ken found himself smiling despite his anxiety. "That sounds like Tyler."

"Exactly! And the way his face changes when he talks about you... Wah, Ken, I'm practically dying of envy over here. Not because I want Tyler - though I absolutely would if he were available - but because I want what you two have, lah."

"You do?"

"Darling, I've been looking for that kind of love my entire life. The kind where someone's face lights up just from hearing your voice on the phone. The kind where being apart for a week feels impossible because you're so used to being a team." Kit's voice got softer. "Tyler told me you've been together three years, and I can tell every single day of it has been real. No pretending, no acting. Just genuine love."

Ken felt tears threatening and blinked them away. "I just... I hate that I can't be there with him. I hate that someone else is taking care of him when that's supposed to be my job."

"Aiya, honey, I get it. I really do. But you know what Tyler told me about you?"

"What?"

"He said you make everything easier for him, lah. That you help him with social stuffs and crowds because you understand how his brain works. He said you're patient with his need for quiet time and all his organizing, and you never make him feel broken or weird for being different."

Ken's throat tightened. "He said that?"

"Word for word. And then he said - and this nearly made me cry into my tea - he said you love him exactly as he is, not as some version of him you wish he could be."

"I do love him exactly as he is," Ken said quietly.

"I know you do. And Tyler knows it too. So when he gets a little overwhelmed by Hong Kong chaos and I help him find quiet spaces, I'm not replacing you, lah. I'm just... filling in for temporary until he can get back to the person who really knows how to take care of him."

Ken was quiet for a moment, processing. "Kit?"

"Yes, darling?"

"Thank you. For calling, for explaining... for taking care of him."

"You're welcome. Now, can I make a suggestion?"

"Sure."

"Tomorrow night - well, tomorrow morning my time - arrange

for longer call. Like, one hour. Make it special. Ask him about his work, let him gush about the city, tell him everything you've been up to. And maybe... maybe start planning something wonderful for when he gets home. Give him something to look forward to besides just getting back to normal routine."

Ken smiled. "That's actually a really good idea."

"I have my moments, lah. And Ken? I'm going to be tied up with work for the next few days, so Tyler's going to be on his own more. Don't worry if he sounds a little lonely - it just means he's missing you."

"Okay. And Kit?"

"Mm?"

"I'm glad Tyler found you. I mean that."

Kit's voice warmed noticeably. "Wah, aren't you sweet. I can see why Tyler fell for you, lah."

After they hung up, Ken sat in the quiet apartment feeling lighter than he had in days. Kit was right - he and Tyler had something special, something real. Two weeks apart didn't change that.

His phone buzzed with a text from an unknown international number: *This is Kit. Forgot to mention - if you want daily updates on how your gorgeous boyfriend is doing, I'm happy to provide them. Consider it as public service, lah.*

Ken found himself grinning as he typed back: *That's probably not necessary.*

The response came immediately: *Aiya, sweetie, it absolutely is. If positions were reversed, wouldn't you want someone keeping an eye on me?*

Ken considered this, then typed: *Actually, yes. I would.*

*Exactly. So we're friends now, and friends look out for each other's boyfriends. I'll call you tomorrow night with full report, lah.*

*You really don't have to do that.*

*Too late, already decided. Besides, I have feeling we're going to get along fabulously.*

Ken stared at the exchange, realizing Kit was probably right. There was something about Kit's directness, his camp humor mixed with genuine care, that reminded Ken of his own approach to friendship.

*Fine. But don't let Tyler know we're talking.*

*Why not?*

Ken thought about it. *At first because I don't want him to worry that I was jealous. But now... maybe because it's kind of fun having our own friendship.*

*I KNEW I was going to like you! Our little secret then. Though fair warning - I'm going to want to hear embarrassing stories about Tyler, and I expect you to want same from me.*

Ken laughed out loud in the empty apartment. *Deal. But I get first dibs on any photos from Macau where Tyler looks mortified.*

*Only if you promise to share the most embarrassing thing Tyler's ever done.*

*Oh, I have stories.*

*Perfect. We're going to be fabulous friends.*

The next evening, Ken's phone rang at exactly 7 PM.

"Ken, darling! It's your daily Tyler report."

"Kit, hi. How did today go?"

"Wah, it was magnificent. Your boyfriend absolutely charmed his Hong Kong colleagues during their big presentation, then got completely flustered when they took him out for congratulatory drinks afterward."

"Flustered how?"

"Well, apparently one of the senior partners made toast specifically praising Tyler's work, and Tyler turned bright red and stammered through thank-you speech that was so sweet everyone at the table fell in love with him."

Ken grinned. "That's very Tyler."

"Isn't it just? And then - aiya, this is the best part - when they asked him what he missed most about home, he launched into this five-minute speech about your coffee-making skills and how you always remember to buy the good cream."

"He talked about my coffee?"

"Honey, he talked about your coffee like it was religious experience. I thought the Hong Kong partners were going to offer you job just to keep Tyler happy, lah."

Ken felt that familiar warmth spreading through his chest. "What else?"

"Oh, we're just getting started, love. So after dinner, I suggested we walk through Central to help him digest, and this adorable businessman started people-watching. But instead of checking out other guys like any normal gay man would do, he kept pointing out couples and saying things like 'Ken would find their dynamic interesting' or 'Ken would have something funny to say about that guy's outfit.'"

"He did not."

"He absolutely did! I finally told him that if he mentioned your name one more time, I was going to start charging him rent for the space you were taking up in his brain."

Ken laughed. "What did he say to that?"

"He blushed - you know that full-face blush he does - and said, 'Sorry, I just really miss him.' Like he was apologizing for being completely head-over-heels in love with you."

"God, I miss him too."

"I know you do, sweetie. Which is why I took some pictures of him looking particularly gorgeous today. I'll mail them to you when I get them developed."

"You don't have to do that."

"Already decided, lah. But fair warning - there's one of him laughing at something I said, and when you see it, you're going to want to fly to Hong Kong immediately. Actually..." Kit paused, his voice getting mischievous. "You know what? You should come visit Hong Kong. Both of you. Maybe next year when you can take proper holiday time. I'd love to show you around properly, and Tyler keeps saying how much he wishes you were here."

"That sounds amazing. I'd love to visit Hong Kong sometime."

"Promise me you'll think about it, lah. I want to meet this wonderful boyfriend Tyler can't stop talking about."

"I will think about it. Really. And Kit? Thank you for calling, for explaining all this."

"You're welcome, darling. Now, tell me something embarrassing about Tyler that I can use for entertainment purposes."

"What kind of embarrassing?"

"Aiya, I don't know... something that would make him turn that
delicious shade of pink he goes when he's flustered."

Ken grinned wickedly. "Well, there was the time he tried to
cook me dinner for our six-month anniversary..."

"Ooh, this sounds promising. Do tell."

"He decided to make lobster pasta, but he'd never cooked
lobster before. I came home to find him sitting on the kitchen floor
having a full crisis of conscience because he couldn't bring himself
to put the lobster in the boiling water."

"Wah, really?"

"Really. He said it looked at him with its 'little lobster eyes' and
he couldn't do it. We ended up keeping it as a pet for three days."

Kit's laughter was delighted and slightly hysterical. "You kept
lobster as pet?"

"In the bathtub. Tyler named it Giuseppe and insisted on giving
it daily pep talks."

"I'm dying. This is the best thing I've ever heard. Your
boyfriend gave motivational speeches to lobster?"

"Every morning before class. 'Good morning, Giuseppe! I hope
you have a lovely day in the tub!'"

Kit was laughing so hard he could barely speak. "Aiya, sweetie,
I am absolutely getting him to tell me this story. Tyler's going to
die of embarrassment when I make him explain it."

"Take pictures when you do. I want to see his face when he's
telling it."

"Deal. This is going to be fantastic."

They talked for another twenty minutes, Kit sharing more
details about Tyler's day while Ken provided increasingly ridiculous stories about Tyler's various quirks and endearing habits. By
the time they hung up, Ken felt like he'd known Kit for years.

The pattern continued for the rest of Tyler's trip. Every evening
at 7 PM, Kit would call with updates, stories, and increasingly
elaborate plans to make Tyler blush for Ken's entertainment. Ken,

in return, provided a steady stream of embarrassing Tyler stories and suggestions for places Kit should take Tyler for maximum photographic opportunities.

"Today I got him to tell me the Giuseppe story," Kit reported on Thursday evening. "I was asking about his cooking skills, and when he mentioned trying to make you dinner for anniversary, I kept pushing for details. He turned so red I thought he might explode when he got to the part about naming the lobster."

"Did you get pictures?"

"Wah, honey, I got whole series. He went through about six different shades of pink. I'll mail them to you - you're going to love seeing his face."

"You're evil."

"I prefer 'creatively mischievous,' lah. Besides, your boyfriend is too serious sometimes. Little embarrassment is good for the soul."

"True. Did he ask how you knew to bring up cooking disasters?"

"Of course not! Our friendship is classified information, remember?"

Ken grinned. "Right. What's tomorrow's plan?"

"I'm thinking of taking him to Temple Street Night Market. Lots of crowds, lots of sensory input. Perfect opportunity to play the protective friend role and send you pictures of him looking over-whelmed and grateful."

"You're terrible."

"I'm thorough, lah. There's difference."

By Friday night, Ken realized he was looking forward to Kit's calls almost as much as Tyler's. Kit had a way of making Tyler's experiences feel immediate and shared, like Ken was part of the adventure instead of stuck at home missing out.

"Last night tomorrow," Kit said during Friday's call. "Tyler flies home Sunday morning your time."

"I can't wait," Ken said, meaning it completely.

"He can't wait either, love. He's been talking about seeing you again all week. Very sweet, very romantic. You two are going to have quite the reunion, lah."

"Kit?"

"Yes, darling?"

"Thank you. For all of this. For taking care of him, for the daily reports, for... for becoming my friend."

"Aiya, sweetie, thank you for letting me. This week has been more fun than I've had in ages."

"Are we going to stay in touch? After Tyler comes home?"

"Are you kidding? You're stuck with me now, Ken Takeshi. I have international calling plans and no shame about using them."

Ken laughed. "Good. I'd hate to lose touch with my Hong Kong correspondent."

"Never going to happen, lah. Besides, someone needs to make sure you two don't get too domestically boring. That's what friends are for."

That night, Ken went to bed feeling more excited about Tyler's return than anxious about the time they'd spent apart. Kit was right - what he and Tyler had was special, and two weeks with a charming Hong Kong friend hadn't changed that. If anything, hearing about Tyler's adventures secondhand had reminded Ken of all the things he loved about Tyler's approach to the world.

His phone buzzed with a final text from Kit: *One more day, then you get your boy back. He's lucky to have you, and you're lucky to have him. Sweet dreams, Ken.*

Ken typed back: *Thank you for everything. Tyler's lucky to have you as a friend too.*

*We're all lucky, darling. Now get some sleep. Tomorrow's the last day of Kit and Tyler show, and I plan to make it memorable.*

Ken fell asleep smiling, already planning Tyler's welcome-home surprise and looking forward to hearing all about Kit's "memorable" final day. Tyler was coming home, Ken had made an unexpected new friend, and everything was exactly as it should be.

# CHAPTER 24
## GET DOWN TONIGHT

Tyler stared at his reflection in the hotel mirror, adjusting his shirt for the third time. Kit had invited him out for the evening —"proper Hong Kong nightlife," he'd said with that mischievous grin—and Tyler was having second thoughts.

The work week had gone better than expected. The KPMG Hong Kong team was impressive, the consultation was proceeding smoothly, and Kit had been the perfect guide to help Tyler navigate the city's overwhelming energy. But this felt different. This felt like crossing a line he wasn't sure he should cross.

Tyler's phone rang right on schedule—Ken's expected evening call. Perfect timing.

"Hey, babe," Ken's voice was warm despite the international connection. "How was your day?"

"Good. Really good, actually. The project is coming together nicely." Tyler sat on the edge of his hotel bed, phone pressed close to his ear. "How are things there?"

"Boring without you. Rebecca made me go grocery shopping with her because apparently I'm the closest thing to you she has available for organizational consultation."

Tyler smiled. "Did you remember to get the good cream for coffee?"

"Of course I did. I'm not a monster." Ken paused. "What are you doing tonight? Please tell me you're not ordering room service again."

Tyler hesitated. "Actually, Kit invited me out. To see some of the nightlife."

"That's great! You should go. Experience the city properly."

"It's... well, he mentioned something about going dancing. At a club."

There was a pause on Ken's end. "A gay club?"

"I think so, yeah."

Another pause. Tyler could practically hear Ken thinking.

"Are you worried about it?" Ken asked finally, his voice careful and gentle.

"A little," Tyler admitted. "I mean, I've never been to a gay club without you. And I don't really know how to... navigate that kind of environment."

"Tyler," Ken's voice was soft but firm. "You can handle this. And besides, Kit will be with you. He seems like good people."

"You're not... you don't mind?"

"Mind what? That my incredibly attractive boyfriend is going dancing with a charming Hong Kong guy who clearly adores him?" Ken's tone was teasing but warm. "Should I be worried?"

Tyler felt his chest tighten. "Ken, you know I would never—"

"I know, babe. I trust you completely. Go have fun. Dance with attractive strangers. Let Kit show you off. Just... be safe, okay?"

"I love you," Tyler said quietly.

"I love you too. Now go get ready for your big night out."

After they hung up, Tyler sat staring at his phone for a long moment. Ken's trust was absolute, unwavering. Which somehow made Tyler feel worse about the complicated feelings he'd been having about Kit all week.

An hour later, Tyler met Kit in the hotel lobby, and immediately felt underdressed. Kit looked effortlessly stylish in dark jeans and a fitted shirt that somehow managed to be both casual and sophisticated. Tyler, in his usual khakis and button-down, felt like a suburban dad who'd accidentally wandered into someone else's much cooler life.

"Wah, Tyler!" Kit's face lit up when he saw him. "You clean up nice, darling. Very handsome."

Tyler felt heat creep up his neck. "Thanks. You look... really good too."

Kit's grin was pleased and slightly predatory. "I know, lah. Come on, we're going to have a fabulous time."

The club was in Central, tucked into a narrow building that Tyler would have walked past without noticing. From the outside, it looked like nothing special. But the moment they descended the stairs into the basement space, Tyler was hit by a wall of sound, lights, and energy that made his pulse spike.

The music was loud—not just background noise, but a physical presence that seemed to vibrate through the floor and into Tyler's bones. The lighting was dim except for occasional flashes of color that strobed across the crowded dance floor. And everywhere, bodies moved in ways that Tyler found both mesmerizing and overwhelming.

"First time in a Hong Kong gay club?" Kit asked, his mouth close to Tyler's ear so he could be heard over the music.

Tyler nodded, trying to process the sensory assault without shutting down completely.

"It's a lot," Kit said understandingly. "But good lot, yeah? Come on, my friends are already here. Let me introduce you."

Kit led Tyler through the crowd to where a group of four guys had claimed space near the bar. They were all around Kit's age, clearly comfortable in this environment, talking and laughing in rapid Cantonese.

"Eh!" Kit called out, switching to Cantonese as he greeted his friends with enthusiasm. Tyler caught his own name in the stream of words, along with what sounded like explanations about his work and where he was from.

One of Kit's friends—slightly older than the rest, with kind eyes and an easy smile—turned to Tyler and extended his hand. "I'm Ted," he said in careful but clear English. "Kit's told us about his handsome American friend."

Tyler felt grateful for the English, shaking Ted's hand. "Tyler. Nice to meet you."

The others introduced themselves with their English names, though Tyler noticed they mostly referred to Ted by what sounded like his Chinese name—something that sounded like "Wai-ming" when Kit said it. Tyler made a mental note to ask Kit about names later, filing away details he could share with Ken during their next call.

Ted seemed to be the unofficial translator, occasionally switching to English to include Tyler in the conversation. He was clearly the elder of the group, maybe five or six years older than the rest, and had a gentle way of making sure Tyler didn't feel completely lost in the rapid-fire Cantonese.

"Tyler works for big accounting firm," Ted explained to the group in English, then switched back to Cantonese, clearly translating for the others.

The guys looked impressed, nodding and making comments that Kit seemed to find amusing. Tyler caught Kit showing him off a little, the way Kit's posture straightened with pride when he gestured toward Tyler.

"What are you drinking?" Ted asked Tyler directly, but before Tyler could answer, Kit was already talking to the bartender in Cantonese.

A moment later, Ted placed a glass in Tyler's hand. "Vodka soda," he said simply. "Easy to drink, not too strong."

Tyler wanted to say he didn't usually drink vodka, that he preferred wine with dinner or maybe a beer, but Ted seemed so considerate about choosing something "easy" that Tyler didn't have the heart to decline. "Thank you," he said instead, taking a polite sip.

It was stronger than he'd expected, but not unpleasant. The vodka had a clean taste, and the soda water made it feel lighter somehow. Tyler took another sip, then another, grateful for something to do with his hands while Kit's friends chattered around him.

He'd been to clubs with Ken before, but not many and definitely not often. In the few times Ken had taken him, they were usually there perhaps thirty minutes before Tyler became overloaded and they'd leave to grab coffee or something to eat. Alcohol was usually reserved for dinner—wine with a meal—so this was a new experience entirely.

After a few more sips, Tyler felt something shift. The overwhelming noise of the club seemed less aggressive, more like music he could actually enjoy. The constant chatter around him felt less like sensory assault and more like the comfortable buzz of people having fun. When Kit's friends laughed at something, Tyler found himself smiling along, even though he couldn't understand what they were saying.

Tyler made a mental note to keep track of everything he was experiencing—the taste of the vodka, the way the alcohol made his head feel slightly light, how the music seemed more enjoyable now. He was eager to share these new experiences with Ken, both because everything was so different from his usual routine and because he felt he owed Ken a full report. Ken was his boyfriend, after all, and this seemed like something he should document and share.

"You okay?" Kit asked, watching Tyler's face carefully.

"Yeah, just... taking it in."

"No rush, sweetie. We can just watch for a while if you prefer."

Tyler was grateful for Kit's patience. Around them, men of all ages moved with an easy confidence that Tyler envied. Some were clearly together, dancing with the kind of intimate familiarity that spoke of long relationships. Others seemed to be prowling, making eye contact across the room, engaging in the ancient dance of attraction and possibility.

Tyler had never been part of this world. He and Ken had found each other in college, settled into their relationship quickly, built their life around quiet domesticity and chosen family. The raw sexuality and open desire on display here was foreign territory.

"Want to try dancing?" Kit asked after they'd finished their drinks.

Tyler's first instinct was to say no, but the vodka had made him feel more relaxed, more willing to try new things. "I'm not very good at it," Tyler said.

"Nobody cares about good, darling. Just move to the music and have fun."

Kit's friends were already making their way to the dance floor, and Tyler found himself swept along with the group. They formed a loose circle, all dancing together, laughing and calling out to each other in Cantonese over the music.

Tyler felt awkward at first, acutely aware of his own stiffness compared to the fluid grace of Kit and his friends. But the group was welcoming, including him in their laughter even when he couldn't understand their jokes. Ted would occasionally lean over and make a comment in English, or one of the others would gesture in a way that clearly meant Tyler should join in whatever they were doing.

When Kit's friends started teasing Tyler—he could tell from their playful expressions and the way they gestured, even though he couldn't understand the words—Tyler found himself laughing along. There was something infectious about their energy, and the alcohol made everything feel less serious, more fun.

"They like you," Kit said, moving closer to Tyler as the music shifted to something with a heavier beat. "They think you're very sweet."

The dance floor was getting more crowded as the night progressed, pushing everyone closer together. What had started as a loose group gradually condensed into a tighter circle, bodies pressing closer as more people claimed space around them.

Tyler was starting to feel the effects of the vodka more distinctly now—a pleasant looseness in his limbs, a warmth that spread from his chest outward, making the music seem to pulse in time with his heartbeat. This was so different from his usual carefully controlled environment, and he found himself enjoying the novelty of it.

As another song began, slower and more intimate, Kit moved closer. The group dynamic shifted, pairs forming naturally as the music demanded more sensual movement. Tyler found himself dancing primarily with Kit now, their friends still nearby but giving them space.

"You're doing great," Kit said, his hands resting lightly on Tyler's hips. "Just feel the music."

Tyler tried to follow the advice, letting the rhythm guide his movements. It was actually easier than he'd expected—the music was designed for this, and his body seemed to know what to do even when his mind was overthinking everything.

As the song changed to something slower, more intimate, Kit moved closer. Not inappropriately, but close enough that Tyler could smell his cologne, could feel the heat radiating from his body.

"You're a natural," Kit said, his voice warm with approval.

Tyler felt something flutter in his chest that had nothing to do with the music. Kit was attractive—really attractive—and the way he was looking at Tyler, the way he moved, the casual confidence of his touch...

Another song began, and Kit's hands moved to Tyler's waist, pulling him slightly closer. Tyler could feel the solid warmth of Kit's body, could see the way Kit's eyes had darkened with something that looked very much like desire.

This was dangerous territory.

Tyler's body was responding in ways that had nothing to do with loyalty to Ken and everything to do with Kit's proximity, his obvious attraction, the sensual environment of the club. Tyler could feel his pulse quickening, could feel heat pooling low in his belly as Kit's thumb traced a small circle against his hip.

"Tyler," Kit said softly, and there was something in his voice that made Tyler's breath catch.

Tyler looked up, meeting Kit's gaze directly for one of the few times since they'd met. Kit's eyes were dark and warm and full of want, and Tyler felt an answering want rise up in his own chest.

Kit leaned closer, his mouth nearly touching Tyler's ear. "You're so beautiful," he murmured. "Do you know that?"

Tyler's entire body went hot. This was exactly what Ken had been afraid of, exactly the kind of situation that tested the boundaries of a committed relationship. And Tyler was failing the test spectacularly, because all he wanted in that moment was to turn his head slightly and kiss Kit, consequences be damned.

Instead, Tyler pulled back abruptly.

"I need to leave," he said, his voice tight with panic and desire and guilt.

Kit's hands dropped immediately. "Tyler? What's wrong?"

"I just... I have an early meeting tomorrow. I should get back to the hotel."

It was a transparent lie, and they both knew it. Tyler was practically radiating conflict, his careful composure completely shattered.

"Of course," Kit said gently, though Tyler could see the disappointment in his eyes. "Let me walk you out."

The cool night air outside the club was a shock after the heated atmosphere inside. Tyler walked quickly toward the street, putting distance between himself and the temptation Kit represented.

"Tyler," Kit called softly.

Tyler stopped but didn't turn around.

"You don't have to explain," Kit said. "I understand."

Tyler finally turned to face him. Kit looked beautiful in the neon light from the street signs, his hair slightly mussed from dancing, his shirt clinging to his lean frame. Tyler wanted him. There was no point denying it.

"I'm sorry," Tyler said quietly.

"Don't be sorry for being loyal to someone you love," Kit replied. "That's actually quite admirable, lah."

Tyler felt tears threatening. "I didn't expect... I thought I could just have fun without..."

"Without wanting something you can't have?" Kit's smile was understanding and only slightly sad. "Desire doesn't follow rules, sweetie. The important thing is what you choose to do about it."

Tyler nodded, not trusting his voice.

"Your Ken is a very lucky man," Kit said. "And you're a good person, Tyler. Better than most."

Kit stepped closer, and for a moment Tyler thought he might

kiss him anyway. Instead, Kit reached out and squeezed Tyler's hand once, gently.

"Good night, beautiful. Sweet dreams."

Kit walked back toward the club entrance, turning to look back once before disappearing into the bar to rejoin his friends, leaving Tyler standing alone on the sidewalk with his heart racing and his body still humming with unfulfilled desire.

Back in his hotel room, Tyler sat on the edge of his bed, staring at his phone. He should call Ken. He should confess everything— the dancing, the attraction, the moment when he'd wanted Kit so badly he could barely think straight.

But what would be the point? He'd walked away. He'd chosen Ken over temptation, loyalty over desire. Wasn't that what mattered?

Tyler set his phone aside and headed for the shower, hoping the hot water would wash away the lingering scent of Kit's cologne and the memory of his touch. Tomorrow he would focus on work, on the consultation, on getting through the rest of his time in Hong Kong without compromising his relationship further.

But as he stood under the spray, Tyler couldn't stop thinking about Kit's hands on his waist, the heat in his eyes, the way his voice had sounded when he called Tyler beautiful.

Some temptations, Tyler realized, were harder to forget than others.

In the morning, he would tell Ken that he'd had a good time, that Kit had been a perfect gentleman, that Hong Kong nightlife was interesting but not really his scene. All of which would be true, in their way.

He just had to work up his courage to mention how close he'd come to kissing another man, or how much he'd wanted to.

# CHAPTER 25
# GROWING UP

The indie radio station crackled through Joshua's car speakers, one of those small stations hanging on despite the death of radio, playing some band he'd never heard of with a mandolin and too much reverb. He wasn't really listening anyway. His brain was still churning over what he'd read last night. And again this morning. And again just before he left to run errands.

Kit's interview. The dancing club story. Tyler's honest admission about being attracted to someone who wasn't Ken.

Now he was driving home through the same suburban streets he'd navigated for years, but he wasn't seeing the familiar strip mall or the intersection where he'd gotten his first speeding ticket. He was seeing a new side of Uncle Tyler, and he wasn't sure how he felt about it.

He wasn't upset or anything. Not disappointed either. Uncle Tyler hadn't done anything wrong—in fact, Joshua was kind of impressed that Tyler had been so honest about his feelings toward Kit. But it still felt... uncomfortable somehow. It challenged Joshua's rock-solid belief that Uncle Tyler and Uncle Ken were hopelessly devoted to each other, that their eyes never wandered, that their hearts never wavered with desire for anyone else.

The more he drove, the more his mind kept working this over like a piece of stale, gritty gum—not enjoying the texture but with no way to spit it out. Joshua "knew" that couples weren't perfect, but what did he really know? He'd never been in a relationship. Hell, he'd never even kissed someone, let alone held hands or felt the rush of having someone tell him he was cute or that they liked him. He'd just assumed that when Uncle Tyler and Ken got together, that was it—they were forever hopelessly in love and it shut off any feelings for anyone else. Ever. Period.

But that seemed kind of silly now, didn't it? Tyler had admitted to Kit that he had a boyfriend and literally ran away from him in the club because he owed it to Ken to do so. But admitting that dancing next to Kit like that... I mean, come on. It sounded like he'd gotten a boner and panicked. Josh figured he probably would've done the same thing. Wouldn't he?

Some guys might have stayed. Taken Kit back to the hotel and... well, what would their boyfriend know anyway? He'd be thousands of miles away. No one would be the wiser, right?

But that seemed wrong to Joshua. And it obviously was to Uncle Tyler, otherwise he wouldn't have bolted from the bar. This made Josh smile a little—not because he was happy about Tyler's choice, exactly, but because he was seeing his uncle more as a real person. Normal. But with integrity. Not the superman Joshua had always imagined him to be.

And it helped him understand something about real relationships—at least the ones that last. Maybe it wasn't about whether partners found other people attractive or felt their hearts skip a beat for someone new. Maybe it was about having the courage to acknowledge those feelings and still choose loyalty to the person you loved. That seemed difficult. Complicated. Joshua felt like he needed to think about it more, but his image of Uncle Tyler was coming into sharper focus, and he felt like he was growing up a little because of it.

Lately, he'd been wondering if he'd ever meet someone the way Uncle Tyler had met Ken. Now it seemed like not only would he meet someone, he'd probably meet several people over the years who made his heart race. It wasn't about meeting people, he realized. Maybe it was about what you did after you met them.

This all seemed so new to him.

And it was.

A stoplight turned red ahead of him, and Joshua slowed to a halt, drumming his fingers on the steering wheel. The radio DJ was saying something about local traffic, but Joshua's thoughts had drifted to that photo of Tyler and Kit in the restaurant booth— Tyler's arm around Kit's shoulders, both of them grinning at the camera, that little heart drawn next to their names.

Now he understood what that heart meant. Not romance, exactly. But something real. Something that mattered enough that Kit had carefully organized those photos, written those captions in his beautiful handwriting, kept it all these years later.

The light turned green, and Joshua pressed the gas, heading home to where Uncle Tyler would be waiting in the attic, probably sitting in that bean bag chair by the window, ready to answer whatever questions Joshua brought him next.

And for the first time since this whole thing started, Joshua wasn't sure what he wanted to ask.

# CHAPTER 26
# GOOD STUFF

**Tyler:** [*Still blushing*] Of course I didn't! I had a boyfriend. I loved Ken.

**Kit:** [*Softly*] I know you did. But it's nice to know the attraction was mutual, even if nothing could come of it.

**Tyler:** It was definitely mutual.

**Kit:** [*Grinning*] Good! My ego needed that confirmation. Now, speaking of mutual attraction, let's talk about that night I took you dancing.

**Tyler:** [*Groaning*] Oh no.

**Kit:** [*Laughing*] Oh yes! You remember - my friends and I dragged you to that gay club in Central?

**Tyler:** I remember being very nervous about it.

**Kit:** [*Nodding*] You were! You kept saying you didn't really dance, that you weren't good at it, that maybe you should just go back to the hotel...

**Tyler:** I wasn't lying. I really wasn't good at dancing.

**Kit:** [*Shaking his head*] Tyler, you were fine at dancing. You were just nervous about being in a gay club without Ken.

**Tyler:** It felt strange. Like I was betraying him somehow.

**Kit:** [*Gently*] Even though he knew where you were going and had given you permission to have fun?

**Tyler:** [*Sheepishly*] Even though.

**Kit:** *[Smiling]* Well, you loosened up after a few drinks. Remember? We were dancing together, and you actually seemed to be enjoying yourself.

**Tyler:** I was enjoying myself. Maybe too much.

**Kit:** *[Leaning forward with interest]* Ah, now we're getting to the good part. You suddenly stopped dancing and said you needed to leave. You said you were tired, that you had an early meeting the next day.

**Tyler:** That's what I said, yes.

**Kit:** *[Grinning]* But Tyler, my dear friend, I knew that wasn't the real reason. I could tell by the look on your face, by the way you suddenly pulled away from me.

**Tyler:** *[Uncomfortably]* Kit...

**Kit:** *[Playfully but gently]* Come on, we're both adults now. This is for your book, right? What really happened that night?

**Tyler:** *[Long pause, then sighing]* You really want to know?

**Kit:** *[Nodding]* I really want to know.

**Tyler:** *[Very quietly]* I was getting... aroused. Dancing with you, being that close to you, feeling your hands on me... and I knew it wasn't right.

**Kit:** *[Softly, but pleased]* Ah.

**Tyler:** *[Still quiet]* I was completely devoted to Ken, but my body was responding to you, and I felt guilty about it.

**Kit:** *[Warmly]* Tyler, there's nothing wrong with physical attraction. Your heart belonged to Ken, but you're still human.

**Tyler:** *[Looking up]* I know that now. But at the time, it felt like I was cheating on him just by feeling that way.

**Kit:** *[Grinning]* Well, for what it's worth, I'm very pleased to know I had that affect on you.

**Tyler:** *[Blushing again]* Of course you are.

**Kit:** *[Laughing]* What? If I can't have Tyler, at least I can feel good knowing I could make Tyler... excited.

**Tyler:** *[Covering his face]* I can't believe we're talking about this.

**Kit:** *[Still grinning]* Oh, it gets better. Guess who I told about that night?

**Tyler:** *[Looking up in horror]* You didn't.

**Kit:** *[Nodding enthusiastically]* I absolutely did! I called Ken the next day and told him everything.

**Tyler:** *[Mortified]* Everything?

**Kit:** *[Laughing]* Well, not the specific details about your... physical response. But I told him that you'd had a good time dancing, that you'd relaxed and enjoyed yourself, and that you'd left when you started feeling guilty about having fun without him.

**Tyler:** What did Ken say?

**Kit:** *[Fondly]* He said that was exactly what he expected you to do. That you were too loyal for your own good sometimes.

**Tyler:** He wasn't upset?

**Kit:** *[Shaking his head]* He was proud of you for being honest with yourself and removing yourself from a situation that made you uncomfortable. He said it proved how much you loved him.

**Tyler:** *[Quietly]* I did love him. So much.

**Kit:** *[Softly]* I know. We all knew. And Ken knew he was the luckiest guy in the world to have that kind of love.

**Tyler:** *[After a moment]* So you and Ken really became friends through all this?

**Kit:** *[Nodding]* Best of friends! In fact, he came to visit Hong Kong the next year, remember?

**Tyler:** Of course I remember. That was an amazing trip.

**Kit:** *[Grinning]* And Ken was exactly as wonderful as I expected him to be. Funny, charming, completely devoted to you...

**Tyler:** He loved Hong Kong.

**Kit:** *[More quietly]* He loved seeing you in your element there. Watching you navigate the city, seeing how confident you'd become... he was so proud of you.

**Tyler:** That trip was perfect.

**Kit:** *[Mischievously]* It was also when I discovered that Ken was incredibly attractive. Like, seriously hot.

**Tyler:** *[Laughing]* You had a crush on my boyfriend?

**Kit:** *[Shrugging]* Not a crush exactly, but... damn, Tyler, you had good taste. If I'd met Ken first, I might have given you some competition.

**Tyler:** *[Grinning]* I'm glad I met him first then.

**Kit:** *[Laughing]* Me too! You two were perfect together. It was beautiful to watch.

**Tyler:** *[More seriously]* What did you think of our relationship? From an outside perspective?

**Kit:** *[Thoughtfully]* You want the honest truth?

**Tyler:** Always.

**Kit:** *[Softly]* I was a little bit jealous. Not of either of you specifically, but of what you had together. The way you complemented each other, the way you made each other better... it was the kind of love that most people spend their whole lives looking for.

**Tyler:** *[Quietly]* We were very lucky.

**Kit:** *[Nodding]* You were. And you both knew it, which made it even more special. You never took each other for granted.

**Tyler:** Ken made me braver. More willing to try new things, to push my boundaries.

**Kit:** *[Smiling]* And you made him more thoughtful. More patient. I could see how you balanced each other.

**Tyler:** *[After a pause]* Kit, can I ask you something personal?

**Kit:** *[Grinning]* After everything we've just talked about? Ask me anything!

**Tyler:** What happened with your love life after we became friends? Did you ever find what Ken and I had?

**Kit:** *[Shrugging, but not sadly]* I've had some good relationships, some fun times. Nothing quite like what you two had, but I'm still looking.

**Tyler:** You deserve that kind of love.

**Kit:** *[Warmly]* Thank you. And you know what? Meeting you and Ken, seeing how beautiful a real partnership could be... it gave me something to aspire to. You raised my standards.

**Tyler:** *[Smiling]* I'm glad we could do that.

**Kit:** *[More seriously]* You also taught me about loyalty, about the difference between attraction and love, about how to be a good friend even when you want something you can't have.

**Tyler:** You were always a good friend, Kit.

**Kit:** *[Pleased]* I tried to be. And I'm honored that our friendship meant enough to you to include me in this book project.

**Tyler:** Of course you're included. You're part of our story, part of our family.

**Kit:** *[Getting emotional]* That means everything to me, Tyler. Everything.

**Tyler:** *[Gently]* What do you want people to know about our friendship? About this time in our lives?

**Kit:** *[Thinking carefully]* I want them to know that real love creates more love. Your relationship with Ken didn't make you closed off to other people - it made you more open, more generous, more capable of forming deep friendships.

**Tyler:** That's beautiful.

**Kit:** *[Continuing]* And I want them to know that you can love someone deeply and still appreciate other people. That attraction doesn't threaten real love, and friendship can exist even when there's chemistry.

**Tyler:** Those are important lessons.

**Kit:** *[Nodding]* They are. And they're lessons I learned from watching you navigate your feelings honestly and ethically.

**Tyler:** *[Softly]* Thank you, Kit. For everything. For being my friend, for taking care of me in Hong Kong, for becoming Ken's friend too...

**Kit:** *[Voice crackling through the phone]* Aiya, stop! You make me cry, and that's not good for my reputation as tough Hong Kong guy.

**Tyler:** *[Laughing]* Your secret is safe with me.

**Kit:** *[Giggling through the phone line]* Good! Now, are we finish with all this emotional stuff? Because this phone call is costing me more than my rent, and I need to go make tea before I start crying for real.

**Tyler:** That sounds like a good place to end.

**Kit:** *[Voice getting mischievous one last time]* And Tyler ah?

**Tyler:** Yes?

**Kit:** *[With audible grin in his voice]* Next time you need to write book, maybe include some steamy details, lah! Your readers might appreciate knowing just how attractive you were back then.

**Tyler:** *[Laughing and clearly blushing even over the phone]* Kit!

**Kit:** *[Laughing through the international connection]* What? I just saying! You were very cute when you flustered. Can hear you blushing even from Hong Kong!

**Tyler:** *[Still laughing]* Goodbye, Kit.

**Kit:** *[Warmly]* Bye bye, Tyler. Thank you for including me in your fancy book. Makes me feel very important.

*[The line goes quiet except for the faint static of the international connection, leaving Tyler with a fuller understanding of friendships and connections he never knew existed during his time in Hong Kong.]*

# CHAPTER 27
# WHAT HE IS NOW

Tyler sat on Joshua's twin bed, looking out the window at the late afternoon light filtering through the maple tree in the backyard. For the first time in years, he was really thinking about how everything was playing out. He wasn't the mastermind of this trip down memory lane that Josh was taking. Rebecca was the one who'd organized it all, primarily as an excuse to do her own dirty work of finally dealing with his belongings, but he didn't blame her for that. Now that the truth was out there, there wasn't really a "need" for Josh—or her, even—to keep looking through all his old stuff, reading all those interviews, the chapters he'd written for the book that never got compiled.

Funny, he thought. It had been Rebecca who'd been the catalyst for that writing project too. Now here she was, guilty as charged again. He smiled to himself.

But this was different. It seemed like this was the only way his voice could be heard. If he'd known that all those years ago, he might have added more... or thought about how he'd written certain sections... or...

But would he, really? Probably not. How often do people get to know they're going away and have one last opportunity to say what they need to say? What do you do with that knowledge? Suddenly become Shakespeare? He didn't really know how he felt.

He just... he felt like his story was no longer his own. It had ceased being his the day he...

*Died.*

How was it possible, he wondered? He'd had a difficult time at first, all those years back, understanding what "this" was—the state he was in. Tyler was too methodical, too scientific and practiced in his approach to life to believe in fairy tales and colorful metaphors about anything beyond death, but here he was. The religious types had it all wrong—smug assholes, he thought. Yet even those kind-hearted people who called themselves "spiritual but not religious" didn't have a clue. And those "ghost hunters" he occasionally heard about... what charlatans. Humans really enjoyed amusing themselves with tales of the unknown.

But what was this? He spent most of his time talking with his nephew when Joshua was home. But he never went away to Joshua's college. Come to think of it, he never went back to the old house he'd shared with Ken. Occasionally, Tyler would find himself wandering around town, walking by the parks or spending time reading in the library. Every so often, some kid would run up to him and wave, the way small children like to meet new friends. But their parents would grasp their hands, retrieving them from whatever they were doing, obviously seeing nothing there.

He remembered the first time he'd spoken with Joshua. He'd been more surprised than Josh had been, wondering how Josh could see him. Tyler had known in his heart that he and Ken had died, even though he hadn't been sure at first. He'd just "woken up" walking along the road the way they'd been driving not moments before—or that's how it felt. But it quickly became apparent that no one could see him, and nothing seemed to bother him the way it used to. Well, sort of. He was still the same Tyler, still had the same traits and mannerisms. His autism still existed. But he didn't feel cold in the winter, nor did rain bother him. He didn't get colds or flu anymore. While he hadn't deliberately tried, he didn't think he'd break his leg if he took a dive on the asphalt or suffer any other physical ailments.

But his mind still functioned normally. He still felt. Felt so much. And that almost seemed worse than the possibility of a broken bone, especially when he realized he could no longer speak with Rebecca... or call Kit... or ask Miss Evangeline for advice... or...

What was the use, he told himself as he leaned back on Joshua's twin bed and used his arms to prop himself up. There were a lot of unknowns he simply couldn't explain. Time seemed "off" to him. Sleep was "off." He always had a fresh set of clothes, but he never did laundry. He never needed to eat or pee or do anything that had made him a man in his physical past, but he could still feel things, touch objects, feel Joshua's comforter under his palms right now. He could smell the Pine-Sol scent of the floors after Rebecca cleaned the hall bathroom. The lasagna coming from the oven downstairs was very pleasant, and he felt his stomach grumble a bit, just like the old days. Hell, he still got horny when he thought about all those nights with Ken, or could cry tears over jokes he shared with Josh. In some ways, he was just as human as before.

But... what was he now?

"Comfy?"

Tyler turned to see his nephew standing in the doorway, pulling his jacket off before walking it over to its assigned hanger in the closet.

"Just thinking."

"About what?"

"Nothing crazy. Just finding it weird, watching you and your mom go through all my old book stuff and stories."

"Yeah... so, can I ask you something about that?"

"Shoot." Tyler swiveled around as Josh sat in his desk chair facing him.

"Mom found the box from Kit. All the Hong Kong stuff."

Tyler's face lit up. "Oh shit, yeah. I totally forgot about that box."

"The pics Kit gave you were... damn, Prism."

"Pics?"

"Yeah, he made this whole little album. Labels and everything, like he was making a scrapbook or something."

Tyler got that "trying to remember" look, so Josh jumped up. "Hold on," and bolted out of the room and up the ladder. Tyler watched him disappear and then scramble back down within a minute, carrying the old shoebox. When Josh sat next to him, Tyler felt that familiar buzz of energy between them. Josh had gotten used to it by now, but still kept enough space so it wouldn't get weird.

Tyler put the box on his lap and started going through everything Rebecca had packed back up—pamphlets, the calligraphy set, and then the photo album. When he opened it to Kit's photo, his whole face changed. He got this warm smile, like he was remembering something really good.

"I read all your stuff about him."

Tyler kept staring at the photo before looking at Josh. "Kit totally saved my ass that day I got lost in Hong Kong."

"Seems like a cool guy."

"Oh man, he was. Hope he still is."

"Mom was pretty confused when she saw these," Josh said as Tyler flipped through pages of Kit's friends, the "Dancing Queens."

"I remember taking this one by Ocean Park. They kept calling me a *gweilo* and making fun of me, but I had no clue what that even meant."

"What's it mean?"

"Just some dumb word for white guy." Tyler was getting lost in the memories.

Then came the restaurant pictures, and finally the one of him and Kit—the one with the little heart drawn next to it. Tyler saw it and his cheeks went red. He glanced at Josh, then back at the photo.

"Kit was... kinda special to you, wasn't he?" Josh asked quietly.

"Yeah, he was. But I loved Uncle Ken. Still do. And Kit knew that."

"But the heart thing?"

"Well, Kit was this massive flirt. And if I'd been single..."

"You would've totally gone for him?"

Tyler went quiet. "I feel shitty saying this, Josh, because I don't want it to sound like I was torn between him and Ken. I wasn't. And Kit knew that. Hell, even Ken ended up being friends with him."

"Yeah, I read about that."

Tyler thought about that for a second. "Well, then you know Kit was a huge flirt, but he respected me and Ken. He was probably more jealous of what we had than anything. Even if I'd wanted to try something with him—which I didn't—I think Kit wouldn't have let me anyway."

"But would you have wanted to?"

"No way. Ken was... is... everything to me. He deserves my loyalty and all my love."

"But...?"

"But I also had to admit that my body... well..."

"You thought Kit was hot, didn't you?"

Tyler hung his head and nodded.

"But," he said finally, "I told Ken everything. I couldn't keep that shit to myself. And even though I found out later that Ken and Kit were having all these phone calls, I didn't know that then. So I came home and just word-vomited all over Ken. I felt so fucking guilty."

"What did Ken do?"

Tyler paused, really thinking. "He listened. Like, really listened. Then he grabbed my hand and said he loved me even more for being honest and letting him in on this whole struggle. That he trusted me and knew I'd been faithful and always would be. That this was more about me figuring out love versus lust versus just being horny, and that it was totally normal to feel that stuff. Said he felt it sometimes too."

"Really? Ken?"

Tyler nodded. "Said his workout buddy had the most perfect ass he'd ever seen, and sometimes in the gym shower he had to stop himself from wanting to just... you know." Tyler giggled, still feeling weird about sharing all this personal stuff.

"Wait, Ken wanted to bang his gym buddy?"

"I think he was just trying to make a point—that it's normal to meet people and think they're hot or feel connected to them, but the person you're really connected to is something totally different. And as long as we were honest with each other about it, we'd never mess up."

Josh really thought about that. Tyler let him have the time, looking back at the heart photo before closing the album and putting everything back in the box.

"Uncle Prism?"

"Yeah?"

"Do you think... this is gonna sound dumb, but do you think there's only one person you're supposed to love? Like, your one true love or whatever?"

Tyler looked up, thinking hard about such a big question.

"I used to think it was super simple: hell yes, one true love per person. But now I think it's more like... a whole spectrum of stuff."

Josh tilted his head, looking interested.

"With Ken, there's no doubt we were... are... in love. But love is just one piece of what it takes to be... I don't know what to call it... a team? A couple?"

"A family?" Josh suggested.

"Perfect word. Family. Love is huge, but it comes in all these different flavors, and it's not just one thing. I don't just love Ken one way. I love him like he's my husband..."

"God, I wish you guys could've gotten married," Josh said.

Tyler stopped. "Yeah... me too." Then he got back on track. "But I also love Ken the way I love you—like family. And I love him as a friend."

"And you think he's sexy as hell," Josh said, wiggling his eyebrows.

Tyler blushed. "Oh yeah, extremely sexy."

"But I also think you fall in love with people all the time, even if it's just for a little bit. Not necessarily romantic love or family love. Maybe you connect with someone at work and fall in friend-love with them. Or maybe you fall in love like I did with your mom—I could never love her any way except like a sister."

"Well yeah, you're gay as hell!" Josh laughed. Tyler rolled his eyes and grinned.

"But Kit?" Josh asked.

"Kit was hot and sweet, but such a flirt, and I could totally see myself getting charmed by all that. And..."

"You could've fallen for him in a sexy way?"

Tyler paused. "Yeah, I could have. But my heart wasn't there, and I knew it. And he knew it. So I told Ken, and because Ken knew exactly where everything stood, and we always talked about everything, he was cool with it."

"Probably helped that he and Kit were secretly talking on the phone without you knowing."

"Oh yeah, that definitely helped. I'm so grateful Kit did that. He didn't have to reach out to Ken, but he wanted to. I think that's why Ken wasn't jealous at all. If Kit hadn't done that, I don't know if it would've gone as smooth as it did."

Josh thought about all this, then looked at his uncle, who'd closed the shoebox and was staring at the lid.

"You know what, Uncle Prism? I always thought you and Ken were like... perfect together, and I still do, but this whole Kit thing makes you seem more... I don't know... real? Like before, you never did anything wrong, but this makes me realize you have feelings and emotions and, like, desires and stuff, just like me or Mom or anybody."

Tyler smiled. "Josh, I'm totally human. So is Ken, and your mom, and everyone you'll ever meet. We just might seem like we have our shit together. Most people don't. But you're growing up. You're already a man, whatever the hell that means." They both laughed. "Seriously though, life is messy as fuck, and people are even messier. Having these feelings isn't something you just shove down and ignore."

"True. I'm still single as hell, so..."

"You know what, Josh? I bet one day you're gonna literally run into 'your Ken' somewhere totally random—like at Target or in some class or at a bar or the library or wherever—and you're gonna feel all these crazy emotions hit you at once."

Josh smiled at that.

"But here's the thing I want you to remember—it doesn't end there. You're gonna have amazing chances to meet all kinds of people who make your life interesting and worth living."

*Living.* Tyler thought about that word.

"Uncle Prism?"

"Yeah?"

"Thanks, man."

"For what? I didn't really do anything."

"Yeah, you did."

Rebecca stared at the ceiling while David's show played on, the familiar blue glow from the TV washing over their bedroom. She had that restless feeling crawling under her skin—the kind that meant her brain wasn't going to shut the hell up, no matter how exhausted she was.

She scrolled through Instagram without really looking at anything. Someone's vacation. Someone's dinner. Some bullshit inspirational quote. The blue light probably wasn't helping, but lying there with just her thoughts felt worse.

*He's an awful lot like Tyler.*

The thought had been bouncing around in her head for hours now, and she couldn't let it go. Not just the obvious stuff—how Josh got that same intense look when he was thinking, how he'd always needed a minute to figure people out, how he'd rather hang out with one or two friends than deal with a big group. She'd noticed all that when he was little.

But now, watching him deal with everything about Tyler and Ken, seeing how his brain worked... it was like looking at Tyler all over again.

Rebecca tossed her phone on the nightstand and rolled toward David, who was half-watching some show she'd already seen twice. She studied his face in the TV light, trying to figure out how the fuck to say what was bugging her.

Tyler didn't figure out he was autistic until he was in his thirties. All those years feeling weird and different, not getting why some stuff was so hard for him. He didn't even think about it until that Australian woman mentioned her brother, and even then it took him forever to actually do anything about it.

What if Josh was going through the same thing? What if he was sitting around feeling like a freak without knowing why?

Christ, how do you even bring that up? *Hey honey, think you might be autistic?* That seemed like a great way to screw up your kid.

But what if he needed to know? What if it could help him the way it helped Tyler?

Rebecca thought about that horrible day when David had to get Josh from school. The locker room thing that completely broke him. The counselor had talked about anxiety and stress, but looking back...

Looking back, it seemed like way more than just being embarrassed. The way Josh just shut down for weeks, staring at nothing. Like his brain just couldn't handle it.

Just like Tyler used to do.

"You're still thinking," David said without looking away from the TV. Twenty-one years of marriage, and he could read her restless energy from across the bed.

"Yeah. Can't turn the damn thing off."

"What's eating at you?"

Rebecca sighed. "I keep thinking about Josh. About how much he's like Tyler."

David hit pause and turned toward her. "Like how?"

"I mean really like Tyler. What if Josh is... you know. What if he's got the same thing Tyler had?"

"You think Josh is autistic?"

"I don't know. Maybe. Think about it—the way he gets overwhelmed, how picky he is about everything, how he's always been better with grown-ups than kids. All that shit."

David rubbed his eyes. "Could just be his personality, babe."

"Or it could be something we've been missing for twenty-one fucking years." Her voice came out more worried than she meant to. "Tyler didn't figure it out until he was way older. What if Josh is going through the same crap—feeling different and not knowing why?"

David shifted to face her properly. "Okay, so what would we even do? How do you tell your kid you think he should get tested for something like that?"

The question she'd been dreading. "I have no clue. It sounds awful no matter how I think about saying it."

"But if it helped him understand himself..."

"Or it could make him think we think something's wrong with him. What if I'm totally off? What if I just miss Tyler so much I'm seeing shit that isn't there?"

David was quiet for a minute, thinking. "What's making you think about this now? Just watching him deal with everything?"

"Sort of. But remember that day I was trying to do the garden thing? I could hear him upstairs talking to someone, except there wasn't anyone there. When I asked him about it, he said he was just working through stuff, but..."

"But what?"

"It reminded me of Tyler. How Tyler would talk out loud when he was trying to figure something out. And Josh has always been weird about changes, needs forever to deal with social stuff, never really dated anyone..."

David nodded slowly, and she could see something clicking in his brain. "Wait. Hold up. He is twenty-one, never had a girlfriend, never even talks about liking anyone. He's gonna be a senior and he's never dated. At all."

Rebecca wasn't following. "Yeah, so?"

"And he grew up with Tyler and Ken. He knows what a good relationship looks like between two guys." David sat up a little straighter, like he'd just solved a puzzle. "Maybe he's not struggling with autism stuff. Maybe he's trying to figure out how to tell us he's gay."

"You think Josh is gay?"

"Would explain everything. Being withdrawn, talking to himself—maybe he's working up the nerve to come out. Never dating girls. Maybe he's scared to tell us even though he knows we were fine with Tyler and Ken."

David had that look now, like he'd figured it all out. Rebecca could practically see him planning the conversation he was going to have with Josh tomorrow.

"Maybe," she said slowly. "But even if he is gay, that doesn't explain the other stuff. How he deals with crowds, the sensory things, all that social shit. Being gay doesn't make you autistic."

"So maybe it's both. Or maybe he's just shy and worried about coming out." David was already moving on, problem solved in his mind. "Either way, sounds like he could use some support."

Rebecca felt some of the tension ease, but not all of it. Something still felt... off.

"So what do we do?"

"I'll talk to him tomorrow. Let him know we love him no matter what, and if he wants to talk about anything—dating, relationships, whatever—we're here for him."

"And if it's not about being gay?"

"Then we figure it out." But David was already reaching for the remote, clearly confident he'd identified the issue.

Rebecca watched him restart the show, feeling like they were missing something. Sure, Josh might be gay. That made sense. But there was still that nagging feeling in her gut, the one that had been bothering her all day.

The conversations she'd overheard. The way Josh would pause, like he was listening to someone respond. The way he'd laugh at things only he could hear.

It wasn't just working through problems out loud. It was... something else.

"David?"

"Mmm?" He was already getting absorbed back into the show.

"What if we're both wrong? What if it's not about autism or being gay or any of that?"

"What else would it be?"

Rebecca stared at the ceiling, trying to put her finger on what was bothering her. "I don't know. Just... something else."

David made a noncommittal sound, clearly done with the conversation now that he'd solved it to his own satisfaction.

Rebecca closed her eyes, but sleep felt far away. Josh was smart and thoughtful and had people who loved him. David was probably right—he was likely just struggling with coming out, and once they had that conversation, everything would make sense.

But she couldn't shake the feeling that there was still something they weren't seeing. Something about those conversations she'd overheard, the way Josh seemed to be responding to someone who wasn't there.

Something that had nothing to do with sexuality or autism or any of the normal things parents worried about.

Something else entirely.

# CHAPTER 29
# MEETING BRONWYN

Tyler was having the kind of travel day that made him question why he'd ever left Portland. The engine flame-out over the Pacific had been terrifying enough—thirty minutes of circling while the crew assured passengers that "one engine is perfectly sufficient for safe landing." Now he was stuck in Brisbane Airport, a city he'd never intended to visit, waiting for a connection to Sydney that might or might not happen today.

The Qantas lounge was his refuge, at least. Quiet, comfortable seating, free wifi, and actual food instead of whatever passed for airplane meals. Tyler had claimed a corner table, spread out his work materials, and was trying to make the best of an impossible situation when a voice cut through the peaceful atmosphere like a chainsaw through silk.

"Are you taking the absolute piss? What do you mean there's no guarantee?"

Tyler looked up to see a woman pacing near the windows, mobile phone pressed to her ear, gesturing wildly with her free hand. She was tall, probably late twenties, with light brown hair pulled back in a messy ponytail and the kind of tan that spoke of genuine Australian sunshine rather than salon visits.

"Look, mate, I don't give a flying fuck about your passenger manifest limitations. I've got a meeting in Sydney that I've been planning for three bloody months, and if I miss it because some dickhead pilot can't keep his engines running properly, someone's gonna hear about it!"

Tyler winced at the volume and tried to focus on his laptop screen. The lounge had been blissfully quiet before this tornado of Australian profanity had blown in.

"No, I will NOT calm down! Do you have any idea what this is costing me? This meeting could make or break my entire fucking quarter!"

Tyler found himself stealing glances at her as she continued her tirade. There was something almost mesmerizing about her complete lack of filter, the way she gestured with her entire body while she talked.

"Fine! FINE! But I want meal vouchers, I want hotel vouchers if this goes overnight, and I want someone with an actual functioning brain to call me the second you know something concrete!"

She ended the call with enough force that Tyler was surprised her phone survived, then stood there for a moment, hands on her hips, staring out at the tarmac like she could personally will the delayed flights into existence.

Tyler tried to return his attention to his work, but he could feel her restless energy from across the lounge. She was now pacing again, muttering what sounded like increasingly creative combinations of Australian swear words.

Without warning, she spun around and marched directly toward Tyler's table. Before he could react, she'd slapped his arm with surprising force.

"Can you believe this shit?" she demanded, dropping into the chair across from him without invitation. "Bloody plane breaks down over the Pacific, and now they're acting like it's my fault I'm stranded in Brisbane when I'm supposed to be in Sydney!"

Tyler blinked, completely taken aback by the sudden invasion of his personal space. "I... uh..."

"I mean, seriously! How hard is it to keep a plane in the air? That's literally their one job!" She was still talking at full volume, seemingly oblivious to the fact that other lounge patrons were now staring. "And of course it happens on the day I've got the most important client meeting of my bloody career!"

Tyler nodded politely, but inside he was calculating escape routes. The noise, the aggressive energy, the rapid-fire questions—it was all too much too fast.

"I'm Bronwyn, by the way. Bronwyn Mitchell. I actually live here in Brisbane—which is fucking ironic since we had to emergency land in my own bloody city—but I was supposed to be heading straight to Sydney for this massive client meeting. And if the idiots at Qantas can't get their heads out of their arses and figure this shit out, I might as well hang it up and head home. You?"

"Tyler," he managed, his voice barely audible.

"Right! So what's your story then? Business? Pleasure? Running away from home?" She was leaning forward now, taking up even more space. "You look like maybe a business type—all neat and organized and whatnot."

Tyler tried to answer, but the words wouldn't come. His hands, he realized, were starting to shake slightly as he gripped his coffee cup.

"So what do you do? And please tell me it's something more interesting than accounting or insurance or some other soul-crushing corporate bullshit."

Tyler's hands were definitely shaking now. He tried to hide it by placing them flat on the table, but that just made it more obvious.

Bronwyn was still talking, asking about his job, his travel plans, his opinion on Australian coffee versus American coffee, but Tyler had stopped processing the words. Everything felt too loud, too fast, too much.

That's when Bronwyn stopped mid-sentence.

Tyler's hands were trembling against the table surface, and he was staring down at them like they'd betrayed him. His breathing had gone shallow, and there was something in his posture that reminded her of...

"Oh, fuck me," Bronwyn said quietly, and for the first time since she'd sat down, her voice dropped to a normal volume. "You're not upset about the flight delay, are you?"

Tyler looked up at her, confused and still shaking.

"Jesus, I'm such a dickhead." Bronwyn leaned back in her chair, putting space between them. "Look at me, coming over here like a bloody hurricane, talking at you like you're supposed to keep up with my insanity."

She watched Tyler's hands continue to tremble and felt her stomach drop. "You remind me of my little brother," she said softly. "He does that exact same thing when things get too much for him."

Tyler's hands stilled slightly, his attention caught.

"I'm really sorry, mate. Can we... can we start over?" Bronwyn's voice was completely different now—warm, gentle, without a trace of the aggressive energy. "I'm Bronwyn, and I just had a massive fucking meltdown about my travel plans, and I took it out on the first person I saw. That was shitty of me."

Tyler looked up at her, seeing a completely different person than the woman who'd slapped his arm five minutes ago.

"You okay?" she asked gently. "You want me to piss off and leave you alone? I'll understand if you do."

Tyler shook his head slowly. "No, it's... I'm fine. Just not good with... unexpected things."

"Yeah," Bronwyn said, recognition in her voice. "My brother Jamie's the same way."

She was quiet for a moment, studying Tyler's face. "My brother Jamie does that exact same thing," she said, settling back in her chair. "The shaking hands, the way you get when things are too much."

Bronwyn settled back in her chair, her energy completely transformed. "Jamie's my little brother—two years younger than me. Growing up, he was... God, we all thought he was just the most difficult kid. He'd never answer when you asked him questions—like, you'd ask him something simple, and he'd just stare at you for ages before saying anything. Drove my parents absolutely mental."

Tyler felt something twist in his chest. That sounded familiar.

"And restaurants? Forget about it. We couldn't take him

anywhere without it turning into a disaster. He'd get all tense and weird, pick at his food, ask to leave before we'd even finished ordering. My parents would get so frustrated."

"What about... other things?" Tyler asked quietly.

"Oh, everything. Concerts, shopping centres, even family gatherings. Jamie would either shut down completely or have these massive meltdowns, and we'd all end up angry and exhausted." Bronwyn's voice got softer, tinged with regret. "I'm ashamed to say this, but for a while there, I started to really resent him."

Tyler's chest tightened further.

"I mean, I was a teenager, you know? I wanted to go out, have fun, be spontaneous. But every family outing had to be planned around Jamie's... quirks. My parents would spend ages preparing him for things, explaining every detail, and even then he might have a panic attack halfway through."

Bronwyn paused, looking uncomfortable. "I used to call him high maintenance. A drama queen. Said he was just being difficult for attention."

The words hit Tyler like physical blows. He'd heard those exact phrases whispered about him—sometimes by friends, sometimes by colleagues who thought he couldn't hear. Even Ken and Rebecca, who loved him, would occasionally tease him about being "particular" or needing "special handling" when they went out.

"Jamie started pulling away from all of us," Bronwyn continued. "Wouldn't come to family dinners, stopped accepting invitations from friends. I thought he was just being an asshole... but... now..." She trailed off in thought, and Tyler saw her entire temperament change.

"Then one night, we had this massive fight. I'd invited him to come out with me and my mates, and he said no, same as always. I got fed up and started laying into him about how he never did anything fun, how he was such a drama queen, how no wonder he couldn't get a girlfriend."

Bronwyn's voice cracked slightly. "That's when he just... broke down. Started crying, really crying, not the dramatic stuff I'd accused him of. And he said something that still keeps me up at night."

Tyler found himself leaning forward, despite his anxiety.

"And when I said the usual bullshit—'just be yourself, Jamie'— he lost it completely." Bronwyn wiped her eyes with the back of her hand. "He said, 'Bullshit, Bron! I can't! I can't get my brain to let me know who that is!'"

"What did he say then?" Tyler whispered.

"He said he sometimes wanted to just end it all because no one understood how hard it was to live in his brain. That he was always trying to be like everyone else but couldn't figure out how."

Tyler felt tears starting to slide down his cheeks without realizing it had happened.

Bronwyn noticed and quietly pulled a packet of tissues from her purse, placing them on the table between them. "That's when it clicked for me. Jamie wasn't being difficult or dramatic. His brain just worked differently than ours, and we'd been trying to force him to operate like everyone else."

Tyler's eyes were starting to burn. This story felt too familiar, too close to his own experience of always feeling like he was making things difficult for everyone. But he was afraid to ask what he really wanted to know.

"What... what happened to Jamie?" he finally managed quietly.

"Well, he finally went to see someone. Got diagnosed with autism." Bronwyn said it matter-of-factly, but Tyler could see the weight behind the words.

Tyler looked confused. "I thought that was... no offense... kids with helmets who couldn't speak..."

Bronwyn tensed, and Tyler felt instant regret flood through him. "I'm sorry. I'm stupid about this stuff..."

"Nah, mate, I thought the same thing," Bronwyn said, relaxing again. "So did my folks. Everyone did, really. In fact, it took some doing to even get Jamie to go see someone. He was terrified of being labeled as 'retarded'—that's what kids at school called people like that."

Tyler winced at the word. He hated hearing things like that.

"But after some tests and conversations with specialists, he was diagnosed as high-functioning autistic," Bronwyn continued.

"What does that mean exactly?"

Bronwyn shifted in her chair, choosing her words carefully. "Basically means he's got all the traits of autism, but he can function pretty well in everyday life. He can work, live independently, have relationships. His brain just processes things differently, especially sensory stuff and social situations."

Tyler was quiet for a moment, processing. He was afraid to stick his nose too far into her brother's business, but he desperately wanted to know. "And... how is he now?"

Bronwyn smiled, seeming to understand his hesitation. "It's still difficult sometimes, and there are still times when I want to strangle him." She laughed. "Just pick pepperoni or sausage already, Jamie! But now that we all understand what's going on, it's easier to know how to talk to him and what to do."

"In what way?"

"Well, he still has the same... I was gonna say 'issues,' but they're not really issues, are they? Just differences. But he understands them better now. He's able to accommodate himself, prepare for things, ask for what he needs. Most importantly, he doesn't feel less than or bad or wrong or stupid anymore." She grinned. "And if he is a drama queen these days, it's because he wants to be."

Tyler got very quiet, staring down at his hands that had finally stopped shaking.

They sat in silence for a moment, Tyler processing this story that felt like hearing his own life described by a stranger.

"Do..." Tyler started, then stopped. "Do you think... I might be...?"

Bronwyn was careful not to jump in with answers. She could see Tyler working up to something important.

"Do you think I might be like Jamie?" Tyler finished quietly.

"I don't know, mate," Bronwyn said gently. "But sometimes it doesn't hurt to learn a little more about ourselves, you know? To help us figure out how to live our lives a little better."

Tyler nodded, still crying softly. For the first time in his life, someone had given him a story that made sense of all the ways he'd always felt different, difficult, wrong. Maybe he wasn't broken after all. Maybe his brain just worked differently.

And maybe that was okay.

## CHAPTER 30
# HAVING IT THEIR WAY

David's car waited in line at the Burger King drive-through, ninth in what seemed like an endless parade of people "Having It Their Way." He drummed his fingers on the steering wheel and glanced over at Josh, who was navigating their spot in line with the kind of focus most people reserved for parallel parking.

Rebecca was at her pottery class with the girls—which was really just an excuse to drink wine and gossip while painting already-made pots. It wasn't like they were getting their hands dirty or anything. So it was just "the boys" tonight, and David had found his son exactly where he'd expected: upstairs in that bean bag chair that had started taking Josh's permanent shape since he'd moved it up there last week.

When David had wrestled his fat ass up the ladder into the attic —okay, that wasn't true, David suffered from what he'd heard Prism's Australian friend call "NASS" once. No Ass Syndrome. Most white guys like him had it, no matter how many squats they did. He'd noticed Josh had inherited it too, though he felt a little weird for checking out his son's rear end. He'd laughed to himself about it.

"What's so funny, Dad?"

"Hmm? Oh, nothing. Let's go grab some food. Your mom's with the girls."

"Drinking?"

"Definitely, but while painting pottery or some bullshit. You know how they do."

Josh had smiled and closed up the binder before standing, and David had noticed the NASS affliction was definitely genetic. He'd chuckled again.

"And you're laughing because...?"

"Nothing. Get your shoes on. I'm driving."

Josh had looked dubious but grinned. It wasn't often he just hung out with his dad like this.

Now here they were, pulling up to BK. Not exactly fine dining, but it got them out of the house. Besides, it felt easier to talk when you were driving—no direct eye contact, no pressure to look at each other. Your mind could admit shit without realizing it because it was doing double-duty with driving.

"So, how's the detective work going with Uncle Tyler's stuff?"

"It's good, I guess. I didn't know he did so much."

"Yeah, that crazy bastard was always somewhere around the world whenever I heard about him."

"Like, I didn't realize he lived in Hong Kong for a while."

"Oh yeah. Made friends everywhere, apparently. I think he took trips all around Asia. Sent some photos of him in the Forbidden City once and..." David tapped his skull, willing himself to remember. Josh found this gesture funny—it never seemed to work, like people's brains were separate entities. "The Ming Tombs or something. Guy was pretty connected."

"Did you know about Kit?"

"Who?"

"The guy in Hong Kong. His friend?"

"Mmm, not sure. I never went there, but I think he mentioned friends. Why?"

"Oh, nothing really. I was just reading about that." Josh decided not to push it. He didn't know how much Prism and Ken had shared with his folks. That was Uncle Tyler's story to tell if he wanted. He stopped and thought quietly. Well, he guessed Tyler already had told it—it was written down. Besides, how else could he tell it now? It wasn't like he could just show up at dinner and say "Remember that time I was in Hong Kong? Well, let me tell you a story!"

David noticed Josh going quiet after shutting down the Hong Kong conversation. He made a mental note to ask Rebecca if she knew who this Kit person was.

"Uh, Josh, I wanted to ask you something, if you don't mind."

Josh snapped back from his thoughts. His dad was always cool with him—never pushy, never gave him crap about being a nerd or not bringing girls home. But they didn't talk one-on-one much. Truth was, they didn't have a ton in common. He loved his dad and felt loved, but David was into the Grateful Dead as much as Oingo Boingo. Josh, most definitely, was not. His dad enjoyed having a beer with friends and didn't mind hanging out during the Super Bowl. Josh would rather drink piss and sit through a lecture on dental floss regulations than deal with sports.

Well, that wasn't entirely true. He enjoyed watching professional tennis sometimes, and he'd started watching Red Bull Cliff Diving on YouTube this week. Something about the way guys would jump off a seventy-foot cliff into the ocean without so much as a splash. It seemed magical. He imagined Prism up there in his little blue Speedo, gauging the wind and a million other variables before jumping.

David cleared his throat, bringing Josh back. "Everything okay, bud?"

"Yeah, just thinking."

"Mind if I ask you something?"

"Sure. Sorry, what was it?"

David felt his balls ascending into his body, hiding from preemptive shame. This was harder than he'd thought. "Well, I uh..." he stammered.

Josh looked at him, then motioned that the car ahead had moved. David pulled forward and finally looked over.

"Listen, Josh, I'm gonna stick my nose where it probably doesn't belong, and forgive your old man if he doesn't know how to do this right, but I just wanted to ask... or uh, tell you..."

Josh looked intrigued. It was kind of cool seeing his dad fumble with words for once.

Finally, David just said fuck it and blurted it out—not the polished, carefully crafted way he'd practiced on the drive home, but the message came out:

"Josh, I just wanted to tell you that I'm really damn proud of you and will always love you."

Josh looked at him awkwardly and half-smiled. "Uh, thanks, Dad. That's... nice."

David nearly kicked himself. He'd said the second part but forgot the first—the part about it being okay if Josh was gay. Shit!

"Uh..." David stammered. "Listen, what I meant to say is... uh..."

Josh stared. This was definitely one weird drive-through conversation.

"Josh, if you're gay, it's completely okay with us." David practically blurted it out, then looked over at his son, who looked a little surprised.

"Dad—"

"Listen son, I'm sorry for being so fucking direct, and maybe I'm wrong, but I get the sense that—"

"Dad—"

"Just let me get this off my chest. I want the best for you, and—"

"Dad—"

"I know you don't really have any girlfriends, at least that your mom and I know about—"

"Dad!" Josh raised his voice slightly. He really didn't like confrontation.

"And that's fine, you don't have to tell us every damn thing about your private life, but I just never told you that—"

"DAD!"

David stopped mid-sentence. "What?"

"The car moved," Josh said quietly, pointing to the vacant spot ahead of them. Feeling foolish, David pulled up and hit the brake. "Sorry, I just... I just wanted to say, Joshua, I love you. Always have, always will. And if you're gay, that's great. Or if you're straight, or whatever the hell you are, I don't give a damn. I just want you to know how proud we are of you and that we'll always love and support you!"

Josh had looked down—his usual thing—but he was smiling a little.

"What? Did I say something wrong?" David worried.

"No, Dad. You said it just right. I just... wasn't expecting it."

"Well, sorry to spring that shit on you."

"Car."

"What?"

"Car moved ahead, Dad."

"Oh." David pulled up to the speaker.

"Welcome to Burger King. How may I take your order?" came a middle-aged woman's gravelly voice. Didn't teenagers used to work at places like this? "Uh, two number threes, one without cheese, and a Coke Zero." He laughed inside. Who orders a greasy hamburger and fries only to drink sugar-free soda?

"Dad?"

David snapped out of his thoughts. "Yeah, bud?"

"I... uh... I don't really know what I am yet."

It took David a moment to switch gears from hamburgers back to their conversation.

"That'll be $19.37," came from the speaker. "Pull around."

David drove to the next window and stopped.

"Joshua, it's totally okay to not know. I just wanted you to know that your mom and I will always be in your corner, no matter what."

Josh smiled again, this time looking a little embarrassed the way you do when your dad tells you he loves you.

"Dad?"

"Yeah, bud?"

"I... sometimes I think guys are... you know. Good-looking."

"Oh yeah? Well, that's something. Some guys are pretty damn handsome."

"Yeah, I guess."

David realized that wasn't quite right. "Josh?"

"Mmm?"

"Did I ever tell you about the first time I saw Prism?"

"No." His face lit up.

"Hang on." David drove up and paid before turning back. "Yeah. I thought he was a really good guy. Treated your mom and Ken well, always seemed so protective of people he cared about."

Josh seemed more interested as they waited for their food.

David laughed. "I remember them grilling me about your mom and my 'intentions,' like it was 1890 or some shit. But I could tell they were just looking out for her. Funny thing is, she'd kick anyone's ass, including mine, if someone tried to mess with them!"

They both laughed, sharing knowledge of Rebecca's fierce protectiveness.

"But Josh, your Uncle Prism... well, if I were gay..." David felt himself blushing.

Josh blushed too. "Dad! Oh my god, stop!" he laughed.

"No, listen. I'm straight and I know it. But I also know that if I weren't, someone like Prism would've been exactly my type."

"Dad! You're embarrassing both of us!" Josh laughed, covering his face.

"I'm serious, bud. I'm comfortable being who I am—took some time to figure that out, but I know I love your mom and she's the most attractive woman in the world to me. But I can still recognize when someone has that... I don't know, that thing that makes you wonder if they're meant for you. And that's perfectly normal."

Josh listened, getting what his father was trying to say.

"Look, Josh, some guys like guys, some don't. But it doesn't matter a damn bit—at least not to me, and you know it sure as hell doesn't matter to your mom."

"Wouldn't... wouldn't..." Josh got shy, his default mode.

"What's that, Joshua?" David looked ahead, not forcing eye contact, knowing this was Josh's moment to share what he wanted, when he wanted.

The drive-through window opened with their bag of hamburgers and drinks, interrupting everything. It always seemed to happen that way—just when you're getting to the important stuff, some trivial bullshit interrupts. Joshua went quiet.

David passed the food to Josh, thanked the worker, and drove away. As they drove home quietly, David wanted to ask Josh to finish his thought, but knew better than to push. Still, this felt unfinished. He took a chance:

"Josh, you seemed like maybe you were worried about something before we got interrupted." He glanced at his son, face lit by the setting sun, casting long shadows that made his thoughtful expression even more pronounced.

"I... well... Dad?"

"Yeah?"

"Would Mom be disappointed if I..."

David knew to stay quiet. Just the hum of the road.

"...if I never gave you guys grandkids?"

There it was.

"I don't think so, buddy. Why?"

"Because I... uh..."

More waiting. More road sounds.

"I... I..." Josh's voice got smaller, and David could see him starting to tear up. He glanced over and saw the way Josh was gripping the food bag, trying to hold something back.

"Josh?"

"Yeah," barely a whisper.

"I love you, son. You're safe with me." David knew not to reach for him yet, but Josh needed to know he was loved and supported. Those were the only words that mattered right now.

Josh slowly raised his left hand, like he was fighting against something invisible. David gently reached over and took his son's hand—something he hadn't done in years. The moment their hands connected, Josh's whole body seemed to relax, his shoulders dropping, and the tears he'd been holding back finally came. Quiet tears, not of sadness, but of something deeper.

David drove one-handed and held his son's hand for the few minutes it took to get home, only letting go when they pulled into the garage. They sat in silence for a moment before getting out.

"Dad?"

"Yes, Joshua?"

"I'm not totally sure yet, but... I think... I think I might be..."

David stood quietly next to his son, letting his presence speak for itself, trying to surround Josh with all the love and acceptance he could manage.

"I think I'm gay," Josh whispered, like he was telling David the most important secret in the world.

David felt his heart swell with pride—not just that Josh was gay, but that his son had trusted him enough to share this part of himself. "Joshua, I'm so proud of you for telling me. And I'm so damn happy that you know I love you no matter what."

David was completely unprepared when Josh suddenly stepped forward and wrapped his arms around him. Josh rarely initiated physical contact, and David wasn't sure how tightly to hold on, but in that moment he didn't care. He pulled his son close and held him tight. Josh's tears continued, but they felt different now—like relief, like coming home.

Saying it out loud, feeling his dad's arms around him, knowing he was loved and accepted—it all became real. More real than anything had felt in a long time.

As real as Tyler, who stood on the back porch watching through his own tears, remembering what it felt like to finally understand who you were and know you were loved for it.

# CHAPTER 31
# THE DIAGNOSIS

The phone rang at 9 AM Brisbane time, which Tyler had carefully calculated was 4 PM the day before in Portland. He'd been clutching the official packet of paperwork in his lap for two hours, waiting for what he hoped was a decent time to call.

"Tyler!" Bronwyn's voice came through the international connection, bright and surprised. "Well, this is a lovely surprise! How are you, mate?"

"Bronwyn," Tyler said, and she could hear the excitement in his voice immediately. "I wanted you to be the first to know... well, aside from Ken." He glanced at Ken, who was sitting beside him on their couch, watching with an encouraging smile. "I got the results back. It's official."

There was a pause on the line, then Bronwyn's voice came through warm and delighted. "Oh, Tyler! You went through with it! How do you feel?"

"Amazing," Tyler said, his voice getting stronger. "Like everything finally makes sense. I have this whole packet of information, and follow-up appointments, and learning exercises for... for high-functioning autistics." He said the words with a kind of wonder, like he was still getting used to them.

"That's bloody brilliant!" Bronwyn's enthusiasm crackled through the phone. "Now you can be a right and proper drama queen whenever you bloody well want to! And to everyone else who doesn't like it? Fuck all!"

Tyler burst out laughing, and Ken grinned at hearing Bronwyn's characteristic response through the phone.

"You know what it's like?" Tyler said, settling back into the couch, the packet of papers spread across his lap. "Learning about all this, finally understanding myself... it's like I've been walking through one of those haunted houses you go through at Halloween. The ones you pay for them to scare you."

"How do you mean?" Bronwyn asked gently.

"Like, you intentionally walk through it knowing you can't see anything about where you're going or who you're with, just so you can feel like you're with other people. And it's so scary, always waiting for something to jump out at you. Sometimes just the fear of knowing something is going to scare you is worse than when it actually happens."

Ken's smile faltered as he listened to Tyler's metaphor, really hearing what Tyler was describing.

"But you keep walking through it," Tyler continued, "because everyone else is walking through it too, and you want to be part of the group. You want to belong. So you just... stumble through in the dark, getting scared out of your wits, never knowing where you're supposed to go or how you're supposed to react."

Bronwyn's voice was softer when she spoke. "And now?"

"Now it's like someone finally turned on the lights. I can see where I am, I can see the path, I can see what was scaring me all along. It wasn't real monsters - it was just... me not understanding how my brain works."

There was silence on the international line for a moment. Bronwyn, on the other side of the world, was wiping tears from her eyes, disguising her emotional response behind the occasional "mmhmm" and "really?"

Ken wasn't so lucky. Tyler's description of stumbling through life in a constant state of fear and confusion, just to be near other people, had broken something open in his chest. He'd always known Tyler found certain things challenging, that he was "particular" about routines and environments, but he'd never understood it like this.

"Tyler," Ken said quietly, his voice thick. "I had no idea it was like that for you."

Tyler looked at Ken with surprise. "What do you mean?"

"I mean..." Ken's voice cracked. "I thought it was just hard sometimes. I knew you needed things organized, that crowds were difficult, but... God, Tyler, you make it sound like you've been terrified most of your life."

"Not terrified," Tyler said gently, finally understanding Ken's distress. "Just... confused. Always trying to figure out the rules that everyone else seemed to know automatically."

Ken wiped his eyes with the back of his hand. "It breaks my heart that you've been going through that alone."

"But I wasn't alone," Tyler said firmly. "I had you. I had Rebecca. And now I have Bronwyn, and Miss Evangeline, and Kit... I was never really alone, I just didn't have the words to explain what I was experiencing."

Tyler paused, looking down at the papers in his lap. "It's like I never learned to speak, and finally someone taught me how."

That's when Ken completely broke down, tears streaming down his face as he thought about all the times Tyler had struggled to explain his needs, all the moments when Ken had been patient but hadn't really understood the depth of what Tyler was navigating.

"Ken?" Bronwyn's voice came through the phone. "You okay, love?"

"I'm sorry," Ken managed. "I'm just... I'm overwhelmed. In a good way. I'm so happy for Tyler, but also... I feel like I should have understood better."

"Ken," Tyler said softly, "you understood perfectly. You made space for me to be myself before either of us had words for what that meant."

Ken nodded, still crying, then gestured for the phone. "Bronwyn? It's Ken."

"Hi, Ken," Bronwyn said warmly. "Tyler's told me lovely things about you."

"I wanted to thank you," Ken said, his voice still thick with emotion. "For what you did for him. For helping him understand himself."

"Oh, love, I didn't do anything special," Bronwyn said. "I just shared my brother's story."

"You gave him words," Ken said. "You gave him permission to explore who he really is. That's... that's everything."

There was a pause on the line, then Bronwyn's voice came through softer. "Tyler's lucky to have you, Ken. Someone who loves him enough to cry happy tears over his self-discovery."

"I'm the lucky one," Ken said, looking at Tyler with such love that Tyler felt his chest tighten with emotion.

Tyler took the phone back. "Bronwyn, I can't thank you enough. For everything. For seeing me, for understanding, for being brave enough to share Jamie's story with a complete stranger."

"You weren't a complete stranger," Bronwyn said firmly. "You were someone who needed to know he wasn't alone. And besides, it's done me good too, talking about it all. Made me appreciate my brother even more."

"How is Jamie doing?" Tyler asked.

"Brilliant. Still driving me mental with his indecisiveness, but brilliant. He's been asking about you, actually. Wants to know how the American who reminded me of him is getting on."

Tyler smiled. "Tell him I said thank you. For being brave enough to figure himself out first, so that when I needed to understand, there was a path to follow."

"I will. And Tyler?"

"Yeah?"

"Welcome to the club, mate. It's a good club to be in."

After they hung up, Tyler and Ken sat quietly on their couch, Tyler's diagnosis papers spread between them like a map of newly discovered territory.

"How do you feel?" Ken asked softly.

Tyler considered this. "Like I've been living in a foreign country my whole life, and someone finally gave me a guidebook written in my language."

Ken reached for Tyler's hand. "I love you exactly as you are. Diagnosis or no diagnosis. But I'm so happy you finally have words for your experience."

"Me too," Tyler said. "And Ken? Thank you for loving me through all those years in the haunted house. For being my light even when I couldn't see where I was going."

Ken squeezed his hand. "Always."

They sat together in comfortable silence, both of them understanding that something fundamental had shifted. Tyler finally had language for his experience, and Ken finally understood the courage it had taken Tyler to navigate the world all these years. It was a new beginning for both of them.

# CHAPTER 32
# COMING DOWN

Despite being his nephew, Prism felt that Joshua had grown up to be one of the most intelligent people he'd ever known. His quiet wit, his excellent academic and research-oriented mind, clever use of rhetoric, insatiable thirst for knowledge and truth - all of it impressed his uncle practically on a daily basis. Until he wasn't, that is. For example, the stupid shit he was attempting to do now.

He'd been digging through one of Tyler and Ken's old boxes, sorting out keychains, old papers, a couple of photo albums and other random shit, but got a wild hair and decided he wanted to keep some of it—at least he'd ask Prism if he could when he saw him next. Even with the box half-emptied, it was still awkward as hell and heavy considering he was trying to walk backwards down the old wooden ceiling ladder with the damn thing basically on top of his head.

Stepping onto the third rung down, he misjudged the step because the box was blocking his view and slipped. It all happened so fast: The box tilted and smacked the access hole in the ceiling while Josh's instinct was to let go and grab at anything to prevent his fall. Unfortunately, there was jack shit to grab onto and Josh nearly ate it backward and down.

That's when he felt it.

A sudden burst of energy caught him—like grabbing a live

wire, but not painful. More like getting zapped by the world's most intense static shock. It slowed his fall and gently guided him down to the floor. The box somehow wedged itself between the ladder opening and the ceiling, balanced like some circus act as Josh looked up and then down again, trying to process what the hell had just happened.

"Holy shit! You alright, bud?"

Tyler appeared beside him, looking like he'd just watched his nephew nearly break his neck, which, let's face it, he had. He was checking Josh over for cuts and bruises like a worried parent. This was the closest Josh had ever been to his uncle physically since... well, since he was little and rode on Tyler's shoulders. And now he got why Tyler usually kept his distance. Whatever Tyler was made of now, it was like standing next to a fucking Tesla coil. Josh could still feel it buzzing through his back and legs where Tyler had caught him.

"Oh fuck! Oh fuck! Oh fuck!" Josh let out a string of swears that would've made his mother proud. His heart was trying to beat its way out of his chest.

"Easy there, sailor. You're okay. I got you." Tyler's voice had that calm, steady thing going on, but Josh could tell he'd been scared too.

Josh stepped back, still feeling like he'd been plugged into a wall socket. He kept rubbing at his back and legs where Tyler had caught him—it wasn't bad, just intense as hell, like every nerve ending was doing the electric slide. While he tried to shake off the weird sensation, Tyler scrambled up and rescued the box.

"So where were you planning on hauling this treasure chest?" Tyler asked, carrying it into Josh's room like it weighed nothing.

"Uh..." Josh was still trying to get his pulse back under the speed of light. "I was gonna put it in my room. Christ, that nearly... Prism, thank you for catching me. I just... holy shit!"

Tyler set the box down next to the computer desk and turned back to Josh with this look—like he cared but was trying to play it cool.

"Here, park your ass and breathe for a minute," Tyler said,

gesturing to the bed. "You're gonna be fine, just need to give your-self a sec to stop vibrating. Hell, if that had been me, I would've shit myself, wet my pants, and probably thrown up for good measure."

Josh couldn't help but laugh at that, even though he was still shaky. He dropped onto the mattress, still working at his legs where that strange energy was slowly fading. It wasn't unpleasant, exactly, just... different. Like his skin was humming some weird tune. Tyler watched him for a moment to make sure he wasn't going to keel over, then seemed to get distracted by his box of old crap.

"So what's in here that was worth risking life and limb?" Tyler started digging through his stuff, his voice taking on this nostalgic tone. "Let's see... random junk, old paperwork, probably some expired condoms from the Clinton administration..."

Josh snorted. "Gross, Uncle Tyler!"

"Hey, better safe than sorry!" Tyler grinned, then his hand stopped on something. Josh watched his uncle's face completely change—part pride, part holy-shit-I-can't-believe-this.

"Well, I'll be damned. Look at this thing."

After a few minutes, Josh's breathing settled and the electric feeling started to fade. His curiosity kicked in—because honestly, watching Tyler get all sentimental was kind of fascinating—and he got up to see what had captured his uncle's attention.

Josh stood next to him, looking over his shoulder. He normally kept some distance from Tyler—being near him was like standing next to high voltage wires on a good day—but after Tyler had liter-ally saved his ass, he didn't give a damn about personal space.

"I hadn't seen that yet. You look... actually happy," Josh said, studying the photo on whatever Tyler was holding.

Tyler held up a KPMG employee ID card, staring at his younger self in the picture. "I was. Happier than a pig in shit to be part of something... well, big. Like I was actually worth something, you know? Not just some weird kid who couldn't figure out how to talk to people without wanting to crawl under a rock."

Tyler had never been big on getting his picture taken. Most of the time he looked like he was constipated or having some kind of medical emergency. But this one—this one had actually come out decent. Thank Christ he never had to deal with all the social media bullshit that came after—the endless quest to look like some Instagram model and pretend you're living your best life while eating avocado toast. He would've told that whole scene to go fuck itself.

"What? Were you actually worried you wouldn't get hired?" Josh couldn't wrap his head around Tyler being scared of anything, especially getting a job. I mean, Prism was basically a walking genius. He knew all kinds of people, had been everywhere, could probably solve world hunger if he put his mind to it...

"Worried? Kid, I was so terrified I practically didn't even apply."

"What the hell?!" Josh couldn't believe his ears. Uncle Tyler was... scared shitless?

"Your mom and Ken got me that job."

"How?" He was completely blown away. "How could Mom and Uncle Ken get you a job? That seems completely insane. You're so... smart and cool and..."

"I was a fucking disaster, Josh!"

"What?!"

"Seriously. A complete mess." Josh looked like he was caught between laughing and thinking his uncle was completely full of shit. Tyler had everything going for him—how could he have been a disaster?

"I really was. I mean, long before I knew I was..."

"Autis... how do you say it again?"

"Autistic."

"Yeah, that."

"Long before I figured that shit out, I just knew that job fairs were basically my personal version of hell. You had to go to this huge campus thing and talk to recruiters with like a million other desperate college kids. It was loud as fuck, crowded, and basically designed to make people like me want to curl up in a corner and die."

"Sounds like a complete nightmare."

"Right? So I told myself I'd just apply online and avoid that clusterfuck entirely. Seemed like a brilliant plan at the time."

Josh was cracking up. It was weird but awesome hearing his uncle talk like this—raw and real instead of polished.

"But Ken and your mom told me I was being a dumbass. Said I needed to show people what I was made of, or some motivational bullshit Ken was always spouting." Tyler laughed, remembering. "I loved Ken to pieces, but goddamn if he didn't sound like a self-help book sometimes."

"So what made you actually go?"

"Your mom threatened to kick my ass."

"Mom? She actually threatened violence?" Josh was dying. "That's fucking hilarious!"

"Oh, she did more than threaten." Tyler grabbed his butt and pretended to wince. "Woman's got hands like a linebacker when she wants to make a point."

They were both cracking up now.

"Actually, she and Ken figured out I was completely fucked up about the whole thing..."

"You're not fucked up, Uncle Tyler."

"You know what I mean, smartass." Tyler stuck his tongue out. "So they went all covert ops on my ass."

"Covert ops?"

"They planned the whole damn thing like we were infiltrating enemy territory. Came in early to scout the location, figured out escape routes, timed how long I could handle being in that madhouse before I'd lose my shit..."

"Holy crap."

"Yeah, and then they took turns being my wingmen. One would walk with me to interviews while the other kept watch for potential disasters. It was like having bodyguards, except instead of protecting me from assassins, they were protecting me from having a complete meltdown in front of corporate recruiters."

"That's actually kind of badass."

"It worked, though I was ready to say fuck it all and bail right before my last interview. You probably would've been right there with me—it was absolutely insane. People everywhere, everyone trying to out-bullshit each other about their qualifications..."

"Sounds like a complete shitshow."

"Oh, it was. Total chaos." Tyler leaned back against the desk, grinning at the memory.

"So what happened? How'd you actually get the job?"

"Well, I was about to tell the whole thing to kiss my ass when Ken and your mom basically dragged me to one last interview. So I sucked it up, walked over to this KPMG guy who looked about as thrilled to be there as I was..."

"Wait, he wasn't into it either?"

"Hell no. Poor bastard looked like he'd rather be getting a root canal. But that's exactly why we clicked—we were both barely tolerating the circus around us. Turned out he was probably wired a lot like me, just better at hiding it."

Tyler held up his old ID again, that proud grin coming back.

"And that's how your uncle went from social disaster to corporate success story!"

"No shit. And thanks to your mom and Ken basically being your personal life coaches."

Josh could picture the whole thing—his mom and Uncle Ken running interference while Tyler tried not to have a panic attack in a room full of suits.

"Christ, they probably needed therapy after that!" Josh was still laughing.

"Are you kidding? They got so drunk celebrating that night, I had to drive them home. Ken kept telling everyone at the bar that he'd just 'launched a future executive into the stratosphere' or some shit like that."

They were both cracking up now, and the room felt warm and easy. Josh was thinking about how this incredible, successful guy had been just as anxious and overwhelmed as he often felt. And Tyler had people who loved him enough to literally engineer his success.

The same way Tyler had just literally kept Josh from breaking his neck.

"Prism?"

"Yeah, bud?"

"I came out earlier. To Dad."

Josh said it casually, like he was mentioning he'd had a sandwich for lunch. After everything Tyler had just shared—after Tyler had caught him when he fell—it felt natural. Easy.

"No shit. How'd that go?" Tyler's response was just as casual, like Josh had told him the weather.

"You already know, don't you?"

"Well, yeah."

"How? Did you always know I was gay?"

"Nah. But I was hanging out on the porch when you and your dad had your little heart-to-heart in the driveway."

Josh's face broke into a huge grin as he grabbed a pillow and whipped it at his uncle, who ducked and started laughing.

"That's totally cheating! No fair eavesdropping!"

"Hey! I was there first. You two just happened to walk into my personal space."

"I didn't even see you."

"You had other things on your mind. Like trying not to have a panic attack about telling your dad you like boys."

"Yeah, pretty much."

"And how do you feel about it now?"

Josh flopped back on his bed, staring up at the ceiling with its glow-in-the-dark solar system stickers that still annoyed him because they weren't to scale.

"Good, I think. I mean, I'm still a virgin who's never even kissed a guy, so it's not like I have a lot of experience to base this on."

"Doesn't matter, kiddo. It's not about what you've done—it's about who you are."

"Yeah, but how do I know who that is?"

Tyler leaned forward, getting serious for a minute.

"You figure it out by paying attention to what feels right. Like we talked about before—someone's gonna find you eventually, and when they do, the best thing you can be is completely comfortable with who you are. The rest of the shit will figure itself out."

Josh thought about that and nodded. "I guess that makes sense. When I told Dad..." he trailed off, like he was trying to find the right words to explain something he didn't quite understand himself.

Tyler could see him working through it, so he kept quiet and let Josh figure out what he wanted to say.

"I just felt like it was right. Like I was finally saying something true instead of just... I don't know, pretending or avoiding it."

"Then that's your answer. That's how you know."

"You really think so?"

"Kid, I know so."

Josh looked over at his uncle and smiled. "Then yeah. I'm gay."

"Welcome to the club. We have better music and way more fun at parties."

Josh burst out laughing. "Oh my god, you're such a stereotype!"

"What's that supposed to mean?" Tyler pretended to look offended.

"You're so gay that unicorns probably follow you around spraying confetti out of their butts!"

"Oh, you little shit!" Tyler jumped up and Josh yelped, but he was laughing so hard he could barely breathe.

Downstairs, Rebecca had just stumbled in from her Uber ride back from girls' night pottery painting. She was pleasantly buzzed and happy, but when she heard yelling and commotion from Josh's room, she figured David was up there goofing around with their son. She tossed her purse on the counter and wandered into the family room, where David was parked in front of the TV, looking like he hadn't moved in hours.

"Hey babe," David said without taking his eyes off the screen. "Have a good time?"

"Yeah, it was fun. We actually managed to talk shit about everyone in between painting those goddamn pots. The things I go through just to be with those women!" Rebecca said, causing David to laugh.

"You're such a martyr," he replied. "I made some popcorn, if you want."

She plopped down on her side of the sofa and belched, giggling at how loud it was, prompting David to give her the 'I know you're buzzed, but that's disgusting' look. Whatever, she thought, but glanced up at the ceiling as more laughter drifted down from Josh's room. Didn't David hear all that commotion? Who the hell does Josh have over at... she looked at her watch... 9:37 at night anyway?

# CHAPTER 33
## CAREERS

Rebecca stirred her latte, watching Ken demolish a chocolate croissant like he hadn't eaten in weeks. Their weekly "girls' night out" had been sacred since before Ken and Tyler moved in together —a chance for them to gossip about hot guys, debate whether Ken's latest fashion obsession was brilliant or ridiculous, and generally talk shit about whatever was currently consuming their lives.

Tonight's agenda was more serious, though.

"Okay," Rebecca said, leaning forward like she was about to share the world's juiciest secret, "I need to talk to you about Tyler and this whole career fair clusterfuck."

Ken paused mid-bite, croissant crumbs on his lip. "What about it?"

"Well, I keep thinking it could be really fucking good for him. Like, really good. Some of the best companies only recruit on campus, and Tyler's got the grades and the brains to blow them away." Rebecca traced the rim of her coffee cup with her finger. "But..."

"But Tyler would rather stick hot needles in his eyeballs than deal with a sweaty gymnasium full of networking assholes," Ken finished.

"Exactly! And even if we somehow convinced him to go, can you imagine? He'd be so freaked out just trying to get from booth to booth that by the time he actually talked to a recruiter, he'd probably grunt out one-word answers and look like a deer in headlights."

Ken sighed dramatically. "You're not wrong, babe. Tyler's fucking brilliant once you get to know him, but first impressions in chaotic shitshows... not exactly his wheelhouse."

"But that's just it!" Rebecca said, getting worked up. "Once people actually talk to him—like, really talk to him—they see how incredible he is. He's methodical as hell, asks these insightful questions that make you think... any recruiter with half a brain would see his potential immediately."

"So what's rattling around in that devious little head of yours?"

Rebecca chewed her lip. "I don't know. Maybe I'm being a nosy bitch and sticking my nose where it doesn't belong. It's Tyler's life, not ours, right?"

Ken considered this while licking chocolate off his fingers. "But you really think this could be huge for him?"

"I do. I think this could be like finding a fucking diamond that he'd never get the chance to dig up anywhere else." Rebecca slumped back in her chair. "I just don't know how to make it work for someone whose brain goes into meltdown mode around crowds."

"What if..." Ken said slowly, "what if we made it less of a complete nightmare? Like, broke it down into manageable chunks instead of throwing him into the whole overwhelming shitshow?"

Rebecca perked up. "What do you mean?"

"Well, we could do our homework first. Research which companies he'd actually give a damn about, figure out the least hellish routes through that madhouse, build in tons of breaks so he doesn't lose his mind." Ken paused, getting excited about the idea. "And maybe—this is crazy, but maybe I could practice interviewing with him beforehand. Help him get comfortable with the usual recruiter bullshit, so he can focus on being amazing instead of freaking out about small talk."

"Holy shit, you think that could actually work?"

"I think Tyler's a hell of a lot better when he knows what to expect. If we give him a real plan—like, a serious fucking plan with backup options and escape routes—he might actually be willing to try it."

Rebecca grinned wickedly. "I love it. But how do we bring this up without making it sound like we think he's some kind of helpless baby who can't handle shit on his own?"

"Very, very carefully," Ken said. "And with really fucking good food."

The following week, Ken spent three days perfecting a chicken stir fry recipe. It wasn't exactly groundbreaking cuisine, but it was new for their dinner rotation, and Ken had learned that Tyler was more receptive to new ideas when he was relaxed and well-fed.

"This is really good," Tyler said, taking another bite. "Where'd you get the recipe?"

"My mom," Ken replied. "She said it was foolproof, even for someone who burns water."

Rebecca laughed. "Speaking of foolproof plans, I was thinking about that career fair coming up..."

Tyler's fork paused halfway to his mouth. "Rebecca, we've talked about this. I'm not going to that chaos."

"I know, I know. But hear me out." Rebecca held up her hands. "What if it didn't have to be a complete clusterfuck? What if we made it actually manageable?"

"How the hell would we do that?" Tyler asked skeptically.

Ken jumped in. "Well, we could do our homework first. Figure out which companies you actually give a shit about, so you don't waste time wandering around like a lost puppy. And we could map out the layout, plan the best routes to avoid the worst of the chaos..."

"And build in breaks," Rebecca added. "Like, we'd hit one or two booths, then get the fuck out for some air. No pressure to stay if it turns into a nightmare."

Tyler looked between them. "You two have really thought about this, haven't you?"

"We just think you're fucking amazing," Rebecca said earnestly, "and we want to make sure you get every shot at showing potential employers how amazing you are."

"But what if I completely freeze up? What if I can't think of what the hell to say?"

"That's where the practice comes in," Ken said. "I could help you prep. We could run through the usual recruiter questions, practice your elevator pitch, get you comfortable with the whole dog and pony show."

Tyler was quiet for a long moment, staring down at his plate. "I don't know, guys. You really think this crazy plan could work?"

"I think you're brilliant," Rebecca said firmly. "And I think once a recruiter gets past the initial small talk bullshit and actually talks to you about your work, your ideas, your potential... they're going to see what we see."

Tyler shifted uncomfortably. "But what if I just... what if I can't do it? I mean, I know you both think I'm smart and everything, but I'm not good at this stuff. Meeting new people, talking to strangers..." He trailed off, looking embarrassed. "I don't know why it's so hard for me when it seems easy for everyone else."

Ken and Rebecca exchanged a quick glance.

"Tyler," Ken said gently, "there's nothing wrong with finding social stuff challenging. Lots of people do."

"Not like this," Tyler said quietly. "Not like me. I can see you guys trying to help because you know I'll mess it up on my own."

"Hey," Rebecca said firmly. "We're not trying to help because we think you'll mess up. We're trying to help because we love you and we want you to have every possible advantage. There's a difference."

Tyler looked up at them, still uncertain. "You really think I won't just freeze up and make a fool of myself?"

"We think," Ken said, "that with the right preparation and the right conditions, you're going to show them exactly how incredible you are."

Tyler took a deep breath. "Okay. Let's try this insane plan. But if it turns into a complete disaster, we bail immediately. And... thanks. For understanding that I'm weird about this stuff."

"You're not weird," Rebecca said. "You're just Tyler. And Tyler happens to be pretty fucking wonderful."

Tyler's eyes got a little watery, and he looked down at his plate again, clearly trying to compose himself. He'd spent most of his life feeling like he was somehow broken, like everyone else had received some manual for social interaction that he'd never gotten. To have people not just accept his differences but actually value them...

"Sorry," he said quietly, wiping his eyes with the back of his hand. "I'm not used to... people don't usually..."

"Hey," Ken said softly, reaching over to squeeze Tyler's shoulder. "You never have to apologize for having feelings."

Tyler nodded, but the dam had broken. "It's just... I've always felt like I was doing everything wrong. Like there was some secret everyone else knew that I missed out on." His voice cracked slightly. "And it's so fucking exhausting, trying to figure out how to be normal all the time. Watching other people to see how I'm supposed to act, what I'm supposed to say..."

Ken and Rebecca exchanged a look of dawning understanding. They'd known Tyler struggled socially, but this... this was deeper than they'd realized. This was a lifetime of feeling fundamentally different, of carrying a weight they hadn't fully comprehended.

"Tyler," Rebecca said softly, her usual bravado completely gone.

But Tyler wasn't finished. The words kept coming, like he'd been holding them back for years. "I watch you guys, and you just... you know how to talk to people. You know when to laugh, what jokes to make, how to read a room. And I'm over here analyzing every interaction like it's a math problem, trying to figure out if I'm doing it right."

His voice broke completely then, and Ken didn't hesitate—he pulled Tyler into his arms without asking, something he'd never done before. Tyler stiffened for just a moment, then melted into the embrace, letting himself be held while he cried.

Rebecca felt her own eyes filling with tears, watching her two boys—Tyler finally letting himself be vulnerable, Ken holding him like he was something precious. She reached across the table and put her hand on Tyler's arm, not saying anything, just being present.

They sat like that for several minutes, Tyler's quiet sobs the only sound in their kitchen. When he finally pulled back, wiping his face with his sleeve, he looked embarrassed but also somehow lighter.

"Shit," he said, laughing shakily. "I'm sorry, Rebecca. I didn't mean to fall apart in front of you."

"Don't you dare apologize," Rebecca said fiercely. "Do you have any idea how brave that was? Letting us see that?"

Tyler took a deep, shuddering breath. "So... you really think this plan can work? That I can... I can actually do this?"

Ken and Rebecca looked at him with such love and certainty that Tyler felt something tight in his chest finally loosen.

"Yes," Ken said firmly. "We've got you."

"We'll always have you," Rebecca added. "Always."

Tyler nodded, a small smile finally breaking through. "Okay then. It's a deal."

The next two weeks became Tyler Anderson Interview Boot Camp. Ken researched common interview questions and helped Tyler craft responses that highlighted his strengths. They practiced handshakes, eye contact, and small talk until Tyler felt more confident navigating those initial awkward moments.

Rebecca studied the career fair layout like she was planning a military operation. She identified quiet corners where Tyler could decompress, mapped out the most efficient routes between target companies, and even timed how long it would take to exit the building if Tyler needed to leave quickly.

But despite all their preparation, the night before the career fair, Tyler was a wreck.

"I can't do this," he said, staring up at the ceiling in their darkened bedroom. "What if I mess up? What if I make a fool of myself?"

Ken lay beside him, their hands linked in the darkness. This was how they had their most honest conversations—no pressure, no need for eye contact, just quiet truth shared in the safety of their bed.

"Tell me what you're really worried about," Ken said softly.

Tyler was quiet for so long that Ken thought he might have fallen asleep. Then, in a voice barely above a whisper, Tyler began to talk.

"It's like... my brain works differently than other people's," Tyler said slowly. "In crowds, with lots of noise and activity, it's like there's too much input and I can't process it all. I start to shut down, and then I can't think clearly or respond normally to questions."

Ken squeezed his hand encouragingly.

"And the social stuff is exhausting," Tyler continued. "I have to think about everything—how long to maintain eye contact, when to smile, what tone of voice to use. Most people do that automatically, but for me it's like... like I'm constantly translating between two languages."

"That sounds really hard," Ken said gently.

"It is. And I'm always worried that people can tell I'm working so hard at it. That they can see I'm different and they'll think something's wrong with me."

Ken turned onto his side, even though he knew Tyler couldn't see him in the darkness. "Tyler, there's nothing wrong with you. Your brain just works differently, and honestly? The way you think, the way you approach problems, the attention you pay to details that other people miss... that's not a weakness. That's a strength."

"You really think so?"

"I know so. And tomorrow, you're going to get a chance to show some very smart recruiters exactly how capable you are."

Tyler was quiet again, but Ken could feel some of the tension leaving his body.

"Will you stay close tomorrow?" Tyler asked. "Both of you?"

"We'll be right there," Ken promised. "Every step of the way."

The career fair was every bit as chaotic as Tyler had feared. The moment they walked into the gymnasium, he felt the familiar tightness in his chest as the noise and activity threatened to over-whelm him.

"Okay," Rebecca said, consulting her carefully prepared map, "let's start with a walk around the perimeter. Get a feel for the layout."

They'd planned to hit five companies over two hours, but by the time they'd visited three booths, Tyler was visibly drained. The conversations had gone well—Ken's interview practice had paid off—but the cumulative effect of the environment was taking its toll.

"I think maybe we should call it quits," Tyler said quietly as they stepped outside for their third break. "I'm starting to lose focus."

Rebecca checked her watch. "What if we just did one more? KPMG is next on our list, and you said before that you'd really like to work there."

Tyler hesitated. KPMG was one of the Big Four accounting firms—exactly the kind of place where he'd dreamed of starting his career.

"Just a quick conversation," Ken encouraged. "If it doesn't feel right, we can leave immediately after."

"Okay," Tyler said, taking a deep breath. "One more."

The KPMG booth was quieter than the others they'd visited. The main recruiter was taking a break, and the booth was being staffed by a younger man who looked almost as overwhelmed by the chaos as Tyler felt.

Tyler approached hesitantly. "Hi, I'm Tyler Anderson. I'm a senior in business administration, and I'm really interested in learning about opportunities at KPMG."

The assistant recruiter looked up with obvious relief. "Oh, thank god. Someone who gets straight to the point." He smiled genuinely. "I'm David Chen. Nice to meet you, Tyler."

What followed was the most natural conversation Tyler had had all day. David seemed to appreciate Tyler's direct communica-tion style and wasn't interested in small talk either. They moved quickly past pleasantries to discuss Tyler's academic background, his career interests, and his understanding of KPMG's client base.

"Your transcript is impressive," David said, reviewing Tyler's resume. "And your approach to problem-solving... it's exactly what we look for in our analysts. Detail-oriented, methodical, but also able to see the bigger picture."

Tyler felt himself relaxing for the first time all day. This wasn't the superficial networking he'd been dreading—this was a real conversation about work, about potential, about things that actually mattered.

"I'm impressed," David said, closing Tyler's portfolio with a nod. "You should expect to hear back from us within the next few weeks." He handed Tyler his business card with a slight smile that Tyler somehow knew meant it was a real promise, not just recruiter politeness.

Tyler noticed that David didn't make much eye contact during their conversation, but he wasn't sure if that was because Tyler himself was struggling with it, even after all of Ken's coaching, or if David was just focused on the resume.

"Thank you," Tyler said, shaking David's hand. "It was really great talking with you."

Walking the few steps over to Ken, who had been waiting just at the edge of the booth and watching, Tyler felt something light and buoyant in his chest.

"Well?" Ken asked, but immediately started walking, knowing they needed to get outside to fresh air and quiet.

"He said he was impressed," Tyler said as they headed toward the exit. "Said I should hear back in a few weeks, but the way he said it... I think he really meant it."

Ken grinned. "I told you you'd be amazing."

And then Tyler did something that surprised them both. Right there, in the middle of the crowded hallway with people streaming around them, Tyler pulled Ken into a hug and kissed him. It wasn't anything dramatic, but it was definitely public affection—something Tyler never did, especially not when he was already socially exhausted.

Rebecca, who had been trailing twenty feet behind and witnessed the whole thing, felt her heart squeeze with pride and love.

"What was that for?" Ken asked, a little breathless and completely swept off his feet.

"Thank you," Tyler said quietly. "For helping me, babe. I couldn't have done this without you."

Ken knew that spontaneous public display of affection had probably used up every ounce of social energy Tyler had left, but it meant everything to him.

"Yes, you could have," Ken said softly. "But I'm glad you didn't have to."

Three weeks later, Tyler got the call. KPMG wanted him for a second interview. A week after that, they offered him a position that exceeded every expectation he'd had for his first job after graduation.

"I can't believe it," Tyler said, staring at the offer letter. "They really want me."

"We can," Rebecca said, raising her beer in celebration. "We've always known how amazing you are. We just helped you show them."

That night, as they celebrated Tyler's success, Ken caught Rebecca's eye across the table. They'd done it—they'd figured out how to create the conditions that allowed Tyler to shine, without making him feel like he needed to be managed or protected.

"You know what this means?" Ken said to Tyler. "You're going to be a big shot corporate executive."

Tyler laughed. "Let's start with surviving my first day."

"You're going to do more than survive," Rebecca said confidently. "You're going to thrive."

And lying in bed that night, Tyler felt something he'd never quite experienced before—the absolute certainty that he could succeed in the professional world, not despite his differences, but because of them. Ken and Rebecca had helped him see that his careful, methodical approach wasn't a limitation to overcome, but a strength to leverage.

"Thank you," Tyler whispered in the darkness.

"For what?" Ken asked.

"For believing in me. For helping me believe in myself."

Ken squeezed his hand. "That's what family does."

And Tyler fell asleep knowing that whatever challenges his career might bring, he wouldn't face them alone.

# CHAPTER 34
# COMING OUT

David sat in his recliner, working his way through a bowl of popcorn and trying to focus on the final ten minutes of the Netflix series he'd been attempting to catch up on with Rebecca. The sound of the front door opening followed by an unmistakable belch made him smile despite himself.

*Graceful as ever,* he thought, listening to Rebecca's slightly unsteady footsteps in the hallway. He loved his wife dearly, but her girls' nights had a predictable pattern—cheap wine, loud conversation, and a return home with all the subtlety of a freight train.

Another belch echoed from the kitchen, and David couldn't help but chuckle. He'd been married to this woman for over two decades, and somehow her complete lack of pretense still charmed him, even when it was objectively gross.

The sounds from upstairs had quieted down about twenty minutes ago. Joshua had been unusually animated earlier—David had heard what sounded like genuine laughter, maybe even some roughhousing, which was decidedly uncharacteristic for his methodical, careful son. Whatever had put Joshua in such a good mood, David was grateful for it.

A sudden burst of muffled laughter echoed from Joshua's room above, followed by what sounded like someone flopping onto the bed. David glanced toward the ceiling as Rebecca's attention seemed drawn upward as well, then adopted his most innocent expression and began humming a little "I know something you don't know" tune under his breath.

"Spill it!" Rebecca demanded, appearing in the doorway with her finger pointed accusingly at him.

David placed his hand over his heart with mock sincerity. "I don't know what you mean? I'm just an innocent young man attempting to enjoy my popcorn while finishing up this wholesome television program."

Rebecca squinted at the TV screen, where two characters were in what could generously be called a passionate embrace. "Bullshit! If you're a young man, I'm Queen Victoria!" She gestured toward the television with her drunk hand. "And that's about as wholesome as soft-core porn in a preacher's house."

David nearly choked on his popcorn, laughing. "Your Majesty," he wheezed.

"Spill it!" she repeated, flopping onto the couch beside his chair.

"Let's just say... your son and I had a nice dinner."

"Yeah? McDonald's or did you upscale it to KFC?"

"If you must know, we met with royalty."

Rebecca's eyes lit up with delight. "Oh, Burger King! How... gross."

They both dissolved into laughter, and Rebecca let out another impressive belch that would have made a fraternity brother proud.

"Jesus!" David shook his head. "What the hell was in that wine you had?"

"I dunno... it sucked, but I did my royal duty and drank it, you know, so the girls didn't feel bad about bringing the cheap stuff."

"You definitely are a saint then, aren't you?"

Rebecca flipped him off with a grin.

David watched as his wife's expression shifted slightly, her senses sharpening despite the alcohol. "So... what did this son of mine have to say? Were you right?"

*Here we go,* David thought. Rebecca had been sensing something was different about Joshua for weeks now, that maternal radar that seemed to pick up on things even when she couldn't articulate what they were.

"Well, it was a good talk... but I think he should be the one to tell you."

"Oh, for God's sake, David. I'm tired. Can't you just give me a hint?"

"Nope."

"You're a dick, you know that?"

"Yep!" David said, grinning. "But I'm *your* dick."

"Good thing you've got something useful about you. Saves me on batteries." Rebecca laughed at her own joke while David just shook his head and turned back to the show.

"Fine!" she said, getting up and making her way toward the stairs with only slightly unsteady steps. "But I expect a full recount tomorrow."

David threw his hand up in a wave. "Night, honey."

She flipped him off again and belched.

David smiled as he listened to her climb the stairs. Twenty-three years of marriage, and that woman could still make him laugh until his sides hurt. He turned his attention back to the TV, but found himself listening to the muffled voices from upstairs. Whatever conversation was about to happen up there, he had a feeling it was going to be important.

Rebecca made her way up the stairs, holding onto the banister more for show than necessity. She wasn't *that* drunk—just pleasantly buzzed enough that everything seemed slightly more amusing than usual. The cheap wine Susan had brought tonight could strip paint, but Rebecca had dutifully consumed her share to be polite.

She paused at the top of the stairs, looking toward Joshua's room. The sounds she'd heard earlier—actual laughter, maybe even some kind of physical activity—had been so unlike her usually quiet, controlled son. It had made her heart lift to hear him being... well, young. Carefree. He was too serious most of the time, too careful, too contained.

*Whatever put him in that mood, I hope it happens more often,* she thought.

She appeared in his doorway and found Joshua sitting up on his bed, his usually pristine comforter rumpled and his hair slightly mussed. He looked... happy. Genuinely, openly happy in a way she hadn't seen in months.

"Hey, Mom."

She started to reply but was interrupted by her own belch, which sent both of them into laughter. David found her crude humor beneath him, but Joshua had inherited her appreciation for the ridiculous.

"Guess you had fun, then," Joshua continued, still laughing.

"You're in a good mood," she observed, walking over to sit on the edge of his bed. He really did look different—not his usual stoic, thoughtful self, but more... joyful. The word surprised her with its accuracy.

"Well... I... uh, guess..." Joshua's smile faltered slightly, as if he'd suddenly become self-conscious about his happiness.

*Don't you dare shut down on me,* Rebecca thought. *Not when you finally look like the twenty-one-year-old you are instead of a forty-year-old in a college student's body.*

"It sounded like you were doing cartwheels up here earlier," she said gently.

Joshua froze for just a moment—so briefly she almost missed it. "Just... watching a funny video online," he said quickly.

Rebecca knew bullshit when she heard it, but she also knew when to let something slide. Whatever had been making her son laugh so freely, she wasn't about to interrogate him out of it. If Joshua wanted to keep some joy to himself, so be it.

"How was your night?" Joshua asked, clearly steering the conversation away from his activities. "Did you paint a lot?"

Rebecca let him change the subject. She'd perfected this particular dance long before she'd given birth to this kid twenty-one years ago. "Oh, it was fun, but the goddamn wine was shit." Another belch escaped, sending them both into laughter again.

"But we wound up painting like... oh, I dunno... fifteen fucking ceramic mugs."

"Fifteen?"

"Yeah, I just painted as they passed them along. I don't even like them, but what the hell? I was too interested in Susan's son."

"Susan's... son? Was he there?"

Rebecca leaned in conspiratorially. Susan had been a godsend after Tyler and Ken died, especially during those late-night phone calls when Rebecca couldn't stop crying. Susan's approach was always the same: "Are we going to be having this same conversation this time next year?" It pissed Rebecca off just enough to pull herself out of the pity party and keep moving forward.

"What about her son?" Joshua asked, curious.

Rebecca lowered her voice like it was top-secret information. "Well... Susan said she got up in the middle of the night last week and heard something going on down the hall. She was out of it, still half asleep, so she wandered to see what it was and discovered him..." She paused for dramatic effect. "In bed fucking another guy!"

Rebecca laughed loudly, delighted by the gossip.

"No! She didn't!" Joshua exclaimed, a big "Let's Gossip" smile spreading across his face.

*There's my boy*, Rebecca thought. Joshua might be his own special breed of peculiar, but these little moments of shared gossip were some of her favorite memories with him.

"Swear to fucking God!" She crossed her heart. "I asked the same thing... I mean, Jesus! What would I have done if it had been you?"

She caught the slight wrinkle in Joshua's brow at that comment but continued without thinking too much about it.

"She said she slowly backed up and walked back to her room."

"That's... it? Didn't he see her?"

"I guess not... they must have been really going at it... I mean... I would've thought that if my MOM"—she emphasized the word, aware of the cheap wine on her breath—"walked in on me fucking some dude! I mean..."

"I'd be mortified!" Joshua finished for her.

"Right?"

As they continued dissecting Susan's son's nocturnal activities, Rebecca noticed Joshua seemed to retreat into what she'd learned to recognize as his "thinking" mode. His face grew thoughtful, and she could see him processing something deeper than their gossip session.

She'd learned this patience from Tyler, actually. You never noticed these thinking patterns until you lived with someone who needed processing time, and then suddenly you saw them every-where. Joshua was doing that thing Tyler used to do—twirling the fabric of his comforter in a pattern with his hands without even realizing it.

"Mom?"

"Yes, darling."

"Uh... what would you really do if that had been me?"

For a moment, Rebecca's wine-buzzed brain didn't follow. "Been you what?"

Joshua's face flushed slightly. "You know..."

Then it hit her. He was asking about Susan's son and what she would really do if she'd walked in on Joshua with another guy.

"Oh... Ooohhhh. Oh. That." The conversation had shifted into serious territory, and Rebecca could feel herself sobering up. "Well... all joking aside, I would hopefully never just walk in on you regardless of who you were with... Well, unless you were being harmed or something... obviously."

Joshua nodded, but she could tell that wasn't exactly what he was asking.

"But... to the 'real' question... I'd be just fine... of course, you know that, don't you? Your uncle Tyler would come back and haunt me if I wasn't!" She laughed, but noticed Joshua scanning the room as if looking for something.

"Is... is that something you worry over?"

"Not... really worry about. I mean... I know about you and Uncle Ken and Tyler... and all that... but..."

He got quiet, and Rebecca felt her heart squeeze. Her beautiful, careful boy was struggling with something.

"But what, sweetheart? Are you afraid of something?"

Joshua seemed to consider the question seriously. "I... I just... I'm the only kid you and Dad have... and there'd never be..."

*Oh, baby,* Rebecca thought, understanding immediately. She leaned forward and brushed his bangs from his forehead—a gesture from when he was small that still seemed to comfort him.

"Baby?"

"Yeah, Mom?"

He might be twenty-one, but he was still her little boy. "Let me set you at ease... I have never worried if we have grandchildren or not. Knowing... no... *loving* your uncles and being part of their world... well... we made our own little family... and..."

The words caught in her throat unexpectedly. Years of carefully contained grief threatened to spill over, and she struggled to maintain composure. This was supposed to be about Joshua, not about her own losses.

"You miss him, don't you?" Joshua said softly.

"I miss both of them... tremendously... and..."

"Mom?"

"Yeah?"

"I'm gay."

The words hung in the air between them, simple and profound. Rebecca felt a single tear escape her left eye. "I know, baby... I know," she whispered.

"Are... is... everything okay? Are you... okay with... that?" Joshua seemed so small suddenly, so unsure.

"Of course I am, Joshua!" She enveloped him in a hug, feeling his worry dissolve as she held him close.

"Why... what are you sad?" he asked timidly.

"I'm not... sad... really... I just wish... I just..." She wiped her eyes, willing herself not to make this about her grief when it should be about her son's courage. "I just wish your uncles could be here to... I dunno... help you with it... or something... They would have been the perfect couple to..."

"What?" Joshua said, and she could hear the smile in his voice.

"Oh... do what those two homos always did!" she joked, trying to lighten the moment. "Shopping... parties... check out guys... you know?"

"Like you and Ken did when you met Prism?"

Rebecca's mind immediately went back to that day in the natatorium, remembering how she had practically tackled that poor, awkward boy in the diving well while Ken stood there completely gobsmacked. What she wouldn't give to see Tyler and Ken put Joshua through the same kind of well-intentioned chaos.

"Yeah... Yes! Exactly like that," she said, her spirits lifting at the thought. "Someone needs to teach you how to scope out guys properly... you know... weed the trash from the treasure. I guess I'll just have to do it myself since those two..."

"Oh my god! I'm not checking out guys with my mom!"

"Why not? I got your uncle Ken his husband, didn't I? I'd say I'm batting a thousand!"

"I cannot even imagine going to a swim meet... with you!" Joshua laughed and fell back onto his bed.

Rebecca loved seeing him this way—genuinely happy and relaxed. Maybe this was why he'd seemed so carefree when she'd first come into his room.

"You told your dad?"

"Oh yeah... earlier..."

"I heard you went to Burger King."

"Yeah... fancy!"

They both laughed. "Did Dad tell you?" Joshua asked.

"No... you know him. I'm the blabbermouth, remember? You did it in the right order, kiddo!"

She gave him another quick hug. As much as Joshua didn't usually care for physical contact, she could feel him cherishing the warmth and connection.

"Mom?"

"Mmm?"

"I wish Uncle Ken and Tyler could be here, too."

Rebecca could only nod, not trusting herself to speak without letting loose the tears she'd been holding back for years.

"But I like to think they are," Joshua continued.

Rebecca assumed he meant it the way most people do—that somewhere, somehow, those we love can look down from heaven and "be with us" in spirit. The comfort of believing their memories live on in our hearts.

But as she sat there holding her son, Rebecca couldn't shake the feeling that Joshua meant something more literal than that. Something in his voice, the way he'd scanned the room earlier, the genuine joy she'd heard when she first came upstairs—it all seemed to point toward something she couldn't quite name.

*Don't be ridiculous,* she told herself. *Grief makes you imagine things.*

But as she looked at her son's face, peaceful and happy in a way she hadn't seen in so long, Rebecca found herself hoping that maybe, somehow, Joshua was right. Maybe Tyler and Ken really were here, in whatever way mattered most.

# CHAPTER 35
## MISS EVANGELINE

Tyler had been in New Orleans for three days, and the city was everything he'd expected and nothing he was prepared for. The KPMG assignment was going well—reviewing financial systems for a mid-sized shipping company—but the sensory assault of the French Quarter, the humidity that seemed to wrap around him like a living thing, and the constant noise had left him feeling perpetually off-balance.

He'd found refuge in his hotel room each evening, ordering room service and calling Ken to decompress from days filled with too much input. The work was interesting, but navigating a city this intense while maintaining professional composure was exhausting in ways Tyler hadn't anticipated.

"You need to get out more," declared Marcus, one of his colleagues from the New Orleans KPMG office, as they wrapped up Thursday's client meetings. "You can't come to New Orleans and just hide in hotel restaurants. That's not experiencing the city."

"I'm experiencing plenty," Tyler replied, already dreading whatever Marcus had in mind. "The client dinners have been very... educational."

Sarah, another colleague, laughed. "Educational? Tyler, we've taken you to exactly one restaurant that wasn't in your hotel. You need real New Orleans food. Street food. The kind of cooking that makes this city famous."

"I prefer restaurants," Tyler said carefully. "Actual restaurants. With menus and... predictable service."

"Exactly the problem!" Marcus was already pulling out his phone. "We're going to fix that right now. There's this food truck that's supposed to be incredible—Miss Evangeline's. Won the food truck championship two years running, gets written up in all the food magazines."

Tyler felt his stomach clench. Food trucks meant crowds, lines, chaos, standing around in the heat while trying to figure out unfamiliar menus. "I don't really do food trucks."

"You do now," Sarah said firmly. "It's lunchtime, we're hungry, and you're getting a proper New Orleans experience whether you like it or not."

Twenty minutes later, Tyler found himself standing at the back of a line that stretched around the block, the lunch crowd pressing close in the humid afternoon heat. Miss Evangeline's food truck sat in a small lot off Canal Street, painted bright yellow with hand-lettered signs advertising gumbo, jambalaya, red beans and rice, and beignets. The smell was incredible—rich and spicy and completely overwhelming.

The noise level was exactly what Tyler had feared. People calling out orders, the truck's generator humming, conversations in multiple languages, car horns from the nearby street, music bleeding from storefronts. Tyler tried to focus on his breathing, on staying calm, but he could feel that familiar tightness starting in his chest.

"Look at that line," Marcus said approvingly. "You know it's good when locals are willing to wait in this heat."

Tyler nodded politely, trying not to show how overwhelmed he was becoming. The line moved slowly, people chatting and laughing around him while Tyler worked to process all the sensory input without shutting down completely.

When they finally reached the front of the line, Tyler got his first glimpse of Miss Evangeline herself. She was exactly what central casting would order for a New Orleans grandmother—a large, comfortable woman with graying hair pulled back under a colorful headband, wearing an apron that had seen serious kitchen duty. Her movements were economical and purposeful as she worked behind the small service window, calling out orders and managing what looked like controlled chaos.

But there was something else about her, something Tyler couldn't quite identify. A quality of attention, maybe, or presence. When she looked at customers, she really looked at them—not just taking their order, but seeing them in a way that made Tyler immediately uncomfortable.

"What can I get for you, honey?" Miss Evangeline asked when Tyler stepped up to the window. Her voice was warm molasses, tinged with an accent that spoke of decades in the Deep South.

"Um," Tyler glanced at the handwritten menu board, feeling overwhelmed by the options. "The gumbo, please. And..." He hesitated, not sure what else to order.

"You want some cornbread with that, sugar? And how about some sweet tea to cool you down in this heat?"

Tyler nodded gratefully, though he had no idea what sweet tea would taste like. Miss Evangeline moved with practiced efficiency, ladling gumbo into a container, wrapping cornbread in wax paper, filling a cup with amber liquid from a large dispenser.

"There you go, baby," she said, handing him the order. "You find yourself a nice shady spot to eat that."

Tyler paid and moved away from the window, following Marcus and Sarah to a cluster of picnic tables set up under a makeshift awning. The crowd was dense here too, people eating and talking, children running between tables, the general chaos of a popular lunch spot.

He took a sip of the sweet tea and immediately understood why Miss Evangeline had called it cooling. It was sweet—incredibly sweet, almost syrupy—and Tyler's entire mouth puckered in shock. He tried to hide his reaction, taking another sip and forcing himself to smile like he enjoyed it.

The gumbo, at least, was incredible. Rich and complex, with a depth of flavor Tyler had never experienced. The cornbread was perfect—slightly sweet, with a texture that somehow managed to be both dense and light.

But as Tyler ate, he became aware of being watched. Not obviously, not intrusively, but he could feel eyes on him from the direction of the food truck. When he glanced up, Miss Evangeline was looking directly at him through the service window, her hands busy with the next order but her attention clearly focused on Tyler.

The eye contact lasted only a moment before Tyler looked away, but something about her gaze was different from what he usually experienced. Most people's direct attention made him uncomfortable, made him want to escape or hide. But Miss Evangeline's attention felt... gentle. Curious rather than invasive.

Tyler tried the sweet tea again, managed to drink about half of it by taking very small sips and trying not to wince visibly. When Marcus and Sarah finished eating and declared themselves ready to head back to the office, Tyler was grateful to escape the crowded seating area.

"See?" Sarah said as they walked back toward their office building. "That wasn't so bad, was it?"

"The food was excellent," Tyler said honestly. "Really incredible."

"And you survived the food truck experience," Marcus added. "Maybe we'll make a proper New Orleans tourist out of you yet."

Tyler smiled and nodded, but as they walked back through the French Quarter, he found himself thinking about Miss Evangeline's gaze, the way she'd looked at him like she was seeing something he didn't know was visible.

That evening, Tyler sat in his hotel room, grateful to be back within the safety of its walls. The day's meetings had been productive but draining, and his sanctuary of a room—quiet, controlled, predictable—felt like a blessing after hours of navigating client interactions and the sensory chaos of New Orleans.

He reached for the phone to order room service, the same routine he'd followed for the past three nights. Room service was safe. No crowds, no noise, no unexpected variables. Just food delivered quietly to his door.

But as his hand touched the phone, something made him pause. He couldn't explain it—just a feeling, a quiet voice that seemed to whisper that he should put the phone down. That maybe tonight was different.

Tyler stared at the phone for a long moment, then slowly pulled his hand away. Instead, he found himself reaching for his jacket, drawn by an impulse he didn't understand but somehow trusted. The night air was marginally cooler than the day had been, and walking might help him process the residual tension from another day of intensive client work.

His feet carried him almost unconsciously back toward Canal Street, back toward the small lot where Miss Evangeline's food truck had been parked that afternoon. Tyler told himself he was just exploring the neighborhood, getting a feel for the city, but he knew he was curious about the woman who'd served him lunch.

The lot was much quieter now, the lunch crowds long gone. Miss Evangeline's truck was still there, but the service window was closed, and only a few small lights were on inside. Tyler was about to turn around and head back to his hotel when he heard a voice from behind the truck.

"I was wondering when you'd come back."

Tyler turned to see Miss Evangeline emerging from around the side of the truck, moving with that same purposeful grace he'd noticed at lunch. She'd changed out of her apron into a simple dress, but she still radiated that quality of presence that had caught his attention earlier.

"I was just..." Tyler started, then stopped, not sure how to explain what he was doing there.

"Just walking off a long day," Miss Evangeline finished for him, her voice matter-of-fact rather than questioning. "Those long meetings can be a lot for a soul who likes quiet."

Tyler blinked, surprised by her perceptiveness. "How did you...?"

Miss Evangeline smiled and gestured toward a picnic table that sat under a streetlight at the edge of the lot. "You want to sit for a while? I was just fixing to have some tea myself. And I bet you haven't had proper dinner yet."

Tyler found himself nodding before he'd consciously decided to stay. Miss Evangeline disappeared back into the truck for a moment, then emerged with two cups, what looked like a thermos, and a container that smelled wonderfully of the same gumbo he'd had at lunch.

They sat across from each other at the weathered picnic table, Miss Evangeline pouring tea that smelled of mint and something else Tyler couldn't identify. The streetlight cast a warm glow over the small space, and the noise of the city felt distant, muffled by the late hour and the intimate scale of their surroundings.

"This is different tea," Tyler said after taking a sip. It was still sweet, but gently so, and the mint made it cooling without being overwhelming.

"Different kind of sweet," Miss Evangeline agreed, settling back on her side of the picnic bench. "Some folks need the sugar rush, some folks need something more gentle."

She was quiet for a long moment, studying Tyler's face in the streetlight. Not staring, not making him uncomfortable, but looking at him with that same quality of attention he'd noticed at lunch.

"You looked a little overwhelmed today," she said finally, her voice soft. "During the lunch rush."

Tyler felt his cheeks warm. "It was pretty crowded."

"Mm-hmm." Miss Evangeline sipped her tea, considering. "Lots of noise, lots of people, lots of everything all at once."

Tyler nodded, surprised by her understanding. "I'm not really... I don't do well with crowds. Or noise. Or chaos in general."

"Nothing wrong with that, honey." Miss Evangeline's voice carried absolute certainty. "Some people are made for the middle of everything, and some people are made to see it all clearly from the edges."

Tyler looked up at her, startled by the observation. For a moment, their eyes met directly—something Tyler almost never managed with strangers—and he felt something he'd never experienced before. Instead of the usual discomfort, the urgent need to look away, Tyler found himself able to hold Miss Evangeline's gaze.

Her eyes were dark and kind, but there was something else there, something that seemed to shimmer just beneath the surface. Tyler had the strangest sensation of seeing light—actual light—emanating from somewhere behind her eyes, as if there was something luminous living inside her.

The moment lasted perhaps ten seconds, but it felt like longer. Tyler didn't feel anxious or overwhelmed. He felt... seen. Understood in a way that had nothing to do with words or explanations.

Finally, Tyler looked away, but gently, naturally, the way other people seemed to be able to do. He took another sip of tea, trying to process what had just happened.

Miss Evangeline was quiet for a long time, and Tyler began to understand that this wasn't awkward silence. This was the kind of quiet that held space for thought, for feeling, for understanding things that couldn't be rushed.

"You're the observant ones of the world," Miss Evangeline said finally, her voice carrying the weight of something larger than casual conversation. "It takes those like you to keep all the rest of us honest."

Tyler looked up, but Miss Evangeline wasn't looking at him now. She was gazing out into the night, her hands wrapped around her tea cup, her expression peaceful but distant.

"We owe a debt of gratitude for folk such as yourself," she continued, still not looking at him. "Seeing what needs to be seen, understanding what needs to be understood."

Tyler wanted to ask what she meant, wanted to understand the certainty in her voice, but something told him to wait, to listen.

Miss Evangeline turned back to him then, and when she smiled, Tyler felt that same sense of being truly seen. "You keep walking your life just as you are, honey. You'll understand who you are one day."

The words settled over Tyler like a benediction, carrying

weight he couldn't explain but somehow knew was important. Miss Evangeline's voice had taken on a quality that seemed to come from somewhere deeper than casual conversation, somewhere that touched the edges of things Tyler couldn't name.

They sat in comfortable silence after that, Tyler working his way through the gumbo Miss Evangeline had brought him from the truck, Miss Evangeline sipping her tea and gazing out into the New Orleans night. The streetlight created a small pool of warmth around their table, and the sounds of the city felt distant and manageable.

Tyler found himself relaxing in a way he hadn't since arriving in New Orleans. The quiet between them wasn't empty—it was full of understanding, of acceptance, of something that felt almost sacred. Miss Evangeline didn't need to watch him eat or make conversation to fill the space. She simply sat in her own peaceful presence, and Tyler could feel that presence like a blessing.

The gumbo was even better than it had been at lunch, and Tyler ate slowly, savoring both the food and the unexpected gift of this quiet communion. Miss Evangeline didn't need to look at him to know he was there, didn't need to speak to communicate her understanding. She felt his presence and that was enough.

Tyler had never experienced anything like it—this sense of being completely accepted without explanation, of being seen without having to perform or justify or explain himself. He ate his gumbo and watched the night, and beside him Miss Evangeline sat in her own quiet wisdom, and the silence between them held more truth than any conversation Tyler had ever had.

# CHAPTER 36
# DISCOVERY

"We owe a debt of gratitude for folk such as yourself," she continued, still not looking at him. "Seeing what needs to be seen, understanding what needs to be understood."

Rebecca looked up at her son, who had found this chapter tucked away in the back of one of Tyler's binders. Unlike every other piece of his meticulously organized collection, this one seemed hidden—stuffed into a pocket without color coding, tags, or bookmarks. Behind it was something even stranger: a story that started typewritten but finished in Tyler's unmistakable handwriting, so perfect it rivaled the machine but warm enough to feel the intent behind every word.

"Did you know about Miss Evangeline?" Joshua asked.

Rebecca set down the papers and leaned back in her chair. "Tyler mentioned her once or twice. Some old lady he met in New Orleans. Ken talked about her more afterwards."

"After what?"

"After Tyler came back from that trip." Rebecca's voice grew thoughtful. "Ken said Tyler seemed different. Not dramatically, but... different."

"How?"

"I don't know exactly. Ken noticed it more than I did. He said Tyler had gotten more... philosophical, I guess? Not religious—

God, no. Tyler would've laughed his ass off at that. But Ken thought he was thinking deeper about things. His place in the world, that kind of shit."

Joshua waited, sensing there was more.

"Ken was intrigued by it more than worried. Like whatever happened in New Orleans, whatever this Miss Evangeline said to Tyler, it had really gotten to him somehow." Rebecca shrugged. "It sounded confusing at the time, honestly."

"When did he go? It doesn't say on this paper."

Rebecca examined the document, turning it over as if dates might materialize. "A few months before..."

She stopped. They both knew what she meant. A few months before the accident. Before everything changed.

Rebecca's mind drifted to those early days after the funeral, when she'd told Joshua that his uncles were away on a long business trip. She'd been so fucking lost, so desperate to protect him from the truth that she couldn't even say the words "dead" or "gone." Just... away. Coming back when they could.

She remembered finding Joshua in his room, talking animatedly to no one. When she'd asked who he was talking to, he'd just shrugged and said it was his imaginary friend. She'd been relieved, actually. Kids needed ways to cope, and if pretending his uncles were still around helped him process their absence, what was the harm?

"Mom?"

Rebecca blinked back to the present. "Yeah, honey?"

"Do you... do you believe in heaven?"

The question caught her off guard. Rebecca almost laughed—not from cruelty, but from the memory of countless philosophical debates around their dinner table. Tyler, Ken, David, and herself, arguing about everything from politics to the meaning of life, usually over too much wine.

"I know what your uncle Tyler would say," she said with a sad smile.

"What?"

"'Heaven is a construct we've created to feel better about our ultimate loss—not being able to be with the ones we love.'" The words came back to her easily. Tyler had said it so many times, usually while gesturing wildly with whatever drink was in his hand.

She watched Joshua's face carefully. He was looking past her, almost like he was listening to someone else say the words along with her.

"But you know," Rebecca continued, "Tyler's thinking changed a little after that New Orleans trip. Not completely—he still thought organized religion was bullshit. But he started talking about energy. About connections between people that might persist somehow. Not some bearded guy in the clouds, but... something. The power we share with each other."

Rebecca found herself staring at the corner of the room where Joshua kept looking. Nothing there but shadows and afternoon light, but for just a moment...

"Tyler always had this energy about him," she said quietly. "This presence. And sometimes, since he died, I swear I can feel it. Just for a second. Like he's... around."

She felt foolish saying it, but also strangely comforted.

"Why do you ask about heaven, honey?"

Joshua was quiet for a long moment, still looking at that corner. "I just... I miss him sometimes. Uncle Prism. I miss them both."

"I know, baby. I miss them too."

Rebecca looked where Joshua was looking, at the empty space that somehow didn't feel empty at all. She thought about Tyler's handwritten words, about Miss Evangeline seeing something special in him, about energy and connections and love that doesn't end just because a heart stops beating.

"Sometimes," she said softly, "I like to think they're still here somehow. Not in some mystical bullshit way, but... you know. In the things they taught us. The love they gave us. The way they changed who we are."

Joshua nodded, tears threatening in his eyes. "Yeah. I like to think that too."

Rebecca reached over and squeezed his hand. In the corner of the room, the afternoon light shifted, and for just a moment, she could have sworn she felt Tyler's presence so strongly it took her breath away. Not supernatural, not impossible—just love, lingering in the spaces between words, in the silence between heartbeats, in the way grief transforms into something that feels almost like hope.

# CHAPTER 37
# DEBRIEF

Tyler was sprawled across their couch with his head in Ken's lap, finally relaxed for the first time in two weeks. Ken's fingers moved through Tyler's hair as they talked, both of them just happy to be together again.

"So tell me about the people you met," Ken said. "I wanna hear about everyone who was nice to you while I was stuck here missing your ass."

Tyler grinned up at him. "Well, there was this old lady who made the most incredible gumbo..."

"Oh yeah? Like a grandma type?"

"Miss Evangeline. She had this food truck, and my work people dragged me there for lunch. But she was... I dunno, special." Tyler paused. "She had this way of like, really seeing people."

Ken's fingers stopped moving. "What do you mean special? Like, magical?"

Tyler considered this. "She sorta was..."

"Like how?"

"Well, she didn't perform spells or anything..." Tyler laughed, and Ken joined him.

"But she told me stuff about myself," Tyler continued.

"Like what?"

Tyler hesitated. "Well... she knew about my..." He trailed off, not sure what to call it. He didn't have words yet for why his brain worked differently, why crowds freaked him out, why he needed things quiet and organized.

"Really? She just knew?"

"Yeah... like right away... didn't even have to talk to me... just looked right through me..."

"Her eyes..." Tyler's voice got weird, remembering. "There was this light..."

"Light?"

"Kinda... hard to explain."

Ken shivered. "That's creepy."

"It wasn't," Tyler said quickly.

"Is she a witch?"

"No, dummy..."

"Well?"

Tyler sat up, turning to face Ken. "Okay, promise you won't freak?"

"Uh... yeah, I guess..."

Tyler took a breath. "She pulled out these old cards after I ate my gumbo that night... they looked all beat up and worn, with writing in like old French or something..."

"Like Tarot cards?"

"I dunno."

"Did she read your fortune?"

"Well, not really, it wasn't like in movies..." Tyler shifted. "She told me that only some people in the world could connect with the cards... Nobody 'reads' them... you just connect with them... and she thought maybe I was one of those people..."

"No way!" Ken got goosebumps and pulled his feet up on the couch.

"And she tells me to take the cards... she can't use them... she's just been protecting them since her great aunt gave them to her like decades ago... and her aunt got them from way back..."

"So... what'd you do?"

"I reached over and took them."

"Weren't you scared?"

"Well, it was kinda weird, but she was so nice and... I dunno, it felt okay..."

"What happened?"

"Nothing really."

"NOTHING?"

"Well... I just opened them up and they were all dirty and frayed, but two cards fell out onto the table."

"And?"

Tyler closed his eyes, remembering. "The Hermit and The High Priestess."

"And?"

"She said the cards just told what I was... like a wise person who knows old stuff, someone who helps other people just by being real."

"You believe that?"

"I dunno... it was kinda... weird..."

"Then what?"

"We just sat there quiet again. I started to put the cards back to give them to her, but they were gone."

"What happened to them?"

"No idea."

"She must've taken them."

"She was looking away at the street."

Ken freaked out, then started laughing. "So you're like some wise old soul?"

"I guess."

"Holy shit."

Tyler grinned. "Oh, I forgot... I got you something..."

Tyler got up and dug through his suitcase, pulling out a small package. "Here."

Ken unwrapped it to find an old Tarot card - really pretty but obviously old, with gold that was wearing off around the edges.

Ken nearly dropped it. "Tyler! Is this...?"

Tyler smiled. "Welcome home present."

# CHAPTER 38
# REVELATION

David was asleep... had been for some hours. He always could sleep... snoring away even if it were a hurricane outside. But not Rebecca. She'd tossed a bit, then finally said the hell with it and pulled out her phone. The "experts" always said to get up... read something... if you can't sleep. But avoid screens... Well, fuck that. Her mind had been too preoccupied to even concentrate on a book, let alone understand what she was reading. Scrolling Instagram was at least mindless... so what if her eyes suffered. At least it wasn't the goddamn TV blaring out. The California King sized bed was so massive, she could be rolling around doing pilates on her side and David would be none the wiser. Whatever was so special about California, she wondered, that they had to make a whole goddamn bed just for them?

Man! The things her mind would drift off to.

But it wasn't any of that shit that caused her to not stay asleep longer than fifteen fucking minutes. So much had changed in a week. So much good, she admitted, but it was still... well... a lot.

At least the whole "Hey honey, your uncles aren't dead... they're just 'away'" bullshit story she'd been fooling no one with for years was over... it was all out in the open. Josh had taken it remarkably well... He said he already had known somehow, but still... it was "finally talked about"... like Prism's name should have been goddamn Voldemort or something. And then there was the whole "coming out" thing...

I mean, it was no surprise to her at all... and... fuck me, she thought, but admitted that David had been right. Yes... she said it. Her husband had been "right"... so sue her! And Josh seemed to be more... joyful... yes, that was the word... he just seemed like a load of shit had been hosed off and the true son... the boy she knew and loved, who had always been there... was somehow released from all the gunk of years past somehow. Which was great. It truly was.

But... there was something else... Those stories that Josh had uncovered... I mean, she was the one who got Tyler to start writing in the first place. She meant it, way back when, that day she nagged and bothered him into writing... He "did" have good stories and "did" go to incredible places... he "did" get to know wonderful people... But, she only knew a partial bit of it all. Funny how when you're living the day-to-day, you don't really under-stand what really happened until you reflect upon it sometimes years later, she thought.

And this last one that Josh had found... the handwritten "sto-ry"... she guessed Tyler intended it to be a story... but it read more like a transcript of a conversation he and Ken had about that magical old lady in New Orleans. She could just imagine her... all voodoo and such... Or maybe not? Maybe she was just a sweet little old woman who spoke truth and lived life? Who knew?

Tyler knew... apparently.

Apparently enough to write it all down... to share some of his philosophy about the afterlife and purpose and meaning and all that other horseshit they'd get in debates over beer and nachos down at the pizza joint. Apparently enough to seem to just... she wasn't sure... but... "make sense" in some way... all that stuff about "energy" and "spirit" and "unknowns" and...

God, would she just go to sleep for Christ's sake? What's the point in rolling this all around in her head?

She clicked off the phone she wasn't even paying attention to and the room went dark, except for the trickle of light from the red LEDs on the bedside alarm clock. That and that fucking little light that never turned off on the bottom of the goddamned TV. During the day, you never noticed it, but at night... it was just bright enough, that once your eyes got used to the little moonlight that made it through the curtains and the rumble of the fan David kept on his side of the room, all your senses could tell was a slight glow, barely able to see the edge of the chest the TV sat on... or the stack of clothes she'd been meaning to hang up laying on the edge of the foot of the bed... or the old chair sitting in the corner that she'd had since college... the same chair that...

Tyler.

She rubbed her eyes... Goddamnit! I'm so tired I'm...

seeing...

Rebecca slowly raised up from her pillow... as if she were being careful not to scare "it" away... whatever it was.

Of course there's nothing there. This is fucking ridiculous Becca, she told herself. I'm just sleep exhausted... and it's been one hell of a fucking week... and my son just...

"Are you okay?"

Fear hit her like ice water. She always heard stories of people freezing up when there's a true emergency, but just thought they were being dumbasses. She'd look at the TV when something like that would be on and yell "Run! You dumb bitch! Get out of the fucking house!" People were stupid, not able to even move, like that.

Except, this was her. Right now. Frozen solid. Her brain knew what it heard... thought she saw... something...

David snored away. The clock still showed the time... the fan kept humming.

"Can... can... you see... me?"

What. The. Actual. Fuck? Becca's mind reeled. She's got to be hearing things... Whatever was in dinner...

"Becca?"

Her lips trembled... No No No No No No... this is just me being stupid... I'm going to sleep... closing my eyes... time to sleep! She rattled off to herself...

Something seemed to move towards the bed... it was so... faint... so...

was she sure she saw something... like "actually saw"?

Her heart hammered against her ribs... she'd realized she had forgotten to breathe and willed herself to just make all this go away... she'd wake up in the morning and it'd all been some stupid nightmare...

Yet... she... wasn't really... scared, was she?

Just then, something pressed down on the bed, right next to her feet... as if...

Someone sat down...

She strained in the darkness... her eyes squinted, but that didn't help.

"Are... are... you there?" she whispered, terrified of actually hearing a response...

"I am."

Jesus Christ! she jolted. She had half hoped she'd get one just to prove she wasn't losing her goddamn mind... but also just wanted everything to be quiet... "explainable"... God... was this really happening?

"Wh... wh... who?"

"Becca... it's me."

The voice seemed as stunned as she was that she could even hear him... or it... or... whatever. She looked over at her snoring husband and back at this... dark... shadow? What was this? She thought she saw the faintest outline of... a...

Oh my God... is this a ghost? For real? Her pulse hammered again, every muscle tightened. Oh Jesus Oh Jesus...

"Becca... calm down... it's okay... I'm... I'm not going to hurt you."

"What? I don't know who..."

"It's me, Becca... Prism."

"Nnnnn nnoooooo it can'ttt be..." she nearly choked on her tears. "No... No No this isn't happening... you're not real... this is some fucked up joke someone is playing... Joshua!" she looked up at her ceiling, as if that would address her son... "if you so much as even tried to prank me I am beating the shit ou..."

"Becca! Josh doesn't know I'm here. He's asleep."

"You... I'm hearing things... is all..." the more Prism pleaded, the more she felt like she was drowning... unmoored... terrified.

"It's me. Look..."

"no... no..."

"Please Becca," he begged, and she could hear tears in his voice. It was a literal once in a lifetime opportunity... he didn't know how... or why or what caused her to see him... or hear him... but he wasn't going to let this slip away... not now... not when he'd spent years aching to talk... to let her know he was there... to... have some piece of their friendship... their family back.

Tyler leaned forward into a sliver of moonlight and the flecks from his chromatic eyes caught the light... the same mismatched eyes she'd only seen in photos in the years since his death... the same eyes that gave him his name... that perfectly captured his soul... that allowed her to believe... it was...

"Tyler? But... how?"

"I... I don't know... I was just sitting there watching over you when..."

"You watch me?"

"Becca... it's not like that... I... I just want to make sure you're safe... happy."

All her grief crashed over her at once... the years of sorrow, the fury she had for him dying... the devastating sadness that he and Ken had left her... that her son had no fabulous uncles to help him grow up... all the gossip and dinners and family barbecues... all of it and more flooded back in one crushing wave... and for years she kept it locked inside... too many others had it worse, she told herself... besides, she had to be strong... for Joshua... for David... for... everyone...

"Becca, it's okay. I've been here all along..."

She couldn't stop the tears if she wanted to... but they came out in that silent cry... where you can't even grasp enough air to let out an audible wail... where everything in your body just wanted to collapse and die along with him...

Tyler moved closer and she felt that familiar electric buzz start to surround her... the same one she felt every so often when...

"You've always been by me, haven't you?"

"I tried..."

"I fucking hated when you left." The words came out raw, years of bottled rage finally spilling.

"I... I know. But I am here..."

"Is... is Ken?"

Tyler's form seemed to sag in the moonlight. "I don't know what happened to him, Becca. I haven't seen him since..."

They both knew the end of that sentence.

"I'm so so sorry Prism..." she let out an audible sob, stirring David, who simply turned away to his side, deep in sleep.

"Becca... it's okay."

"But... I feel like... I need to tell you everything... like... I was such a shit friend sometimes and I never told you how much you meant to me and how proud I was when you finally found Ken and how scared I was when you got sick and..."

"I know already."

She stopped mid-sob... only her tears and heartbeat filled the silence now.

"How?"

"I've been there... I've always been there..."

"But Josh and..."

"We talk sometimes."

Well, there was that little bombshell that nearly knocked her flat.

"You... you talk?"

"Yeah... he was afraid to say anything to you... you... you know... might think..."

She knew... crazy... just like she felt right fucking now... No one would believe it. She wasn't even sure if this was real or some grief-induced breakdown.

"When?"

"Oh... He's been able to see me almost from the beginning..."

"You mean..."

"That he knew I was..." Tyler hated saying the word because it felt so wrong, so incomplete for what he was...

"dead."

"I'm afraid so."

"And... I spent all those years pretending..."

"He knew..."

"But... why didn't he..."

"Say anything? Because he knew it would destroy you."

"I... I don't understand..."

"Joshua is... is the most incredible person, Becca. He knew this would shatter you... and he wanted to protect his mom... so... he played along..."

This sent her grief spiraling into another crushing round... She had thought she was protecting him... but it really was for her... and she felt selfish... like the worst mother... Oh god, how could she have been so blind...

"Becca, it's okay. It actually... it helped us both."

"How?" she gasped through her tears.

"Josh and I have been able to talk over the years... and... well... I hope I've helped him as he's grown up... I know he's saved me."

"Saved... you?"

"Yeah... How do you think I feel knowing the family I love more than anything... is never able to speak to me... to hear me... to touch me... to know I'm right fucking there..." His voice broke. "But Josh... he could. I don't know how or why... but... he could. And I could still be Uncle Tyler... it's... it's kept me from losing myself completely." He said this through his own tears...

"So... you know about him coming..."

"Out? Yeah... We've talked about it a lot lately."

"I knew it! I fucking knew it!" she said fiercely. "I just... knew it..." and fresh tears flowed...

"Jesus fucking Christ, I can't stop crying. Damnit, Prism... why can't we just go back? Why can't you just... come home?"

"Because I can't... but..."

"But what?"

"But at least we get this moment, right? At least we get to talk now."

"Oh fuck you and your sentimental heart, you beautiful bastard!" she sobbed and laughed at the same time.

"Now there's my Becca!" Tyler's voice cracked with laughter and tears. "I've missed you so fucking much."

"Tyler?"

"Yeah?"

"Will you still be here tomorrow?"

"What do you mean?"

"Like... when I wake up... will I be able to see you again?"

"I hope so... but I don't know... this is brand new to me too."

She was quiet for a long moment, processing. "I really hope so... but even if I can't... I'll know you're around."

"Becca..."

"No... I don't need explanations... and I don't care about the how or why... I just..."

She reached out desperately, unable to see clearly, just needing to hold his hand... or touch him somehow... to make it real... to connect with him one more time. Suddenly, she felt like she'd grabbed a live wire... not painful, but electric... alive... and fuck it all if she cared... she felt... him...

"Becca?"

"Yeah..."

"Can you maybe... not grab my crotch? I know I'm dead, but it's still kinda weird..."

She yanked her hand back from the darkness and burst out laughing despite her tears. Tyler giggled... that sweet, infectious laugh she hadn't heard in years... and it felt like coming home.

"Goddamnit, Prism! I try to have a tender moment and we still end up talking about your junk! Jesus, what is it with you gay boys?" She was laughing and crying at the same time.

"Bitch!" he laughed, wiping his eyes. "Some things never change."

"Tyler?"

"Yeah?"

"Will you... stay here while I sleep?"

"I'm not going anywhere."

"Promise?"

"Becca, I've been here for years. I'm sure as hell not leaving now."

"I love you, Prism. I love you so fucking much and I'm sorry I never said it enough when you were... when I could..."

"I love you too, Becca. More than you'll ever know."

After a moment, she couldn't help herself...

"But not like 'that'... I mean, I do have standards, you know?" She let out a watery laugh.

"You're such an asshole!" he laughed, and for just a moment, it was like no time had passed at all.

"Tyler?"

"Mmm?"

"Thank you. For watching over us. For being there even when we couldn't see you. For... for everything."

"Becca, you don't need to..."

"Yes, I do. Just... thank you."

And in the darkness, surrounded by David's snores and the hum of the fan, Rebecca finally felt something she hadn't felt in years... complete.

# CHAPTER 39

# BRIGHT EYES

**The Japanese Name - Hospital Waiting Room**

The hospital cafeteria was nearly empty at two in the morning, fluorescent lights humming overhead and casting everything in that peculiar institutional glow. Tyler sat across from Ken at a small plastic table, both of them running on coffee and nervous energy. Rebecca had been in labor for eight hours now, and David had stopped giving them updates an hour ago.

"God, I'm tired," Ken said, rubbing his eyes. "How are you holding up?"

"Tired too," Tyler admitted, methodically arranging the sugar packets they'd accumulated throughout the evening. "Just keep thinking about everything that could go wrong."

Ken reached across the table to still Tyler's hands. "Becca's tough. And the doctors seem to know what they're doing."

Tyler looked up, meeting Ken's eyes. "I know. It's just... this is going to be our nephew. That's kind of a big deal."

Ken felt something warm settle in his chest. Even exhausted and worried, Tyler was thinking about their little chosen family. "Yeah, it is. We're going to be uncles."

"Actual uncles," Tyler said softly. "Not just... I don't know, family friends or whatever."

"My mom's already excited about being a grandmother," Ken

said with a tired smile. "She keeps asking when she can visit and meet the baby."

Tyler smiled at that, the first genuine smile Ken had seen from him all evening. "She's going to spoil him rotten."

"Oh, absolutely." Ken stretched in his plastic chair. "So... Joshua. Do you know why they picked that name?"

Tyler's expression shifted slightly. "Actually... I may have suggested it."

"Really?" Ken perked up, interested. "How'd that happen?"

"We were having dinner a few months ago, and I mentioned this book I'd read—'Joshua' by Joseph Girzone. It's about this guy who shows up in a small town and just... loves people. Takes care of them. Makes them feel seen." Tyler paused. "Rebecca asked about it, and I guess it stuck with her."

Ken was quiet for a moment, processing this. "So you basically named our nephew."

"I guess I did." Tyler looked surprised by the realization.

"That's... that's really cool, babe." Ken studied Tyler's face. "Speaking of names... I never asked you about Ken. Is that short for something?"

"Kenshin, actually. My parents gave it to me." Ken stretched again. "A lot of Asian kids pick English names for school, but I never did. Just went with Ken."

Tyler's curiosity was clearly piqued, his usual social reserve lowered by exhaustion. "How do you pronounce the full name? Properly, I mean."

"Ken-shin," Ken said slowly, emphasizing each syllable. "It means 'wise heart.'"

"Ken-shin," Tyler repeated carefully. "That's beautiful. What made your parents choose it?"

"My grandmother, actually. She said I had an old soul, even as a baby." Ken found himself enjoying this more relaxed version of Tyler, the way tiredness made him ask questions without over-thinking them.

Tyler was quiet for a moment, then: "If I were to have a Japanese name... what would it be?"

Ken blinked, surprised. "You want a Japanese name?"

"I mean... hypothetically. What would fit me?"

Ken studied Tyler's face—those distinctive mismatched eyes, the thoughtful expression, the way Tyler saw everything so clearly. "Akira," he said after a moment. "Definitely Akira."

"What does that mean?"

"Bright. Clear. Like the way you see things, the way you understand people." Ken felt his chest tighten. "It suits you."

Tyler was quiet, processing. "A-ki-ra," he said slowly, practicing the pronunciation.

"Yeah, that's it." Ken watched Tyler's face. "You could use it, you know. If you wanted."

"Really?"

"Of course. I mean, you're part of my life now. Part of my family." Ken felt suddenly emotional, probably from the exhaustion. "It would... I'd like that."

Tyler's smile was soft and wondering. "Could you teach me some Japanese? Like... how to introduce myself?"

For the next twenty minutes, Ken found himself teaching Tyler basic phrases, watching with growing affection as Tyler approached learning Japanese with the same methodical focus he brought to everything else. Tyler's pronunciation was careful and precise, and he asked Ken to repeat things until he got them exactly right.

"Watashi no namae wa Akira desu," Tyler said slowly. "My name is Akira."

"Perfect," Ken said, meaning it.

Tyler was quiet for a moment, then: "Could you... could you show me how to write it? Akira, I mean?"

Ken stared at him. "You want to learn the characters?"

"If that's okay. I just... if I'm going to use this name, I want to do it right."

Ken felt his throat tighten. "Yeah. Yeah, I can show you. But I'll need paper."

Tyler was already standing, that determined energy Ken recognized. It took three tries and conversations with two different nurses, but Tyler returned with a stack of napkins and a ballpoint pen.

"Not exactly proper materials," Ken said, accepting the supplies.

"They'll do," Tyler said, settling back with focused attention. "Show me."

Ken spread a napkin flat and began drawing the first character, explaining each stroke. Tyler watched intently, then tried it himself on a fresh napkin. His first attempt was shaky but recognizable.

"Like this?" Tyler asked, already reaching for another napkin to try again.

"Close. The proportions need to be a little different..." Ken guided him through it, and Tyler practiced with the same patient determination he brought to everything he wanted to master.

After about an hour of Tyler filling napkins with increasingly confident characters, Tyler looked up. "Could you show me how to write your name too? Kenshin?"

Ken's heart did something irregular in his chest. "You want to learn my name?"

"Of course I do."

Watching Tyler work so diligently to learn not just his new name but Ken's own name as well, Ken felt like his chest might burst from how full his heart was. This beautiful, methodical man who approached everything—even love—with such careful attention and genuine desire to understand.

"There," Tyler said finally, showing Ken a napkin with both names written in careful characters. "How's that?"

Ken stared at the napkin, at their names side by side in Tyler's precise handwriting. "It's perfect," he said softly. "You're perfect."

"Tyler," Ken said suddenly, looking down at the napkin. "Can I tell you something?"

Tyler looked up, curious. "Of course."

Ken hesitated, feeling suddenly emotional. "Watching you learn this... learning my name, wanting to get it right... it means everything to me."

Tyler's expression softened. "Really?"

"Really. I've never... no one's ever cared enough to learn this part of me before." Ken's voice got quieter. "You wanting to know my real name, wanting to have one yourself... it's like you want to understand all of me. Even the parts that are different."

Tyler reached across the table and took Ken's hand. "I do want to understand all of you. Every part."

They sat in comfortable quiet for a moment, the weight of the night and their feelings settling around them. Tyler carefully folded the napkin with both their names and tucked it into his wallet.

"I'm going to practice until I can write them perfectly," Tyler said.

Ken squeezed his hand. "I know you will."

Just then, David appeared in the cafeteria doorway, his scrubs rumpled and his face exhausted but radiant.

"He's here," David said simply. "Joshua James Brennan. Seven pounds, two ounces. Rebecca's tired but fine. Everyone's perfect."

Ken and Tyler were on their feet instantly, the scattered napkins forgotten in their rush to meet their nephew. But as they hurried toward the elevator, Ken caught Tyler's hand.

"Uncle Akira," Ken said quietly.

Tyler's smile was brilliant. "Uncle Kenshin."

And walking down that hospital corridor at three in the morning, Ken knew they'd just crossed another threshold in their relationship. Tyler wasn't just his boyfriend anymore, or even just his partner. He was family in every sense that mattered—chosen, claimed, and named with intention and love.

When they finally got to hold Joshua, taking turns in the quiet hospital room while Rebecca dozed, Tyler whispered something in the baby's ear—practicing, Ken realized, the pronunciation of his new name. Making it real through repetition, through the same careful attention he brought to everything important in his life.

Later, when they were finally home and collapsing into bed as the sun came up, Tyler pulled out the napkin with his practiced characters.

"I want to frame this," he said. "The first time I wrote my Japanese name."

Ken pulled Tyler closer, pressing a kiss to his temple. "We'll get you proper calligraphy paper. You can practice until it's perfect."

"It's already perfect," Tyler said softly. "Because you gave it to me."

And falling asleep in Ken's arms as the morning light filtered through their bedroom windows, Tyler understood that he'd been given more than just a name. He'd been given a place in Ken's heritage, a connection to generations of history and culture, and a way of being that honored both who he was and who he was becoming.

Akira. Bright and clear.

It fit him perfectly.

# CHAPTER 40

# ABSOLUTELY PERFECT

"Akira?"

Tyler nodded.

"I... I never knew..." Rebecca said.

"I... never really... well... it came up the night you were born, Josh. I just... wanted to be..."

"What?" Josh looked over at his uncle, but saw something tender there, something vulnerable. He remembered reading about uncle Ken giving Tyler his Japanese name, but it was... well... all of "this" was different. Especially because...

"You and Ken did this while I was in labor?" Rebecca looked up from the notebook she was reading for the second time, sitting cross-legged on the attic rug while Josh lounged in his bean bag chair that had become his permanent residence over the past two weeks.

Josh had been watching his mom since she came upstairs twenty minutes ago, and something was definitely different about her today. She seemed relaxed in a way he hadn't seen in years, like some invisible weight had been lifted off her shoulders. But the really mind-blowing part was that Tyler was sitting right there next to her, and she was actually talking to him like he was visible.

Which was completely fucking insane.

Josh had spent years having conversations with Uncle Tyler that nobody else could hear, always careful never to respond out loud when other people were around. He'd gotten pretty good at the whole "pretend you're texting while actually talking to your dead uncle" routine. But watching his mom casually chat with Tyler like it was the most natural thing in the world? That was a whole new level of weird.

And now she was responding to something Tyler had just said about the night he was born, like this was perfectly normal.

"Mom," Josh said carefully, "what exactly is happening here?"

Rebecca followed his gesture between her and Tyler, then laughed like she'd just remembered something obvious. "Oh shit! I completely forgot to tell you. I can see Prism now."

"She takes forever to explain anything," Tyler added with a grin.

"Fuck you, Prism! I was getting to it," Rebecca shot back, nearly swatting at him before remembering the whole electric shock situation.

Josh stared at them both. "You can actually see Uncle Tyler?"

"Well yeah, and don't give me any of that 'I don't know what you're talking about' bullshit. I know you two have been having your little conversations behind my back for years."

"What's the matter, kiddo?" Tyler asked, clearly enjoying Josh's expression. "Never seen your mom hang out with her dead best friend before?"

They were both laughing now, acting like teenagers sharing gossip, and Josh felt like his brain was trying to process too much information at once.

"How is this even possible?"

"You want to tell him or should I?" Rebecca looked at Tyler.

"Last night I was keeping watch over your parents like I always do, and your mom suddenly started talking to me. Not talking to herself about me, but actually talking to me. I have no fucking idea why or how, but there it is."

"You were watching them?" Josh made a face. "Please tell me they weren't doing anything gross."

"Jesus Christ, Josh! Of course not! What kind of perverted uncle do you think I am?"

"Hey!" Rebecca tried to punch Tyler's arm. "I'm not gross, you asshole!"

"Can't hit me!" Tyler stuck his tongue out while Rebecca nursed her tingling hand.

"You two are acting like children," Josh said, but he was grinning. There was something magical about watching them fall back into their old friendship dynamic.

"Admit it, you're just jealous that you don't get me all to yourself anymore," Tyler teased.

"Besides," Rebecca added, "if it wasn't for Tyler here, you wouldn't exist." They both stuck their tongues out at Josh.

"You're both completely hopeless."

They giggled like idiots until Rebecca calmed down enough to return to the notebook. "God, I've missed this so much."

"Me too." Tyler's smile faded slightly. "I just wish Ken could be here too."

The mood shifted, and Josh knew they were all thinking the same thing. "You miss him."

"Every day. But I've got you two, and that's pretty amazing."

"Okay, enough sappy shit!" Rebecca declared. "I don't know how long this whole seeing-you thing lasts, so we're making the most of it."

"Eww, I don't do pussy!"

"Oh my god, Tyler!" Rebecca shrieked, half-laughing and half-scandalized. Josh completely lost it at hearing something so crude come out of his usually proper uncle's mouth.

"And in front of the boy!" Rebecca spelled out B-O-Y like Josh was four years old, which made everything even funnier.

Soon Tyler was rolling on the floor laughing, Josh had sunk so deep into the bean bag he was practically horizontal, and Rebecca was trying to scold them both while cracking up.

"What kind of uncle are you? Look what you're teaching my son!"

"I'm the perfect uncle! I'm teaching him how to be a proper gay!"

"Watch it," Rebecca warned Josh through her laughter, "or I'll make Uncle Tyler tell you about the first time Ken topped him."

"Oh, I already know about that!"

Rebecca spun toward Tyler. "What the hell have you been telling my innocent child, you perverted ghost?"

"Mom, I'm twenty-one!"

"You'll always be my baby!"

"He asked!" Tyler protested between giggles.

"I can't believe my dead best friend is corrupting my son with sex stories."

"Mom, I'm not that innocent."

"What?" Rebecca's head whipped around.

"Oh please, Becca, you were fucking everything with a pulse when I met you!"

"Moi?" Rebecca tried to look innocent, fooling absolutely no one.

"Wait, Mom, you were a..."

"Complete slut!" Tyler finished, earning another attempted punch.

"I give up!" Rebecca threw her hands in the air.

"We win!" Tyler reached for a high-five with Josh, then thought better of it. "Right, electric ghost, forgot."

After they all caught their breath, Rebecca looked back at the chapter about Josh's birth. "Am I saying Akira right? Ah-kear-rah?"

"Yeah, that's perfect. Ken was always better with pronunciation than me."

"Bright," Josh said softly, remembering the story.

"That's what Ken saw in me, I guess. Said my eyes were like light breaking into different colors."

They sat with that for a moment, the weight of memory settling over them.

"Do you remember any other Japanese?" Josh asked.

"Ken taught me a few phrases. Like this one: Chiisai chinpo ga suki desu."

"Ooh, what does that mean?" Rebecca looked impressed.

"Ken told me it meant 'I enjoy life's small pleasures.'"

"Aww, that's sweet."

"Bullshit," Tyler said flatly.

"What do you mean, bullshit?"

"I thought it was sweet too, until I tried to impress Ken's father with my Japanese skills. The poor man looked horrified and Ken nearly died laughing."

"Oh no," Rebecca started grinning. "What did Ken actually teach you to say?"

"The bastard taught me to say 'I like small dicks!'"

"No fucking way!" Josh doubled over. "That's so Ken!"

Rebecca was belly-laughing now. "I can absolutely see him doing that to you!"

"What did you do to him when you found out?" Josh managed to ask.

"Let's just say I showed Ken exactly what size dick I preferred, right up his ass!"

Even Rebecca blushed at that one while wiping tears from her eyes. "Tyler! I cannot believe you just said that!"

Josh was cracking up not just at what his uncle said, but at seeing this completely different side of him. This was Uncle Tyler unfiltered, the way he must have been with Ken and his mom back in the day.

But what Josh loved most was being here in the middle of this chaos, watching his mom and Uncle Tyler be themselves again, sharing inappropriate stories and laughing until they cried. He felt like he'd been let into their secret world, the one that had created the family that led to him existing. Not just being born, but being here, surrounded by this crazy, loving, completely inappropriate family where he felt absolutely and utterly loved.

There would be time for all the big questions later. What would Dad think? Would Tyler be around forever, or would he eventually find his way to Ken? All of that could wait.

Right now, looking at his mom and Uncle Tyler sharing old memories and being ridiculously inappropriate together, Josh knew one thing for certain: this was his family. Unbelievable, impossible, and absolutely perfect. And he wouldn't trade them for anything in the world.

# ABOUT THE AUTHOR

Michael Manosca first pursued a career in the arts, studying in Chicago, but storytelling has always been at the heart of his creative expression. His travels across the world have shaped his perspective, infusing his writing with the depth and nuance of the people and cultures he has encountered.

Michael writes in a deeply personal format, inspired by the relationships and experiences that shaped his upbringing. He explores the intricacies of friendship, the search for identity, and the quiet moments that define us. Through vivid characters and emotional depth, he hopes to craft stories that linger in readers' minds long after the final page.

When not writing, he can be found wandering the northern woods, exploring new cities, or enjoying a lively conversation in a tucked-away café. He currently resides along the western coast of the United States and is already working on his next story.

## ALSO BY MICHAEL MANOSCA

www.ingramcontent.com/pod-product-compliance
Lightning Source LLC
Chambersburg PA
CBHW070533260626
47161CB00002B/359